BED of ROSES

BED of ROSES

KATHERINE STONE

WARNER BOOKS

A Time Warner Company

Warner Books, Inc., 1271 Avenue of the Americas, New York, NY 10020
Visit our Web site at http://warnerbooks.com

 A Time Warner Company

Printed in the United States of America

First Printing: February 1998

10   9   8   7   6   5   4   3   2   1

Library of Congress Cataloging-in-Publication Data

Stone, Katherine
    Bed of roses / Katherine Stone.
      p.   cm.
    ISBN 0-446-52179-5
    I. Title.
  PS3569.T64134B43   1998
  813'.54—dc21   97-29649
                              CIP

Text design by Stanley S. Drate/Folio Graphics Co., Inc.

BED of ROSES

ONE

*N*ot one of the celebrity journalists recognized him, and they would have, had he been a power broker in this town of glittering fantasies and celluloid dreams. The reporters assembled outside the ICU were the best of the best, celebrities in their own right, so renowned they had been permitted to congregate here, close to *her* and far from the hordes of lesser media huddled outside in the rain.

Quite obviously this man, this tormented stranger nearing their elite circle, had come from that torrential storm. Raindrops spilled from his night black hair onto his stunning yet ravaged face. It was a treacherous journey past ice gray eyes to unshaven cheeks to jaw muscles rippled with worry. The tempest had drenched his charcoal gray suit as well. But with the clothes as with the man, the dampness in no way diminished the elegance, the sophistication, the style.

1

This man was not a force in Tinseltown, the journalists knew; but he was a force *somewhere*. The savvy band of reporters recognized power when they saw it. This was a man accustomed to being in command—a man for whom doors opened, crowds parted, even as *they* were parting.

There were, of course, other patients in the ICU. But not one of the select assembly of newspeople entertained for an instant the notion that this man was a player in another—but anonymous—human drama. He was here because of the drama that engaged them all . . . the life-and-death struggle of Cassandra Winter, the actress who had appeared from nowhere to take Hollywood by her own dazzling storm, a five-year tempest of talent—and of success—that had seemed unstoppable.

Until now.

The journalists' assumption that this gray-eyed stranger was here because of Cassandra might have remained just that, for he had almost reached the double doors through which they could not pass. But then he spoke.

It was a command, hoarse, harsh, laced with a desperateness that seemed as foreign to him as he was to them. "How is she?"

"Out of surgery," the most seasoned reporter replied.

"That's all we know," another embellished.

"Alive," a third whispered, a response uttered less to report than to reassure.

But it was a false reassurance, for even though the journalist didn't qualify "alive" with "still" or "barely," the unspoken words haunted the air like gossamer ghosts, invisible yet menacing.

The elegant outlander vanished then, as precipitously as he had appeared, leaving in his wake a bewildered silence. Indeed, the media luminaries were beginning to wonder if he had been a phantom in his own right—a mirage of their own fatigue—when they heard through the closing double doors a startled greeting from within.

"Sir? May I help you?" The ICU clerk sat at a desk in the nurses' station. When her words had no impact on the sudden intruder, she rose to make her presence known.

Perhaps he sensed her movement, perhaps not. He certainly didn't look at her. But he did stop. To get his bearings, the clerk realized. His eyes, wild and searching, scanned the vast expanse of gleaming technology until he found the glass-walled cubicle in which their celebrity patient lay.

Loudly and urgently, the clerk repeated, *"Sir?"*

His gaze did not falter, did not flicker. The wildness had not been conquered, but it was contained, and something else, new and fearsome, smoldered in the dark gray depths: rage at those who blocked his view—the famous man who stood without and the physicians and nurses who hovered within.

"I'm here to see Cassandra."

"Oh, well," the clerk temporized as she awaited the reinforcements summoned by her fervent plea. They were almost here, and it was a gratifying show of support—two uniformed police officers, the unit's head nurse, and Natalie Gold, agent to an elite and glittering galaxy of stars.

"Is there a problem?" the head nurse asked.

"He wants to see Ms. Winter."

The police officers, who had sauntered over with deceptive nonchalance, shifted subtly yet ominously; and Natalie Gold frowned; and the head nurse, although mindful of the potential significance of his request, behaved according to protocol.

"I'm sorry, sir. Only family members are permitted to see her."

A bitter coldness glinted in his winter gray eyes as he

gazed at the man who stood outside the glassy walls. "He isn't family."

"Well, no," the nurse conceded. "But he's Robert Forrest. The actor? And, more important, Ms. Winter's—"

Lover. Chase preempted the pronouncement with a dismissive wave of his hand. The gesture was slight, and not menacing on its face. But from the man who had been standing statue still, even the faintest motion was startling; and so commanding that the nurse recoiled and was silent.

"Robert Forrest is not her family," Chase repeated.

"Nor has he been permitted into her room." The new voice was quiet, like Chase's own, yet filled with authority; and it belonged to a man, like Chase, accustomed to being in charge.

A cop, Chase decided even before he turned. The conclusion was undeterred—in fact, enhanced—by the Ivy League clothes the man wore and by the serene appraisal of his intelligent gaze. *The top cop.*

"I'm Lieutenant Jack Shannon." Jack edited the usual tag line, "Homicide." Cassandra Winter was not dead—yet, although murder was clearly what her assailant had had in mind. "And you are . . . ?"

"Chase Tessier."

"Tessier," Jack echoed. The surname and its pronunciation were French, although Chase was not. "Tessier" was familiar to Jack on a number of counts. He selected the common thread, the fertile land that sustained the roots of the majestic family tree. "From Napa Valley?"

"Yes."

"And you feel you should be permitted in Ms. Winter's room because . . . ?"

"Because she's my wife."

"That's a lie!" Natalie Gold broke her silence with a burst of righteous indignation. Her annoyance crescen-

doed as the elegant man—with the heart-chilling eyes—
shifted his glacial gaze to her. "I would *know* if Cass had a
husband, had *ever* had a husband."

"Apparently you wouldn't, whoever you are."

Natalie Gold did not deign to offer her name. It had
been years, decades, since anyone who was anyone had
failed to recognize her. Nor did Natalie concede that she
might not have known about a husband; that, unlike her
other celebrity clients, Cassandra Winter never confided in
her at all. "She is my client, and my friend. I *would* have
known, as would Robert, whom I also represent and with
whom Cass has been sexually—"

"We have an open marriage."

Hollywood's premier talent agent narrowed her eyes
and looked significantly at the other commanding presence in the uneasy circle. "You know who he is, don't you,
Lieutenant Shannon? He's the monster who assaulted
Cass, who broke into her home *and beat her.* He's come to
finish what he started—he *has* to, because if he doesn't,
she'll identify him the moment she wakes up. Maybe he *is*
her husband, a *terrible* mistake she made years ago."

It was Natalie Gold who then made a terrible mistake.
She looked from the impassive homicide lieutenant to
Chase Tessier—at which point any fantasy Natalie might
have harbored that men with lethally good looks were in-
capable of murder was savagely dashed.

"Talk to me, Mr. Tessier," Lieutenant Shannon suggested calmly. "Convince me I should let you see her."

Chase reined in his fury, an act of immense control, its
only release the single, impatient pass of a powerful hand
through rain-soaked hair. "I was in Paris when I heard the
news. I had just arrived. There was a flight leaving for L.A.
within the hour. I was on it. I cleared customs at LAX forty-
five minutes ago."

"You were in Paris on business?"

"Yes." *To receive an award, meaningless without her.* Was that why he had thought of nothing but her throughout the flight? That—and the fact that the gaily costumed flight attendants sent the constant reminder that it was Halloween. Her birthday. His thoughts on that long transatlantic flight had been haunting, urgent . . . and prophetic. She was in trouble. She needed him. On his return from Paris, he would go to her, talk to her, help her. *To hell with his pride.*

"During the brief time you spent in Paris—or on either of the flights—did you happen to see anyone you knew?"

"A colleague met me at Charles de Gaulle. He's the one who told me about Cassie."

"No one calls her Cassie," Natalie interjected.

"I do." *I did.*

"Do you have your passport, Mr. Tessier?"

Chase answered by plumbing the depths of the inside pocket of his rain-drenched charcoal suit, an exploration that yielded both his passport and airline ticket.

Jack studied the documents, then looked at Chase. "I'll need the name and phone number of that colleague. Sometime. For the record. But I believe you, Mr. Tessier. I believe you were en route to Paris at the time of the assault."

"Just like that?" Natalie queried.

"Just like that," Jack confirmed. "Passports are examined fairly critically these days."

And Jack had been studying Chase Tessier fairly critically as well. He saw tightly controlled emotion, and frantic worry, and a desperateness that had nothing to do with a murderer worried about loose ends. And if, this time, Lieutenant Jack Shannon's uncanny instincts were dead wrong? Cassandra Winter was under constant guard, a relentless surveillance designed to thwart a killer's bedside assault.

"I assume you can prove that you're married."

"Yes." Chase frowned, shrugged, and confessed softly, "I don't carry our marriage certificate with me." *I carry only the memories.* "It's in a safe-deposit box in St. Helena. As soon as the bank opens I'll have a copy faxed to you." *As soon as the bank opens.* It was just dawn on this storm-ravaged Southern California day, hours until the bank opened, and he needed to be with Cassie now, *now.* "May I . . . ?"

Jack nodded. "Assuming her doctors say it's okay."

Chase whispered his gratitude even as he began his journey toward the glass, toward her. Emotionally it was a solitary journey. But he was accompanied by Lieutenant Shannon, who informed the officer stationed beside the door that Chase Tessier would be permitted to pass.

The exchange was overheard by the man, the lover, whose vigil at the glassy wall was so intent that he had been unaware of the commotion—until now. Now the famous blue eyes, dark circled from lack of sleep, blazed with the passion for which Robert Forrest was so renowned. "What the hell is going on?"

"I've just informed the officer that Mr. Tessier may be permitted into her room."

"Instead of me?"

"Mr. Tessier is her husband."

"Her *what?*"

"He has a legal relationship—and therefore a legal right—to be with her."

"And I have *no* rights, even though I love her? And *she* loves *me?* What about Cass, Lieutenant? *Her* rights? I can assure you she doesn't want him at her bedside, whoever he claims to be. She wants me, *me.*"

Chase barely heard the actor's outraged queries—although later the words would taunt and goad. Every ounce of his being, of his heart and of his soul, was focused on her.

He was so close now, close enough to see at last . . . and what Chase saw—at last—evoked a silent scream deep within.

Save for the rise and fall of her chest, forced by the rhythmic sighs of a breathing machine, she was absolutely still. Motionless. Without life. Her gold and sable lashes—the tiny fans that could dance, could flutter, could conceal—hid everything now. They were as lifeless as she, aflicker neither with nightmares nor with dreams—and yet, in their stillness, so very far from peace.

Her skin, always so pale, was translucent, except where savage blows had created massive purple blotches, gravestones of violence on pristine snow. A silvery helmet shrouded her head, and a spiderweb of brightly colored wires floated in the air above, rainbowed conduits between her wounded heart—so wounded before this—and the cardiac monitor pulsing nearby. Her heartbeats raced across a tiny screen, emerald green symbols of shock and despair.

Cassandra Winter wore bruises, and a helmet, and tubes and wires, *and little else.* The flimsy cotton gown provided by the hospital was functional, of course, and perhaps even necessary—permitting professionals virtually unimpeded access to her neck, her limbs, her chest, her heart.

But don't you know how modest she is? Chase's own heart implored. *And that she is cold? Always . . .*

Except when I am loving her.

Except when we are one.

His silent queries to mere—and well-intentioned—mortals were eclipsed by anguished demands to a more malevolent force. What monstrous whimsy of fate had chosen her for this torture? By what cruel destiny had she, *she*, come to this place?

She. His forlorn and lovely Tinkerbell. His bold and sassy vixen. The droopy-faced enchantress who had sauntered into his life eight years ago. . . .

TWO

NAPA VALLEY

JUNE, EIGHT YEARS AGO

*T*he sun shimmered in the indigo sky, its golden rays caressing the vines like whispered kisses, nourishing the sugars of the nascent grapes, awakening the delicate sweetness that slumbered within. The air was fragrant with the promise of that awakening; and with the intoxicating scents of blossoming roses and sun-warmed earth.

It was a perfect summer day, an artist's inspiration, a poet's dream. But Chase Tessier loved this land, this valley, every day: in spring, when wild mustard blooms carpeted the vineyards in bright yellow; and in fall, at harvesttime, when the vines surrendered their magnificent bounty; and even in winter, when healthy plants became mere skeletons and diseased ones were burned to ash.

And yet, on this day of incomparable beauty, worry cast a dark shadow. Would Hope see the splendor? Could she? Or was her vision forever tainted by loss?

Chase would know, soon. For the first time since leaving for college last September—for the first time since Frances Tessier's death—his sister was coming home. Hope might have made the journey before. UCLA was, after all, an easy six-hour drive away. But the drive was not easy for Hope. In fact, it was impossible. As each school holiday had neared, Chase sensed her crescendoing dread and suggested alternate venues: Thanksgiving in Aspen, Christmas in Paris, a weekend in late January in Santa Fe.

It was during that Santa Fe weekend that Hope vowed to spend spring break in Napa—a brave promise, which she did not keep.

"Cassandra and I are just going to hang out here," Hope told him by phone, in March. "If that's okay?"

"Sure. But wouldn't you—and Cassandra—like to get away?"

"Not really. Cass has just gotten a terrific job at a restaurant on Rodeo Drive, and there's lots of reading I should do in advance of my spring quarter courses."

"You work too hard, Hope Tessier." The brotherly tease was fueled by an aching truth. Reading was Hope's retreat—her escape—from pain.

"I don't work nearly as hard as you—or Cassandra."

Cassandra. Since February the name crept into every conversation and monopolized many. Hope loved talking about her new friend. Her only friend.

Cassandra Winter was twenty-one to Hope Tessier's eighteen; and after only three collegiate years she would be getting her degree, in art history, in June.

Cass arrived late in her parents' life, Hope told him: an only child and such a welcome surprise that, in an eagerness shared by the entire Vermont town, the doctor had used forceps and squeezed a little too tight. The result was a crushed nerve, with a lingering facial droop.

The droop was only on one side, Hope explained, and hardly noticeable, except when Cass was tired. It didn't bother Cassandra; *nothing* did—especially not a crushed nerve that symbolized how wanted she had been.

The portrait of Cassandra, as painted by Hope, was a tableau of supreme confidence and soaring self-esteem— which were the very gifts Hope herself needed. But it seemed an unlikely friendship, Chase thought: the self-assured upperclasswoman and his reserved little sister. And even though he was grateful for the optimism in Hope's voice, courtesy of Cassandra Winter, he worried as well.

Hope was determinedly reluctant to reveal precisely how the friendship had begun. "We just met, Chase. We just *met*." And there was that astonishing coincidence: the death of Cassandra's father—who was more like a grand-father—when she was only four, and of her mother when Cass was just seventeen. So like Hope's own losses.

Chase was troubled by the coincidence. Suspicious of it. But he kept his worries to himself and looked forward to the June day when Hope returned to Napa for the summer and Cassandra "headed back east" to begin whatever— undisclosed—career had compelled her to finish college in just three years.

Now that day had arrived.

This perfect day.

This glorious day in Napa that his sister might not even see.

*H*ope! Someone has scattered *diamonds* on that vine-yard."

"What, Cass?"

"Diamonds," Cassandra repeated softly, achingly. Hope

wasn't seeing the rare beauty of this June day—not the indigo sky, or the golden sun, or the treasure trove of diamonds that sparkled atop the glossy green vines. Hope saw
only the gray ribbon of highway on which she drove and
all the somber memories that lay ahead.

In response to Cassandra's pronouncement, however—
that precious gems glittered amid the newborn grapes—
Hope glanced away from the solemn pewter pavement.

"Oh," she murmured. "Those are silver streamers, like
tinsel, to scare away the birds. They do look like diamonds."

Hope's assertion was polite, as always. Gracious, despite
her pain. This homecoming was so difficult, Cassandra
knew. The apprehension was etched on Hope's face, and
in the tautness with which she clutched the steering
wheel, and even in the way she drove, sometimes at the
speed limit, sometimes far below. Approach, avoidance.
Part eagerness, part dread.

There was only one reason Hope was making this bittersweet journey: the big brother she scarcely knew but admired so much.

*Don't you dare let her down, Chase Tessier. She's doing this
for you.*

And perhaps, Cass thought, Chase was doing this for
Hope as well—encouraging her to return, knowing there
were ghosts to be exorcised, pain to be laid bare, a necessary divestiture of ancient shadows so that a brilliant future could be hers. Or maybe Chase Tessier simply believed
that the place that had stolen so much from Hope was
ready to give something back—its healing bounty, its
nourishing warmth, its diamonds in the sun.

Chase loved his valley, his vineyard, his home. Hope
had told her so. For Chase, who had lived here his entire
life, the losses that so devastated Hope were isolated

threads of darkness in a vast and vivid tapestry . . . whereas for Hope, who had been a rare visitor since age four, loss and Napa were inexorably entwined.

Hope rarely visited, and Chase rarely left. Which made the twenty-six-year-old heir, who could have been a jet-setter par excellence, what instead? A man so socially encumbered, or so physically unexceptional, that he preferred the sanctuary of his vines to the ski slopes of Mont Blanc? A man without alternatives, or worse—one lacking in imagination, curiosity, even a soupçon of adventure?

Or maybe the man who had taken the dull road—the high road?—to tradition and family was a wizard of sorts. Maybe Chase sensed, without needing to sample the rest of the planet, that he already lived in paradise.

"We're here."

Hope's quiet announcement drew Cassandra from her reverie.

Here. Domaine Tessier. The mansion and winery lay ahead, imposing stone structures separated by an immense courtyard, its sparkling fountain spilling even more diamonds into the sunlit air. Olive trees lined the private road to the estate, an arcade of emerald feathers. Beyond the fluttering plumes stretched the vineyard, vast, orderly, and dotted at precise intervals with surprising pastel blooms.

"Roses," Cass murmured.

"Yes, that's because—Oh, there's Chase."

He was shadowed by the portico, and shadowed still, by the mansion itself, as he walked to greet them. In a few more strides, however, sunlight would illuminate the golden—if socially tarnished—heir, and all would be revealed.

But Cassandra did not witness that sunlit revelation. Even before her friend's sigh, her gaze had shifted to Hope.

"Hey, Hope."

"He's going to be so disappointed. I'm even heavier than I was when we met in Santa Fe."

"You look terrific."

"Well . . . as good as I *can* look . . . thanks to you."

Cassandra dismissed with a frown her own contribution to Hope's appearance. It was trivial, remedial, the obvious suggestion that green would complement nicely her fair skin and emerald eyes, and that a matching satin ribbon, braided into her cinnamon hair, would add a certain flare.

"You look beautiful, Hope Tessier. You *are* beautiful." A butterfly within a cocoon of unhappiness . . . a butterfly who could have flown, could have soared, no matter what her weight, had such flight been fueled by confidence. "Beautiful. *Ravishing.* Inside and out. Chase is not going to be disappointed. He's going to be thrilled to see you, and we're going to have a sensational summer watching the grapes grow."

And putting the *fun* back into dysfunctional, Cass mused. The irreverent quip, used often before meeting Hope, had been long since abandoned, because of Hope. There was really nothing fun about Frances Tessier, the mother who, in Cassandra's estimation, had defined selfishness; or Victor Tessier, the father who wasn't really a father. And as for Chase? He would be as kind, as wonderful, as Hope always claimed. *He had better be.*

"Sensational," Cass repeated decisively.

"Well," Hope whispered. The tentative syllable lingered in the air as she doused the ignition, set the parking brake, and curled her fingers around the handle of the door. "Here goes."

Cass witnessed the brother-sister reunion from within Hope's car. And what Cass saw, all she saw in those first few moments, was the character of Chase Tessier: his relief that Hope was home, his pride in his little sister—and nothing else, not disappointment, not surprise, not the slightest shadow of concern. His arms encircled Hope as if she were the tiniest of creatures . . . and the most cherished of treasures.

It was then, as brother and sister embraced, that Cass saw the greater measure of the man, the emotions that Chase Tessier would never permit Hope to see. Sadness. Worry. And something else, urgent and fierce. If he could assume Hope's pain, every aching ounce of his sister's hurt, he would—and gladly. And until such time? Chase would do everything in his power—such immense power—to protect her from further harm.

Longing stirred within Cass. No, it tore at her soul. *May I be part of this? Please? Please.*

Did Chase Tessier hear the silent call of her lonely heart? Was that why, at that precise moment, he noticed the shadowy figure within the car?

The glass was tinted, preventing all but gauzy access to his searching gaze. But Cass saw him clearly. The physical being in which he dwelled. The coal black hair. The intense gray eyes. The sensual elegance. Poet. Panther. Predator. Prince.

"Cass? Come meet Chase!"

Hope's invitation floated in the balmy air. Soft. Melodic. And in exquisite harmony with the astonishing music that hummed within. Cassandra's entire being was singing, *singing* such joyous songs, unknown yet wondrous carols from places she did not know—and awakened by him . . . the brother whose fierce protectiveness of his sister made her ache with unfamiliar longing . . . the sensual man whose piercing gray gaze evoked another foreign longing, even deeper, even warmer, and so amazingly bold.

Cass almost leapt out of the car, almost made a brazen

dash toward the maestro himself. But reality crashed in on her. Strident, discordant, the end of the music.

Remember who you are, what you are.

At this moment Cassandra Winter was a refugee, rescued from the uncertain storm of the rest of her life by the lovely generosity of a friend.

Cass wasn't even supposed to have seen Hope today. Last evening, as they'd watched the sun fall into the sea, they had said their good-byes. They'd promised to keep in touch, always, beginning the moment Cass knew where she would be and shared the news with Hope.

That was last night. Good-bye. Farewell. But this morning Hope had appeared unannounced at Cassandra's dorm room door . . . and Hope Tessier was not nearly as expert as her brother at concealing her surprise, her worry, her shock.

"It's my transit outfit," Cass had said by way of explaining her own shocking appearance.

Cassandra Winter enjoyed campuswide acclaim for the flamboyance with which she dressed. Her eclectic potpourri of garments was, in reality, quite small. But from that meager yet vivid palette, Cass created an ever-changing array of ensembles, a daring kaleidoscope of texture and hue.

Her rainbowed clothing was fashion statement enough. But there was that crowning glory, her wild, dancing hair, the luxuriant mane in all the shades of amber, from rich sable to brilliant gold. Cass never subdued her amber bounty, never tamed its exuberance in any way.

Spectral plumage and flowing hair—that was the Cassandra Hope knew, had known, until today. Today Cass was dressed in black: tights, sweater, jumper, boots. The clothes were wintry, tattered, and, save for the high-heeled boots—Cass's favored footwear—entirely unfamiliar to Hope.

Her hairstyle, too, was foreign. Still wet from washing, dark from washing, the amber strands were subdued, imprisoned, bound in a tight black ribbon at the nape of her neck.

"Your transit outfit?" Hope had echoed at last.

Yes. This is what I wear whenever I leave . . . whenever I must begin again. "I don't want to attract attention on the bus—to have to speak to strangers from whom there's no escape—and you know the air-conditioning will be going full blast, so it will be positively frigid inside."

"Why don't you come with me?"

That had not been Hope's plan. She was merely going to give Cassandra a final chance—previously declined—to accept a ride to the Greyhound terminal. But everything changed when Hope Tessier saw her friend, and Hope's gentle query took on an uncharacteristic forcefulness, becoming a quiet command. "Come to Napa, Cass. Come spend the summer with Chase and me."

Cass had grabbed at the gossamer lifeline, clutched it so desperately that she hadn't thought to change her clothes or unbind her hair.

Now she was here, in this place where diamonds sparkled and roses bloomed. This place, where this brother, this man, would see her soon.

The sunlight that beamed its most gentle smile at Chase, its glowing gold approval for the Tessier prince, would glare upon *her* with arch disdain. Her drooping face. Her sleep-starved eyes. Her tautly punished hair. Her witch's garb.

If only she could remain forever in the shadows, watching but unseen, touched by the music, healed by it.

It wasn't possible, of course. Besides, this man did not need sunlight to pierce the shadows. Even now Cass felt his heated gaze, penetrating the tinted glass, searching for the truth.

And what if Chase Tessier saw the truth? The real Cassandra? And what if—maybe, maybe—he wanted to cherish and protect what he saw?

The music began anew. Delicate. Fragile. Bold.

Go to him, the joyous chorus sang. Abandon the shadows. Dance in the sunlight. To him.

To him.

THREE

*Y*ou were brilliant, Hope. Absolutely stunning."

Hope smiled faintly at Meryl Atwood, San Francisco's district attorney and Hope's boss. "It was just the opening statement, Meryl. We have a way to go."

"But the beauty is you know precisely where you're going, and now the jury knows it, too. You've given them a crystal-clear road map to conviction. You've probably already written your closing statement . . . haven't you?"

Hope shrugged. Of course she had. How else could one possibly prepare a coherent prosecution? The jury needed a beginning, a middle, an end; a story that flowed and made sense. Hope had an aptitude for such storytelling, an inheritance, perhaps, from her mother—except that Frances Tessier's domain had been fiction, over which she'd had complete control, whereas Hope was at the mercy of

21

the surprises—and imperfections—inevitable to any criminal trial.

"Just the first draft," she admitted. "The defense is going to have something to say about the clarity of my road map to their client's guilt."

"But given that Detective Craig Madrid is as guilty as sin, and every shred of evidence proves it . . ." The district attorney's smile was wry. "Admittedly, there's precedent for an entire mountain range of evidence not being enough. But not in this office, and not with you trying the case."

"At least the judge nixed cameras in the courtroom."

"I wish he hadn't. I have a feeling this is going to be a case the entire country should see, especially those who've lost faith in the criminal justice system."

"Well. I hope so."

"Listen, I know—we all know—that spousal rape is a difficult conviction in any circumstance, and when the accused just happens to be the cop who won the admiration of the entire city for heroism during the quake . . . well, nobody said it would be easy. I dropped by to congratulate you on a spectacular start, not to weigh you down with even more pressure than you already feel. I'm afraid my plan backfired."

"No. It didn't. I'm just distracted."

"Of course you are, with good reason. And trust me, I have no intention of *un*distracting you, since your focus is dead on. We could, however, do lunch at Mama's."

"Thank you, Meryl, but no. I think I'd better spend the noon hour uncluttering my mind so that I can hear between the lines when the defense presents its opening this afternoon."

It was the truth. She needed to unclutter her mind. But what Hope didn't say was that the thoughts that distracted her had absolutely nothing to do with the biggest case of her career.

As soon as Meryl left, Hope closed her office door, locked it, a signal to all other well-wishers that she needed privacy—to think, they would assume, to concentrate.

Not one of Hope's colleagues would imagine that she wanted privacy for a phone call, much less a personal one. As far as anyone could tell, the compulsive prosecutor had no personal life. Besides, given her devotion to the law, its letters and its rules, Hope Tessier seemed the most unlikely of all state employees to indulge in personal issues while at work.

The taxpayers of California were getting their money's worth from Hope, far more than they paid for. Indeed, if presented with the facts—her round-the-clock commitment to her job—none would have begrudged Hope either the time or the cost of the long-distance call.

But Hope billed it to her own credit card and felt guilty—yet determined—as she dialed. She needed to know, needed more than the recorded message she had listened to repeatedly throughout the night: "Cassandra Winter is undergoing emergency neurosurgery. Further information will be provided as events merit." Finally, just before dawn, the new message: "Cassandra Winter has been admitted to the ICU. Her condition remains extremely critical."

Throughout the night, on her own time and from her own phone, Hope had dutifully complied with Westwood Memorial Hospital's recorded request that the famous actress's worried admirers listen to the prepared messages rather than flood phone lines to the operating room or ICU. Staff members were prohibited from providing any additional information, the recording noted, and bombarding them with inappropriate inquiries would only deprive Cassandra—and other patients—of essential care.

From the night-shadowed darkness of her Pacific Heights apartment, Hope had felt like one of Cassandra's anxious fans, with no more right to privileged information than anyone else. At work, however, Hope was an attorney: assertive, proactive, and fully aware of her rights.

Now, without the slightest hesitation, Hope followed the sequence of menus that guided legitimate callers with the instruction "If you are a relative seeking information on a patient in the Surgical ICU, press one."

Hope pressed and was swiftly connected.

"Surgical ICU. This is Tamara. How may I help you?"

"My name is Hope Tessier. I'm calling to inquire about Cassandra Winter." Hope stopped abruptly, halted not by the learned behavior of an attorney—never to volunteer more than was necessary—but by emotion, fear. She had been in court all morning and had assumed that during those hours Cass had improved. But what if . . .

"You must be related to Chase Tessier."

"He's my brother," Hope murmured, stunned. "Is he there?"

"Yes. In fact, he's just finished speaking with her neurosurgeon, so he's more up-to-date than I. And he's right here. Mr. Tessier? It's your sister."

Hope heard muffled dialogue—she was on line three, Chase could take the call in the quiet room—then echoing silence as she was placed on hold; then the stark echoes of her brother's pain.

"Hello, Hope."

"Hi," she said softly. She had been debating phoning him in Paris, just to let him know. But somehow Chase had heard and . . . "You're there."

"Yes."

"How is she?"

Dying. He couldn't say it, wouldn't say it. But her doctors had said it, as gently—and euphemistically—as they possibly could. Her chances were very slim, they warned. The trauma was so immense that even the most aggressive therapeutic interventions, which she was definitely receiving, were unlikely to succeed.

"Chase? The initial news reports speculated that there was blood—bleeding—in her brain."

"There was. A clot, which they removed. But there's something else, a rare complication called malignant cerebral edema, a massive swelling of the brain."

Rare. Malignant. Massive. The words were harsh enough, ominous enough. But Hope heard a greater harshness in her brother's voice: fury, toward himself, for failing to protect Cass from the vicious assault.

"If the doctors know what it is, they must know how to treat it."

"They can try, Hope. They are trying."

"By doing what?" she pressed, less concerned about the medical specifics than the specific anguish of the brother who had not uttered Cassandra's name in years. "How do they treat it?"

Horrifically. Barbarically. The words didn't form in Chase Tessier's mind. They merely bored, like sizzling hot acid, into his heart—even as he repeated, with astounding calm, what the doctors had told him.

"They've removed bone"—*the top half of her skull*—"to relieve the pressure. And they're controlling her breathing, hyperventilating her, to decrease the carbon dioxide in her blood. And they're giving her drugs." Including barbiturates, in overdose amounts. Overdose. The word had shaped Chase's life, sliced it to threads—some glittering, some gray.

"It sounds like they know what they're doing."

"It's an impressive team."

Hope sensed there was something more. Something worse. "But?"

But they're cooling her, chilling her.

Medical science supported the barbarism, of course. By lowering her body temperature, one slowed her metabolic rate, which, like manipulating carbon dioxide and overdosing with barbiturates, diminished the demands on her savagely injured brain.

Cassandra would not shiver, no matter how chilled. That primal reflex, the instinct to increase heat, was blocked by even more drugs.

But Chase knew how cold she was. How she hated to be cold.

"But nothing, Hope. She's very precarious, that's all."

"Is Eleanor with you? Or Jane?"

"No. This isn't about me, Hope." *It's about Cass. Cassie. And Robert. The man she loves.* The actor was at her bedside, touching her, whispering to her, imploring her to awaken and return to their love. Chase had authorized the visits. How could he not? Robert Forrest was her love, and more. He was the man who had rescued her, saved her—at least given her the chance to be saved.

"Well," Hope said. "*I* want to be there. I will be, as of about eight tomorrow night."

"Didn't the People versus the rapist cop begin today?"

"Yes, and I've already given my opening. Whatever preparation I need to do this weekend, I can do in L.A. So, please tell Cass I'll see her tomorrow night."

Tell? "She's not awake, Hope."

"But you *are* speaking to her, aren't you?"

His heart was, frantic whispers, desperate prayers.

"She can't hear me, Hope." *She's beyond sleep, beyond coma, in the oblivion of overdose . . . where the prayers of small children go unheard . . . and from which loved ones do not re-*

turn. "And even if she could hear, mine wouldn't be the voice she wanted."

"But yours *is* the voice that could provoke her into waking up—even if it's just to tell you to go to hell. Don't you remember the first time you two ever met?"

Did Chase Tessier remember that glorious June day?

Of course he did.

How could he ever forget?

FOUR

DOMAINE TESSIER

JUNE, EIGHT YEARS AGO

*C*hase, this is Cass. She's going to spend the summer with us."

"Oh?" *Good.*

It was a surprising thought. But she was a surprise, this uncertain waif dressed in black. Her facial droop was more noticeable than Hope had forecast; and despite Hope's assertion to the contrary, it seemed to bother Cassandra after all. This Cassandra, that is: the one who stood before him so delicate, so hopeful . . . and so very unexpected.

Where was the woman that Hope had described? The creature of soaring confidence and unsurpassed self-esteem?

Chase's silent musing was answered with the suddenness—and the regret—of a rainbow vanquished by a too bright sun.

She was that gilded dazzle. That sudden drama. With a

grand flourish, the once uncertain waif swept the ebony ribbon from her hair, freeing the bounty of sable and gold. And she smiled. Brilliantly. Seductively. A provocative lushness that erased all memory of her droop. Even her outfit seemed transformed, her body changed beneath it, from anguished penitent to self-assured vamp.

Her blue eyes followed suit—eventually. But the segue from pastel hopefulness to flirtatious sparkle was hesitant, reluctant—as if she, as he, would have preferred to linger amid the delicacy of rainbows.

Cassandra would have preferred it, wished for it, ached for it. She had followed the joyous—goading—music from shadows to sunlight. To him. And she had stood before him. Vulnerable. Drooping. Exposed.

And for several glorious moments he seemed to be welcoming her, welcoming *her* . . . her tattered clothes and battered soul.

Then he frowned, with gentle wonder, with soft surprise. But Cassandra saw neither wonder nor surprise. *Could not.* Her entire life had taught her to perceive frowns—at her—in only one way: as disapproval, as rejection, as disdain.

The same life lessons that tainted her vision taught Cassandra Winter how to respond. How to survive.

Even as she wept inside, an aching disappointment she would not permit him to know, she became someone else: a smoky, sultry, southern belle.

"That's right, sugar," she purred. "When Hope invited me to the ranch, why, I just couldn't say no."

"The ranch?"

"The ranch," Hope confirmed. "Cass has decided that the notion of taming wild wine is a little more romantic than farming docile clusters of grapes."

"Not to mention the fact," Cassandra embellished sug-

gestively, "that wine wranglers are more—shall I say interesting?—than farmers."

"I see," Chase replied, torn between conflicting images—the oh-so-welcome reality of his sister's dancing
smile . . . and the unwanted, yet real, image of Cassandra
bewitching the crown princes of the valley while Hope hid
in her room, reading romance novels, until her *friend*
deigned to beam a little golden dazzle her way. "I thought
you were going back east, Cassandra, to begin the career
for which you raced through college."

Chase hadn't spent much time pondering what, precisely, his sister's friend planned to do with her art history
degree. But he had assumed Cassandra had a plan.

Apparently not, he realized as his comment was met
with silence by Cassandra—and clarification by Hope.

"Cass is like *you*, Chase," Hope explained. "She can *do*
anything, *be* anything. It's just a question of deciding
where her passion lies—which is what she's going to figure
out, this summer, while she's here."

Chase Tessier knew all about passion: that it offered no
choices, took no prisoners. One didn't decide where passion lay, nor did one wait for inspiration to light—as if passion were a timid muse, a tentative Tinkerbell, fluttering
uncertainly in the ether.

Chase gazed at the woman who had seemed, at first, a
tentative Tinkerbell; an image that was now a rainbowed
mirage.

"Do you have any ideas, Cassandra, about where your
true passion might lie?"

Her true passion? No. She had no such thing. She knew,
for she had searched, taking course after course and declar-
ing major after major, a frantic exploration that scrupu-
lously avoided even a single class in the dramatic arts.

Cassandra Winter needed no lessons in acting. She had

been an actress all her life, pretending not to care, learning that such pretense was the only way to endure—to survive—the loneliness and the hurt.

Wasn't acting, then, her true passion? No. It was merely a bewitching monster that could consume her—as if a passion—could devour her so completely that she might spend her entire life pretending to be someone else.

Anyone else.

Cass might have succumbed, had she not left UCLA when she had; might have surrendered to the intoxicating, if destructive, promise of losing herself entirely—acknowledging, with that surrender, the aching belief that losing herself, her self, would be no loss at all.

Chase Tessier seemed to share such a belief. He wanted her gone, lost forever, away from whatever imagined threat she posed to his sister.

A threat to Hope? Me? Never! Cassandra might have screamed the astonished protest. But the actress within, that brazen creature born of pain, imposed restraint. The southern seductress was on stage now—on stage and in control.

"Why, yes, Chase. I most surely do have some ideas on the subject of passion. I believe I'd like to make the acquaintance of a wrangler or two, and this being Northern California and all, I thought I might just try my hand at a little gold-digging while I'm here. That's what's got you so worried, isn't it, big brother? The notion of little old me mining for gold?"

"Cass! Chase would never think that. *Never.* Would you, Chase?"

You bet I would. And Chase wasn't troubled in the least that Cassandra so precisely understood his concern.

Hope, however, was another matter.

"No," Chase reassured his sister, then addressed her friend. "Welcome to the wine ranch, Cassandra."

"Thank you," Cass murmured, even as Hope confessed:

"Actually, Chase, you haven't really met Cassandra. The southern accent—and, I suppose, the type of dialogue—has been brought to you by Blanche DuBois. You know, from *A Streetcar Named Desire*? She's good, isn't she?"

"Very."

"That's probably enough Blanche for now," Hope mused. "Chase doesn't seem to think it's as funny as we do."

Not funny at all, Cassandra thought. Merely disdainful, disapproving, wishing her gone.

And yet the gracious host had welcomed her, and now he was luring her ever deeper into his lair.

"So," Chase Tessier said, "why don't I grab your luggage while the two of you go inside? Eleanor—"

"I'll grab my own luggage."

"—is in the kitchen, making dinner."

"She's *making* dinner?" Hope asked.

"We can still go to the Auberge," Chase replied. "Whatever she's making, she says, will keep. She was so pleased that you wanted to include her on your first night home that—she says—she was overcome by a euphoric urge to cook. Basically, she thought you'd be tired from the drive and might prefer to stay home."

"I guess I would prefer that."

"Good. So while I grab everyone's luggage, why don't you go inside? Eleanor can't wait to see you." His glacial gray gaze shifted to Cass, to do battle over the issue of luggage. A battle he would win. But Cassandra was a rainbow once again. Delicate. Fragile. And lonely, *lonely*—and so very much alone. "You too, Cassandra," he said softly. "Eleanor can't wait to see you, too."

The sentiment was echoed by Eleanor herself the mo-

ment Cass walked into the kitchen and repeated, by Eleanor, forty-five minutes later, when Cass needed it most.

Cassandra stood at a windowed alcove in the spacious lilac bedroom adjacent to Hope's. She saw vineyards from the alcove, and diamonds; and, below in the garden, Chase and Hope strolled in the fading rays of the setting sun.

"Knock, knock," Eleanor's voice sang in the doorway. "May I come in?"

"Oh, Eleanor. Yes, of course."

Eleanor McBride was a contemporary blend of fairy godmother and Mrs. Claus, the best of each. Merry. Forthright. Wise. She waltzed in, assessed the situation, and frowned.

"You haven't unpacked? Are there no hangers in the closet?"

"No. I mean, I'm sure there are. It's just . . ." *that I have to leave.*

Cassandra hadn't quite figured out how she was going to vanish into thin air. Only that she needed to. Such a vanishing act was undoubtedly something a fairy godmother could accomplish in the blink of an eye. But this fairy godmother's eyes—kind, unblinking, and shrewd—were focused squarely on her.

And far from orchestrating a deft disappearance, Eleanor seemed determined to convince her to stay. "It's positively wonderful that you're here, Cassandra. It's going to make this summer so much better for Hope. And for Chase."

"For Chase?"

"Absolutely. His top priority is Hope. Of course. But Chase Tessier also happens to be responsible for the Domaine, and all its wine. Given the rains we had this spring, and the heat that's forecast for this summer, an early—and possibly precipitous—harvest is likely. Chase has to decide

precisely when to harvest each and every varietal in each and every Tessier vineyard—from the Carneros to Mendocino and key locales in between. It's not something he can delegate. *He* is the wine maker. *He* has to decide. There's no one else as good as he is, anyway."

Eleanor's endorsement shimmered, unquestioned and unchallenged, in the burnished hues of twilight. "So there's *that,* the whimsical harvest, on top of which phylloxera is devastating the crops—and livelihood—of other valley vintners. And since this is Domaine Tessier's centennial year in Napa, there's the gala to plan. And as if we—Chase—needed more distractions, there's the *movie.* But now that you're here, Cassandra, Chase can spend quality time with Hope, and not worry so much—at all—when his other responsibilities take him away. Which is lovely. Wonderful. Perfect."

And false, Cass amended. Hope didn't need her, not really, not nearly as much as she needed Hope. And Chase didn't want, or need, her at all. Did he?

"Chase is a remarkable man, Cassandra. A remarkable brother, vintner, grandson, friend."

I know that, Eleanor. The problem is me, not him. Me. Don't you see?

Quite clearly, Eleanor did not see. And not only was her fairy godmother vision fatally flawed, she seemed singularly oblivious of her deficiencies in sight—because, of course, Eleanor McBride was neither fairy godmother nor Mrs. Claus. She was merely a very kind woman . . . who was now patiently awaiting Cassandra's reply.

Cass murmured an assertion that she believed to be true. "You've known Chase all his life."

"Not quite—but for eighteen years, since Chase was eight, the year Hope was born. Why don't I tell you how we met?"

No. Thank you, Eleanor. I really must be going. Even though I wish I could stay.

Eleanor didn't wait for Cassandra's answer, although perhaps she sensed the silent wish. Without further ado, she walked to the closet, extracted several hangers, and looked at Cass . . . at which point the ersatz—but lovely—fairy godmother's treacherously determined gaze drifted to the bed—where, atop a comforter abloom with lilacs, sat the duffel bags Cassandra had hoped Chase would never see, much less carry.

But Chase *had* carried them, and he had chosen to place them on the comforter, not the floor, even though they were as alien to this luxury as was she. The bags were army surplus, the calico of camouflage fatigues, and they were packed with her own combat gear—a masquerade of floating fabrics and vivid hues.

"Why don't you unpack, Cassandra, and I'll hang?"

Faux fairy or not, Eleanor had magical powers. Without warning, Cassandra's black-clad legs staged a mutiny against reason, and by the time she reached the lilac bed, her hands had joined the revolt.

"Oh, my," Eleanor raved as Cassandra's renegade fingers withdrew from the treasure trove of color a plum jumpsuit sashed in mauve. "This would be perfect for this evening. It really says *celebration.*"

For many amazing minutes Cass became a helpless—but not unhappy—marionette. Her arms, controlled invisibly yet absolutely by Eleanor, unpacked the vivid palette of flippy skirts and gauzy blouses. And, at Eleanor's request, her puppet arms even removed her tattered black sweater to illustrate precisely how she created her never-ending wardrobe, the mix and match of fabrics and hues, often in layers, accessorized with sashes and scarves.

The impromptu fashion show was such fun. And so dys-

functional. As if she belonged here, as if she belonged anywhere. As if Cassandra Winter could ever belong.

But reason, and remembrance, were still in hiding.

"You were going to tell me how you and Chase met."
*And how remarkable he is, this man who mistrusts my friend-
ship with Hope and wants me gone, lost forever.*

"Oh, yes. Well. My husband . . ." Eleanor faltered,
swamped by a flood of emotion that came without
warning.

"Andrew," Cass provided gently. "Hope told me."

"Did she? Hope remembers him?"

"Of course!"

"You're a dear girl, Cassandra Winter. But Hope was
only four years old when she saw my Andrew last. She
can't possibly remember him."

"But she *does*, Eleanor. She remembers the happiness of
that time."

Eleanor drew a steadying breath. "It was a happy time.
I'll never know what made Jean-Luc Tessier decide to include Andrew and me in his family. But he did. And I'm
forever grateful."

"Jean-Luc," Cass echoed. "He was Grandpère?"

"Yes. Grandpère was Chase's name for him. It means
Grandfather in French. Well, of course you know that. The
name caught on throughout the Wine Country. He became Jean-Luc and Grandpère, spoken interchangeably
and with great affection. In any event, Andrew and I had
recently moved to the valley. Andrew was editor in chief
of the local newspaper, and I baked desserts for a caterer in
town. We had no children, despite trying for almost three
decades. Andrew claims he never shared that sadness with
Jean-Luc, who was then only a casual acquaintance. But
for whatever reason, when baby Hope arrived, and was
obviously going to stay for a while—while Frances accom-

panied Victor on his concert tours around the world—
Grandpère invited us to the Domaine. And we stayed,
too—emotionally, not literally. We lived at our home, a
mile from here, and worked at our jobs. But whenever we
had a free moment, and every free moment we had,
we were here, playing with Grandpère and his grandchildren."

Eleanor stared thoughtfully at the bright blue blouse
she held in her hands, as if in boldness and hue it mirrored
perfectly those happy years. "Jean-Luc was Peter Pan. He
had no intention of growing up, not this time around, and
neither did we. Chase was the grown-up of our frolicking
fivesome, but even he had lots of fun. No Captain Hook
haunted our Never-Never Land, although there was that
wretched crocodile, with its relentlessly ticking clock. We
grew up, every one of us, when Jean-Luc died. In an instant, the fantasy was over. Within days, even Chase and
Hope were gone."

Eleanor stopped speaking.

But it took Cass several moments to hear silence where
she had been hearing laughter, and several more to reconcile what Eleanor had just said with what she had learned
from Hope.

"Chase was gone?" she asked at last. "I knew that Hope
went to New York, but I thought Chase remained here."

"Chase *returned* here."

"He ran away?" *Ran home?*

"Oh, no. Running is not Chase Tessier's style. It wasn't
even when he was twelve and his entire world had shattered. Chase was a grown-up, remember? He simply told
Frances he was going to live in Napa—with Hope. Frances
let him go, and promised that Hope could follow later,
when she was older. Not that Frances believed there would
ever be a later. Victor was already here, meeting with real-
tors to determine a fair asking price for the Domaine."

"Victor was going to sell the winery?"

"He was. But somehow Chase talked him out of it."

Hope hadn't told her *that,* a detail a four-year-old was unlikely to know. Hope had simply explained that following Grandpère's death, no Tessier—except Chase—ever again lived at the Domaine, and that, ever after, she—and Victor and Frances—visited the estate, and the valley, only rarely.

Hope had moved at age four to the Manhattan penthouse where Victor lived still; and later, while Frances Tessier was writing her best-selling novels and Victor was dazzling worldwide audiences with his gift for the violin, Hope attended boarding schools—the same ones attended by her patrician mother—in Connecticut and France. Hope's girlhood summers were frequently spent at camp, and family holidays almost always happened in luxury hotels—or in villas, or on yachts.

That was Hope's story, at least the basic fabric; a tapestry into which Chase was woven by letters, and phone calls, and journeys, when he could, to the hotels, villas, and yachts.

Chase. In Hope's recounting of her childhood Chase was always the older brother she admired so much—so centered, so confident, so mature. But, Cassandra realized, as grown-up as Chase might have seemed, as persuasive as he had obviously been in convincing Victor not to sell the Domaine, he was only twelve when the rest of his family moved away.

Cassandra frowned briefly, then smiled. "So Chase lived with you and Andrew."

"We wanted that, of course," Eleanor replied. "But Chase had already lost too much—Hope and Grandpère. I think he was afraid of getting even closer to us, only to lose us, too. He remained here, at the Domaine, with a small army of staff he never really knew, until he was old enough to live alone."

"But you saw him."

"Oh, yes. I insisted that he sample every culinary extravaganza I concocted, and Andrew showed him every op-ed piece before it went to press." As Eleanor reached for the marionette's discarded black sweater, her smile faded, and her mind journeyed to memories as dark and as somber as the garment she held. "There came a time, long after Chase could possibly have needed us, when he suggested that we live together after all."

"When Andrew became . . . ill?"

"Ill," Eleanor echoed, speaking to the blackness. "It's an odd word, isn't it? Alzheimer's is an illness, a disease, and yet until three months before he died, Andrew was so very healthy." She looked up. "Anyway, yes, that was when Chase made the offer. And when I—we—refused, Chase simply began dropping by to help. After Andrew died, Chase offered me a job, created it for me."

"The Blue Iris."

Eleanor smiled. "You and Hope have been talking."

"I hope that's all right."

"*Of course,* Cassandra. It's lovely. But I'll bet Hope didn't tell you—because how would she know?—that Chase's decision to open a gift shop and tasting room had nothing whatsoever to do with business. A winery of Tessier's stature needn't be open to the public. Ever. But I wasn't doing well. And Chase knew it. And Chase Tessier is simply not afraid of old people. He may be an old soul himself."

"Eleanor! You're *not* old."

"No one is old, Cassandra, not inside, not unless they permit themselves to be. But there I was, feeling every bit a sixty-eight-year-old fossil. Decrepit. Useless—"

"But you don't feel that way now."

"Heavens, no! I feel about your age. Thanks to Chase. He's really quite wonderful, Cassandra."

I know that, Eleanor! It's not him. It's me.

"Chase is so very much like Grandpère," Eleanor persisted. "Honest and generous and fair."

At last, at last, Cassandra understood. The wise and wily woman who stood before her was the genuine article after all—a fairy godmother whose vision was twenty-twenty; beyond twenty-twenty, for Eleanor saw the delicate wishes of even the most battered of hearts.

Chase is remarkable, Eleanor told her, and honest and generous and fair. And what Eleanor meant, the moral of her story was this: Chase Tessier will give you—even you, Cassandra—a chance.

*M*ay I help you?"

"Oh! Chase. What are you . . . ?"

"Doing here? Well, Cassandra, I live here. And, as it turns out, my office is directly across the courtyard. So when I noticed the kitchen light, I decided to wander on over."

"You were in your office at one A.M.?"

"I was. And you're here. So, Cassandra, how may I help you? Are you foraging for food? I wouldn't be surprised. You barely touched your dinner."

Yes I did. She had eaten more than usual, had forced herself to eat, even though her stomach twisted and churned. But she hadn't consumed enough for the appraising gray eyes. Chase had noticed that she ate like a bird—at least in front of Hope.

And what of his assessment now, in the middle of the night, having discovered her in his kitchen? Would he conclude that she was a secret eater? A classic bulimic? Classic, but with a cruel streak, maliciously mindful that her clandestined binge would be attributed to Hope and never exposed.

Cassandra's own conclusion might have seemed excessively paranoid, had it not been for the icy glitter of his dark gray eyes. The glitter was triumph—having caught her in the act. And the ice? A frigid foreboding of an appropriate punishment for this most selfish thief of his sister's already ravaged self-esteem.

"Cassandra?"

"I was looking for something to drink. Some wine . . . or something."

Cass hadn't consumed a drop of alcohol during dinner, had specifically declined. Perhaps, to the master vintner, closet drinking was a lesser offense? Cass couldn't tell. His expression was cool, impassive, calm.

Yet she felt judged. Condemned. And she ached.

It was time, past time, for the actress within to saunter onto the stage. But the usually brazen Thespian was nowhere to be found. Blanche DuBois and the myriad other guises Cassandra could so effortlessly evoke were fairweather phantoms far too terrified of the granite gray eyes to come out to play.

Cassandra was on her own, and now there was that other pain, tearing not at her heart but at her womb, its knife-sharp claws piercing, twisting, piercing anew.

Surprise. Hurt. Defiance. Fear. Chase saw them all, in a whirling flutter of luminous wings. Then something new: pallor. And breathlessness. And fists clenched tightly, as if in mimicry of a clenching within.

Chase Tessier had been on the planet for a while. Twenty-six years. He had known women, intimately, for over a decade. His guess was an educated one and would have been casual, leisurely . . . had she not been in pain.

"You're having your period, aren't you?"

Her pale cheeks flushed pink, even as her fists curled into smaller, tighter, bloodless knots. Despite her crescendoing pain, she was embarrassed—surprising him again, enchanting him anew.

The sultry Blanche would not have been embarrassed.

But Cassandra was.

Tinkerbell was.

"Yes," she murmured. "I am. I've heard that alcohol sometimes helps."

"I've heard that, too." Testimonials from lovers, women for whom the subject was not embarrassing at all. Indeed, they told him in lavish detail about the paroxysms of pain, the fury and the peace. Chase's lovers raved about the salutary effects of alcohol for menstrual cramps—but they invited him to ply them with any old Tessier vintage any old time, a gourmet accompaniment to pleasure, not pain. "You've never tried it before?"

"No. My period only shows up once in a while." *Every six or eight months, a token—if taunting—appearance.* "This is the first time since I heard about trying alcohol."

"Well. You've come to the right place. Follow me, Cassandra."

His graceful strides were swift, wanting an end to her pain. But during the short journey to the Blue Iris, the piercing claws relinquished their fury.

"Oh," Cass whispered when they reached the gift shop and tasting room. Three walls were glass, providing daylight vistas of roses and vines, and there was more glass inside: display cases filled with knickknacks for sale; glass-top tables adorned with crystal vases, abloom with irises, where guests were invited to linger over a glass of wine; and, of course, a wall of bottles, filled with Tessier's best, behind the tasting counter. The floor was iris blue, and what wood there was, the framework that held the glass, was cream, and the entire room sent a message of welcome and cheer. "This is beautiful."

"Thanks to Eleanor."

Thanks to you, for giving Eleanor this chance. For giving everyone a chance.

"How are you feeling?"

"Fine . . . for the moment."

"Let's seize the moment, then. What wine would you like?"

"Oh, anything. I don't really drink much."

"Are you twenty-one?" Hope had said she was, but everything about this creature was so different from what Chase expected.

Her chin lifted. "Of course I am."

"For aeons?"

"Since Halloween."

"Halloween." He gazed at her—the plum jumpsuit, sashed in mauve, the black boots with their high, high heels, the luxuriant chaos of amber, the vulnerability of bright blue eyes. "What are you, Cassandra? Trick or treat?" *Penitent or peacock? Temptress or Tinkerbell?*

I'm a trick, can't you tell? Cassandra's girlhood acquaintances—and her parents—had made the devastating diagnosis at first glance. How else to describe a skin-and-bones girl with a droopy face and unruly hair? How else? Witch. *Witch.*

Chase saw her sudden sadness and felt an astonishing urge to curl her into his arms—and murder whoever had caused her such pain. Whoever. At the moment he was the culprit.

Chase embraced her not with his arms, but with his voice.

"Treat," he said softly. "You're definitely a treat."

"Oh! Well . . ."

"Well. So, Cassandra"—Chase gestured to the wall behind the tasting counter—"what's your pleasure?"

"Whatever's cheapest. I mean, least expensive. I'll pay for it, of course."

"All the prices are the same. On the house. Make a choice."

She knew nothing about wine. Not one thing. But when her gaze fell on light pink liquid in a bottle so lovely it could have been a vase for roses . . . "Some of that pretty pink stuff? Maybe?"

"Ah." Silver shafts of amusement glittered in his dark gray eyes. "The white zinfandel."

Chase moved as he spoke, ever mindful of the claws of fury that might seize her once again. He retrieved a perfectly chilled bottle from beneath the counter, opened it, and poured a glass.

"Aren't you having any?" she asked as he handed her the shimmering crystal glass.

"White zinfandel is a bit too pink—and too sweet—for my taste."

"Not a guy drink."

His smile was slow, sexy, utterly—and devastatingly—male. "Not a guy drink."

Cass wanted to return the smile, its soft, seductive, feminine twin. But Blanche, and all the others, were still in hiding, and before she could find the courage to try such a smile on her own, a fierce—if taunting—reminder of her womanhood stole her breath.

"Drink," Chase commanded gently.

And she did, discovering in several urgent—yet ladylike—sips the truth about Domaine Tessier's white zinfandel: its taste was as delicate as its color, but its potency rivaled that of any other wine, especially for someone unaccustomed to alcohol and exhausted from pain. *"Oh."*

"You can't possibly be feeling it that quickly."

"But I am. I *am.*"

"And?"

"It's working." The claws were floating in a light pink pool of warmth. She was floating, too, and the joyful chorus within sang a lovely serenade.

This is your chance. He is giving you a chance.

A chance to float, in this glassy wonderland, amid a garden of irises blooming in crystal vases by Lalique. Chase floated beside her. Elegant, graceful, unhurried. A perfect host. A leisurely sentry.

Cassandra set the course and the pace, a meandering stroll from flowers to gifts, a floating pink journey that brought a lovely pink smile when she spotted a display of dangling glass earrings—a tiny vineyard of them—dainty clusters of grapes painted in every shade of purple and cream.

"These are wonderful," she murmured as she studied the whimsical yet delicate array.

Eventually her gaze fell to more hand-painted glass in the display case below: wineglasses, goblets, elegant flutes designed for champagne. There was no whimsy here, only delicacy, and the improbable—yet so beautiful—intertwining of roses and vines.

As Cass leaned over for a closer look, a curtain of amber impeded her view. Leaning still, she set her own wineglass on the countertop, freeing her hands; then, with both, she grabbed the renegade strands and swept them over her shoulders.

Away.

But the banished strands did not stay away. Could not. This time, however, as gravity began to wreak havoc anew, the amber curtain was captured, such a gentle imprisonment, by fingers that were strong, and lean, and very male.

"You like the stemware?" he asked.

"Yes," she breathed, barely.

"The artist is Jane Parish," Chase said. Jane Parish . . . an extraordinary artist . . . unless one happened to compare her talent, any talent, to the creator of this silken cloud of spun gold. The golden cloud seemed to flutter in his hands, as if *she* were fluttering at his touch. Fluttering, trembling, wanting—*what the hell was he thinking?* That he needed to learn the truth about Cassandra Winter. Temptress? Or Tinkerbell. "I've asked Jane to paint a special collection of champagne flutes for the centennial celebration in September. Each guest will keep his—or hers—as a memento of the evening. That includes you, Cassandra, if you're still here."

His voice was soft, husky, welcoming, as if he wanted her here. Now. Then. Always.

"I will be."

"Even if passion strikes?"

His voice was soft still, deep and low. But she heard the edge, the warning, the taunt.

And she floated no more. And her world, once so pink, turned as gray as his eyes. She straightened and spun. Her hair spun with her, unrestrained and free . . . for Chase Tessier had already let go.

"Do you really believe I have some ulterior motive?"

I don't want to believe it. But I have to be sure. "I have some concerns."

Why? she wanted to scream. But she knew why. Because Chase Tessier could see into her soul. He could see her lies.

"Hope has been quite vague about how the two of you met."

"Because she was protecting me."

"Protecting you?"

"Yes!"

"Meaning you're not going to tell me, either."

This is your chance, the chorus admonished. The choir was not so merry now, its music more chant than song: Your only chance. Your *only* chance. Tell him what truths you can tell.

"We met in the Sculpture Garden. At dawn. Hope had never been there before. But I went there often." *To watch as the first rays of dawn caressed the statues. To watch the night-dark copper come to life.* "I was . . . unhappy. Hope offered to help."

"So Hope befriended you."

"Yes. *She* befriended *me*."

"Unhappy," Chase repeated quietly. "Why, Cassandra? Were you thinking about your parents?"

No. Of course not! She had no reason to mourn her fictional parents and their fictional deaths. The lie began long before she ever met Hope . . . long before she learned that Grandpère had died when Hope was four, and Frances when she was seventeen.

And if she confessed to Chase the astonishing—yet unwitting—coincidence? The false—yet compelling—bond? *An honest lie, Chase! A fiction I needed—for me—so I could reinvent myself and begin again.*

To confess the lie would be to confess *that* she lied.

Cass met his harsh silvery gaze and spoke the truth. "I was unhappy, that's all. I wasn't thinking about my parents. Nor was I bemoaning the fact that I had yet to entrap some scion of Bel Air. I'm not a gold-digger. That was a joke." *A silly tease from the irrepressible Blanche—before she fled, in terror, from you.* "If you knew anything about me, Chase, you'd realize that the notion of my searching for some man to support me is absolutely ludicrous."

"Oh? Because?"

"Because I'm never getting married."

"Because?"

Because no one would want me. "Because of the *monotony,* of course. The monotony of monogamy."

Chase gazed at her. Proud and fierce. Fragile and brave. And a woman with such vast sexual experience that she knew already she could never be satisfied by just one man? No. Not Tinkerbell. Not this luminous creature who fluttered at his touch.

"What," he asked softly, "about children?"

Children? What child—what baby—would want me for a mother? "I guess I'm old-fashioned when it comes to children and matrimony."

"Meaning no children? Ever?"

"No children," Cassandra confirmed. *Ever.*

Her gaze fluttered away, for a moment, then returned, determined and proud . . . and prepared to answer whatever other questions this concerned older brother might have.

But Chase Tessier had a comment, not a question. And it was spoken gently, without a hint of concern. "Hope is very lucky to have you as a friend."

Cassandra's blue eyes shimmered with surprise. "I'm the lucky one, Chase. Hope doesn't need me. Not really. She's so strong."

"Too strong sometimes."

"I suppose."

"And sometimes, Cassandra, I'm too protective."

"That's not possible."

"Sure it is. Witness the past few moments. For which I'm very sorry."

"It's *okay.*"

"No. It's not. And I'm sorry." Chase looked at her, watched her, waited until he saw delicate flickers of hope. "Okay?"

"Yes," she whispered. "Okay."

Okay. Chase was being fair, giving her a chance. But what would happen, she wondered, if—*when*—she let him down?

FIVE

DOMAINE TESSIER

JULY, EIGHT YEARS AGO

*I*s anyone interested in a field trip?"

"Sure," Hope enthused.

Sure, Cass echoed silently as her entire being sang.

As Eleanor had forewarned, Chase Tessier, wine maker and CEO, had been endlessly occupied. Cassandra had not seen him, even from a distance, for eighteen days. She wasn't actually seeing him now. She and Hope were on the veranda of the Blue Iris, sipping lemonade in the summer twilight, and he was standing behind her.

"How about you, Cassandra?"

Yes. Yes! She fashioned her reply, a study in nonchalance, before she turned to him. "What field?"

His black hair held prisoner every fading glimmer of sunlight, and his eyes glittered with a light of their own—amused silver fire. "Well, I have to check our Russian River

51

vineyard—I beg your pardon, the herds in the south forty—after which I thought we might go to Bodega Bay for the night."

"We want to go," Hope said. "When?"

"Tomorrow morning, returning Saturday."

"Oh." Hope's enthusiasm faded. "Is that a problem for you, Cass?"

"Well, yes. I mean, I'd have to be back here by four."

"Hot date, Cassandra?" The query sounded idle, casual, polite. But there was nothing casual in the eyes that darkened from silver to steel.

"Hot *job*," Hope clarified. "Even though Cass should be relaxing this summer, relaxing for once, she's not. She even has this fantasy about paying room and board."

The steel glinted. "Divest yourself of that fantasy, Cassandra, as well as any burgeoning fantasies about paying for Bodega Bay. It's my treat. I'd like the company. And as it so happens, I too have to be back by four Saturday afternoon. So, we leave—pardon me, saddle up—at ten in the morning."

Then Chase was gone, riding off, metaphorically, into the sunset.

*T*he summer sky, on that night, was mauve satin . . . which became ebony velvet sprinkled with stars . . . then glowed pink again, at dawn, with lacy lavender ruffles at its edge.

By ten A.M., the heavens shimmered cobalt.

Cassandra chose, for their journey, to sit in the backseat of Chase's car.

"Seat belt, Cassandra." It was a soft command, issued before leaving the Domaine, and his dark gray gaze smoldered not with censure, but with concern. "Please."

"Okay."

"Thank you."

"You're *welcome.*"

The terrain changed as they neared the Russian River. Forests appeared, lush and dense; towering islands of pine with oceans of vineyards in between.

"I won't be long," Chase explained as he stopped the car in the shade of such a majestic island. "I just need to check the vines here and on the hill."

"Hold it!"

Chase turned, his expression serious, patient, intense. "Cassandra."

The undivided attention—and interest—of Chase Tessier was unsettling. Awesome. She managed, however, to match his solemnity in kind. "Chase."

"Is there a problem?"

"Well, yes. I was wondering why Hope and I can't check the vines with you. I mean, is this a field trip or isn't it? Of course, I recognize that this is probably a *men*folk thing, another crystal shard in the glass ceiling that has created a wine-making universe composed—with rare exceptions— almost entirely of males."

Without a word, but with a glitter of gray, Chase got out of the car.

"What a chauvinist! I'm sorry, Hope, but your brother is really—" Cassandra stopped abruptly as her car door and Hope's simultaneously opened.

"Ladies," Chase said.

Hope giggled and Cass sniffed, as imperiously as possible, "Thank you."

Chase smiled. "You're *welcome.*"

Cassandra was dressed as a cowgirl—of sorts—on this summer day: the inevitable high-heeled boots, the requisite blue jeans, a hot pink blouse floating over an emerald tee. As she strode toward a row of vines, however, the flamboyant cowgirl became the princess of Wales.

When she spoke, her accent was British, her manner arch. "I daresay, Hope, this is a rather fine example of vertical trellising. Wouldn't you agree?"

Except for the threat of a new round of giggles, Hope Tessier made a credible lady-in-waiting. She thoughtfully studied the sculpted vines, pruned to afford the perfect exposure to—and protection from—the summertime sun. Her Majesty's faithful sidekick did not attempt the royal accent. But her affect was precisely right. "A fine example, Cassandra."

"Just the sort of canopy the finicky pinots adore. These *are* pinot noir, I presume."

"Why do you presume that?" Chase asked.

Cassandra looked at him with the noblesse oblige of an astonished royal. "Deep purple grapes. Cool river mists. A maritime microclimate. An oceanic *terroir*. What else could they be?"

"What else indeed."

Her intelligent blue eyes narrowed as her scanning gaze came to rest on a cluster of vines planted halfway up the hill. "Hold on. We're growing some pinot meunier, too, aren't we? I can't see the grapes per se, but that white dusting, that miller's flour look, is a dead giveaway."

"I'm impressed, Cassandra. What happened to the pretty pink stuff?"

"It's still pretty . . . and pink."

As are your cheeks, Tinkerbell. Pretty, and pink, and utterly intoxicating.

"And is there some pinot gris as well?"

"Perhaps," Chase conceded. "Why do you ask?"

"Well, as I'm sure you know, several other champagne houses are adding a little pinot gris to their *cuvées*."

"Do you happen to know what percent of their blends is gris?"

"No." *But I could find out, Chase!* I could become a champagne spy, a merlot Mata Hari. I *would*, for you—if it would make you look at me as you are looking now, with such interest, such approval, such . . . "I might be able to find out."

"I'm sure you could. But I go by taste, Cassandra. My taste."

Of course he did. The lips and mouth that set a breath-taking standard for sensuality did so, as well, for wine. And as for corporate sabotage? Chase Tessier would deplore the notion, deplore whoever—

"I repeat, Cassandra." Those lips, that mouth, spoke softly. "I'm impressed."

"This is just the tip of the iceberg of what she knows," her lady-in-waiting advised.

"Of what we both know," Cass amended. "You've been right there, Hope, on every tour, and given your incredible memory, there isn't a fact you've forgotten."

"Every tour?"

"Every tour," Hope confirmed. "While you've been holding down the Tessier fort, Cass and I have been checking out the competition."

"Why? Are you thinking about becoming a wine maker, Cassandra?"

She smiled in reply, provocatively, beautifully, as Blanche DuBois made a rare return. It was a surprising time for such a cameo. The sultry belle appeared only when there was pain. But there *was* pain now—a longing, a *wanting* that hurt far more than all the familiar disdain.

"Would that threaten you, Mr. Tessier?"

"Not at all, Ms. Winter. In fact, in the interest of fair play, feel free to drop by my office any time. I'd be delighted to show you the business aspects of making wine, and you might enjoy my library of videos and books."

"Why, thank you, sir."

"You're most welcome," Chase replied pleasantly, easily—but he was conflicted. It was fun for Hope, good for Hope, to be a lady-in-waiting for a princess or the friend of a temptress from New Orleans. But Chase didn't like—in Cassandra—the pretending, the *games*. He looked from the provocative Blanche to his unpretentious sister. "So, from your travels, how does Tessier stack up?"

"Tessier is the best."

It was Cassandra who answered, Cassandra who felt the desperate, aching loss when he looked away.

She was Cassandra now, just Cassandra, without accent, without embellishment, without pretense of any kind. So earnest were her sky blue eyes, so clear and so bright, that—although Chase knew she wasn't lying—he sensed a qualification of sorts.

"But, Cassandra?"

"But nothing. Tessier is the best. By far."

Chase smiled. "But?"

"Well. Why doesn't Domaine Tessier offer tours?"

"You think people—other than future wine makers—are actually interested?"

"Yes," Cass said.

"Definitely," Hope asserted.

"It seems," Chase replied, "that we have a consensus. I wonder if Mark or Alec would like to give tours."

"Maybe," Cass murmured.

"But?"

"Well, it's just that they're both so terrific—and indispensable—in the tasting room. Besides, finding guides would be a snap. Enology majors from Davis and Stanford drop by the Blue Iris every day, trolling for jobs, trying to convince Eleanor that there should be tours. Frankly, it would be much easier for Eleanor if there were—less time explaining to people why there aren't."

"So Eleanor likes the idea as well?"

"Absolutely."

"Okay." Chase smiled. "Done. Now, ladies, let's see what else you've learned."

Nothing, they realized. Absolutely nothing compared to what they learned during those sunlit hours from the master.

Taste the grapes, Chase told them, and tell me what you taste.

Their answers, at first, were tentative. But encouraged by the silver-eyed magician who believed that within each grape dwelled the flavors of everything it had known from birth to harvest, his apprentices became quite bold.

"I taste the river," Cassandra whispered.

"Good," Chase coaxed softly. "Very good. What else?"

"The pines," Hope offered.

"Yes. Absolutely. The pines are there, too. Now try, this time, to taste the wind."

*I*t was evening when they reached Bodega Bay. They separated, to settle into their respective ocean view rooms and agreed to meet, for dinner, just before sunset.

Chase was seated at their window table when Cass appeared. He stood as she approached and pulled the chair out for her when she arrived.

"Is your room all right?"

"It's lavish. Thank you. Far fewer birds, however, than I'd imagined."

"Rumor has it Hitchcock imported a few. Where's Hope?"

"In her room. She'll be down in a while, definitely in time for the green splash."

"Flash."

"Whatever. A figment by any other name."

"You've never seen it?"

"A bright green flash as the setting sun splashes into the sea? No, and neither has Hope, although we've given it the old college try. Literally. Study breaks, precisely at sunset, at the palisades. Have you seen it?"

"Never." His gray eyes narrowed. "Is Hope all right?"

"Oh. Yes. She just needs a little time alone. She'd like us to order a Diet Pepsi for her."

"Cassandra?"

"She's *fine,* Chase. Keeping one's own counsel is all part of being so strong."

"True," he conceded quietly. "So. Diet Pepsi for Hope. And for you? A glass of white zinfandel?"

"Yes. Please. Unless . . . is it too awful for you to have something so pink sitting on the table?"

"A threat to my masculinity, you mean? I think I can handle it. I wonder, though, if you'd like to try our blanc de noirs. It has the sweetness, and the pinkness, of the zin-fandel—plus bubbles."

"*And* has won all sorts of awards."

Chase smiled. "That, too."

"I'd like to try it."

When their drinks arrived, Cass raised her bubbly blush champagne to his sedately crystalline chardonnay.

"To Hope," she whispered as their glasses met.

"To Hope," he echoed solemnly. Solemn still, and toasting *her* with his serious gray eyes, he said, "It's won-derful that you've gotten her to get out. I was afraid she'd spend the summer reading romance novels in her room."

"Hope doesn't read romance novels."

"No? She did. Used to."

"I know. But not anymore. Hope doesn't read fiction at all—unless it's assigned."

"But she reads."

"Ravenously. Anything and everything to do with the law. Has she told you she plans to go to law school?"

"Yes. But not why."

"I don't know, either. Truth. Justice. The American Way. Maybe?"

"Maybe." Or maybe, Chase thought, it was the certainty of the law that appealed. Its rigid codes. Its unambiguous rules. Its absence of emotion. Its inability to betray. "In any event, thanks to you, Hope hasn't spent the summer immersed in jurisprudence."

His gray eyes caressed her, appraising, approving, enveloping her in a floating pink euphoria that had nothing to do with the dancing bubbles in her glass . . . and which she had done nothing to deserve. "It's not thanks to me, Chase. It's thanks to Hope. She's . . . trying. And it's been good for her, I think, *fun.*"

"I think so, too. And I think—no, Cassandra, I know—that it wouldn't have happened without you." His words embarrassed her, confused her, and if he persisted in his praise, she might look away, or go away, and Blanche would appear. He shifted the topic slightly, just enough to permit Cassandra, only Cassandra, to stay. "Eleanor says you've met Jane Parish."

She was floating still, would float forever. "Yes."

"And like her?"

"Very much. She's so talented, and so *together.*"

"Together?"

"Yes," she murmured. So serene, and so fearless. Jane, who was forty-three, had never married—despite offers, Eleanor said, from gorgeous, kind, wonderful men. Jane's men, according to Eleanor, remained important in her life: lovers turned friends whose children adored their aunt Jane and whose wives trusted her never to lure their husbands back to her bed.

"Meaning?" Chase pressed gently.

"Meaning Jane couldn't care less if she happens to have a little paint, or even a lot of paint, on her face, her hands, her hair. Nothing—and no one—intimidates Jane Parish. If only she'd been with us the day we encountered the witch."

"The witch?"

Cassandra's blue eyes widened. "Did I say witch? Excuse me. That was an insult to witches everywhere. I meant bitch."

"Ah." Chase smiled. "And who might that be?"

"Napa's very own cover girl. Sibyl 'My face should grace *Vogue*' Raleigh."

The description was apt. There was no denying Sibyl's glamour and style. But Cassandra's other description was apt as well.

"Not one of my favorite people."

"But Eleanor says that she is in charge of Tessier's centennial gala. That our Ms. Raleigh has a gala-giving business called It's My Party."

"She is. She does."

"Not that I'd ever tell *her*, but—for anyone familiar with the lyrics—It's My Party is a ridiculous name."

"Ridiculous," Chase concurred, "but hardly a liability. Sibyl has gone from San Francisco's premier society hostess to the Bay Area's businesswoman of the year. Which means, I guess, that her clients aren't put off by the name."

"Just as you weren't."

"Actually, it was Victor's decision. Victor's call."

Victor, Cassandra mused. Not Father, not Dad, not Pops, not *Père*. "Victor."

"He and Sibyl go back a long way."

"Oh, that's right. In between bitchy remarks, party-woman did demand—more than once, now that I think of it—to know precisely when Victor would be arriving for the gala, how many days, or weeks, in advance. Is there an answer to that, in case we see her again?"

The faintest frown shadowed Chase's face. "No." The shadows became deeper. Darker. "Tell me about the bitchy remarks. Was there something Sibyl said to you?" *About you?*

"Well, yes, but . . ." Cassandra shrugged dismissively, as if disapproval of her were entirely expected. "Anyway, it's what she said to Hope that was truly malignant—especially since it was cloaked in concern. The word 'weight' was never mentioned, but there was abject pity on her cover girl face as she raved about how *obviously* difficult the past year had been for Hope, and how *upset* your mother would have been had she known."

"Maybe Sibyl won't be handling the centennial celebration after all." His voice was dangerously calm. "In fact, she won't be."

"*No,* Chase. It would be awkward for Hope if you made this a cause célèbre. And it's not even the end of the world for her to learn to deal with bitches. Or, for that matter, to hear your mother's friends—I assume Sibyl was a friend?—ascribing reactions to her that simply would not have been true."

"Not true?" Chase repeated. "Frances wouldn't have been upset about the weight Hope has gained?"

Frances, Cassandra mused. Not Mother, not Mom, not *Mère*.

"Cassandra?"

"No," she replied. "Frances wouldn't have been upset. In fact— Oh, Hope, here you are!"

"Hi. I feel like I interrupted. . . ."

"Not at all," Chase assured her with a smile. "Cass and I were just discussing the elusive green flash—and hoping you'd arrive in time to see it."

"Which you have," Cass murmured. *So, Chase Tessier, you too tell lies—smoothly, expertly . . . for love.* "Just in time."

Just, for in seconds the sun would vanish beyond the horizon, and this magical day would end, its heat, its light, its floating pink joy, drowned forever in the icy sea.

Cassandra watched with dread this ending, this death. It was almost done, the loss irrevocable and complete. Only a tiny rim of the fiery star remained, and that was disappearing, too, so quickly, a free fall now, a plummeting surrender to the inevitable.

Then it happened, and they all saw it—the glorious splash, not the anguished drowning. Emeralds scattered into the twilight sky, an infinity of dancing jewels, each precious gem sending a shimmering green promise to the world.

There will be light—again.

And heat. And joy.

And magic.

*C*hase and Cassandra discovered, twenty-four hours later, the reason each needed to return to Napa by four. Cassandra's hostessing job at Courtland's commenced at five . . . and Chase needed to deal with whatever loose ends had unraveled during his absence before his own arrival, at Courtland's, at eight.

Cass saw him the moment he entered the posh Napa Valley eatery—many moments before he saw her. They might have collided, for Cass had just noticed the departing diner, an elderly woman with a cane, and would have held the door herself, had Chase not gotten there first. He made the woman's wobbly journey easy and pleasant. His smile told her there wasn't the slightest need to hurry, he was in absolutely no rush, she could take all the time she wanted. As relief—and gratitude—flickered in her ancient eyes, she did just that.

Which gave Cassandra time to adjust, to prepare, to try to. As always, Chase Tessier wore his midnight black hair, and his intense gray eyes, and his elegance, his power, his grace. Inconsequential adornments worn tonight included an impeccably tailored charcoal gray suit understated further by a blue gray tie.

It was only as the door closed behind the departing matron that Cass noticed Chase's other adornment, not inconsequential in the least, merely beautiful, merely regal, merely stylishly self-assured. The woman, who was Chase Tessier's date, rested a perfectly manicured hand on his charcoal-cloaked arm—rested, but did not cling . . . for she was far too confident to cling.

Chase saw Cassandra then, at last. Surprise—and something she could not possibly read—flickered deep and dark in his silver gray eyes.

"Hello, Cassandra."

"Good evening, Chase. I hadn't noticed your name in our reservation book. Did you . . . ?"

"Yes."

"Oh, yes. Here it is." In blue and white, and with embellishments that made her ache. "Let's see, according to this asterisk, you called last night." *After* our sunset dinner in Bodega Bay? *After* we saw a treasure trove of emeralds splash from the sea? "And requested the table in the gardenia alcove."

"If available," he amended gently.

Cass looked up from the reservation book and smiled. Brilliantly. "Of course it is. For Chase Tessier? Of *course.*"

"Oh, good," his date graciously enthused. "It's our favorite."

"We aim to please."

"Thank you. I'm Paige, by the way."

"Sorry," Chase murmured. "Paige, this is Cassandra Winter. Cassandra, Paige Roderick."

"You're Hope's friend," Paige said.

"Yes," Cass confirmed softly. "That's who I am."

And who was Paige Roderick?

Just about the most well-liked heiress in the valley, Cass learned as Paige and Chase dined in gardenia-fragrant seclusion. The information came—in unqualified raves—from employees and guests alike.

Paige was quite sensational: classy and smart. Her summa cum laude graduation from Vassar had been followed, with comparable brilliance, by a Harvard MBA. She had held, and distinguished, the title of chief financial officer at her family's winery for almost three years, and she and Chase had been an item since March . . . an item Hope had never mentioned—why would she?—if, in fact, she even knew.

Hope probably didn't know, Cassandra decided. His love life, even with someone as fabulous as Paige, was not something Chase was likely to discuss with his little sister—unless and until there was something she needed to know . . . which there would be, any day now, it seemed, for the union of Paige Roderick and Chase Tessier was a match, everyone agreed, made in vintner heaven.

When Paige ventured from the alcove—a posture-perfect journey to the powder room—Cass defied every survival instinct she possessed.

Even after reaching the alcove, Cass had ample opportunity to retreat from her self-destructive madness. Chase was staring at his glass of champagne, his gray eyes grave and intense. Another man might have been merely lost in idle thought. But this man, never lost, never idle, seemed on the verge of a monumental decision—a marriage proposal, perhaps, amid the gardenias.

"Hi."

Chase looked up. Stood up. "Cassandra."

"May I?" She gestured to the cushioned chair vacated by Paige. May I sit with you in this lovers' haven, just long enough to remind myself who I am? *And who I will never be?*

"Sure." He held the chair as she fluttered into the cushiony softness. She was fluttering still, he decided as he sat across from her; *trembling* beneath the many vivid layers of chiffon. "Are you cold, Cassandra? Would you like my jacket?"

"No, thank you. It is a bit chilly. By design, I suppose, for cuddling."

Damn you, he thought, infuriated—yet enchanted.

Enchantment won. He wanted her here, with him, her asymmetric face aglow with candlelight, her blue eyes shining from the luminous glow within.

He smiled welcome, and reassurance, even as curiosity compelled him to ask, "Aren't you supposed to be manning—excuse me—*woman*ning—the entrance?"

"An important aspect of my job is making certain that our patrons are happy. Deliriously so. So here I am, making certain that you are." The questioning tilt of her head created a dance of candlelight in amber. "Are you?"

Yes. Deliriously. Now. "Of course."

The dancing stopped, and the shining blue glow started to fade—then brightened. She made it brighten. "Well,

good. Besides, we're full, and since reservations are virtually required—as native Napians know and every tourist
guidebook says—the only likely drop-ins are the Hollywood crowd."

"Who aren't big readers?"

"Who believe the rules don't apply to them."

"I see. Do I detect a certain disapproval of our visitors
from Tinseltown?"

"It's rational analysis, Chase, not random disdain. I
mean, doesn't it seem just a tiny bit aberrant to spend your
life pretending to be someone else, wanting to be, *choosing*
to be?"

"You don't enjoy being Blanche DuBois?"

*Enjoy? No. But sometimes being me—just me—hurts so
much I have to be someone else. Anyone else.*

"Cassandra?"

Her shrug was a battle of frail shoulders against an immense, invisible weight. In the midst of the valiant struggle, her droop became more pronounced, a sagging
sadness.

Chase wanted to kiss her lovely lopsided mouth, to vanquish all unhappiness, to transfer every ounce of anguish
from her delicate shoulders to his.

"Tell me," he whispered.

"What? Oh. Nothing! Anyway, except when I'm working here, or when a road's blocked off for filming, I don't
have much to do with the tinselly wonders."

"I hate to tell you this, Cassandra, but beginning next
week *Duet* will be on location at the winery."

"At *your* winery, Chase?"

"Domaine Tessier is not mine."

"But you run it." *You love it.*

"With Victor."

"He's an awfully silent partner, isn't he?" *Silent partner,* silent father, silent vintner. "As far as I can tell, Victor Tessier couldn't care less about the Domaine." *Or anyone—or anything—except himself.*

"That's really not true," Chase countered quietly, knowing the source of her contempt for Victor, understanding it, and appreciative of her fierce loyalty to Hope. But Chase had loyalties as well. "Victor and I talk all the time. He's very aware of the decisions I make—the decisions we make together."

"You talk? I guess I imagined Victor Tessier to be an e-mail kind of guy." *Silent, evil missives sent in the dead of night.*

"We talk. Frequently."

She narrowed her bright blue eyes. "These Hollywood types are his friends, aren't they?"

Chase smiled. "Victor does, from time to time, compose Academy Award–winning sound tracks for their films—including for *Duet.*"

"So why isn't Victor here, composing?"

"He wrote the music last summer."

Last summer, Cassandra mused. When Frances had died, and so much had been lost—for Hope. So much hope. But Hope was here, this summer, and maybe given enough time, happier times in paradise. . . .

"Domaine Tessier will be yours, though, one day."

"I wouldn't count on it, Cassandra. I'm certainly not."

"Is . . ." She shrugged as she battled a dangerous goading deep within, evoked by her own fantasy, her own pain. The fantasy was glorious: summer after summer here, in paradise, with Hope—and with Chase—tasting the wind and watching emeralds soar from the sea into the twilight sky.

"Is what?"

Is your fiancée counting on it? The sultry Blanche wanted

her to purr, to provoke his fury so irrevocably that every glorious, foolish fantasy—with its aching, longing pain—would end once and for all.

Cassandra wouldn't, couldn't, utter the insulting taunt. She didn't need to. "What are you doing, Cassandra? What game?"

The only game I know, the one that protects my heart from being shattered.

"Paige is very beautiful," she murmured, aching, shattering. "And she seems . . . quite pleasant."

"She is . . . quite pleasant."

Cassandra nodded and smiled a brave and lovely smile—for him, for his happiness, with Paige.

"As," Chase embellished softly, "are you. Quite pleasant. Sometimes." Then, with a gentle smile and so softly still, he added, "And, sometimes, Cassandra, you are impossible."

SIX

SURGICAL ICU

WESTWOOD MEMORIAL HOSPITAL

FRIDAY, NOVEMBER SECOND

I like it better when you're with her."

Chase was in a quiet room, seated on the edge of a chair, staring at the floor. A kaleidoscope of images, and memories, swirled in his sleep-starved mind.

The voice compelled him to look up. Politeness compelled him to stand.

"I beg your pardon, Dorothy?"

The ICU nurse didn't know if it was her sixty-three years or her gender that made this exhausted man, this gentleman, come so swiftly to his feet. He stood before her, impeccably bred, desperately worried.

"I said," she reassured him, "that I prefer it when you are at Cassandra's bedside. She's better when you're there. Better. Stronger. More calm."

Chase frowned, bewildered. A pharmacy of drugs filled

Cassandra's veins, medications expressly designed to thwart every normal physiological response. Her heart could not race with recognition, nor could her blood pressure soar, and even a gasp of breath-held surprise was precluded by the ventilator's carefully programmed puffs and sighs.

There was no way to assess better, stronger, more calm. But softly, reverently, Chase asked, "How can you tell?"

Dorothy's reply was gentle and wise. "Call it the art of nursing, an aptitude acquired after years—decades—on the job. She's better when you're with her, Chase. Even her color is better."

Her color? Cassie was white, *blue* white, the fragile translucence of ice stretched thin over a wintry lake. She was as cold as the frigid waters beneath that icy veneer. They were making her that cold. The thoughts screamed, pierced his soul. But Chase gazed at the seasoned nurse as if she were a high priestess and he was her most fervent disciple.

"Better," he whispered.

"Better," Dorothy confirmed.

"And better still when *he's* there?" *He.* Robert. The lover. The beloved.

Chase's query was a hope, a prayer, for Cassandra. Whatever, *who*ever, made her better was all that mattered.

But the high priestess was shaking her head.

"She's worse when Robert is with her. Agitated. Perhaps because he's so upset. Of course, no one's more upset than you." She smiled slightly at his surprise. "Call it the art of nursing. The point is, you're hiding your worry from Cassandra—which means that what she senses is your courage, your confidence, your calm."

"I'm not any of those things."

"Well. To her you are. Even without speaking. You don't speak to her, do you?"

"No." *Not aloud.* "Do you think I should?"

"Absolutely. If Romeo's anguished soliloquies are making her anxious, which they definitely are, then your words, your confidence, your calm—" Dorothy frowned.

"What is it?"

"I'm assuming there's some . . . difficult . . . past history between the two of you?"

"Yes."

"I guess I'd suggest steering clear of that, at least the truly thorny parts. Tell Cassandra about the things, and the people, she cares about. I'm sure you know what—and who—they are."

Chase knew. How he knew. He had seen Cassandra's passion for Hope *and for him* on that summer night, eight years ago, when he'd returned to the Domaine following his dinner with Paige. . . .

$\mathcal{I}$t was two o'clock in the morning. Cass was in the family room, sitting cross-legged on the carpeted floor in front of the mammoth television screen. Her feet were bare. Her bathrobe was *thread*bare. And her hair was a tangle of moonbeams.

A thoughtful expression touched her face. Thoughtful—and drooping. As Chase perceived the full measure of her damaged nerve, he understood the immense effort she must expend—every waking minute of her life—to overcome it.

At this waking moment, however, when she believed herself to be quite alone, Cassandra's vast energy was focused on the screen and whatever would be revealed once her slender fingers released their determined pressure on the VCR remote.

What engaged the ever-vigilant Tinkerbell so completely that he could stand, watching her, undetected and unseen? A romantic movie, perhaps. The frosty fate of Yuri and Lara. The sultry saga of Scarlett and Rhett.

No, Chase realized with an uneasy jolt when she reached her desired spot in the tape.

What riveted Cassandra was authentic drama, not Hollywood fare, although in production values this particular video rivaled Tinseltown's very best.

Chase had never viewed the tape. But he had been at the lavish gala and knew at a glance precisely where—in the celebration of Frances Tessier's forty-second birthday— they were. Victor had just given his wife the diamond necklace, and now the birthday girl was bestowing grand gifts of her own, promises of gifts, to her children.

The uneasy jolt became a rush of fury as Cassandra tilted ever closer to the screen, a divining rod seeking water . . . a Geiger counter sensing gold. Quite obviously this was not her first screening of the tape. And she was choosing to return to this sequence of frames, knowing what lay ahead, eager to see it anew.

"These are presents, not inheritances," Frances Tessier assured her guests. "I definitely plan to be around to watch Chase and Hope enjoy them. Chase can begin enjoying his gift any time. Except for one *tiny* little provision, Chase has complete control over when—and if—his gift becomes his. Hope's present, however, will be deferred until her thirtieth birthday. Fourteen years from now. That seems an eternity, doesn't it, my little love? But time passes so quickly, too quickly. It's simply impossible that you're already sixteen. *Sweet* sixteen, my sweet Hope. I remember so clearly the day you were born."

The camera remained on Frances, even as she posed rhetorical questions to her daughter, and now it zoomed even closer, revealing her own ageless beauty. Frances could be sixteen. Still. Always.

"Thirty will come soon enough, my darling. And these next fourteen years are so terribly important—a chance to discover who you are without the distraction of a fortune . . . and the unsavory men who hunt for such things. I know you won't be counting the days, my Hope, who *is* my hope. Money is not, nor ever will be, who you are. And despite its value, neither is my gift. It's about dreams, not about money. Career dreams, that is."

The best-selling novelist smiled. "So, enough prologue! On her thirtieth birthday, my daughter will receive every penny ever earned from my writing. *Every* penny, *ever*. Books, movies, audiotapes, the works."

As the professionally crafted video scanned the audience, other microphones, silenced during Frances's speech, captured the astounded murmurings of the be-gowned, bejeweled, and tuxedoed guests. *That's millions. Already. Millions.*

Eventually the camera found the beneficiary herself. Hope stood beside Chase, in his sheltering aura. She managed an awkward smile, and as applause—edited to an artful flutter—rippled through the ballroom, her plump cheeks turned bright red.

The obvious next move would have been for Hope to weave through the silk-and-satin sea to Frances, for an elaborate mother-daughter hug. But Hope was spared that mortifying journey as Frances spoke again.

"Now for Chase's gift, and the proviso—which the mothers among you will understand. Grandbaby lust, I believe it's called. Don't worry, Chase, it's not that bad. I know that children are not in your immediate plans—or, for that matter, perhaps not even in your eventual ones. Your life is full, satisfyingly replete, with the care and nurturing of grapes. I would not be so foolish as to mandate a Tessier grandbaby, much less a cluster of same, as a requirement for this gift—your gift, Chase—the gift of Black Mountain."

As Frances paused for effect, the audience microphones transmitted, amid the rustle of designer silk, whispered oohs and murmured aahs.

"That's right," Frances whispered above the whispers. "Black Mountain. As most of you know, Jean-Luc Tessier could not read. So Chase read to him. Grandfather and grandson learned, together, about the geology of the valley, the veins of volcanic ash laced throughout. Grandpère predicted—correctly, we now know—that grapes would flourish in that ash. He also predicted that a treasure trove of ash lay beneath the obsidian shell of the mountain, just waiting to be planted with vines. Jean-Luc Tessier shared his bold, if fanciful, vision with many of us. But mostly with Chase. Black Mountain was a gift to me, from Grandpère, on my wedding day. It will be my gift to my son on his."

Frances's tapered fingers caressed the diamonds encircling her neck, an entire strand of one-carat stones, free of flaws and crystal clear. "That's the requirement, Chase. A bride, a wife. It must be a *real* marriage, based on committed love. That's what Grandpère would have wanted—and, of course, it's my greatest wish for you as well."

Her fingers traced her gemstones still, the birthday present from her husband, as if the strand of perfect diamonds symbolized *her* marriage, how flawless a marriage could be. "True love, Chase. That's all I ask, with not a demand for a grandbaby anywhere in sight. I'll leave that immense— and quite possibly *im*possible—task to my future daughter-in-law, whoever she shall be."

Frances smiled, a provocative hint that there was something more. "In the meantime, while you're ushering the Domaine into its second century—and finding, with comparable care, the love of your life—I'll be adding an improvement or two to the mountain itself. My dear friend Sibyl's even *dearer friend* Gavin is building me—building you, Chase—a château. Not just any old château, of course, but a modern-day rendition of the Tessier château—and winery—in Champagne. Its grand opening will be celebrated with a Christmas ball to end all Christmas balls, a Sibyl Raleigh extravaganza so magnificent that even Victor will be compelled to spend a Christmas in the valley—at last."

The camera remained on Frances as she cast a teasing glance at her husband, whose reply was not recorded, only the fleeting frown that furrowed his beautiful wife's porcelain brow. "The château is for you, Chase—and for your bride. A home for your winery, and maybe for my grandchildren, and if nothing else, it could be the most elegant hotel the valley has ever seen. It's all terribly presumptuous of me. I know. But Grandpère would have loved this magnificent incarnation of his ancestral home—so I have to imagine that you will love it, too." A new tease sparkled, fondness for her handsome son. "So, Chase, your old mother isn't *too* awful, is she?"

The camera began its journey toward Chase, a leisurely sweep across faces shining with admiration for Frances's amazing largesse, a meandering crescendo that would peak when it captured the son's reaction to his monumental gift.

Chase knew his reaction. How he had felt inside. Elation. Gratitude. Joy beyond words.

But he had no idea which—if any—of the soaring emotions had been revealed on his face. Nor did he want to know. Or for Cassandra to know. But she did know already.

She had seen—already, at least once. And now she was leaning ever closer in anticipation of seeing it again.

"That's enough, Cassandra."

His voice was hoarse, harsh, and Chase moved as he spoke, toward the VCR, where he found the rewind button without a falter. The screen turned indigo as a quiet whir signaled the return of family secrets and fortunes to their celluloid vault.

"Oh!" she gasped. "Chase."

Such a different Chase from the man who had been dining at Courtland's with Paige. The jacket of his charcoal suit had been forsaken, as had his stylishly elegant tie. His shirt was open at the collar, rolled at the sleeves.

He was home now, in his luxurious castle, a man—a prince—whose every passion, every desire, had been gloriously satisfied. Gourmet food. Gourmet wine. Gourmet sex.

Except that Chase Tessier seemed hungry still.
Ravenous.

"So, Cassandra. Talk to me."

"I . . . couldn't sleep." *I kept seeing you kissing her, touching her, making love to her.*

"And?"

And it hurt. "Well, I decided to watch a movie. But then I saw this cassette—right here, on the shelf, in plain view."

Once having discovered a video labeled "Frances's forty-second, gifts to Hope and Chase," she had, of course, looked for something devoted exclusively to the Tessier children. But with the exception of Frances Tessier's birthday, the videotapes chronicled career, not family: Victor's concerts; Frances's appearances on *Oprah, Larry King Live, Entertainment Tonight;* their joint appearances at the Academy Awards.

"And this was more interesting to you than a movie?"

"Yes."

"Because?"

He towered over her, fierce and daunting.

But Cassandra stood, and even though Chase towered still, she met his searing gaze.

"Because," she said, "I wanted to learn something about Hope. Call me impossible."

She was so delicate in her bare feet, so fragile without the floating plumage she always wore. And so wounded, so terribly wounded by what he had said. It had been a gentle tease—at least he'd meant it that way—but it had pierced her. Deeply.

"If I may, Cassandra, I would very much like to retract that comment, or at least amend it. To *difficult,* maybe. Or better yet," Chase said softly, "and in the tradition of the finest of wines, *complex.*"

In the tradition of the finest of wines, she blushed a faint and lovely pink. "I . . . thank you."

"You're welcome. So, you wanted to learn something about Hope."

"Yes."

Chase gazed at her proud, defiant, drooping face—and believed her. Believed her.

"And," he asked gently, "did you?"

His gentleness was more fearsome than his fury. Cassandra moved, a few barefoot steps away, to the majestic piano the color of his hair. She traced a thoughtful finger along a brightly polished edge. "Indirectly, I suppose."

"Meaning?"

"Well, the video was mostly about your mother." Cassandra frowned at gleaming black wood, then looked at him. "She was so young when you were born. I mean, assuming this was really her forty-second birthday, and Hope was really sixteen, then you were twenty-four. Which means your mother was only eighteen when you were born, and your father couldn't have been much older."

"Frances was eighteen, and Victor was twenty. But my mother was thirteen. I don't know how old my father was—or who he was."

"You're . . . adopted?"

"Yes."

"Hope never told me."

"She could have, though. It's hardly a secret. I was six at the time."

"And your mother?"

"Died of a heroin overdose."

"I'm sorry."

"So am I. For her. She was too young to have a baby, and far too young to die. She was a good mother, even though she was only a child herself. She fed me, clothed me, protected me."

"Loved you."

"Loved me," Chase echoed softly. Even as she was dying, she had held him close to her, in a sheltering cave of warmth and love—which became a cavern of ice in which he had dwelled for many hours after she died. "I remember how patiently she taught me to read."

"And you"—*so patiently*—"taught Grandpère."

"I tried to teach him. But he was truly dyslexic. I know that now. All the letters looked the same to him."

"But it didn't matter. Because he had you." *The solemn, grown-up six-year-old boy.*

A soft glow lighted the dark gray eyes of the man that boy had become, a shaft of pure silver.

"We had each other," Chase said. "I taught Grandpère science. He taught me French." *And together we learned about love.* "So, Cassandra, tell me what the video taught you about Frances."

She had to move farther away. Had to. If not, she might move closer, too close, to the glowing silver gaze.

Her journey, this time, took her to a mahogany wall of books.

"It was all really about *her*, wasn't it?" she asked as she scanned the works of Frances Tessier. "Even when she was giving gifts to her children?"

"Yes, it was. Did you get that just from watching the tape? Or has Hope said something to you?"

She turned from the books to him. "Hope has said things, of course, but never critically. I think it's still too soon for her to recognize—or maybe simply admit—how selfish, how self-centered, her mother truly was."

"But you recognize Frances's selfishness from the tape?"

"And from her novels. Have you read them?"

"No."

"Neither has Hope. Frances told her not to until she was at least eighteen, something about their being 'R' rated and Hope being so innocent. Which is ludicrous, given that Hope was only seven when Frances decided to share with her the truth about her paternity."

"Hope was seven?" Chase asked.

"Yes. She knew, of course, that Victor wasn't her father. He had always been 'Victor,' not 'Daddy'—for both of you, I guess. But she wondered *idly*, at seven, about the man she had never known. It was curiosity, not torment, and Frances could have satisfied her inquisitiveness in all sorts of fictional ways. Instead, Frances told Hope everything: her anger that Victor ignored her in favor of some concerto he was composing; her retaliatory trip to Europe to research a book; the sexual nature of that study; the many men who could have fathered Hope—all of whom were fabulously rich and incredibly handsome . . . and some of whom, Frances said, were even royal." The tangled cloud of moonbeams tilted thoughtfully as Cassandra envisioned her lovely, generous, regal friend. "He probably *was* royal, whoever he was."

"Probably," Chase quietly agreed. The ice in his dark gray eyes melted, with love, for Hope. "Was Hope terribly upset?"

The moonbeams shook decisively. "No. Not at all. She *was* innocent, and the words had almost no meaning."

"Still," Chase murmured as, with love for Hope, the glacial gray froze anew. "I can't believe Frances told her everything—ever."

"You mean Frances Tessier?" Cass asked, pacing now, restless strides before the bookshelves. "Best-selling paragon of family values—and of love? If her books are any indication, she was not a paragon, much less an expert."

"Oh?"

"I mean, love should be unselfish, shouldn't it? And giving? And kind? Her characters are always so greedy, so self-indulgent—especially when it comes to . . ."

Her pacing stopped.

Everything stopped.

"Sex, Cassandra?" he asked softly, captivated by her passion, by *her*—barefoot, and fluttering, and so luminous as she offered her bold and breathless definition of love. But when it came to defining physical intimacy, Tinkerbell became tentative anew. "Tell me how sex, making love, should be."

"Well, I . . ." Her gaze fell away, a flutter of gold and sable lashes over shining blue eyes.

"Unselfish, Cassandra? And giving and kind?"

"Yes." She spoke to the heather green carpet. "I suppose." She looked up, impassioned again—for her friend—and not moving now, absolutely still, as she spoke to the man in the indigo moon. "In any event, although Frances was clearly a stylish, savvy, talented writer, her books left me feeling a little . . . empty."

"Which is the way Hope felt as her daughter." His voice was very quiet, very still. "She's told you that?"

"No," Cass admitted. "Not in so many words. But . . ."

"Her weight."

"Yes," Cassandra confirmed quietly. Her weight. "Food is, has been, a comfort—and a torment—for Hope. A way to fill up the emptiness, to try to, at least for a while."

"You started to tell me, at Bodega Bay, that Frances wouldn't have been upset about the weight Hope has gained since her death. That surprises me."

"But it's *true*. For some reason Hope believes that Frances disapproved of the way she looked when she was thin."

"When she was thin?" Chase asked. "When was that?"

"I don't know. You never saw Hope when she was thin?"

"Thin? No. She was slender as a little girl, during the four years she lived at the Domaine. Slender, not thin. And after, until she was thirteen, she was plump, a lovely, healthy, girlish plumpness." Chase saw, in his mind's eye, images of that girl, her cheerful spirit, her ready smile, her uncomplaining acceptance of her life of boarding schools and summer camps. "She was a tomboy, very active in sports, very good at sports."

"And then?"

"And then," Chase said softly, "we all met in Paris, in March, when she was thirteen. It was a good visit, for all of us, or so I thought. Hope seemed particularly happy, especially since, as a surprise, Frances told her she would be spending the summer at Willow Ranch, a camp for teenage girls in northwestern Montana where Frances had spent her teenage summers. We made plans to meet again in late August, here, all four of us. But a week before they were scheduled to arrive, Frances and Victor had a major parting of the ways—probably for the same reason Frances had gone to Europe to conduct her own sexual research thirteen years before. Frances—and Hope—spent the remainder of that summer in London, after which Hope returned to boarding school at Val d'Isère. I didn't see her again until Christmas."

Chase drew a breath, his gray eyes darkening with sadness as he saw more images of Hope. "She'd gained weight, quite a bit of weight, and she had abandoned sports in favor of reading, and she was uncertain, wary, on guard. It wasn't anything she could talk about, and even the most gentle inquiries about how was she doing made her retreat ever deeper into her wary cocoon. Frances, who would discuss it, attributed Hope's unhappiness to her own troubled marriage."

Cassandra, too, saw images—of a radiant and cherished Frances Tessier being presented, by her husband, a necklace of flawless diamonds. "Which was much better, less troubled, by Frances's forty-second birthday."

"Yes," Chase confirmed. "Much better. And Hope seemed better, too, finally, toward the end of last summer." *The summer that was an end.* "Has Hope talked to you, Cassandra, about the day Frances died?" *When the butterfly, who seemed on the verge of soaring free of her cocoon of such unhappiness, became weighted anew, crushed by betrayal and loss.*

"No. Not really." Cassandra hesitated. Then, emboldened—and determined—for her friend, she asked, "Can you tell me, Chase? Would you?"

He answered at once, this man in the moon who gave everyone, even droopy-faced witches, a chance. And his voice was very soft. "I would, Cassandra." *I trust you, Tinkerbell, with my sister's heart.* "But Hope wouldn't talk about it. Neither of them would."

"Neither of them?"

"Victor was there, too. After the accident."

"Victor," Cassandra echoed. *Victor.* "You like him, don't you?"

"Yes. I like him, and respect him."

"Hope's not too fond of him."

"I know," Chase said quietly. "It wasn't always that way."

"It *wasn't?*"

"No. Admittedly, he wasn't always around. His concert tours took him all over the world. In another life, I imagine, Victor wouldn't have had children."

Because his life was full, Cassandra mused, with the care and nurturing of the violin—just as, according to the birthday videotape, Chase Tessier's life was full, satisfyingly replete, with the exquisite vintages he created. And was it a crime to decide not to have children? Not at all, at least not to her. Cassandra Winter had abundant—and anguished—reasons to admire any potential parent who recognized in advance they wouldn't have the time to properly devote to a precious young life . . . and who believed that anything less than such devotion would be unfair to a child.

"So, like you, Victor didn't really want children."

"Like me, Cassandra," Chase confirmed softly. "And like you."

Want? She had never permitted herself to imagine a time when she might actually have a choice.

"Cassandra? You're frowning."

"Oh." Her thoughts scattered as she met the too interested gray eyes—scattered, then regrouped. They had been discussing Victor, the father who, perhaps, never wanted children. But who had them nonetheless. "I know that Hope was unplanned, most of all by Victor. But you . . .

Victor and Frances adopted you, chose to adopt you, two years before Hope was born."

"It was Grandpère who adopted me. Not literally. But in fact." *It was Grandpère who saw the little boy on the evening news . . . the little boy who wanted only to die.* That little boy had become Jean-Luc's shadow—Peter Pan's shadow—and he had learned the shadowed secrets of Grandpère's heart. "Grandpère loved Victor very much, and Victor loved Grandpère."

So that, Cass realized, explained Chase's allegiance to Victor—a solemn loyalty based on love for Grandpère.

Love, not blood, bound Chase and Victor Tessier. But there was more, a discovery she had made as she watched the video image of Victor Tessier giving to his wife a strand of perfect gems.

"You and Victor look so much alike."

"I know."

"Do you think it's possible?"

"What? That twenty-year-old Victor Tessier impregnated a thirteen-year-old Haight Ashbury flower child? No. It's not possible."

"Because?"

"Because Victor Tessier never would have abandoned her . . . or me."

SEVEN

*I*f you could just step outside, Mr. Tessier, Ms. Tessier."

Any illusion of calm the doctor hoped to convey was shattered by the frantic beeping of the cardiac monitor over Cassandra's bed—and by the battalion of doctors and nurses who descended on her room even as Chase and Hope made their retreat. They didn't retreat far, just to the other side of the wall of glass.

During the past two days, Chase had learned numerous new words, medical terms subsequently shared with Hope. "Edema," "blood gas," "vasospasm"—and myriad others—dutifully defined by Cassandra's physicians the first time each unfamiliar term was used.

But now, as Chase and Hope overheard snippets of urgent dialogue from within the glass-walled room, there were other new words, foreign and terrifying. Words that no one had the time to define.

"She's bradyied down to twenty."

"Twenty?"

"With ectopy."

"She must be coning."

"But she can't be. *Can't* be."

"Atropine?"

"It's in. No response."

"Okay. Let's try Isuprel."

New words, foreign and terrifying, with emotions to match. Such a sharp contrast, piercing and cruel, to the foreign yet wondrous feelings awakened within Chase in the weeks following their late night encounter in the family room at the Domaine. . . .

*T*hey saw each other only in passing.

Chase was busy, preoccupied. The sparkling wine harvest was imminent, and precarious, waiting only for him to decide. Still, whenever their paths crossed, his graceful gait slowed, and he would stop—no matter how rushed he was.

His gray eyes would focus on her, intense and clear—as if *she* were the master vintner's sole concern.

"Cassandra," he would say.

"Chase," she would reply.

"How are you and the Hollywood types faring?"

"Fairly well. So far they haven't trampled any vines or tapped any barrels."

"So you're keeping an eye on them? Watching the filming?"

"Keeping an eye on them, yes. Watching the filming? Only when there's absolutely nothing else to do. My role is insignificant, however, since Hope has them positively mesmerized."

"Hope?"

"Ms. Nicole Haviland—*actress*—is lusting after Hope's hair. The greedy Ms. Haviland wants it all. The length, the curl, the color, the shine. She keeps demanding to know the name of Hope's hairdresser, and what bottle the cinnamon comes from. Naturally, I've advised Hope to string her along. Forever. But you know Hope. She's *so damned honest.*"

"Unlike you?"

"*Moi,* Chase?"

"*Tu,* Cassandra."

Tu, not *vous.* He was fluent, she knew; and her high school French was sufficient to recognize his use of the intimate pronoun—the *tu* reserved for dear friends and passionate lovers.

Cass basked in that glorious knowledge for ten days, into the impossibly hot August, a steamy heat that kept Chase on the road, tasting the sun-baked grapes for just the right flavors of wind, of river, of roses, of moonlight.

Chase was supposed to be away, on that August afternoon, when Cassandra journeyed to his office, as he had invited her to do, to read his books and screen his tapes. She had just finished viewing a comprehensive video on the *méthode champenoise* when he appeared.

"Cassandra."

"Chase!" *Chase.* Unshaven. Shadowed. Exhausted. "I thought you were in Andersen Valley."

"I just got back."

"How are the herds up north?"

A deep light sparked in his tired gray eyes. "They need a little more grazing time. Are the tapes helpful?"

"Yes. Thank you. Very." His fatigue, she knew, came from his wine-making responsibilities for the Domaine. But his worry—and she saw such worry amid the exhaustion—had nothing whatsoever to do with his ability to determine the perfect sweetness of the Tessier fruit. In fact, what troubled Chase Tessier had nothing to do with him at all—except that he cared. "How's the phylloxera?"

"It's bad, Cassandra. Following this season's harvest, the skies above Napa will be black with smoke."

Vines would be killed, burned to ash.

"Not *all* the skies. Not the ones over Tessier land."

"We're very lucky."

"But it's not luck, is it? Didn't you invent a magic potion that protects against the pesky root louse?"

"I didn't invent it. It's a naturally occurring compound."

"Well, you *discovered* it, then, and knew it would work."

"Grandpère discovered it, and knew it would work."

That wasn't exactly the way Cass had heard the story. "How bad will it be, this year, for the other vintners?"

"Disastrous, especially for the smaller ones."

"Is there some way Tessier can help?" Cassandra knew the answer. Eleanor had told her. She just wanted Chase to admit it.

"Sure."

"How?"

"By giving them some of our grapes."

Giving, not selling. "And giving them some magical root potion, too, for the vines they plant next spring?"

"If they want it."

"They will."

It was eight days before she saw him again. Indeed, she crashed into him first . . . then saw him.

She was rounding a corner, staring at the floor, her lips moving in imaginary conversation.

"Whoa."

"Oh!"

Oh, he echoed silently, his every sense did, as her body collided with his.

"Cassandra," he murmured.

"Chase," she whispered.

He released her reluctantly, and the silence that followed shimmered with a wondrous heat—astonished and lingering—until, for her, the dangerous, foolish longing became too much.

She shrugged, a soft flutter that drew his attention to her clothes. Her loose, long-sleeved blouse was the richest shade of cream, and her flowing trousers were a lustrous ebony, and the silken shell beneath was both ebony and cream. The look was stylish, elegant, subdued—and chosen with great care.

In the hope that he might approve.

Which he did. Appreciation glittered in his eyes—even for the flamboyant touches: the blush pink ribbon that bound her hair, a gentle captivity, so that her dangling earrings, the lavender clusters of hand-painted grapes, could be amply revealed.

Chase approved. But would the glittering silver endorsement become molten fury if he discovered *why* she was dressed this way?

"Is there a problem with the Hollywood folks?" Chase asked in response to her sudden frown—and recalling the fierceness of the imaginary conversation in which she'd been engaged.

"Oh. No. Not more than the usual sociopathy, that is. But . . . you remember the bitch?"

"That would be Sibyl."

"That's the one. I now know why her company is called It's My Party. The 'my' is *her.*"

"The bitch."

"Yes! Since when is *she* the grape goddess? I mean, is

her name Tessier? Is this *her* centennial celebration? Does she have one single drop of wine flowing in her pretentious veins?"

Chase didn't answer at once, mesmerized by Cassandra's impassioned protectiveness of all things Tessier. "Actually, she does. Her maiden name is Courtland."

"As in Courtland Cellars? Courtland Medical Center? Courtland Lane?"

"All of the above. Her cousin runs the winery, and everyone in Napa drives on the lane, and although her father sold, years ago, the medical center he founded, Sibyl sits quite prominently on the hospital board."

"Oh, *no*. The restaurant."

"I believe that was sold as well—the name being part of the very pricey price tag. Still, I'm afraid, Sibyl Courtland Raleigh's veins are flooded with wine. Is there some dispute about what vintage to serve our guests?"

"No. I figure that's up to you."

"That's right." His expression was calm, faintly amused. "So, Cassandra, what seems to be the problem?"

"Jane's champagne flutes. Sibyl says there is *no way* we can use them, much less give them away as mementos to the guests."

"And Sibyl's reason for this? Other than her aforementioned personality disorder?"

"Because, she says, Victor would be upset. She claims there's some ancient history between Jane and Victor, something that should preclude not only the flutes, but Jane herself, from attending the gala."

"Jane is on the guest list I gave Sibyl."

"Not anymore. Sibyl removed it before the invitations went out."

All traces of amusement vanished. "What does Jane say?"

"Eleanor hasn't discussed it with her. But that's clearly the next step, at which point we'll discover something petty—on Sibyl's part—something in the category of 'Welcome to junior high school.' Of course, it could just be old-fashioned bigotry."

"Bigotry?"

"Jane's mother was a full-blooded Lakota."

"I didn't know that."

"Well, Sibyl does, which means bigotry is a definite possibility. Still, I think it's something else—like Jane gave a party and had the nerve to assume it was hers and not Sibyl's. I honestly think Sibyl is using Victor's name to give her pettiness a weight it doesn't deserve. I mean . . . you don't know anything about Victor and Jane, do you?"

"No. But I've only known Jane since March, when Eleanor decided to sell her art in the Blue Iris. I don't even know how long Jane has lived in Napa."

"Most recently, for less than a year. But Jane was born here, grew up here. Just like Sibyl. So even though Jane's a couple years younger, it really could be a junior high school thing. Anyway, you're right. The logical next step is to ask Jane."

"Why don't you let me ask Victor instead?" It was phrased as a question but spoken as a command. The decision had been made. "In case there is something to it."

"You have more important things to do with your time than adjudicate a cat fight."

"Not really," Chase replied. *Nothing more important— except for kissing you.* "The chardonnay harvest began, two nights ago, at midnight."

"I know," Cassandra murmured, barely, for it seemed that desire was glittering in his dark gray eyes—desire, and longing, and *wanting*. And surely it was an illusion, a magnificent mirage crafted from her own impossible wishes and fanciful dreams. "I've been watching from my window. It's so beautiful. The lamps in the vineyard look like a thousand tiny moons."

Beautiful, *yes*. But Chase didn't see myriad tiny moons. He saw instead, in the fluttering luminescence, a dancing field of Tinkerbells.

"If you'd like a closer look, we could meet, at the fountain, at midnight. Unless you have other plans."

At midnight? When the carriage becomes a pumpkin? And Cinderella is left in rags?

"No. I don't." *Not at midnight.* "I wonder if I should ask Hope to join us?"

Chase smiled. "Sure. Good idea."

He smiled, even as he wondered if she was afraid to be alone with him in the glow of a thousand tiny moons, if she sensed—and feared, for she was so delicate—his immense desire, his astonishing need.

You are safe, Tinkerbell . . . unless and until I have something to offer you . . . and then I will be so very careful with you.

Cassandra was safe with him. Now. Then. Always. But Hope was their link, their gently shared concern, and when Cassandra Winter talked about her friend, she played no games. There was no pretense in the fierceness with which she cared about his sister, no acting at all.

"How's she doing?" he asked.

"Well, I think. *Very* well. She's lost quite a bit of weight."

"I know."

"That's *so* significant, Chase. She wanted to lose weight this spring, to return to Napa thin and svelte. But she couldn't do it. *Couldn't.*"

"So losing weight here, this summer, may mean she feels less empty. More safe."

"Yes," Cassandra whispered, amazed. This man, so confident, so centered, so strong, understood about feeling safe? And about feeling *not* safe? "I think it does mean that."

"But Hope is never truly going to feel safe here, is she?"

He knew so much, saw so much . . . but now he was looking at her, his gaze serious and intense, wanting the truth.

Demanding it.

"Cassandra?"

"No," she confessed softly. "She's not."

Your sister is never going to truly feel safe in this paradise that is your home.

$\mathcal{T}$hree hours later Chase happened by the family room. *Family.* For years it had been a misnomer. But not now. For there they were, *the girls*—Eleanor, Cassandra, Hope, Jane—seated on the floor and on the couch in front of the mammoth screen.

Chase had unwittingly intruded on some planned event. But he was welcomed—by all save one: Cassandra.

"Chase!" Hope greeted him. "You're just in time. Tonight's five-star movie features our very own Cass Winter."

"Oh?" His cool, interested gaze drifted to the star who could have invited him to join the screening. But hadn't. Had, quite specifically, *not.* Cassandra wouldn't acknowledge that truth, wouldn't acknowledge *him,* except in the anxious words she spoke.

"Let's not watch the tape tonight. In fact, let's not *ever* watch it. Hope, you're the future attorney. There must be some law against videotaping a human being without her consent. If so, this is probably my opportunity to become a major shareholder in a major motion picture company."

"Who's going to tell me what we're talking about?"

Eleanor complied. Fondly. Proudly. "The videotape of Cassandra's winery tour."

"Cassandra's winery tour?" Chase Tessier did not speak again until she looked at him; until her sky blue eyes confessed that *her* tour of *his* winery was something she should have mentioned. "I guess I didn't realize you were giving tours, Cassandra. I thought you were working at Courtland's."

"She's doing both," Hope explained. "Cass always has more than one job."

"The tours aren't a job."

"Only because you're refusing to be paid."

"I don't *want* to be paid."

"What Cass should do," Eleanor informed Chase, "is negotiate with you for a percent of the gift shop proceeds. As I'm sure you've noticed from the books, sales have sky-rocketed."

"Yes. I have noticed." But he had attributed the boost in revenue to a robust tourist season, a movie—directed by Academy Award winner Adrian Ellis—in production on the estate, and the ever-crescendoing reputation of the Blue Iris itself. "And now we have a tape of the tour?"

"We do." Hope gestured to a nearby tabletop. "Many tapes. Adrian took the tour, realized it was wonderful, and decided to get it on tape. He wanted it to be spontaneous, exactly the way Cass gives it, so when his cameramen went along, they pretended they were just getting test shots of various locales."

"Which I *believed*, because they were so devious. They made occasional shows of looking into their cameras and fussing with the lenses. But the cameras, sitting so innocently on their shoulders, were running the entire time."

"And capturing exactly what Adrian hoped," Eleanor

embellished. "In fact, Hollywood's premier director has already announced that if Cass ever wants a role in an Adrian Ellis production, she can simply consider this her screen test—passed with flying colors."

"I would *never* want a role in *any* film."

"And," Jane Parish said, speaking for the first time, "we're not going to watch the tape. Not tonight. Not ever. Not if Cass doesn't want us to."

"It's not us," Chase said quietly. "It's me."

"Cass?" Hope queried. "Is that true? Because Chase will love your tour. I know he will."

"But Chase has other things to do," Cassandra murmured. "Better things. An evening, perhaps, with—"

"As I recall, Cassandra, you—and Hope?—and I have a midnight rendezvous."

"Yes, but it's only eight o'clock."

"And I have work to do." His gaze, fierce and cold and gray, held her prisoner as he walked to the table stacked with tapes. "Is one of these for me?"

His question was to her, and Cass knew she had no choice. "Sure."

"Good." Then, softly, before turning to leave, Chase Tessier murmured, "Showtime."

The Oscar-winning director's artistic embellishments were evident from the opening frame—a soaring zoom through olive boughs to the mansion, the winery . . . and Cass.

She stood in the courtyard, before the diamond-bright fountain, encircled by an already captivated throng. *She* captivated them even before she spoke: her cream-and-ebony ensemble, the blush pink ribbon in her hair, Jane's lavender earrings chiming at her ears.

"I'm Cassandra," she began. "Your guide for the next forty minutes. First, let me welcome you to Domaine Tessier. We're delighted you've chosen to visit our winery, and want you to know that this tour is *for you*. So, if you have questions, please feel free to ask. I know one question you're all far too polite to ask: Why in the world is Cassandra carrying a heavy black sweater on this sweltering August day? The answer is that I'm always a little cold—which means, for me, the wine cellars feel downright chilly. But don't worry. I'm sure you'll find them quite perfect, just as our wines do, a welcome respite from the summer heat. We're going to spend just a few moments in that heat, because I want you to see our grapes up close and personal. So, please, follow me."

With that, Cassandra led her flock of tourists, and the sneaky cameramen, into the vineyard. "This lovely purple beauty is pinot noir. Would it surprise you to learn that inside this violet skin the pinot is crystal clear? I can see that it would. It surprised me, too. So why don't you investigate, as I did? Look *and taste*—for yourselves . . . yes, right here and now."

The camera zoomed in for a close-up of a lush cluster of pinot noir, then panned to amazed tourists sampling grapes from Tessier vines.

"While we're still outside, please notice the roses. Since roses are my favorite of all flowers, you can imagine my delight when I arrived in this paradise and saw rosebushes adorning each and every row of vines. How perfect, I thought. How *romantic*. And how unexpectedly beautiful, the intertwining of roses and grapes. However, as you'll discover, a theme of our tour is the exquisite blending of the art—and the science—of making wine. In keeping with that theme, I must confess that the artistic marriage of vines and roses serves a decidedly scientific purpose as well. Are there any rose gardeners in the group?"

Cass waited for a few hands to raise, smiled approvingly, and asked, "You know the black—or powdery—spots that sometimes appear on the leaves? Well, it turns out that grapes and roses are susceptible to similar diseases. Roses are more susceptible, however. Which means that if there's a fungus—or whatever—floating around, the roses will catch it first. So, beyond adding pastel romance to the vineyards, the roses are noble sentinels, planted to detect disease before it hits the vines. You will note—please, note this!—that every Tessier rose is healthy, fragrant . . . perfect."

The camera followed her slender hand to a nearby rose. It was a not-quite-touching touch, an invisible caress that lingered, thoughtful and hovering, as if the enchantress herself were entranced. Suddenly, as if giving herself a mental shake, she spoke anew. "Okay, time to go inside. As we walk toward the winery I'd like you to look beyond the rooftop and to your left. See that mountain? The one with the obsidian cliffs at its peak?"

When all eyes, and the camera lens, obeyed her command, Cassandra explained. "That's Black Mountain, although it has a much *better* name, one you'll know by the end of the tour. So stay tuned. Film at eleven."

The enraptured pilgrims followed their amber-haired leader through the heated air.

But as she watched her image on the family room screen, Cassandra Winter had never felt more cold.

Chase, too, was watching the tape. She knew it. Felt it. Felt his astonishment, and his disdain.

It gets worse, Chase. Much, much worse.

Cass shivered as she—and the traitorous cameras—reached the winery.

"It's time to define a few terms. First of all, we are now 'in crush,' meaning the harvest has begun. 'In crush' should really be 'in press,' since that's what we actually do. Slowly, gently, *carefully*. Grape stomping is incredibly sensual, of course, something to savor in the privacy of your own homes. But it's not in the best interest of the grapes—or of the wines—at least, not Tessier wines."

Cassandra paused briefly before introducing more wine-making terms. "Within the industry, wines are referred to as 'still,' as in motionless, and 'sparkling.' Still wines are good, *wonderful*. Tessier's white zinfandel, for example, is beyond compare. But I must confess a preference for the sparklers, alive—dancing—with bubbles. My favorite is blanc de noirs, a pretty pink blush champagne."

Her blue eyes widened, sparkled, danced. "Yes, you heard me, *champagne*. For all intents and purposes, sparkling wine *is* champagne. According to the French, however, the only *true* champagne comes from the Champagne region of France. In fact, the French felt *so* strongly about this that—years ago—they convinced a number of other nations to sign an agreement promising never to apply the C-word to their sparkling blends. As a result, Italian champagne is known as *spumante,* and in Spain it's *cava,* and in Germany *sekt.* Now, as it so happens, the agreement was signed during Prohibition—which means, of course, that the U.S. wasn't involved. Therefore, it's perfectly all right for California vintners to label their bubbly 'champagne,' and some do. Those with ties to French champagne houses—or, like Tessier, with French roots of their own—generally go with sparkling wine."

She smiled. "Confused? I hope not. A rose—which is not to say a rosé—by any other name, and all that! *Anyway,* at Tessier, we make both still and sparkling wines, which is a bit unusual. But when you have a wine maker—a wine *master*—as talented as Chase Tessier, it would be a shame to do anything less. Which brings us to the history of Domaine Tessier. For those of you who've visited other wineries, this is the point at which I should lead you to our museum, filled with black-and-white photos of the early days, as well as displays of ancient wine-making tools. But winery tours are quite new to Tessier, so will you please just pretend that *I'm* a museum? Or, better yet, close your eyes and let your imagination go."

If any of the rapt tourists followed the command to close their eyes, the camera didn't capture it. The lens, like the tourists, remained fixed on Cassandra . . . hardly a museum, but most definitely a muse.

She was Scheherazade, spinning wonderful tales.

"Picture this: a man named Etienne Tessier, born in Champagne, one hundred thirty-four years ago. Etienne was both incredibly handsome and incredibly bold. At age thirty, he—and his wife, Louise, and his infant son, Jean-Luc—left their Gallic homeland and sailed to San Francisco. Four years later, one hundred years ago this September, Etienne founded Domaine Tessier. For almost sixty years Etienne and Jean-Luc ran the vineyard together. Longevity runs in the Tessier men, just as handsomeness, *gorgeousness,* does. Gorgeousness and *danger,* I might add, a rather significant blend of pirate and poet, gentleman and rogue."

No photographs—neither black-and-white nor living color—could have conveyed as vividly as her words the fierce yet tender maleness of Tessier men. Her words, embellished by some secret knowledge aglow in her bright blue eyes. "Talent, too, flows in the Tessier veins. Whereas Etienne and Jean-Luc created liquid symphonies of color and texture and taste, Victor Tessier—Jean-Luc's son— composes the real thing. Jean-Luc was immensely proud of his virtuoso son. He encouraged Victor to pursue his musical gift and to forget all about the symphonies of wine. So it was Victor's son, Chase, to whom the wine-making baton was passed. Chase took the baton willingly, eagerly. From the time he was a young boy, Chase read to his be-loved—and dyslexic—grandfather, and helped Jean-Luc with winery paperwork, as well as the care and tending of the vines.''

Cassandra paused to permit images to catch up with words. ''Robert Louis Stevenson said it best: 'Wine is bottle poetry.' Which makes Chase Tessier the poet laureate of the Domaine. Chase learned the *art* of wine making from his grandfather, and the *science* from the books he read and the courses he took. In Chase, the art and science are per-fectly blended—an exquisite *cuvée*.''

Cass could no longer sit still. Her heart raced, and she was trembling. Shivering.

''I'm going for a walk.''

''Would you like company?''

''Oh! No, Hope, thank you.''

Hope smiled softly at her friend. ''He's going to love it, Cass.''

''He will,'' Eleanor affirmed.

''Trust him, Cassandra,'' Jane advised. ''Trust yourself.''

*A*s she crossed the courtyard toward his office, Cass saw the flickering light. Chase was watching still. Good. At least he would see the technical part of the tour, her elo-quent, accessible, and absolutely accurate descriptions of making wine.

But nothing would erase the foolishness he had already seen: her breathless, presumptuous adoration of him—as if he were *her* pirate poet, *her* gentleman rogue.

The rogue would be amused, the gentleman flattered.

The gentleman, of course, would prevail. With impeccable politeness Chase Tessier would explain that he and Paige were virtually engaged—as if Paige Roderick were all that stood in their way.

It's my fault, he would gallantly say. I think of you as a little sister, Cassandra, and you know my affection for Hope. I'm sorry if I misled you. Terribly sorry. Really.

I know, Chase!—somehow, somehow, she would reply. It was just *theater,* you know? For the tourists? I'm an actress, and it was a performance. That's all. That's *all.*

But Cassandra Winter wasn't an actress, hadn't been, not really, not since the gray-eyed Tessier pirate had stolen that talent away; had looted the once powerful witchcraft from the once empowered witch.

I have to steal it back, to conjure again that part of me that can pretend not to care.

It was what she had done best, once, before Chase. Bravura performances that said, to those who taunted and teased, I don't care! It doesn't hurt!

I don't care, Chase. It doesn't hurt.

But it did.

It did.

His office door was open, as if he knew she would come. Cassandra believed he sensed her arrival. But he didn't acknowledge it, didn't turn; did not, even for a racing heartbeat, draw his gaze from the screen.

"One final thing," she was telling Domaine Tessier's bedazzled guests, "before I turn you over to Mark and Alec, our tasting room gurus, after which I hope you'll wander amid the wonderful gifts and goodies of Eleanor's Blue Iris. I want to tell you about a future sparkler, a champagne so magnificent that the term 'champagne'—with all its controversy—will simply become obsolete.

"You remember Black Mountain? You'd better! In French, Black Mountain is *Montagne Noir.* That's *mone,*

rhymes with phone, *tayn,* as in train, *nwar,* like film *noir.*
Shall we try it together? *Montagne Noir.* . . . Good! The time
will come when, instead of asking for champagne, you'll
just ask for Montagne Noir. I'm not certain how soon this
time will come. But it will. It *will.* From vines planted on
the obsidian slopes, their roots buried deep in lacy veins of
volcanic ash, Chase Tessier will discover, and you will
know, the 'inimitable soft fire' that Robert Louis Stevenson
described—soft fire, dancing with bubbles. Perfect poetry
from volcanic shale. You'll see. *You will see."*

Her faraway blue eyes seemed to see the dream, then—
see it and want never to awaken.

She did so, finally, with a start.

"So! On to the Blue Iris, and a taste of Tessier's best.
Although authentic enophiles—wine lovers—Alec and
Mark aren't pretentious in the least. Oh, they *know* all the
proper ways to describe fine wine, and to assess its aroma,
its appearance, its bouquet. But Mark and Alec also know
the truth: that one's personal taste is all that really matters.
Personal taste, and personal descriptions. So be inventive!
For the men in our group, if you taste something you really
like, really love, may I suggest describing it as your
wife—or girlfriend—would want to be described? Like *irresistible,* maybe? Or soft, lovely, delicate, smooth . . ."

The cameras captured the Pied Piper leading her merry
band of devotees across the courtyard, then swept up for a
final shot of Montagne Noir. It was a still shot, but not a
silent one, filled with ever more suggestions from Cass.

Perfectly aged.

With great character.

Elegant. Sexy. Lush.

"Chase?" she whispered. *Turn it off! Please?*

He heard her but did not move, and the tape ran still,
the shot of Montagne Noir and her foolish, dancing voice.

"And, last but not least, the highest compliment that can be paid to a woman—or to a wine—that one truly loves: complex. *Complex.*"

Then it was over, and he turned to her, at last.

Cassandra had expected amusement amid his annoyance; a familiar silvery glint despite his irritation at having to find a gentleman's way—the poet's way—to extricate himself from her idolatry.

But neither gentleman nor poet stood before her.

Only pirate.

Only rogue.

No humor sparked in the rogue's dark eyes, just cold, glittering fire. And the pirate's mouth promised to plunder her with harsh words and cruel disdain.

"I'm *sorry.*"

"Sorry, Cassandra?" His voice was ice. "It's not really your fault."

Of course it is. I'm the one who said whatever it was that enraged you so. But what was it? Surely not her lavish praise of him—monumental for her, trivial for him. So something else, perhaps everything else. Her mind whirred, replaying the tour, finding fault in every remembered frame.

Her apology was breathless, whirring, too. "I didn't mean to sound irreverent—like stomping grapes in the privacy of one's home? I just thought a little humor would make it more . . . interesting. And I know I said *our* vineyard, Chase, and *our* wine, as if . . ." *I belonged.* "But that's the way *all* tour guides talk. *Truly.* Oh! And what I said about Grandpère's dyslexia? I'm *so sorry.* I didn't think it was a secret. I mean, Frances mentioned it on her birthday tape, and . . . I would never intentionally betray a trust. *Never.*"

"You didn't, Cassandra. Eleanor did."

"Eleanor?" My lovely fairy godmother? The merry Mrs. Claus? "Do you mean by letting me give the tours, without checking with you first? I really *insisted*, Chase, and Eleanor is so nice that she would never have said no."

"I didn't even realize that she knew." Chase spoke almost to himself. "Grandpère must have told Andrew."

"Told Andrew what?"

"The name, Cassandra, the translation. Montagne Noir."

"Oh," she whispered. "But Eleanor *didn't* know, not until she took the tour."

If not Eleanor, if not Andrew, then . . . "Hope told you?"

"Yes. And I'm *very* sure she didn't mean to betray—"

"I know," he interjected softly. "I know. When did she tell you about Montagne Noir?"

"Let me think." But it was so hard to think. The ice had melted, but the fire glittered still, silvery bright, blindingly intense. Chase wasn't angry with Hope—she could read that much in the searing brilliance. But that was all . . . except that he was awaiting her answer, and that it was very important to him that she be precise. "Oh, I know, how could I forget? It was shortly after our charming little encounter with Sibyl. Hope took me there."

"To the mountain?"

"Yes."

"Did you drive up?"

"No." Cassandra had assumed it was the massive gate that prevented their ascent. But now Chase had asked if they'd driven up, meaning they could have, that Hope knew the code. So there was another obstacle entirely. "Oh, *no*. That's where Frances died, isn't it? On the mountain?"

"Yes."

"Hope drove us there, Chase, and she didn't *mention*

the accident. She just told me the name, in French, and that someday you would grow vines in the volcanic ash."

A deep light glowed in his silvery eyes.

Glowed. Glittered. Faded.

Died.

And Cass knew the truth. Chase's dream—Grandpère's dream—had died with Frances. Hope hadn't known. And she, Cassandra, hadn't checked, had merely raved blithely about something Chase wanted so much, but which now would never be.

"I'm *sorry*."

"It's okay."

"I won't ever mention the mountain again."

"I want you to mention it, Cassandra. At least for the next few moments—to me. I want you to tell me how you knew Grandpère planned to make champagne, and to call that champagne Montagne Noir. Hope couldn't have told you that. She didn't know. No one knew, except Grandpère. And me. And you. How?"

"Well, I . . . haven't gone up the mountain, but I've seen the mists that shroud the peak. They seemed so dense at first, too dense, impenetrable to even the most determined sun. But then I saw what happened—what happens—almost every afternoon."

"The rainbows."

"Yes," she echoed. *The rainbows.* The pastel arches that adorn the mountain like shimmering crowns. "So it seems, given the cool maritime mists, parted by sunlight, that one would logically plant champagne grapes."

"That's what you would do, Cassandra? As wine maker of Montagne Noir?"

"Well. Yes."

"Has anyone ever told you that you were 'complex'?"

"Well," she whispered. "Yes."

"But has anyone ever added the vintner's most coveted embellishment—'yet not confused'?"

No. How could they, Chase, when I am so confused? When the way you are looking at me makes me believe that the dream—every dream—hasn't died after all? And that there can be magic and rainbows and . . .

"No," she murmured. "No one ever has."

Chase saw the shimmering blue glow of hope.

"Well," he said softly. "They should have. I should have. Because that's what you are, Cassandra. Complex, yet not confused."

EIGHT

*T*hey couldn't see beyond the circle of white coats. But they would have sensed commotion within the circle, surely they would have, had there been frantic pumping on Cassandra's frail and slender chest. The screams of the cardiac monitor had been silenced, and the crash cart, crowned by a shining white defibrillator with gleaming silver paddles, had been hurriedly wheeled in.

But neither Chase nor Hope had heard the medical words that needed no translation: "Shock her." Nor had they seen the horrific pantomime as the circle widened just seconds before an electrical current jolted Cassandra's flesh.

"Chase?"

The quiet voice was familiar, though unheard for years, *years.* It was, perhaps, the only voice that could, as it did, compel Chase to look away—however briefly—from his wife.

"Victor."

Even a sophisticated observer would have sworn the two were related. Father and son. Brothers, perhaps. Mirror images of masculine elegance and sublime grace.

Victor had always acknowledged the sameness, embraced it in remembrance of Grandpère. But never, in Chase, had Victor seen the mirror image of his soul. Never, until now. Now, in Chase, Victor Tessier saw the man *he* once had been—a man deeply, desperately, in love.

The Tessier men faced each other, speaking in silence, until another voice, astonished and soft, intervened.

"Victor?"

Victor turned to her, saw the bewilderment that matched the voice, and greeted her gently. "Hello, Hope."

"I . . . don't understand why you're here." *How dare you?*

"I'm here to help," Victor Tessier said quietly. "If I can."

But what, Hope wondered, can you possibly do?

They were going to find out, it seemed, for Victor was about to be put to the ultimate test—helping the man who was not his son survive the death of the woman he loved. An ominous transfer of blankets was taking place through the white-coated wall, a shroud of privacy—at last.

The wall began to crumble, as nonessential personnel turned to leave. Cassandra's once naked feet, shrouded now, came into view—as, cloaked too, did her legs, her abdomen, her chest—which moved still.

The ventilator, not yet disconnected, puffed away calmly, rhythmic heaves and sighs that would persist until someone realized the oversight . . . or worse, until rigor mortis thwarted the charade.

Except that it wasn't a charade, for as her neurosurgeon left his post at the head of her bed, to make the short journey to her loved ones, those loved ones saw clearly the silver helmet, her gleaming crown that was uncovered, *not* covered, by the cotton shroud. Indeed, the blankets stopped at her neck, as if someone had tucked her in, a precious daughter being sent, with love, to dreams.

"She became bradycardic," the neurosurgeon explained when he reached them. "Which means her heart rate dropped. It's back up now, and her blood pressure's okay. Our best guess is that the bradycardia was caused by her extremely low body temperature."

"What does coning mean?" Hope wondered.

"Coning? Oh, it refers to brain stem herniation from increased intracerebral pressure. That's not an issue here. The removal of bone basically insured that wouldn't happen, and the cerebral edema has responded very nicely. In fact, we began barbiturate withdrawal last evening, and since midnight we've decreased the hyperventilation as well."

"So even if her heart rate hadn't dropped . . ."

"We would have begun warming her today. This afternoon. The bradycardia has encouraged us to speed up the process."

"How quickly?" Chase asked. *Let her be warm. Now. Please.*

"Slowly," the doctor replied. "But steadily."

Slowly. Steadily. Hope heard the surgeon's words, his wise caution, and forced herself to apply the sage advice to the emotions that raged within.

Hope had believed she would never see Victor Tessier again . . . would never be compelled to confront the ambivalence she felt. Not that she was obliged to confront such emotional ambiguity now—at least not in any overt way.

Victor was here because of Chase, not because of her, and Chase welcomed his presence, welcomed this man who, eight years before, had made Chase's entire world fall apart.

*W*here *is* he?" Sibyl glared at her diamond watch. "All the guests have arrived and we haven't offered them a drop to drink or a bite to eat. I know you had hoped to begin the evening with a toast, Chase. But . . ."

"That's precisely how it's going to begin, Sibyl. I assume the champagne is ready to be served?"

"Yes."

"In Jane's flutes?"

"*Yes.* But what about *Victor?*"

"He's not coming."

"*What?*"

"He's not coming."

"Since when?"

"A while."

"You should have told me."

"Really? What difference would it have made? Fewer ice sculptures? Less extravagant hors d'oeuvres?"

"No, of course not. It's just that everyone, all the guests—"

"Are here because of Chase." The new voice belonged to Hope—and it was a new voice, a glimpse of the assertive attorney she would one day become. "Most of the guests don't even know Victor."

"Yes, but Victor Tessier is—"

"An accomplished musician." Hope smiled slightly as Sibyl blanched at the understatement. "And tonight is about the celebration of wine."

"And it's time," Chase observed. "Past time, for the celebration to begin. Where's the champagne, Sibyl?"

"Awaiting my signal."

"Then give it."

Sibyl Courtland Raleigh was accustomed to giving orders, not receiving them. She bristled, but withdrew. Chase watched long enough to make certain that she was en route to the kitchen, then grinned at his sister.

"You are one tough cookie, Hope Tessier."

Hope exhaled in a rush. "Not really. *Not at all.* That was pretty scary. I wonder if Cass feels this anxious when she's pretending to be Blanche, or whoever—even when she's speaking the truth, which I definitely was."

"Well, here's a truth: You look sensational."

"Oh! Thanks," she murmured, embarrassed yet pleased. "I . . ."

"What?" he pressed gently.

"Well, I told Cass this, but I asked her to not tell you until I was sure it would work. Anyway, remember the sunset at Bodega Bay? When we all saw the green flash?"

"Of course I remember."

"I made a decision, Chase. Right then. Or maybe the decision came to me in a flash. Whatever, I decided to lose weight, once and for all, for the rest of my life. I know I'll feel better about myself if I do. No matter how I look."

"No matter how you look?" Chase echoed, remembering Cassandra's impression—her conviction—that Hope believed Frances Tessier had disapproved of her appearance without her bulky cocoon. "I repeat, Hope Tessier, you look sensational."

Sensational, he thought, in an emerald gown the color of that sunset sky. More sensational, however, was the sparkling emerald hope in her shining eyes.

"For the record," he said quietly, "you look good—beautiful—no matter what you weigh. But if losing weight will make you feel better . . ."

"It will. It's what I want."

"Then go for it, Hope." Chase smiled. "Sensibly."

"I will." She smiled, too, and blushed, and changed the topic—sort of. "Meanwhile, have you seen Cass?"

"No."

"I think she's in the kitchen, making sure Sibyl doesn't do a last minute switch of the flutes. Anyway, just wait until you see her."

"You two went shopping?"

"We went renting. We only have the gowns for tonight. Which, as Cass pointed out, is all we need. Oh, here she comes."

The Cassandra who came to them shimmered and glowed in billowing folds of gold lamé.

"See, Chase?" Hope enthused when her fluttering golden friend arrived. "Isn't she stunning?"

"Yes," he said softly. "Stunning."

As was he, Cassandra thought, in the tailored tuxedo the color of his hair. But Chase Tessier was equally stunning in denim, or charcoal, or, a sight she would never see, clad only in his glinting silver eyes.

The insistent—almost impatient—clanging of a small crystal bell brought an appropriate end to her inappropriate thoughts. Sibyl stood on a riser designed just for this moment. The remarks, to be made by Chase, would begin the centennial gala . . . and launch Domaine Tessier's next one hundred years.

"It's *her* party, isn't it?" Cass murmured.

Chase smiled. "Actually, she's just following my orders. A bit passive-aggressively, more than a bit, but to the letter."

Cassandra knew, from her foray into the kitchen, just how exacting Chase's orders had been. Tessier's best champagne, a vintage reserve, had been chilled to perfection.

"So," he said, "that's my cue."

The crowd parted for Chase and hushed to respectful silence as he spoke. Ever gracious, Chase Tessier began with a welcome to all his guests and with thank-yous to Eleanor, to Sibyl, to Jane—who, despite Chase's personal invitation, had declined to attend.

"Like Jane, Victor is unable to be here tonight. His decision to be absent, like the other decisions I'm about to reveal, is one we reached together. It was most appropriate, we decided, that I be the one to tell you that Domaine Tessier is closing its doors."

There was a collective gasp, a harsh gulp that seized every molecule of air.

"The Domaine, and the Tessiers, have enjoyed a spectacular century in Napa. Spectacular," Chase repeated softly, "but not without its share of sadness. Jean-Luc almost left the valley thirty years ago, after his beloved Margaret died. It was his son—their son—who convinced him to stay. And fourteen years ago, following Jean-Luc's death, Victor himself was on the verge of selling everything. But he didn't. Because of me. Because this valley, this vineyard, had become my home. It's been a wonderful home."

Chase Tessier drew a breath. To steady himself, perhaps. But there was no oxygen in the ballroom. His guests, the ones who could breathe, exhaled what they could. "For many years Domaine Tessier has had standing offers from French champagne houses, as well as from wineries over here. But Victor and I tried to make the choice Grandpère would have made. And we believe we have. Jean-Luc Tessier believed in sharing his good fortune. And so, in his memory, we will share ours—this year's harvest, as well as our land, with our neighbors. I will be solely responsible for this disbursement, and I promise to be fair.

"As for the house and winery, Adrian Ellis, who has just

finished filming *Duet,* will take possession of both on November first. Although there's ample precedent for a celebrated Hollywood director to become an excellent vintner, Adrian has no such plans. The mansion will be his home, the winery a soundstage."

Chase looked down for a moment, and afterward there were those who would contend that—during that moment—his hands trembled and a glistening mist touched his eyes. But the guests who stood closest knew it wasn't true. Chase Tessier was as calm, and as hard, as granite. When he looked up a faint smile curved the unyielding stone. "So, that's it. Thank you—and best wishes—from Victor and myself. Now, may we begin this party with a toast to Jean-Luc Tessier, our beloved Grandpère?"

With that, Chase raised his hand-painted flute. "To Grandpère."

Grandpère. Grandpère. Crystal chimed against crystal, a delicate caress of vines, and roses, and vintage champagne.

As the echoes faded, and before applause—for him—could begin, Chase stepped off the riser, and Cass turned toward Hope, to where Hope had been. Her emerald-gowned friend was gone. Indeed, she must have left the instant Chase announced the closing of the Domaine's century-old doors—for even now Hope was reaching Chase.

"This is what he wants."

Cass spun in the direction of the reassuring voice. "Eleanor! You knew?"

"Chase told me earlier today. He was, typically, worried about me. But thanks to Chase, I know I can do whatever I like. Anything. How's that for self-esteem? Who knows, maybe I'll give Sibyl a run for her gala-giving money."

"That would be . . ." *terrific,* Cass would have murmured, but the superlative drifted away as Eleanor's attention was summarily commandeered by a valley shopkeeper determined to commiserate.

Then Cass herself began to drift, tossed about in a glamorous sea, a fluttering golden leaf in a churning ocean of silk.

It was a talkative ocean, where even the most quietly whispered tidbits crashed like storm-ravaged waves.

"Talk about grapes of wrath. I had no idea Victor's hatred of Chase ran so deep."

"But why wouldn't it? Chase was the son to Jean-Luc that Victor could never be."

A physician from Courtland Medical Center offered a succinct—if medically explicit—summary. "Chase has just participated in his own vivisection, and we watched. Before our eyes, Chase Tessier cut out his heart and dismembered his dreams."

"So you don't think Chase was really part of the decision?"

"Hardly."

"To the Victor go the spoils, as they say."

"Yes, and you also know what they say about the thickness of blood. Victor obviously could not abide leaving anything to an impostor heir—especially one born with heroin, not wine, in his veins."

Cassandra's voyage through the silken sea was not as random as it felt. With each step she drew ever closer to Chase . . . who stood in the shadows with Hope.

They were talking. *Hope* was talking, an impassioned, imploring speech. And Chase? He was a tuxedoed statue of grace and pride. Was he even breathing? It didn't seem so. How could he, without a heart?

Cassandra's view—and her thoughts—were unceremoniously extinguished by the disdainful yet smug visage of Sibyl Raleigh.

"I hope you're happy, Cassandra. This is *your* doing, you know. Your fault."

I know. I know!

"You just had to go to Chase about Jane, didn't you? And he just had to go to Victor. I *warned* you what would happen if Victor ever learned that Jane Parish had insinuated herself into the Domaine."

It was true. Sibyl *had* warned her. And she had dismissed the warning as petty, shades of junior high; and now Chase stood in the shadows without a heart. "But Victor told Chase that it was *fine* to use Jane's flutes for the toast."

"And quite a toast it was, wasn't it? Too bad Jane wasn't here to witness the devastation."

"What *happened* between Victor and Jane?"

"Nothing that's any of your business, Cassandra. I told you that. But you refused to listen, and now . . . well, now it's all over."

"It *can't* be. Will you talk to him, Sibyl? To Victor? *Please.* Tell him it was my fault, not Chase's. *My* fault."

"What was your fault, Cassandra?"

"Oh, Chase!"

"Well," Sibyl purred like a cat glutted with canaries. "I think I'll leave you two. *Enjoy,* Cassandra."

With that Sibyl sashayed away, leaving Cass alone with him.

Him. Chase. Who stood before her, alive and breathing.

His heart sent strong, slow pulses to his neck.

And molten silver glowed in his seductive gray eyes.

And he smiled.

"You know what?" His voice was the soft fire of the finest wine. "It's time for you and me to take a walk."

Chase guided her through French doors into a garden of roses. Rose-fragrant perfume scented the night air, as did the sweetness of moon-ripened chardonnay. The fountain chattered in the distance, a sparkling flow not of sunlit diamonds, but of starlit champagne. And behind them, in the ballroom, the orchestra was beginning its repertoire of love songs.

"Now, Cassandra, tell me what's your fault."

She stood apart from him, separated by roses. But she faced him bravely, across the blossoms and the thorns, fully prepared to accept the responsibility, and the wrath, that was her due.

"Not listening to Sibyl's warning about Victor and Jane. Asking you to speak to Victor."

"But you didn't ask me to."

"Well. Still, Victor was *furious* when you did, wasn't he? So furious that . . ." *he did this to you, the man to whom you have always been so loyal. Victor Tessier betrayed you. Killed you. Made you kill yourself.*

Except that this sensual man, limned by autumnal moonlight, was decidedly not dead.

"Victor was something, Cassandra," Chase conceded as he watched her across the blooms. Watched and waited. Intensely . . . yet patiently. There were, apparently, words she wanted to say, a fluttering catharsis of guilt. Her undivided attention would not be his, and Chase needed every ounce of it, until her catharsis was through. "Something very quiet. But it wasn't fury. He asked me to send him one of Jane's flutes."

"And, in the same breath, to close the Domaine?"

"No."

"But it wasn't your decision, was it?"

"It wasn't my idea. I warmed up to it, though."

"Because of Hope. Because of what I told you about her never truly feeling safe in Napa."

"As I recall, I told you that. You merely confirmed what I already knew."

"But you're leaving the valley, aren't you? Once the Tessier lands and harvest are fairly"—*dismembered*—"distributed, you'll start making wine in some non-Napa locale. Washington, New Zealand, France. You need to *own* the vineyard, Chase, own *everything* this time."

She was fluttering still, not with guilt but with purpose. Such luminous purpose: to help him recapture his dreams. "I do?"

"*Yes.* I know that's enormously expensive. But . . . I have a little money, Chase. Not much, but some—all of which I'd be happy to invest."

She was offering him her life savings. Willingly. Joyfully. As if she truly believed that was all she had to offer him.

Oh, Cassandra, you have so much more. Will you offer it to me with such joy?

"Thank you."

"You accept?"

"No. Actually, I'm fairly solvent. My profit-sharing arrangement has—"

"Made you rich. *Of course.* I . . . that was silly of me."

She faltered, embarrassed by her trivial offer of help, and looked down, away, to a blush pink rose the color of her cheeks.

Chase reached for her across their perfumed chaperon of petals and thorns, and when his fingertips touched her chin, he lifted gently, coaxingly, until she met his molten silver gaze. His hand fell away then. His hand. But not his heat.

"No. That was lovely of you. Unselfish, giving, kind." The words were hers, *her* definition of love; but now, with exquisite intimacy, they were spoken by him. "I don't need money, Cassandra. I need a mountain."

"Montagne Noir," she whispered. "But I thought when

Frances died . . ." *your dream died.* But Chase Tessier's
dream had not died, it had merely been abandoned—by
him, because of Hope; because, for Hope, his mountain of
dreams was a venue of loss. And now? Now Cassandra remembered an impassioned conversation in shadows.
"Hope wants you to remain in Napa, doesn't she? To live
on the mountain, and plant vines, and . . . that's what she
was talking to you about."

"That's what she was talking to me about," Chase confirmed quietly. "She says she needs to return to Montagne
Noir—someday—and that it will only happen if I'm
there."

"She *means* it, Chase. You know she does. It's what she
wants. What you want."

It's part of what I want, Cassandra. The insignificant part.

Chase would tell her the rest. Soon. But his lovely Tinkerbell fluttered still, as if afraid to stop, as if fearful of what
he might say when, at last, she came to rest.

"Do you know who Cassandra was?" she asked.

"Sure. The prophetess no one believed."

"Even though she was *always right.* You *will* grow grapes
on Montagne Noir, Chase."

"You think so?"

"I *know* so."

The prophetess had spoken, and such a lovely prophetess she was, her moonlit blue eyes aglow with happiness—
for him.

And now, at last, she was silent, and still, fluttering no
more, her work complete, his destiny decided.

*And now, Cassandra, my prophetess, the discussion of my
destiny truly begins.*

"Do you remember how Montagne Noir becomes
mine?"

"You have to get married." *To a woman you love. It's so
easy, Chase—you've already found her.*

Was it his imagination, or did the moon flicker? No, Chase realized, the heavenly glow was quite constant. It was the glow within, that delicate luminescence, that threatened to fade.

Yet she looked at him still, unwavering and determined, as she met her fate.

"Frances added a little fine print when the time came to prepare the legal papers. Since Montagne Noir had been a gift to her on her wedding day, she decided it should be a gift not to me, but to my bride, on mine."

"Oh! Well. Is that a problem?"

"Not as long as the marriage lasts ten years. The mountain becomes mine on my tenth wedding anniversary, and—by prenuptial agreement—is exempted from community property adjudications should a divorce subsequently occur."

"And if there's a divorce *before* the ten years?"

"My bride, my wife, gets everything—the mountain, the winery, the château."

"Which she can give to you, or sell to you?"

"No. Neither. Not ever."

"And if you *murder* her?"

Chase smiled. "Assuming I get away with it, I inherit everything."

"Good old Frances," Cassandra murmured. "It was still about *her*, wasn't it? She needed to *control*, even from the grave. You outfoxed her, though."

"I did?"

"Yes. By"—*falling in love with*—"choosing Paige. I mean, she doesn't seem the divorce type, and she's so nice you'd never be tempted to murder her—not that you couldn't commit the perfect crime. But you won't need to, because Paige herself is quite perfect."

The stars twinkled, and the moon glowed, and his dark gray eyes had never been more intense.

"There's just one small problem, Cassandra. I'm not asking Paige to marry me. I'm asking you."

"Me?"

Chase didn't touch her, did not reach for her anew across their fragrant abyss of petals and thorns.

Distance was important now. Necessary.

"You, Cassandra. *Tu.*"

But you can't want me, Chase. You wouldn't—you won't— not for one night, much less for ten years.

"Talk to me, Cassandra."

"Talk to you?"

"About why you look so confused." Complex . . . and so confused. For a glorious heartbeat there had been no confusion at all. Just pure, luminous joy. And then confusion. Then pain.

"Confused? *Moi?* Not at all." Her smile was bright, courageous, false. "And as for your proposal, Mr. Tessier, why *of course* I'll marry you."

Chase banked his fury. But it smoldered in the soft danger of his voice. "I'm not asking Blanche, Cassandra. I'm asking you. I don't need your answer now. I just need you to think about it. Okay?"

"You'd get tired of me."

It was a whisper of pain, spoken so softly in the night air that another man, one who wasn't already in love, might not have heard it at all.

"Never, Cassandra. I will never get tired of you."

"But you and Paige . . ."

"Broke up, that night, after our dinner at Courtland's."

That night? When you returned to the Domaine looking so hungry still? So ravenous? "Paige found someone new?"

Chase smiled. "I did, as well you know. At least I've assumed you knew, Cassandra. I assumed you knew, as I did, from that very first moment in June."

That very first moment, Chase? When I was a refugee from the rest of my life, alone and drooping and dressed in black?

"But . . ."

"Why haven't I told you? I suppose I thought it was obvious, even though it shouldn't have been."

"Shouldn't have been?"

"You were a guest in my home. My sister's best friend. And there was the matter of my uncertain future. And yours."

"Mine?"

"Your passion, Cassandra, and where it might take you. There was that other issue, too, your fairly ferocious feelings about marriage, and the monotony of same. I have to confess that of all the issues that's the one that's worried me the least. Which isn't to say I don't care about monogamy. I do. Very much. I just doubt—very much—that it would ever become monotonous . . . with you."

"You want to . . ."

"Make love to you?" His laugh was soft, low, raw. "Don't you know how much?"

But she didn't know, his tentative Tinkerbell, and a faint shadow of fear passed across her face.

"Cassandra?" Gentleness filled the deep, dark richness of his voice. "Have you ever made love?"

Made love? No. Had sex? Oh, yes. Many times, beginning in junior high, when the most popular boy in school wanted her, *her* . . . Sandra, the teenage witch. It was all a joke, of course, a dare fueled by cruelty—and adolescent hormones that would touch anything, even a witch, in darkness. She hadn't known, until after, when the sexual escapade, and the joke, was shared with the entire school.

Eventually Sandra Jones became Cassandra Winter, a makeover of loneliness and despair. Men wanted the flamboyant collegiate vamp, especially when she enticed

them as Blanche DuBois. But she was destined to disappoint, Cassandra was—a witch still beneath her brightly layered plumage, a bony creature made of ice.

"Cassandra?"

"Yes. I have."

"And would you be interested, do you think, in making love with me?"

Chase Tessier was making love to her now, with his voice, with his eyes, with a tenderness she had never known.

"Yes," she heard herself whisper. *Yes . . . please.*

"Just me?"

Her nod was a courageous dance of amber, a ballet of hope caressed by moonlight. *Just you . . . only you . . . always you.*

"Good." Chase spoke softly, across the roses, to the blooms on her cheeks. He looked at her lovely lopsided mouth, a gentle gaze filled with promise, then smiled at her bright blue eyes. "What about your passion, Cassandra? Is it something that might lure you away from Napa?"

"No."

"No?"

Because you are my passion. Just you. Only you. Always you. She smiled a smile that was all her own, a fluttering enchantment of courage and joy. "I think I'd like to make champagne."

"Then marry me, Cassandra. We'll shatter the glass ceiling all to hell."

NINE

SAN FRANCISCO

SEPTEMBER, EIGHT YEARS AGO

Stage fright, the bride confessed; the same bride who had been an actress all her life—until Chase.

She didn't want to speak aloud her wedding vows, not even in front of Hope, the best friend who was thrilled, and amazingly unsurprised, that Cassandra and Chase were planning to wed.

Still, the bride queried, it would be better, wouldn't it—less . . . awkward—to marry after Hope returned to school? To begin sharing a bed, and she *was* going to share his bed, after Hope was gone?

Chase conceded that it might be better, and that private vows were the only ones that mattered, but he offered instant resistance to Cassandra's final prenuptial request: a loophole-free document giving Chase exclusive decision-making rights for Montagne Noir—beginning the moment they were wed.

"That's not necessary," he said.

"But better," she asserted. "What if I decided that Montagne Noir would be the ideal location for California's largest amusement park?"

"You wouldn't."

"Or what if I slipped into a coma and—"

"You won't." Chase took her hands, frowned, and asked of his bride-to-be, "Are your feet this cold?"

"No."

"You're sure?"

"I'm positive." So terrifyingly positive—for she was beginning to believe that midnight would never come, that darkness would never fall, that Cinderella would dance forever.

It was Jane Parish, painter of glass slippers and other crystal delicacies, who found the answer to the bride's wishes for unwitnessed wedding vows and a marriage that would be consummated only after Hope was gone.

The wedding party would celebrate the impending nuptials in advance, with a lavish luncheon at the Fairmont, where—later—the bride and groom would spend the night. Then three of the five—Eleanor, Hope, Jane—would begin the drive south, to visit art fairs in Carmel and Santa Barbara en route to UCLA. Chase and Cass would meet with their attorney, sign the requisite prenuptial paperwork, after which a judge, with little fanfare but with the full force of the law, would pronounce them wed, and . . .

And now it was that Friday evening.

Bride and groom were husband and wife. Alone, together, in their suite atop the Fairmont Hotel. Roses bloomed everywhere, the bedroom included, where a few perfect petals had fallen—a floating pinkness—onto the white satin comforter of the bridal bed.

Chase and Cassandra were in the living room, she on

the couch, he on an adjacent chair, champagne chilling in silver between them, crystal flutes nearby.

"I have something for you," he said.

The something was a wedding ring, made just for her by a goldsmith in Oakville who had listened attentively to Chase Tessier's vision, then met it precisely, in a marriage of precious metals, the molten matrimony of all three hues of gold.

The roses were pink gold, delicate blooms of joy; and the leaves were pure gold, the purest gold; and both blossoms and leaves were embedded, a flawless smoothness, into a white gold circle that shone like silver.

But Cassandra's wedding ring did not shine as brightly as her wondering blue eyes. Nothing did. Nothing could.

"Chase," she whispered, not touching it, unable to, overwhelmed and trembling.

"I don't remember a prohibition against private vows," he said as he slipped the ring onto her finger. It fit perfectly; made for her from his perfect memory of her delicate hands. "With this ring, Cassandra, I thee wed."

"Chase . . . I didn't . . . I don't have a ring for you."

"This will be our wedding ring, Cassandra, worn for both of us, by you. I think you should say the vow."

She wasn't an actress. Not with him. Nor did she need to be.

She was a bride.

His bride.

"With this ring, Chase, I thee wed."

He gazed at her, studying her, a silvery glint in his eyes. "What?"

"I'm trying to figure out how to get you to say those other words."

You mean, *I love you, Chase?* Because I do. *I do.*

It was, in fact, those latter two words—those wedding vows words—that he was trying to induce.

"Would you care, Mrs. Tessier, for a little champagne?"

"Yes. I would." Her blue eyes sparkled, a brave tease, then glowed, steady and sure. "I do."

The champagne bottle bore a makeshift label inscribed by him. The name of the winery: Montagne Noir. And of the vintage: Cassandra.

"You've already planted vines on the mountain? Planted and harvested . . ." *and vinted at least one bottle, this precious bottle that bears my name?*

"Grandpère and I planted the first vines when I was seven, and when they flourished we planted more, and I've kept planting ever since."

"So Grandpère knew, before he died, that his dream would come true?"

"Yes," Chase said softly. "Grandpère knew."

"Who else knows?"

"No one. Not a soul. The vineyards are where you said they needed to be, in the misted valleys of the western slope, quite hidden until you're actually there."

"Even Hope doesn't know?"

"No. We took her there only once. She was a scampering two-year-old, and the hillside was too steep, too treacherous, for her to be anywhere near the vines. She returned to the mountain with us many times, all the time, but never again to the vineyard. No one else knows. Just you, Cassandra." *My prophetess. My bride.* "Would you like to taste?"

"Yes. Please."

Chase Tessier opened the champagne the way it should be opened, pointed far away from all eyes—especially the lovely blue ones alight with wonder. The cork fell gently into his hand, a quiet sigh, not an explosive pop, because he had done that correctly, too, turning the bottle, not the cork.

Then Chase poured the bottled dream, the bubbles that danced in crystal pink.

Pink.

"This is blanc de noirs," she said.

"The bride's favorite."

"But not the groom's."

He smiled. "I'm an adaptable kind of guy . . . especially on my wedding night. To you, Cassandra."

"And you."

Crystal caressed crystal. Then Chase watched, and waited, as the blush pink dream touched her lips, and floated into her mouth, and spilled gently, a delicate swallow, down her long pale throat.

"Oh," she whispered. "Chase."

"Tell me, Cassandra. Tell me what you taste."

"I taste mists," she murmured, closing her eyes, sipping again. "And the soft fire of the ancient volcano." Her eyes opened. "And rainbows, Chase. I taste rainbows."

"Let me taste," he said as his lips touched hers. "This way."

Let me taste this dream by tasting you.

"Mists," he murmured as he discovered her delicate sweetness.

"And fire," she whispered, tasting him, welcoming him, tasting and welcoming and knowing—at last—his sensual heat.

"And rainbows," Chase told his luminous pastel Tinkerbell. "And you, Cassandra. *You.*"

You. You. You.

Cassie, Cassie, Cassie.

As he made love to her, in their white satin bed adorned with pale pink roses, Chase whispered the new name, a symbol of their intimacy. Whispered it again and again. As he loved her.

Again and again.

Cassie.

Cassie. In all the ways it could be spoken.

Raw, needy.

Wanting, dying.

Cherishing, soaring.

Cassie. With wonder. With love.

She whispered his name, too, in all the ways Chase spoke hers, bravely, eagerly, and with shimmering joy . . . which faded, after, as she lay in his arms, so aware of the discoveries he had made as they loved, the meagerness he had felt—and was caressing so gently even now.

"Does it bother you that I'm so thin?"

She was *so* thin. He hadn't realized, had not begun to guess. She looked slender in her layered plumage—slender, not thin—and her hair sent a message of golden abundance, and her energy was so boundless, so vast. But she was terribly thin, her skin gossamer silk draped over small, prominent bones.

And now she was wondering if her thinness bothered him, disappointed him.

Chase found her lovely, worried eyes and smiled. "Are you asking, Cassandra Tessier, if I could possibly find you more attractive? If I could want you more than I do?" He stroked a loving finger on a pale pink cheek. "If so, you haven't been paying attention. If I wanted you any more, it would kill us both."

"Oh," she whispered with relief, with joy.

"Yes, Cassie. *Oh.*" He kissed the corners of her eyes, the soft, lovely droop of her mouth. In a moment they would begin to love again, both wanting to, needing to. In a moment. "You don't eat much."

"No. I never have." *I've never felt safe enough, you see— never safe enough to eat.*

"I wonder if you should try eating more." Chase vanquished her sudden worry—and her impending free fall from joy—with the gentlest of smiles. "No, Cassandra, not for me. For you. For your health, and so you wouldn't always be so cold." Worry pierced him then, more worry, for her. She was thin, and naked, and the white satin comforter had fallen away—they wanted it away—while they had loved. "Are you cold now? Were you cold when we were making love?"

"No. Not now. Not then."

Then as now she was warm, for the first time in her life. Thin. Naked. Warm.

For the first time.

Cassie was warm . . . and Chase was whole.

TEN

*I*t was not yet dawn. Victor and Hope were in their hotel rooms, asleep. Chase was at her bedside, needing to see her, to touch her and talk to her, before her early morning journey to the operating room. The bone that had been removed to relieve pressure from her swollen brain would be replaced. The swelling had resolved. Her skull would be intact.

But Cassandra had yet to awaken.

She might never awaken.

But you're warmer, aren't you, my love? Chase implored silently as he reached for her hand. Her hands. He held them both in a cave of warmth created by his own, cradled carefully, taking special care to protect the left, so badly wounded during the assault.

Cassandra's hands were free, unencumbered by the probes and needles of intensive care. The plastic line

133

through which she received intravenous nourishment—and, until recently, drugs—was "central": a large-bore conduit that dove through her chest and into her subclavian vein.

Cassandra's arms, too, were unrestrained, and perhaps it was an image of those arms, pale and graceful and reaching for him, that had awakened him, reaching into the nightmares—or unremembered dreams—that haunted the few hours when he attempted sleep . . . when her physicians banished him from her bedside and insisted that he try.

Something *had* happened during last night's tormented sleep, something that had made his heart race with hope as he had neared the ICU. Maybe she was awake, reaching, wanting . . .

But Cassandra was not awake, despite the frantic predawn activity in the unit itself. Saturday night had brought, to the City of Angels, a torrent of rain and a tempest of trauma. Purpose—and crisis—surrounded her. But still she slept.

She *will* awaken, Chase vowed as he cradled her small, pale, wounded hands in his. The thought continued of its own accord, unbidden and unwanted. She will awaken—for Robert. She will reach, with grace, with joy, for Robert.

Robert. The renowned actor's bedside vigil had been less constant of late. But, thanks to the media, his anguish was broadcast everywhere.

Chase didn't speak to Cassandra on this stormy Sunday dawn. Not yet. This silent touching, this cradling warmth, was the way they began each day—the way Chase began these ICU days for them—just as, together, they had greeted every day of their love, their loving, at Montagne Noir.

Eventually Chase would whisper hello, good morning,

and the tender assurance that she was doing well, so very well, and would wake up soon. Chase had to prepare himself to speak such words, to speak at all. His sleep-starved emotions were ever more ravaged, ever more raw, and she needed to hear from him only strength, only calm.

Chase had told her, many times already, about the people she loved.

Hope is an attorney, a dazzling success. And she's dazzlingly beautiful, too, slender and fit.

And Eleanor is terrific, lively and young. Her catering business is the toast of Napa, and she's met someone, a man named Samuel. He's eight years younger than she, a semiretired professor of archaeology who, according to Eleanor, simply could not resist a fascinating fossil such as herself.

And Jane is thriving, too. Still unmarried. Happily unmarried. Her hand-painted glassware is in demand everywhere—especially in France—and the gifted artist has become a patroness of the arts as well. Her gallery, in St. Helena, is a showcase of works by other valley artists.

In the beginning Chase shared only positive news, the barest bones of happiness and success. But his Cassandra, his fluttering Tinkerbell, glowed most brightly when she was needed, when she could help. So Chase added layers of flesh to the stark skeleton, as once Cassandra had added vivid layers to her own fragile frame.

Chase shared the truth of Eleanor's new love: how difficult it had been, for both Eleanor and Samuel, to ever love again; to permit themselves such love; to cherish the memories of his beloved wife—and her beloved Andrew—and yet find happiness with each other.

And Chase told Cassandra the truth about Hope.

She's devoted to her work. Consumed by it. It's her life . . . and her escape. She's slender because she decided to be slender, because she made a pledge, that day, as the sun splashed into the sea at Bodega Bay. And for similar reasons—sheer will—she visits Napa, and the mountain, as if no painful memories lurk there at all. She's stronger than ever. But not safe. Not happy. And so empty still. She needs a friend, Cassandra. She needs you.

As I need you.

Chase never shared that most bare and naked truth. Nor did he taunt her with its layers. Never once, although the question screamed, did Chase Tessier ask his sleeping bride why she had left him. *The truth, Cassandra. Not the lie.* And never did he tell her how he ached when she vanished, how he raged, and searched, and worried . . . until, one day, she was found: a glittering star in the Hollywood heavens. Bright. Dazzling. Flourishing without him.

"Mr. Tessier?"

Chase looked from their entwined hands to the unit clerk who stood in the door. "Yes?"

"Lieutenant Shannon is on the phone—for you."

"Oh. All right. Thank you."

Chase left without speaking to Cassandra. He would speak to her upon his return. But by the time Chase returned, Cass was gone, whisked off to the operating room, without hearing his hello . . . or his good-bye.

*J*ack Shannon's message was mysterious but decisive. The homicide lieutenant wanted to meet with Chase—and whatever other family members Chase chose—as soon as it could be arranged.

Chase asked both Hope and Victor to be there. The meeting began at eight A.M., in a conference room adjacent to the ICU. The unit's quiet rooms were all taken, by friends and family of last night's victims of excessive alcohol, extravagant partying, and the lethal abundance of rain-slick streets.

"There are some things I need to tell you about the investigation," Jack began. "All of which must be held in strict confidence."

"Of course." Impatience edged with worry fueled Chase's voice. "Tell us, Lieutenant."

"Okay. As you know, we found evidence of forced entry into Cassandra's home, and her jewels—including a very valuable piece that was on loan to her—were taken. It appeared, therefore, as if she surprised a burglar."

"Appeared," Hope echoed. "Past tense."

"Not completely past. We're still pursuing the botched burglary possibility. All possibilities . . . including the one in which Cassandra knew her assailant."

"Robert." Victor Tessier's voice was quiet, yet emphatic.

Jack Shannon gazed at the gifted musician. "Yes. Robert. What makes you suspect him?"

"Isn't he the most likely suspect?"

"Sure. In the real world. But this is Tinseltown, where actresses are stalked by psychotic fans. It's a world you know, Mr. Tessier. And yet you guessed—and, quite frankly, it didn't even sound like a guess—that her assailant was Robert. I have to wonder why."

"No reason. Nothing of substance."

"What does that mean, Victor?"

"Nothing, Chase. Nothing."

Nothing . . . yet Jack Shannon waited, patiently, in the suddenly charged silence. Only when it was abundantly clear that Victor had nothing else to say, nothing else he would say, did the lieutenant continue.

"There were skin fragments under Cassandra's fingernails. DNA will confirm that they belong to Robert. We have photographs of the corresponding scratches on his torso, as well as his statement—willingly proffered, by the way, without an attorney in sight."

"He was happy to talk," Hope murmured.

"Delighted to," Jack confirmed.

It began then, the dialogue between professionals—the attorney turned homicide lieutenant and San Francisco's brilliant assistant DA. Experts both on domestic violence and its related crimes.

"What did Robert say about the scratches?" Hope asked.

"That they were a result of her passion—and desperation. Their relationship was volatile from the start, he says. Too volatile, in the final analysis, to last. He told her he wanted out. She wanted him to stay. Hence, the scratches. Of course, her subsequent assault by the brutal intruder made him realize how much he loves her."

"Of course," Hope whispered. "How good is his alibi?"

"It's good. Just about exactly what he needs. It conforms perfectly to our timeline—although with a different scenario—and he has corroborating witnesses when he needs them. His story is that he and Cassandra had sex, at her Brentwood home, between one and two Wednesday afternoon. They argued, before and after, and he left, angry, at about two forty-five. Cassandra's next-door neighbor—who writes for the soaps and works at home—confirms that Robert drove away, sped away, at approximately that time.

"He drove around for a while, he says, eventually ending up at his place in Malibu. He was feeling guilty by then, sorry about some of the things he had said—especially since it was her birthday. He claims to have called her several times between five-thirty and six. It's a toll call, and he's very sure—as am I—that phone records will confirm the calls. When he got only Cassandra's answering machine, he assumed she'd already left for the charity benefit she was hostessing that night. He hadn't planned to attend the benefit, but decided to after all, to see her and apologize. When he reached the Beverly Wilshire, she wasn't there. He dialed her home, then 911. A squad car responded immediately, and the paramedics were called, and by the time Robert—and several celebrity friends—arrived, Cassandra was en route to the hospital."

"And Robert Forrest became the hero of the piece," Hope said. "Not the first time a villain recasts himself in that role." She looked at the man known for his uncanny instincts when it came to murder, even in this town of fiction and facade. "You think he left her to die, don't you, Jack? That he expected the paramedics to discover . . ."

"Yes, Hope, that's what I think. What I believe."

"Is there physical evidence beyond the scratches?"

"Some. All pretty soft. There's the assault itself. It *was* an assault, the kind of vicious beating that bespeaks emotion, rage, the intent to kill. A surprised burglar would have cared only about making his escape. Then there are the scratches on Robert's torso. They seem defensive to me. Defensive, not passionate."

"I wonder . . ."

"What, Hope?"

"Well, I'm sure, given the neurosurgical emergency, no one was really thinking about sexual assault."

"Actually, they were. Cassandra was examined by Dr. Amanda Prentice, one of the very best. Although she isn't prepared to call it rape, she says the sex was quite rough." As was hearing about rough sex and vicious beatings, Jack realized; rough for everyone in the conference room, including the savvy prosecutor who was also a sister-in-law. Jack shifted to a less graphic topic. "Finally, there are the skin fragments themselves. For various microscopic reasons, the county's forensic pathologist feels that the scratches and the assault occurred at the same time."

"So Robert Forrest is under arrest." Chase spoke at last, breaking an eloquent silence of clenched fists and dangerous eyes. "In jail." *About to be executed.*

"No."

"Why the hell not?"

"Because what we have is circumstantial—and speculative. But," Jack assured him, "Mallory Mason, the deputy DA assigned to the case, is already actively involved."

"It's true, Chase," Hope concurred. "There's not enough for an arrest."

And, Hope knew, without Cassandra's side of the story, there might never be enough. But if Robert Forrest had done this to her, and if . . . well, if Cassandra was unable to speak for herself, Hope Tessier—with Jack Shannon's help—would find a way to testify for her, to accumulate such a mountain of circumstances that the path to conviction would be swift and clear.

Hope looked at the homicide lieutenant. "What about a history of physical violence?"

"He says no, of course. And no one has come forward, not even a single anonymous call."

But if Robert Forrest did hit her, Chase told himself, if he even threatened to, Cassandra would have left the relationship and called the police. His Cassie would not have permitted such abuse. *Would she?* "I want him behind bars, Lieutenant."

"So do I, Chase. But it's simply too soon."

"I don't want him anywhere near her."

Jack Shannon smiled slightly. "As her husband, that is entirely within your control. My officers will be happy to enforce your decision."

"They'd better. Because if I so much as see—"

An urgent knock on the door preempted the potential consequences of an encounter between Robert and Chase.

The intruder was Cassandra's nurse, Dorothy.

"She's back from the OR. She needs you, Chase. She needs you *now*."

*C*assandra's neurosurgeon stood in the doorway of her glass-walled room.

"She came out of anesthesia with a vengeance," he said. "So much so that we've already extubated her. She's close to consciousness, Chase, very close. Maybe if you would talk to her . . ."

Talk to her. A recitation of bare bones—and worrisome layers—already shared? Or an update on Sibyl, perhaps, the wry revelation that bitches could, apparently, finish first?

No. Not now. Not *now*. For now, as his lips brushed her translucent temple, emotion flooded reason, wishes drowned restraint.

"Cassandra?" he whispered. "Can you hear me, sweetheart? Wake up, Cass. Cassie. *Cassie, wake—*"

The reply came in a scream from the cardiac monitor overhead. A strident signal of her distress? Of the immense—and perhaps irreparable—trauma his injudicious words had caused her gravely wounded heart?

Yes, apparently, for her doctor rushed in, as did a trio of nurses, a whirlwind of starched white worry amid the frantic cry of the anguished alarm—alarm*s*, for now there was second warning, and a third.

Look what you've done! They screamed. They hissed. Look. Look. *Look.*

Chase obeyed, his own heart screaming—looked at the

frenzied dance he had evoked, the pale green heartbeats that raced across the screen and the blood pressure sensors that quivered with fright.

Racing.

Quivering.

Screaming.

Dying.

No.

"Chase?"

It was a grace note amid a symphony of madness, an enchantment that beckoned him from chaos to calm, from seizing monitors to bright blue eyes.

And there was even more magic, more grace, for as Chase gazed at the shimmering, wondering blue, the screaming monitors shrieked no more, silenced by able fingers—and the truth. Their cries had come not from death, but from life, from an awakening that came with a vengeance, and with exquisite clarity.

"Hi," Chase whispered as all four health care professionals, worried no more, left the room. "You remember me."

A soft smile blossomed on her pale pink lips; half a smile, for the other side drooped. "I remember. Where..."

"The hospital."

"Oh," she murmured without alarm.

She was floating in a warm, swirling mist, drifting in a slow, lovely dream. So lovely, so warm, for Chase was with her, and his gray eyes glittered with—*Chase.*

Pain—and remembrance—shattered the loveliness, froze the warmth. Cassandra looked down, away. But when her gaze fell on her hands, her mind started floating again, drifting, entranced, by what she saw. Hands. Her own hands. Although her floating mind scarcely made the connection.

They were oddly beautiful, these slender, pale, translucent hands. The left, especially, intrigued, its ring finger a vivid if violent tapestry of texture and hue. The flesh was torn, as tattered as her soul, but the shreds of skin were ruffles of lace, snow white frills adorning a purple lake of blood.

"What happened?" she asked of her own tattered flesh.

"What do you remember?"

His beloved voice, so gentle and so soft, floated overhead. Cassandra stared, still, at her hands—and then beyond, into the swirling fog. The mist was impenetrable at first, unreadable. Then, without warning, an image appeared, brilliantly clear.

"Victor."

Victor? Had her memory simply dismissed the past eight years? Chase wondered. Had her traumatized brain—or heart—decided to journey to a faraway time, a better, happier time: the rose-fragrant night when she had agreed to become his bride. *We'll begin there, Cassie. Begin again. And this time . . .* "You're wondering why Victor didn't come to the party?"

She looked up, her eyes as clear and bright as the image she saw. "No. Victor was at the party. He wanted to meet me, but I said *no*. I wouldn't have been so rude, Chase, if I'd known."

"Known what?"

"The secrets," she murmured decisively, then frowned. "I don't remember what they were." But she searched the shadows, tried to, a journey of frustration and fatigue. Her lashes fluttered closed, then opened with a start. "He came to my house."

At that moment Chase Tessier knew how it felt to be filled with ice—every vein frozen—lungs tinged with frost.

"Victor went to your house?" *And told you secrets?* "When was that?"

"Today . . . this afternoon." She gave a thoughtful tilt of her white-turbaned head, an achingly familiar gesture of concern, despite the luxuriance of amber that was no more. "I asked him what kind of man he was. What kind of father. Do you know what he said?"

"No. Tell me."

" 'Not a very good man, Cassandra. And a despicable father.' "

"Then what?"

"We . . . talked." And it was so important what they had said. So very important . . . and hidden in the midnight shadows that shrouded her memory. "Then I heard your voice." *Then I began to dream.* "Chase?"

"Yes?" *My love?*

"I'm really tired."

"I know," he whispered, hiding his fear, all his fears.

Was it safe for her to sleep? Or might sleep mean a return to coma? Had his questions about Victor—*Victor,* that other monstrous fear—pushed her too far?

Chase watched, saying silent prayers, as her eyelids fluttered closed; and watched still, with silent gratitude, as the flickering golden lashes signaled the beginning of dreams.

When at last he looked up, Chase saw Jack Shannon. The lieutenant's solemn expression sent the clear message that he had been standing there for a while. Long enough.

A quiet room was available, a windowless sanctuary recently vacated by a family for whom the tempest's trauma to a loved one had proved too much.

This was where families died.

But the Tessiers had never been a family.

Not even close.

Chase glared at the man he had respected, had defended—the son Grandpère had loved.

"You were with her, Victor. *You.*"

"On Monday, Chase. Not Wednesday. I was in New York when she was assaulted. In rehearsal in New York."

Had Chase known, in his heart, that violence was impossible for the son of Grandpère? Perhaps, for he greeted Victor's revelation with neither relief nor surprise—and his fury raged still. "But whatever you talked about was important, wasn't it, Victor? *Relevant?*"

"Important, yes." Victor's voice was quiet, his expression grave. "But relevant to her assault? No. At least, I didn't think so. I believed, until today, that she had been attacked during a robbery."

"But today," Hope said, "when Jack told us that her assailant might have been someone she knew, you named Robert, *Robert,* without the slightest hesitation. She must have told you something."

"No, Hope. She didn't."

"Then *why,* Victor?"

"Because," Victor Tessier confessed softly, "in all the hours that Cassandra and I talked, not once did she mention Robert's name."

ELEVEN

SAN FRANCISCO COURT HOUSE
THURSDAY, NOVEMBER EIGHTH

*T*his is Beth Quinn, reporting live from the windblown steps of the San Francisco Court House." Global News Network's senior legal correspondent smiled gamely into the camera. It was windy. It was cold. And rain was imminent.

"After seven days of trial, the *People* versus *Detective Craig Madrid,* the San Francisco police officer accused of spousal rape, has gone to the jury. As the jurors begin their deliberations—and we begin our verdict watch—we are expecting press conferences with both the prosecution and the defense. As our viewers know, however, a gag order has been in effect; and since presumably neither side wants a mistrial, the attorneys may remain extremely cautious in their remarks. There are, however, other questions to pose to Hope Tessier. Will she answer them? It looks as if we're about to find out. Prosecutor Tessier and District Attorney Atwood have just appeared."

The initial questions, tossed into the gusting wind by the battalion of reporters, focused on the trial. Were they confident of the outcome? How long did they expect the jury would be out?

"We have a winning case," Meryl Atwood replied. "We wouldn't have gone to trial if we hadn't. We have no idea how long the jury will deliberate, but we're absolutely confident that they'll render the appropriate verdict."

"Meaning guilty?"

"On all counts."

"In your closing argument, Ms. Tessier, you told the jurors that rape is murder. The murder of spirit, you said. The slaughter of innocence. The killing of the soul. Is that what you believe?"

Hope Tessier did not answer. Not with words. But her expression of quiet passion spoke eloquently for her: *Yes,* she believed what she had said about rape. She would not have made such an assertion if she didn't believe it with all her heart.

"If the verdict *is* guilty, Ms. Tessier, won't that cause a rift between the DA's office and the police? In fact, isn't there a significant schism already? Detective Lawrence Billings—the defendant's partner—has been quite vocal about the damage he feels this case has caused so far."

"I hope we all believe, we all *know,* that no one is above the law. Not presidents. Not prosecutors. Not police. Not the press."

It felt like a warning. It was—as the assembled media was soon to discover. . . .

"How is your sister-in-law, Ms. Tessier?"

"She's doing very well. Thank you."

"What does she remember about the assault?"

Nothing. "I'm afraid I can't comment on that."

"Sources claim that Robert Forrest, Cassandra's lover,

has been questioned by the police. Is he a suspect in this brutal crime?"

"You know I can't discuss the police investigation." Hope paused, knowing there were other questions that might be asked, ones that she and Chase had decided she could answer. But the rain was starting to fall, and she had an important message to impart. "What I can discuss, however—what my brother has asked me to discuss—are the plans for Cassandra's convalescence. I'm going to tell you precisely where she will be—and when. None of us has the slightest interest in playing games with the press. In response to this candor, we are all very hopeful that you will respect Cassandra's privacy in the weeks, perhaps months, that lie ahead."

"Months?"

"She sustained significant trauma. She very nearly died. Any physician will tell you that it takes a great deal of time to recover fully from such a catastrophic event. Her pro-longed, and necessary, convalescence will begin today. At Montagne Noir."

"Today?"

"Today. Again, just because she has been discharged does not mean that she's well. Physicians from Courtland Medical Center will be visiting her on a daily—perhaps twice daily—basis."

"The doctors will be making house calls?"

"Yes." Château calls, Cass had quipped; a rare glimpse at the old Cassandra, the irreverent spirit she once had been. The glimpse was so poignant, so rusted, and so ach-ing that sudden tears had misted in the new Cassandra's cloudy blue eyes. "Which brings *me* to the issue of Mon-tagne Noir. The mountain is private property. Trespassers will be prosecuted—and gladly. I am fully aware of the First Amendment rights of the press. As is my brother. But neither of us is willing to permit that right to trample over Cassandra's right to privacy—which, I trust we all agree, is the most sacred right of all. Cassandra has always been gracious, and generous, with the press. On her behalf, I would like to thank *you* for graciously respecting her wishes now."

With that, the prosecution press conference came to a soggy end—at least in its live format. Most Bay Area stations, however, as well as Global News Network and Court TV, chose to replay selected parts—every frame, in fact, in which Hope appeared.

It was spectacular television. The prosecutor stood on the courthouse steps, ladylike, regal, resolved. The wind ravaged her sedate French twist, lashing tendrils of fire on her rain-dampened face. But Hope Tessier did not flinch, did not blink, and her voice was soft yet strong.

Quiet . . . yet formidable.

And so very determined—as always. The thought belonged to Nicholas Wolfe, who watched from a carriage house in Napa, the equestrian estate on Zinfandel Lane where he worked and lived. *Hope has always been so determined.*

Nick watched until there were no more images of her to see—and then, as memories flooded his mind, he saw other images, so many images of Hope, beginning with the first, thirteen years ago, that summer at Willow Ranch. . . .

*H*ope's introduction to Willow Ranch was reminiscent of her experiences at other camps she'd been to—the soccer camp in Tours, the sailing camp near Lake Geneva.

The first few hours—whether in Montana, Switzerland, or France—were devoted to greeting the campers at the airport, transporting them to camp, and permitting them to settle in their cabins before assembling them all for the official orientation and welcome.

Hope's inaugural hours at Willow Ranch were better, of course, because her mother had spent *her* teenage summers here. And now, at last, Hope was old enough to follow in those beloved footsteps—thirteen, at last, although barely, the minimum age required for spending the summer at the ranch.

The closest airport was in Great Falls, seventy miles away, and given that organization and efficiency were administrative hallmarks of Willow Ranch, this season's one hundred campers all arrived at approximately the same time. With comparable efficiency, the girls and their luggage were loaded into the small fleet of willow green vans and soon were on their way.

Each girl learned, during the drive, the cabin that would be her home for the summer—Hope's was Meadowlark—and the table—hers was twelve—at which she and her cabin mates would dine.

Hope loved Willow Ranch before she arrived, loved the stories, spun by her novelist mother, of moonlit campfires, sugary marshmallow roasts, and summertime sails. The reality did not disappoint. Lake Wilderness shimmered blue beneath the vast Montana sky, and the fluttering leaves of the famous willow waved in welcome, and the distant mountains glistened white with snow.

Her lakeside cabin was *perfect,* and the four girls with whom Hope would be living this summer were *wonderful.* All were older than she, by at least three years, the oldest being—already—eighteen.

Hope had never before lived with older girls. At boarding school—Edwina Barclay's School for Girls in Greenwich and most recently, in France, at Val d'Isère—the girls were separated by age, just as when her mother had attended those same prestigious schools. The dividing point, then as now, was fourteen.

But at Willow Ranch Hope would live with older girls, and it would be such fun, she would learn so much, for already the other Meadowlarks were welcoming her warmly, fondly, as if she were their long-lost little sister.

There was something else, Hope thought, in their welcome: sympathy. *Of course* sympathy, she realized—with relief—as she watched the others unpack. These older, sophisticated girls cared, very much, how they looked, from their carefully applied makeup to their color-coordinated clothes to their long glossy hair.

Hope Tessier wore jeans and soccer shirts, whenever the choice was hers, and she was far too young for makeup, and her hair was as short as a boy's. It was her short-cropped hair, Hope decided, that evoked the greatest sympathy—and alarm—from her surrogate sisters. But the severe cut was what Hope wanted, what she chose, the wash-and-go style of the athlete—and student—that she was.

It troubled Hope, briefly, that these older girls might feel sorry for her.

But she vanquished her worry with a silent *Oh, well!* This was part of the fun, the thrill, of being at Willow Ranch—meeting new people, learning what mattered to them, accepting them for who they were, and being accepted, welcomed, in return.

Hope's single suitcase had long since been unpacked, and her young athletic limbs were restless, too long idle during the flight from France. The formal orientation, in the ranch house dining room, was thirty minutes away, and even if her wristwatch suddenly stopped, the shining chrome triangle would sound in advance, summoning all campers as ranch hands had been summoned, for generations, by such clanging.

Hope bid a fond adieu to her cabin mates—they would rendezvous again at table twelve—then she began to wander, a journey that took her to the majestic willow tree, the living symbol of the logo that had been familiar—and beloved—ever since her eighth birthday, when her mother had given her a T-shirt from Willow Ranch.

Hope wore a new version—at least a new size—of the cream-and-teal shirt. The loose-fitting garment was part of the elaborately gift-wrapped package her mother had given her in March, an early birthday present—and a glorious one. A copy of the Willow Ranch rule book was wrapped inside the shirt, and the cream-and-teal luggage tags confirmed that Hope would be spending the summer at the place she'd been hearing about for years.

Now she was here, standing beneath the famous willow, looking up, debating—and recalling the words, the rules, she had read repeatedly since March, committing to memory even the admonitions that did not apply. Indeed, most rules did not apply, having been established for older girls—like her glossy-haired cabin mates—who were interested in boys.

Under no circumstances, the rule book said, were campers and counselors permitted to date. It seemed an unnecessary admonition, Hope thought, since every counselor was at least twenty-one—Chase's age—and hence not boys at all, but men. Far too old, she imagined, for even a most sophisticated teenage girl. But the rule, an absolute prohibition, appeared more than once, as did guidelines—which were not prohibitions—regarding friendships with the teenage boys summering at Ravenwood, the camp across the lake.

Jeans were permitted in the Willow Ranch dining room, as long as they were clean, as were shorts, providing they were the specified—Bermuda—length. "Lights out" meant lights *out,* and there was page after page of other, obvious, rules.

But nowhere, Hope was quite certain, did there appear a prohibition, or even a caution, about climbing the majestic willow.

So she did.

$\mathcal{N}$ick saw, from a distance, the trembling tree, its leaves quivering so vigorously that he feared a lost cougar kitten—or an abandoned bear cub—was stranded in the tangle of limbs. His concern about a forsaken young creature increased as the quivering traveled ever higher, a rapid ascent, as if the frantic animal were disoriented and perhaps even being chased.

Nick abandoned his chores, crossed swiftly from the corral to the tree, and peered up through its heavy curtain of leaves when he arrived.

Nicholas Wolfe had been a Willow Ranch employee for under a day. But even an hour at the sprawling estate was ample time to conclude that "ranch" should have been "country club"—a posh summertime venue for daughters of wealth and privilege. Pampered daughters . . . who, Nick would have assumed, would be most unlikely to climb willow trees.

This *was* a daughter, however, despite the shortness of her cinnamon hair. She was quite young, this heiress, and friendly—for she greeted his appraising stare with an enthusiastic wave and a brilliant smile.

"Hi!"

"Hi," Nick murmured, taken aback. Had *anyone* ever greeted him with uncluttered enthusiasm? Such undemanding joy? "Are you okay?"

"Yes! I'm *fine*. The view is really great from up here and—" The triangle sounded, a clear, crisp chime in the pure Montana air. "Ooops. Time to come down."

"Be careful."

"I will!"

She *wasn't* careful, Nick observed as he watched her scamper down. She was merely fearless—an agile, sure-footed athlete who moved with the unaffected grace of the cougar kitten she might have been.

Hope jumped from the final limb, landing in front of him, her face flushed with exhilaration, her eyes shining bright and green. She looked at him, a forthright gaze, and before galloping off, the intrepid tomboy offered polite proof of the lady she was bred to be.

Polite—and breathtakingly sincere.

"Thank you for worrying about me."

Then she was gone, and although the triangle signaled him as well, Nick returned to the corral to finish feeding the stable of horses in his care.

*T*able twelve was situated toward the back of the spacious dining room, a windowside location overlooking the stable, the pastures, and the snow-capped Rockies beyond. Hope was admiring the equestrian view when the sound of a spoon tapping—softly—on a water glass hushed the ambient hum and drew her attention to the front of the dining room.

Mrs. Fairchild, the ranch director, flanked by a battalion of counselors and other assorted personnel was about to begin her formal remarks.

"Ladies, if I may have your attention, please?" Alicia Fairchild was not, herself, a Vassar graduate. But she knew she was speaking to future alumnae of that college and of others comparably esteemed: teenage heiresses who already attended the finest boarding schools on earth. "Thank you. And welcome. What a pleasure it is to have such a select group of young women at Willow Ranch. You are truly the best of the best."

"She says that every year."

The comment came from Trish, a Meadowlark, who was eighteen, pretty, confident, blond—and quite expert in this, her third summer, on all things having to do with the ranch. With her remark, Trish demonstrated yet another area of expertise—the ability to whisper, while someone else was speaking, without causing any distraction at all. At least, Mrs. Fairchild did not seem distracted. In fact, she seemed completely unaware.

Such whispering was impolite, and something Hope would never do. But Trish accomplished it so discreetly, and had so much to say, that Hope discovered herself quite capable of listening to the camp director and editorial comments by Trish all at the same time.

"We have rules at Willow Ranch," Mrs. Fairchild said.

"Rules that must be followed," Trish admonished as the director uttered the identical words.

"I know that all of you have read the rule book, as requested, in advance of your arrival today. But tonight, during the hour before lights out, I want each and every cabin to go over it once again."

"That'll take us ten minutes—max," Trish announced. "After which it's secrets time."

"Secrets time?" Robyn asked somewhat uneasily, and with far more volume—and lip movement—than was desirable.

But Mrs. Fairchild did not seem to notice, and Robyn's ineptitude was forgiven. She was, after all, only sixteen.

"Don't worry, Robsy," eighteen-year-old Jenna replied. "Sharing secrets is completely optional. Besides, Trish has enough secrets for us all."

Jenna knew. She was Trish's best friend: confident, too, and pretty, and nice. It was particularly nice of Jenna to reassure the newest Meadowlarks that secrets need not be revealed.

Robyn—henceforth nicknamed Robsy—exhaled her relief at Jenna's reassurance. And Hope, too, felt relieved. She had no secrets, and it would have been awkward to appear unwilling to share.

"Okay, listen up," Trish commanded, in a whisper but a command nonetheless. "Mrs. Fairchild is about to introduce this summer's studs. And," she added as she scanned the assembled counselors, "I'm happy to report there have been some changes since last summer's crop—which was truly grim."

"Campers and counselors aren't allowed to date," Robyn—Robsy—murmured.

"Oh, *puhleeze*. Besides, who said anything about *dating?*"

Willow Ranch's counselors came from the same impeccable pedigrees—and staggering wealth—as the campers themselves. It was an all-American, if privileged American, array, and a beautiful one, both female and male, a show of patrician bloodlines, perfect grooming, with exquisite attention to shape, to hair, to teeth. The counselors were dressed as one, a uniform that was country club chic—khaki slacks, lake blue polo shirts embroidered with the willow, and designer tennis shoes, of the cross-training variety, in unsullied white.

"I want *him*," Bonnie, who was seventeen, spoke for the first time.

"You can *have* him," Trish said as she arched a disdainful eyebrow at the Princeton-educated lifeguard who would enroll, in fall, at Harvard Law. "He was here last summer. A nerd, I'm afraid, in wolf's clothing."

"Oh! I . . . didn't know."

"Trish," Jenna whispered, "what about *him?*"

Jenna gestured discreetly toward the man Hope had met beneath the willow tree and who had not, Hope felt quite certain, been present at the beginning of Mrs. Fairchild's remarks.

He stood apart from the rest, in every way. In fact, he leaned, a casual, insolent slant, against a distant wooden wall. He wore denim, not khaki, and boots that were sullied and scuffed. His hair, tousled and long, gleamed sable around his unsmiling face, and he was smoking, *smoking,* in the dining room, breaking a rule known to them all— these patrician girls who went to finishing schools—even those who had not yet read the Willow Ranch book of rules.

"What *is* he?" Robyn asked. "Cowboy? Or Indian?"

"Who knows?" Trish countered. "Who *cares?* He's gorgeous, whatever he is."

"Gorgeous?" Bonnie queried, still stung, perhaps, from Trish's remarks about her lifeguard. "He looks arrogant, and mean."

Arrogant? Hope echoed in silence. *No. Not arrogant. Merely proud.* And mean? This man who had worried about her at the willow tree? No, she knew. He was not mean.

"We call that *dangerous,* dearest Bon-Bon," Trish clarified. "And incredibly sexy. And I, for one, don't have a problem with either danger—or sex. He's mine, ladies. The cowboy is *mine.*"

Trish's possessive pronouncement coincided with more words from Mrs. Fairchild.

"That concludes the introductions—except, of course,

for Sabrina." Mrs. Fairchild frowned as she saw a hand, polite yet insistent, waving in the air. "Yes, Trish?"

"I'm *sorry* to interrupt, Mrs. Fairchild, but I know he is *not* Sabrina." Trish's debutante hand waved in the direction of sable hair and curling smoke—as giggles tittered throughout the room.

"No," Mrs. Fairchild murmured. "He's not. And now *I* must apologize. I didn't see you come in."

Alicia Fairchild's words were polite, but her expression spoke volumes: he was late, he'd sneaked in, he was smoking, and his clothes were a disaster, as was his hair. Indeed, and quite possibly, her apology had far less to do with her own impoliteness at having failed to introduce him than her heartfelt regret that this—he—was the best they could do at the last minute, when Joe, who had been with the ranch for decades, had suddenly taken ill.

Mrs. Fairchild consulted a scrap of paper on the podium. "This is Nicholas Wolfe," she said.

"Yes," Trish enthused in her whisper. "A wolf in wolf's clothing—at last."

"Nicholas—oh, sorry, I see you go by Nick." Mrs. Fairchild could not conceal, despite finishing school training of her own, how distasteful—how *common*—it was to prefer "Nick" to "Nicholas." Nick suited him, of course, this man who was so unsuitable in every way. "Nick will be taking care of the horses for the summer. He's here for the horses, not for you."

"But I want Nick here for me," Trish implored to table twelve. "I *want* Nick to take care of me."

Mrs. Fairchild became more than slightly flustered as the suddenly humming dining room signified that Trish was not the only enthralled teen to have made such a remark. "By this I mean Nick won't be giving riding lessons. For legal reasons, only experienced riders may ride at Willow Ranch, and no matter how experienced you may feel you are, we must have signed releases from your parents before you can ride."

"But I want riding lessons from Nick," Trish moaned. "*With* Nick. I'm sure he could teach me to become even more experienced than I already am."

"He's *beneath* you," Bonnie insisted.

"I'm not planning to *marry* him, Bon-Bon! And whether he's beneath me or on top is his choice." Trish's expression transformed from teasing to serious—and so sympathetic—as her worldly gaze fell on the youngest Meadowlark. "Oh, Hope! I've embarrassed you. You don't even know, do you, what I'm talking about?"

"Yes, I do," Hope replied, although in truth she only *sort of* knew. Hope Tessier knew enough, however, to feel uncomfortable for Nick, the way they were talking about him, as if he were merely an object, merely a toy, without any feelings at all. "I do know."

"But you're embarrassed, aren't you? Don't be. *Please.*" Trish looked worried now, as if she had stepped over some fundamental line. "Your innocence is so charming, Hope. So *precious*—as are you."

Hope blushed and was silent, for Mrs. Fairchild was speaking.

"Now," the camp director said, "it's my pleasure to turn the microphone over to Sabrina Blyth. As all of you know, for the past five years Willow Ranch offered, to a select number of campers, an innovative—and sensational— weight loss program. We call it 'Win,' which makes its graduates *win*ners. Thanks to Sabrina, Win has been a stunning success—so successful, in fact, that this year sixteen of you have chosen to enroll. But why don't I let Sabrina tell you? . . . Sabrina?"

Sabrina Blyth had a degree in psychology, was twenty-eight years old, and, as she told the assembled—and now reverently silent—campers, although she herself had always been slender, she had watched, in agony, the misery of a little sister who was overweight.

"Which is why I'm so passionate about our program. I know how difficult it can be, especially for a teenage girl, to be heavy. Such anguish can be overcome by enhancing self-image, self-*esteem*—by feeling happy about yourself, *loving* yourself, no matter what you weigh. Or, of course, it can be conquered by losing the unwanted weight. In Win we believe in doing both—teaching you to love yourself *and* lose the weight. All sixteen of this year's enrollees share such a belief, and will achieve both goals, *this summer,* with the help of everyone in this room. Everyone benefits in the Win program at Willow Ranch. Everyone *wins.* We all learn to understand each other, to help each other, to trust and support and grow—even as sixteen of us shrink! It takes courage to come to a place where the majority of girls are not overweight. *Great* courage. So, you courageous young women, may I ask you to stand as I read your names and tell the others a little about you?"

Sabrina's request was intended to celebrate, not to mortify, and the Win enrollees, who felt so lucky to have been accepted into the highly competitive program, bounced right up when their names were called. Their courage—and optimism—were greeted with applause; and there was more applause, and authentic murmurs of sympathy, when Sabrina read heart-wrenching excerpts from the personal essays written by each overweight girl.

"And finally," Sabrina said, "and last but not least, is our youngest camper of the summer, Hope Tessier. I'm afraid, Hope, that your personal essay has been misplaced. So I'll just read from the Win application itself. Let's see. You were born in California's Napa Valley, it says, and weight has been a problem for you for many years. Your mother is—oh, my—best-selling novelist Frances Tessier, and your father—what a talented family, Hope!—is concert violinist Victor Tessier, and . . . Hope? Will you stand, please? So everyone can welcome you while I read the rest?''

Hope stood, because she always did what she was told, always tried—how she tried—to do everything right.

But as she stood, as she trembled, her young heart cried. *No. No! It can't be me!*

She had never even heard of the Win program, much less submitted a personal essay of anguish. In fact, she had filled out no application at all, had merely opened an elaborately wrapped package. And weight had *not,* for her, been a problem . . . not at all, much less for *many* years . . . had it?

Yes, apparently, *yes.* For here she was, at this innovative fat farm cloistered in the elegance of Willow Ranch. This place where losers became winners—and where her mother believed she belonged, chose for her to be.

Hope hadn't known, hadn't realized. Her beautiful slender mother had never said a word. *No one had.*

But now, suddenly, Hope Tessier had a secret after all—a secret known to everyone but her, a shame that everyone could see.

She didn't know where to look! There *was* nowhere to look. There was only sympathy, and understanding, and knowing expressions that acknowledged, with sophisticated sorrow, that she had been unable to control this terrible problem no matter how hard she had tried.

But I've never even tried!

Then she was looking at him.

Nick.

And he was looking at her.

Nicholas Wolfe was no longer leaning casually against the wall. He was on alert, powerful yet still, and his eyes, intent and fierce, were glittering blue. Nick did not clap, even though everyone else did, at certain junctures in Sabrina's recitation of Hope's problem—and her pedigree.

Nick just looked at her, as if wanting to take her far away from this cruelty that—his fierce eyes told her—she did not deserve.

It seemed an impossible feat, whisking her away from this torment. But Nick accomplished it, by simply wanting to rescue her—for as Hope looked at him, something bubbled up from deep within, from a dancing spring of cheer that was not, quite yet, completely dry.

Oh, well!

It was, perhaps, Hope Tessier's final "Oh, well!" But at that moment it was the only way to survive.

And Hope did survive, and now she was sitting down, and the other Meadowlarks were saying all the right things—reassurance perhaps suggested in Win program materials sent to the slender campers who were destined to win, as well, by encouraging their overweight comrades.

"You're not that heavy," Jenna said.

"She's right," Bonnie concurred. "In fact, we were all talking about it when you went for your walk. You have a little left-over baby fat—that's all!"

You were all talking about me?

"A fluffiness," Jenna asserted, "that will come off easily now that you really want it to."

Fluffiness? No. I'm fat. Obese. Hope felt her heaviness now, how massive it was, every cell laden—she felt *every* cell—immense . . . and jiggling.

"I'm not sure why you even want to lose the weight,"

Trisha said. "I mean, it obviously doesn't interfere with your ability to play—and excel in—any number of sports. And, precious, innocent Hope, you're not yet interested in boys. So who cares?"

My mother cares! Don't you see? I've been embarrassing her, humiliating her, for all these years.

"I agree," Robyn said. "As long as you're happy, Hope, it couldn't matter less."

Happy? Hope had no memory of the word.

Even Sabrina came over, rushed over, worried that Hope's enrollment in Win might have been a surprise, which would have defeated the purpose, because the program—and its success—was based on commitment and choice.

"Maybe there's been a mistake," Sabrina said. "I have no idea how it could have happened, but—"

"No," Hope insisted. "There's no mistake."

Frances Tessier had not told her. But the best-selling novelist had provided ample foreshadowing—plot clues, all those many years. Hope saw now—only now!—her mother's scowls at her overweight classmates . . . and the frowns, then, that turned to her. And she heard, only now, her mother's accompanying critiques—that there was absolutely no excuse for permitting oneself to look that way.

And there were the fruit plates her mother always ordered, for both of them; and the salads. And, the most revealing clue of all, her mother's delight—or was it relief?—that, at long last, Hope was thirteen . . . and could spend the summer at Willow Ranch.

"I want to be here," Hope told them all, the Meadowlarks and Sabrina alike. Here . . . where she had wanted to come for so long, this place of marshmallows roasts and summertime sails and being welcomed, accepted, for who you were.

Aching anew, desperate anew, Hope gazed beyond the sympathetic faces to the wooden wall. But Nicholas Wolfe was gone.

She saw him later, though, during the dinner at which she ate nothing at all. He was in the pasture beyond the corral. And he was talking, it seemed. Talking to a horse.

TWELVE

WILLOW RANCH

LAKE WILDERNESS, MONTANA

THIRTEEN YEARS AGO

*N*ick found her, a week later, in her hiding place in the hayloft above the stalls.

Nick knew she was there, as she had been for the past six days. Alone. Hidden. For hours on end. She was not hidden from him, however. He knew when she climbed the wooden ladder to the loft, and he checked, after she was gone, for clues to her choice of this sanctuary.

Nick found no clues, only the indentation in the hay, the nest where, alone and silent, she curled.

Thank you for worrying about me, she had said, so politely, beneath the willow tree—and again, with her devastated green eyes, in the dining room.

Nick had not, beneath the willow tree, been worried about her. His concern had been for a baby creature—frantic and alone.

But Nick had worried about Hope, young and frantic and desperate, ever since.

On this day, when Nick found her, Hope was sitting in her nest of hay, hunched into a tight, fierce ball, her tomboy body trying so hard to be small even as her bright schoolgirl mind was focused, intently, on her task.

She pored over a cream-and-teal notebook, emblazoned with the willow tree, poised to write, wanting to write, her fingers squeezed, tight and fierce, against her pen . . . so absorbed that she did not hear his approach.

"Hi."

"Oh!" She looked up, alert and wary, the once intrepid climber of willow trees so fearful now. "Is it bad for me to be here?"

"Bad? No." *Nothing about you is bad.* "Not at all. Can I sit?"

"Oh, yes. Of course."

"Thanks." It was not large, the nest created by this baby creature, this wounded fawn; merely a golden patch of straw rimmed by bales of hay. Nick sat against a bale, across from her, and faced her, looked at her, as he lighted a cigarette. "I'm Nick."

Hope nodded her cinnamon-capped head. He was the reason she had come here, a desperate journey when she needed to run away and could think of nowhere else to go. But when she ran to the stables, to the man who seemed to care, he was in the corral, talking to Trish. So she climbed the ladder to the loft, to this place, this safe place, the only safe place . . . near him.

But now Nick was introducing himself as if he didn't remember her.

"I know," she said softly.

"And you're Hope, who climbs willow trees"—*used to*—"and who was born in Napa, and gets top grades wherever she goes, and plays terrific soccer . . ."

Somehow, every word Sabrina said had been etched in

his brain, even as Hope's anguish was being carved in his heart. His heart? That cold and empty place that did not care? Had no *reason* to care?

"What are you doing?" he asked.

"Working on my assignment for today."

"Assignment? I thought the only assignment at Willow Ranch was to have fun."

"But . . . I'm in the Win program."

"I know." *I have not forgotten.* Nick looked at her, the baby creature whose plumpness was a luxuriant coat of health, a lush and lovely cloak of her exuberant youth. "I don't see why."

"Why what?"

"Why you're in the Win program." His comment seemed to bewilder, not reassure her—for she had surrendered, he realized. Her wound was so grave, the betrayal so crippling, that her only hope of healing, of even going on, was to yield without protest to whatever Sabrina—and Win—had in store. "So, Hope, what's your assignment? Or is that a secret?"

"No." *There are no secrets.* Not anymore. That was an assignment, too: talking about the "problem," the *fat,* dealing with it in a forthright manner, confessing every shame, every weakness, right out loud. "Today I'm writing down all the reasons I eat—trying to. First I have to figure out what they are. I haven't made much headway."

"Does being hungry count?"

"I guess," she murmured, and smiled, a pale ghost of the radiance that had glowed at him from the willow tree. "Is that why you eat?"

"Sure."

"That's *wonderful.*"

No, little fawn, there is nothing wonderful about me. "You must eat when you're hungry, too. Like after you've spent the afternoon playing soccer?"

"Yes," Hope confessed, and frowned. She couldn't imagine ever playing soccer again, ever wearing shorts, ever running across a field with her jiggling, laden flesh. "But . . . I eat at other times, too, for other reasons. At least I've found one other reason so far." She drew a breath, then admitted in a rush. "I eat when I'm lonely."

Oh, Hope Tessier, don't be lonely. Nick felt an astonishing urge to hold her, to cradle and to comfort. Nick . . . who touched only rarely, and with such a different purpose.

But she didn't need to be cradled, to be comforted, for with her admission—that she ate when she was lonely, and that there were lonely times in her life—came a flicker of relief. She had succeeded after all, this earnest schoolgirl who always got A's. She had found a secret reason and confessed it out loud.

As Hope glanced at her wristwatch, her relief faded to worry—and, Nick thought, a whisper of regret.

"I have to go," she said. "Today's nutrition lecture begins in ten minutes."

"Okay. Hope? It's all right for you to come here, whenever you want. It's fine."

She came every day for the next three weeks, and they talked in her loft, where Nick joined her, uninvited but always so welcome. And one day Hope found him first, searched for him in the stables, discovered him grooming an Appaloosa mare.

"I brought an apple for the horses—well, for one of them, I guess."

"Your apple, Hope?"

"I'm just eating when I'm hungry, and I wasn't hungry."

Nick studied her, his blue eyes dark and intense. She wore jeans despite the heat, and a Willow Ranch T-shirt that had always been too large and hung almost to her knees. Her body was concealed, but there was proof that she was losing weight in her face, in her hands, and in her eyes . . . bright eyes, starving eyes, determined—and achingly hopeful.

"Are you eating at all?"

"Yes!"

"Okay," Nick said softly, relenting—softly—despite his worry, unwilling to further pierce her already betrayed young heart—especially since she was doing everything in her power to cause the weeping wounds to heal. "Why don't you give the apple to Freckles here?"

Hope answered by extending to him, not the mare, her polished red apple. "You'd better give it to her."

"Are you afraid?" Nick asked the tomboy who was fearless no more. "Were you thrown?"

"No. I've never ridden at all. But one of my mother's friends was injured, riding, when they were girls. She was *okay*, eventually. But my mother never rode again. And she doesn't want me to, either."

"Do *you* want to?"

Hope shrugged. She had never wanted to ride, had never even thought about it. But when she watched Nick ride, it looked like dancing—for both man and horse—floating, soaring leaps of immense power and majestic grace.

"Is that a yes?" Nick asked. "Because if so, I'll teach you."

"But you *can't*. My mother would never have signed the release, and you'd get in trouble if you let me ride without it."

Nicholas Wolfe's smile was gentle and wry. "I've been in trouble before."

But she hadn't been, this girl who tried so hard to follow the rules and who was so determined never again to make a mistake.

"Oh. Well. No. I shouldn't. I'd better not." *I could never dance like that.* "She'd be really upset if I did. But thank you."

His smile, now, was only gentle. "Sure."

Nick learned, in those weeks, about Hope's family—Chase, the brother who was Nick's age and whom she admired so much. And Frances.

"She's *incredible,*" Hope raved. "Wonderful, and beautiful, so very beautiful, and funny—*witty*—and amazingly smart. Everything is brighter when my mother walks into the room."

And you're just like her, Nick thought but did not say. Hope wouldn't believe it. *Couldn't.* Even if, with a gentle tease, he admitted that she was right in one respect: she wasn't all *that* witty.

Hope Tessier might have been witty, once upon a time, in the life that existed before that night at table twelve. But life had become serious business for the wounded fawn. Hope was fighting for her life; struggling never again to fail—to never again disappoint the dazzling mother she loved so much.

But just how incredible, Nick wondered, how *wonderful* could Frances Tessier possibly be?

"Was it your mother's idea for you to come here?" *To be emotionally ambushed so thoroughly that you may never trust again?*

"Yes."

"But she didn't tell you, did she?"

"About Win? Not specifically. No." *But I should have known, and it's good that she sent me here.* "What about your family, Nick?"

Nick took a deep drag on his inevitable cigarette, a breath of soot, of heat, of flames. "I don't have a family."

"What do you mean?"

He exhaled. Slowly. Not at her. Never at her. And, indeed, Nicholas Wolfe exhaled far less smoke than he had taken in. The flames and the fumes were held inside, searing his lungs, burning his veins.

"I guess I mean there's nothing to tell. Really. Not a thing." *There are so many things I cannot tell you.* He inhaled again. "So, Hope. Tell me about your father."

"My . . . oh, you mean Victor. He's not actually my father."

"Who is?"

"I don't know. I never knew him. Which is *fine.* It doesn't matter. My mother and Victor have been married since before I was born."

"What's Victor like?" Nick's query was interested but casual. He expected, as had been the case for Frances and Chase, an immediate—and enthusiastic—reply. But Hope's response, for the moment, was to tug thoughtfully at a golden strand of hay that was pressed, crushed, in a nearby bale of hay. "You don't like him?"

Hope tugged still. "Well, yes, I do." She looked at Nick, at the dark blue eyes behind the veils of smoke. "I haven't really spent that much time with him. But he's always been . . . nice . . . to me."

Hope recounted her most recent memory of Victor, in March, when they were all scheduled to rendezvous in Paris during her spring break. Chase and Frances would arrive first, then Hope, and eventually Victor, during a three-day hiatus from his European tour.

Frances was flying to Paris from Los Angeles, where she'd been screening the miniseries of her latest book, and Chase would accompany her on that flight. But shortly after Chase's flight from San Francisco landed at LAX, the airport was closed because of fog, a tenacious shroud that forecasters feared might last for days. Frances informed her daughter—and the administrators at Val d'Isère—that Hope should stay put until she and Chase reached Paris.

"A few hours later," Hope said, no longer tugging at the still imprisoned straw, "Victor called. He was in Vienna, and when he learned I might be in an empty dormitory for several days—it was safe, though, since the headmistress was still there—he invited me to join him. I'd never been alone with him before."

"And?"

Hope paused, uncertain how to put this into words. *He* had been uncertain, too. Victor. Uncertain, and almost shy. But he seemed to want her there and wasn't embarrassed in the least by the way she looked. Victor Tessier hadn't gazed at her, not once, with the disappointment, and disapproval, that, Hope realized now—oh, how she realized—her mother so often had.

"And it was nice," she answered at last. "He was nice. We went to the museums, and the palaces, and he told me about Mozart, and Vienna, and the music he performs— and writes. I went to all his performances, too. He's *really* talented."

Hope's endorsement of the father who was not her father was glowing—and bewildered.

"But," Nick said quietly, "there's something about Victor that you don't like."

"It's not me. *I* like him. But . . . he makes my mother unhappy. Not *all* the time, of course. Just sometimes. He gets so involved with his music that she feels ignored. She *is* ignored. And she shouldn't be, not someone like her. She shouldn't be wasting her life waiting for him."

The words, Nick guessed, as well as the passion—and indignation—came verbatim from the novelist who had a talent for such things . . . and who had the blind devotion of her daughter.

But, he wondered, was Hope's blindness a total darkness? He suggested gently, "There must be times when your mother gets involved with her books."

"Yes. There are."

"Does that make Victor feel ignored?"

Hope's smile was faint, weary—and far older than her thirteen years. "No. He doesn't. Which makes her even more unhappy, as if Victor couldn't care less if she's there. He *does* care. I know he does. How could he not? But . . . when I was visiting him in Vienna, I saw how consumed he is by his music. It was an effort for him to pay attention to me."

"But he did pay attention."

"Yes. He did." Hope paused, then said again, and decisively, "He was very nice to me."

Who wouldn't be very nice to this lovely girl? Who wouldn't want to keep her safe and make her smile?

Just Frances . . . the mother who had sent her here, to spend this summer trying to change, to be better, to *win* her approval and her love.

"I really hope they're having a good summer."

It was a soft wish, and such a charitable one, a stark contrast to the harshness of his thoughts. "What did you say?"

"That I hope my mother and Victor are having a good summer. They're spending it together. She's put her writing on hold, and he's cut way back on his concerts. And in August the four of us are going to spend ten days together at the Domaine."

"The Domaine?"

"Domaine Tessier. Where Chase lives. In Napa."

The harshness returned to Nick's thoughts. But it didn't touch his voice. "Do you spend much time there?"

"No. Hardly any time at all. Do you know Napa, Nick? Have you ever been there?"

Do I know Napa? No. Have I been there? Only in my night-mares. "No."

"Well, if you ever *do* go, you have to visit the Do-maine—to meet Chase—and be sure to go to the very top of Black Mountain. You can see the entire valley from there."

"The entire valley?" In the nightmares of Nicholas Wolfe Napa Valley was immense, monstrous—and very, very small. "How big is it?"

"Pretty big, I guess. From the tidelands to Mount St. Helena is about thirty-five miles, and there are a number of towns. Napa is the largest—maybe it's even a city—and then, and these are smaller, there's Yountville, Oakville, Rutherford, St. Helena, and Calistoga." Hope smiled a rare, bright, untarnished smile. "You really should visit Napa, Nick. I *know* you'd like it."

It was an astonishing assertion, and such a confident one, a glimpse of the cheerful girl she once had been—the optimistic tomboy who, perhaps, had believed it was possible to change nightmares into dreams.

Was there a reason for her conviction that he would like what he found in the valley? The scatter of equestrian estates, perhaps, amid the vast sea of vines?

Nick would have asked her, planned to ask her, had Hope come to her loft the following day. But she didn't come. Not that day. Or the next. Or the next.

A week passed. Ten days. Hope Tessier was still at Willow Ranch and still a "winner."

Nick could see her from the corral, sitting with the other Meadowlarks at table twelve, not eating, merely pretending to eat, and not looking, ever, toward the stable, the hayloft, *him.*

Nick missed her. But the loss, he knew, was his—not hers. Hope needed to be with the other Meadowlarks, not with him; needed to be laughing, singing, soaring with joy.

Nick's dark blue eyes searched for her in the sailboats that glided on the wind-caressed lake, and beside the aquamarine tranquillity of the swimming pool, and on the tennis courts, and even in the tree.

But Hope was nowhere to be found. Not laughing. Not singing. Not soaring. Just hidden still. Hidden somewhere else, somewhere new, away from him.

Nick wanted to know why Hope had forsaken her golden nest. And he needed to know that the abandonment was not because of him.

On the eleventh night he waited outside the ranch house, a wolf in the shadows, unseen by the rest of the herd, waiting until a straggler, a solitary fawn, became separated from the others, as he knew she would, because she was—so separate—from them all.

"Hope?"

"Nick," she whispered even before she turned.

And when she turned, Nick saw her sadness.

"Come to the stable, Hope. We need to talk."

They didn't talk, not a word, as they walked across the emerald lawn beyond the willow tree, and into the stables, and up the wooden ladder to her abandoned loft.

They assumed their familiar positions, as far apart as the small nest would allow.

"You've stopped coming here," Nick said. "Why?"

Her young veins had been opened this summer. She had been compelled to open them, to reveal all secrets, expose all faults, to never be secretive again.

She answered honestly, as he knew she would—had to.

"Everyone thought it was . . . strange."

"What was strange?"

"That I could really be your . . ." She shrugged and blushed—an aching contrast to the roses that had bloomed when she'd scampered up a willow tree. This blush was a splotchy red, a smudge of crimson on her pale and worried cheeks.

"My what, Hope?" Anger pulsed within, raged within, as Nick considered the cruel imaginings of teenage girls. Had they envisioned, and shared with her, some strange sexuality between the innocent tomboy and the far from innocent man?

No, Nick decided, Nick hoped—as she seemed worried, but not confused, by the word she had yet to speak. Whatever it was that was strange was, at least, something she understood.

"Your friend," she confessed, as if "friend" were the most important word in the English language.

And it was, Nick thought—and foreign, to him, until now . . . when it was so treasured. "But you are, aren't you? *We* are."

"Really?"

"Yes," Nick said softly. "Really. Okay?"

"Okay," she whispered, then shrugged anew. "Everyone wants to be your friend."

"You mean Trish."

Hope nodded. And others, she thought. So *many* others, older girls who approached her, amazed that she could be friends with the wolf, doubting it, and yet—because Hope did, inexplicably, seem to have Nick's attention—imploring her to put in a good word. Hope's allegiance, of course, was to Meadowlark Trish.

"Trish is really—"

"Not for me."

"Oh. Too young." Hope's assertion was earnest, quiet, wise.

"Way too young," Nick confirmed, quietly, too. They were all too young, these spoiled heiresses who flirted and teased; so young, too young, in so many ways, and uninteresting to him in every way.

"I guess Sabrina is more your type," said Nick's young—and so wise—little friend. "Older, more mature. And she's *so* pretty and . . ."

Hope's words drifted off in the embarrassment, her own, that shimmered in the air . . . and in the smoke, his, swirling from his just lighted, ferociously lighted, cigarette.

As euphemistic as this conversation was, Nick didn't like it one bit. The lovely innocent was right, of course—Sabrina shared, precisely, Nicholas Wolfe's vision of sex: pleasure—no more, no less—between consulting adults. Pleasure without emotion, without caring, without affection of any kind.

Nick never pursued his lovers—never seduced, never teased, never cajoled. Nick's women found him, pursued him, and only when he was certain they truly understood how dispassionate their passion would be did he take them to his bed.

Sabrina seemed to understand the rules, even before she and Nick ever spoke—before she proposed a roll in the hay, a long, hot summer of such unencumbered lust.

But this summer, both literally and figuratively, the hay belonged to Hope. And Sabrina, who might, another summer, have held some appeal, was—this summer—an unwitting conspirator in Hope's betrayal and pain.

"I'm not involved with Sabrina. Or anyone. And I'm not going to be, not this summer."

Perhaps it was the way her weight loss had aged her, leaving her gaunt face both ravaged and wise. But it was as if she understood the loneliness of being wanted, being desired . . . but never as a friend.

"You should probably stop smoking," she said.

"I should? Why?"

"It would make things easier. Everybody thinks you look"—*incredibly sexy*—"good when you smoke."

"That's reason enough to quit."

"Really? You mean you *will?*"

"You don't like it when I smoke?"

"*No.* Of course not! I mean . . . it's not good for you. It's *dangerous* for you."

"Well," Nick murmured. "How about if I promise never to smoke when you're around?"

*I*t began again, the friendship between the wolf and the fawn. Hope told Nick everything he wanted to know about her, and Nick told her what little he could about himself.

He moved from job to job, he told her; the fitful pacing, he permitted her to believe, of a restless cowboy . . . not the truth of a man who could not, dared not, stay in any one place for very long . . . who could not, not ever, find a nest of his own.

Did Nicholas Wolfe, who trusted no one—who had no reason to trust—mistrust as well his earnest tomboy friend? Did he believe that, armed with the truth, Hope would rush to Mrs. Fairchild, who would in turn, and happily, summon the police?

It would, of course, be the right thing to do. But Hope would not betray him. Nick knew it and was humbled by it.

Nick knew, too, what the truth—his truth—would do to Hope. He would not burden her with the sadness he knew she would feel . . . nor would he taint her with horrors she could not possibly understand.

Ten days before the Willow Ranch summer would come to its inevitable end, Nick discovered her in the loft, absorbed in a task—and troubled.

"What's wrong?"

She looked up, startled, even more worried.

"Did you see what I wrote? Because I need to explain."

"It's okay, Hope. I didn't see."

"Oh." *Good.* She should have known. He never looked at her journal, which was a diary; was too gentlemanly to look . . . even though, sometimes, she left her notebook open so that he might read the words, about him, her friend, that she could not possibly speak.

"But you could explain what's wrong anyway. . . . Hope?"

"Okay." It was an assignment, one of the last the winners would be required to do, the one that would prove how far they had come in the arena that mattered most: self-esteem. "First, we have to pretend that we're sitting across from someone we like, looking at them as we tell them everything we like about them—everything we can think of in ten minutes, that is."

That was easy, *so* easy. Except that ten minutes wasn't nearly long enough to chronicle all the things she liked about her mother, her brother, and Victor . . . and Nick. "Then we have to pretend we're sitting across from ourselves, and do the same thing."

"Ten minutes of telling yourself everything you like about yourself?"

"Yes." Everything you like, Sabrina had said; everything you *love.* "You can't list accomplishments—like the grades you get in school or the weight you've lost at the ranch." Every Win girl had lost weight. Hope, who'd had the least to lose, had lost the most. She was the undisputed champion, the dazzling star—even though, Sabrina proclaimed in the same breath, weight loss was not a competition. Hope was that star pupil now, reciting perfectly the lessons she had learned. "People with low self-esteem measure themselves by what they *accomplish,* not who they *are.* You know, like you're good, *worthy,* if you lose a pound, and worthless, *bad,* when you gain? And you also can't list things over which you have no control—like whose daughter or sister you are, or if you inherited your intelligence from your parents. You have to list good things, positive things, about who you are inside, all the time, whether you succeed or fail."

"You still haven't explained the problem."

"Yes, I *have.* I need to give Sabrina my self-esteem word. This afternoon. *Soon.*"

Nick wanted to help his terribly anxious friend. He would—once he understood. Which he didn't. Not yet.

"Your self-esteem word," he repeated softly.

"Yes. We have to give her the one we like the best, so she can read all sixteen at the farewell dinner."

"And, since there may be duplications, you're trying to be creative? To find a word no one else will choose?"

"No."

"Then what? I'm sorry, Hope. I'm just not getting this."

"I can't find any word!" And she'd been trying for hours. Seeing herself in her mind's eye. She'd finally found something positive, something wonderful—"Nick's friend." But that was an *accomplishment,* and it was positive because of him, not her. So she had crossed it out, drawn heavy lines through their friendship and his name.

"Well," Nick said, understanding at last. The Win program poster child, the most glittering winner of them all, was on the verge of failing her most important assignment. Nick banked the fury he felt and said, very gently, "I can think of at least a thousand."

"What?" Her query was disbelieving and breathless— for even though she was fat, would always be *fat* inside, she *had* lost weight. She was breathless, as a result, and couldn't always concentrate. Hope concentrated now on the fierce blue eyes that had rescued her before. "You *can?*"

"I can," Nick repeated softly. "At least a thousand. But you just need one? Okay. Let's see."

He looked at her, so worried about the gaunt, breathless, panicky girl he saw. The lovely girl, who was so generous, so good. And gracious, and caring, and courageous, and loyal, and—

"It's hard, isn't it?"

Oh, Hope. "To find just one? Yes. Very hard. And to decide which of all of them you should give to Sabrina? Almost impossible. In fact, I think I'll just tell you my list so far and let you decide."

"No, Nick. No. *Please.* You decide."

She was so desperate, so hopeless, so needy.

"Okay." Nicholas Wolfe chose, for his friend, the word she had used to describe the father who was not a father. Wonder had touched her voice when she'd told him about Victor Tessier, a wonder that had not been present, despite the superlatives and the raves, when Hope spoke about her mother.

"Nice," he said softly. "Very, very nice."

*N*ick learned from Sabrina, the following afternoon, that Hope had used his word, his "nice." The Win program cheerleader—and psychologist—was in his room in the stable, the windowless room that held little more than a bed.

Sabrina had come at Nick's invitation, and with a self-assured smile. At last the sensual cowboy had seen the light. And, she promised herself, she and Nick were going to make up for lost time, beginning this afternoon, when all the teenage campers were in their cabins planning their skits for the farewell show.

But Nick greeted her not with lust, but with questions.

"Yes," she confirmed impatiently. "Hope *has* lost weight. Lots of it. That's the *point,* Nick. And in group discussions her comments are always perceptive. *Astute.*"

"Because she's so bright," Nick countered. *And so desperate to please.* "And because she's taken such careful notes."

"And," Sabrina insisted, "because she believes what she's learned. Hope is thrilled about the way she looks, Nick. *Thrilled*—as she should be. She looks terrific, and will be leaving here a lifelong winner, with sky-high self-esteem."

Thrilled? Nick didn't think so. Despite her weight loss, the fawn was wary still, worried and anxious—and so hopeful that, this time, she had gotten it right. Maybe Hope would be thrilled, once Frances Tessier saw her and approved—a celebration of Hope's accomplishment, Nick mused, not of her *self.*

No matter the reason, Nick wanted that thrilling—relieved—moment for Hope. And he wanted it soon. She had been starving too long, starving her anxious heart and her precarious flesh.

"Nick?" Sabrina queried with a seductive pout. "Did you really invite me here to talk about Hope?"

Her pout became a frown as Nick moved to answer the soft knock on his door. He didn't have to move far in the windowless closet designed for sleep—or sex.

Hope had never been in Nick's room. Had never before even knocked on his door.

But she had knocked now, a soft and timid intrusion, and she reddened with mortification when Nick opened the door—and she saw them both.

"I'm *sorry,*" she whispered.

"It's okay," Nick reassured her. *We were just talking—about you.*

How betrayed Hope would feel if she knew: mommy and daddy discussing their problem daughter, after which—although it wasn't going to happen, had never been his plan—they would enjoy each other.

"Let's walk," Nick suggested, pulling closed the door on his room, his bed, and Sabrina.

They didn't walk far, just to an empty row of stalls.

"What is it, Hope?"

"I just came to say good-bye."

The pain of it pierced him, stunned him. "You're leaving? Today?"

"Yes. Right now. The limousine is waiting."

Nick drew a breath, a harsh, punishing wish for flames and smoke. He would smoke, could smoke all he liked, once she was gone. "Tell me what happened."

"My mother called. She's leaving Victor. He ignored her—all summer—neglected her despite the promises he made. Why did he do that?"

Because, Hope Tessier, people break promises. All the time. "I don't know. Maybe he got so tied up with his music he couldn't help it."

"He *could* have helped it, and now it's too late."

"Where are you going?"

"To London." In her fist, curled so tightly that Nick would never see her foolishness, was the slip of paper on which she had written—for him—Frances's Knightsbridge address, where she would be until summer's end, and, as well, the address of her boarding school in Val d'Isère. "I have to go! My flight from Great Falls leaves at four."

"Okay. Hope?"

"Yes?"

"Eat."

A faint smile curved on the thin face that was a gaunt forecast of the beautiful woman she would become but which, now, was merely a wan gravestone of the plump and healthy girl she once had been.

"Nick?"

"Yes?"

"Don't smoke!"

Nick smiled, then grew solemn. He said very softly, "Take care of yourself, Hope Tessier."

She became solemn, too, and so very wise—as if, suddenly, she knew all the lonely, sordid truths about him. "You too, Nicholas Wolfe."

Then Hope turned and ran, breathless, starving, gasping for breath as she vanished from his sight . . . and from his life.

THIRTEEN

MONTAGNE NOIR
THURSDAY, NOVEMBER EIGHTH

*C*assandra returned to Napa
Valley as she had first arrived—by car, from Los Angeles. It
was the most private way, Chase decided, and the safest,
her doctors concurred, relieved that her healing vessels
would not be subjected to the barometric vacillations inevitable to flight.

On that long-ago day Cassandra Winter had been
dressed in black, and today she wore lavender—one of a
wardrobe of bright, fluffy bathrobes purchased by Hope.

Cassandra's hair, then—that luxuriance of amber silk—
had been pulled tightly against her skull. And now she had
no hair at all, only a badly damaged skull, wrapped in pale
flesh and beribboned with the dark purple slashes of recent
scars.

No diamonds sparkled on this gray November day; and
every vine had long since surrendered its sweet bounty, as

187

Cassandra had surrendered hers; and even the leaves, brilliant with the fiery hues of autumn, like the vivid plumage she once had worn, had fluttered away.

Only skeletons haunted the once green vineland.

Only winter.

Only loss.

I should not be here! I can't be.

The frantic thoughts pierced the mists that—still—shrouded her brain. The lingering mistiness was expected, her physicians assured her—and necessary, a billowy cocoon that would blanket all worries until she was well enough to confront the sharp edges of truth.

Cassandra knew vaguely, and without alarm, that some crime had been committed at her Brentwood home. Except for wanting to be assured that no one was injured—no one else—the floating mists rendered her remarkably uninterested in details of the event.

The mists didn't care. She didn't care.

But the gauzy cocoon of complacency did not surround her heart . . . and as Chase navigated with care the winding ascent up the mountain, frantic thoughts pierced anew.

I should have said no.

She had tried to say no, in a floating, swirling way. She would convalesce, she mused vaguely, in a secluded bungalow at the Hotel Bel-Air. Her doctors could drop by from time to time, or a hotel limousine could whisk her to them. Room service would deliver her meals, and the rest of the time she would be sleeping anyway. . . .

Gently, oh-so-gently, Chase told her she would be convalescing at the château. He told her in person, his gray eyes intense and searching and worried—but without disgust, never with disgust, even though she was a pitiful sight. And by phone, gaily yet decisively, Hope and Eleanor told her, too.

Hope would come to the mountain the moment the verdict was in; and Eleanor would come any old time at all, she promised, as soon as Cass had the energy for company. While Chase tended to winery business—neglected, forgotten, since Halloween—they would have lunch, and tea, and fun.

They, the girls: Cassandra. Hope. Eleanor. Jane.

But I don't want to see Jane! The jolting assertion came with the brilliance of lightning—a stunning brilliance, and so blinding that Cass could not see beneath its glaring surface to its perplexing truth.

She did not want to see Jane. That was certain. But why? *Why?*

She didn't have the answer. Didn't have so many answers. And now they were here, at the obsidian summit, where the gleaming white château shone like a perfect pearl against the wintry gray sky.

Cassandra felt his gaze . . . and the searing heat of their silence . . . and finally she heard his voice, raw, soft, tender, fierce.

"Shall I carry you, Cassandra?" *Can't you even look at me? Won't you?* But Chase knew, *knew.* The eyes that had awakened with such crystal blue wonder had become opaque and cloudy, with him, *for him.* Cloudy, and fearful—as if *he* were the monster who had beaten her. "Cass?"

"No." She spoke to the glimmering pearl. "Thank you."

It was impossible enough to be here, to return to this fairy-tale castle where for those three magical months before midnight, Cinderella and her prince had loved.

How they had loved. . . .

*T*hey had been, for those magical months eight years ago, explorers in a sprawling mansion of marble, searching the vast luxury until they found a perfect home.

They were pioneers then, nesting in the bedroom they had chosen for their loving. Their room faced west, its vistas of maritime mists and the promise of rainbows. They couldn't see the vineyards, not even from their top-floor perch, but they knew where the vines flourished on the volcanic slopes. The rainbows pointed, precisely, to the spot.

And Chase and Cassandra learned from the windows of the bedroom where they loved even more about the rainbows of Montagne Noir. When the golden rays of sunlight brightened the gray mists to the color of champagne, they knew, a shimmering pastel arch would soon appear.

They were farmers, too, for those enchanted months—yes, farmers, not wranglers, even though their first task was to tame the wild fury of the abandoned vines. The misted vineyards of Montagne Noir had been neglected for over a year, since the death of Frances Tessier had signaled, as well, the death of Chase's dreams.

Side by side the Montagne Noir farmers pruned the overgrown tangles, sometimes making wondrous discoveries within—clusters of grapes, amethyst shards of rainbows, lush and plump and ready to be plucked. It would be small, this honeymoon harvest of Cassandra and Chase, but precious, and come spring they would plant an entire mountainside of vines.

Chase promised his bride more roses, too. A mountain, too, of roses.

Explorers. Pioneers. Farmers.

And lovers.

Cassandra came to him with eagerness, with joy and surprise, every time he touched her. Wanted her. Every time, and Chase wanted his Cassie all the time. Wanted her, needed her, a longing for closeness, for oneness, unlike anything he had ever known.

Cassandra never made the first move in their bedroom beneath the rainbows. She didn't need to, for Chase reached for her always . . . until one night. They lay in silence, not touching, not loving.

"Cassie? Do you want to make love?"

"Yes." It was a whisper of joy.

"You can initiate it, you know. I want you. I will want you, always." *I love you.*

He hadn't told her, not with those three words. But Chase assumed she knew. How could she not? Because, he realized, she was his tentative Tinkerbell, the uncertain waif who had come to him, to his life and to his love, in tattered clothes and with a wounded soul.

Chase didn't whisper those words, that promise, that night in their bed. He waited until morning, in broad daylight, in the vineyards—that were dreams—planted on the obsidian slopes.

Cassandra stood before an exuberance of untended chardonnay, her intelligent eyes narrowed in thoughtful contemplation as she decided how best to prune the renegade tangles.

"I love you."

She looked up. With certain disbelief. And tentative hope. "What did you . . . ?"

Chase smiled. "I said, I love you. I'm in love with you." He saw joy then, pure and blue, and so radiant that when he spoke again his voice held gentle apology. "I should have told you before. All day, every day."

Her cheeks flushed pink, and her own exuberance of tangled moonbeams fluttered—as if some invisible being had whispered something in the autumn air—and her eyes glistened with sudden tears.

Chase cupped the lopsided face he loved so much. "Or maybe not," he said softly. "Is it really so bad?"

"No. *No*. It's just that . . ." *no one has ever loved me.*

"It's just that what, Cassie?"

"Nothing." Radiance glowed anew beneath the glistening mists, a valiant ray from a tiny sun. "You do? You love me?"

"I do. More than I ever believed it was possible for me to love."

"I . . ."

She faltered. But Chase knew what she was going to say. He saw what the luminous glow within was doing to the soggy mists that dampened her eyes.

"Say it," he whispered to the rainbows that shimmered in the brilliant blue. "Say it."

"I love you, Chase. I love you, too."

The fairy tale would not last.

The rainbows were destined to fade.

Cinderella's midnight would come, eventually, and with a vengeance.

Cassandra had known those truths, that destiny, from the very start . . . from the moonlit moment in the rose garden at the Domaine when Chase Tessier proposed to her across a bounty of petals and thorns. Since that rose-fragrant moment, her heart had raced with love, with joy, even as her stomach had churned with its ominous—and relentless—forecast of doom.

The prophetic nightmare began the night Chase told her he loved her. She was standing on a cliff, a shiny obsidian precipice overlooking the lush vineyards of Montagne Noir. For several breathtaking heartbeats she felt unsurpassed happiness, and safe, so very safe. Then the shiny ledge began to crumble beneath her feet, and she was falling, falling. And would her free fall from the mountain be cushioned by the bountiful tangle of vines? No. The vineyards were gone. She was falling into darkness, into blackness, faster, farther, deeper. Help me! Please! *Help me!*

Her cries went unheard, for she was alone, and falling, and—

She awakened, damp and gasping, and Chase was holding her, his lips pressed gently to her fear dampened temple as he whispered, "Cassie, *Cassie.* It's all right, my love. It was only a bad dream."

No! the nightmare screamed still. It was the truth. *Her* truth.

Chase held her closer, tighter, and felt the frantic trembling of her fluttering heart. "Talk to me," he said gently. "Tell me."

"I'm so afraid. Everything seems so . . ." *precarious, so fleeting, so fragile.*

"So what?" he asked. "So perfect?"

"Perfect," she echoed softly, a whisper of hope against his chest.

"Yes. Perfect. At least for me it is. I have everything I ever wanted—and much, much more. The mountain, the rainbows . . . but most of all you."

"So you're happy?"

Chase found her chin, lifted gently until he saw her eyes in the shadows, and smiled. "Deliriously." His expression became solemn with love. "But what about you, Cassandra? Are you happy, too?"

"Yes," she whispered. "Deliriously."

Deliriously happy, and breathlessly afraid, and determined to make certain that nothing ever changed.

But everything did change. And it was all her fault.

Cassandra Tessier reached for her husband the night before she left him, reached for Chase in those few heartbeats before he reached for her.

"So," he whispered on a soft laugh. "You want me after all."

"I want you." And she needed this night, this memory, to sustain the journey of the rest of her life.

It was a night like no other, a loving that was fierce and tender, solemn and desperate, and when Chase rose, at dawn, his reluctance to leave their bed, to leave her, was edged with fear. He had a meeting with his attorneys in the City by the Bay, the final bits of paperwork in the fair and generous disbursement of the Domaine.

"Come with me, Cassie. I know you were planning to spend the day with Eleanor and Jane, but . . . come with me. We'll stay at the Fairmont, in our wedding suite if I can get it, and we'll do some Christmas shopping." He smiled. "Maybe."

"I . . ." *can't.* She had to leave on this day, when Chase wouldn't be home until evening—long after she was far away—and when unanswered calls to the château would be explained by her fictional plans with Eleanor and Jane. "No. Thank you."

"Are you okay?"

"Yes! I'm *fine,* and you'd better go, or you'll be late . . . but drive carefully."

Chase left—only to return an hour later, just as Cassandra had finished packing her duffel bags. The camouflage luggage, her combat gear, lay on the floor beside the bed where they had loved, and she wore black, her transit outfit, as she had when she'd first arrived, and a taxicab idled in the smoke gray mists that swirled outside.

Smoke gray mists, and ominous ones—but quite trivial compared to the menace of his dark gray gaze.

"Chase! Why are you here?"

"I live here, Cassandra. I thought you did, too."

"But . . ."

"I'm supposed to be in San Francisco. I know. But I was

worried about my wife." And despite his smoldering fury, Chase was even more worried about her now. She was so fragile, so vulnerable, *so false.* "I sensed she was lying to me. It appears I was right."

"I wrote you a letter," Cassandra murmured, as if that explained everything, *would* explain everything, even though it explained nothing at all. The letter couldn't reveal her reasons for leaving. *She* couldn't reveal them. She could not even reveal the barest bones of the truth—that the silver-eyed sorcerer had given her a chance at magic . . . and she had let him down. "It's in your office downstairs."

"Why don't you tell me what it says?"

"That I have to go."

I see that, Chase thought. I see how desperate you are, how frantic to flutter away. "That's not very enlightening, Cassandra. Tell me why."

"I . . . there's someone else."

Her quiet words were thunder, their impact a stunning blow. *You're lying!* he wanted to rage, would have raged. *You have to be lying.*

But in her unflickering gaze Chase saw that Cassandra, who could act, who could pretend, was doing neither now.

"I guess it's a measure of my own arrogance that this comes as a complete surprise." His wry, sexy smile didn't begin to travel to his ice gray eyes. "Anyone I know?"

"No. But . . . Montagne Noir is yours, Chase. It *will* be yours."

He shrugged. "Do whatever you like, Cassandra."

Oh, Chase, I cannot do whatever I like. "I have to go."

"I'll carry your bags."

Her worldly belongings weren't heavy, just the feathery plumage of her battle fatigues. "That's all right. I can."

Chase stared at her for a long, unreadable moment.

Then he said, very softly, "Dammit, Cassandra," and crossed the carpet to get her bags.

FOURTEEN

MONTAGNE NOIR
SATURDAY, NOVEMBER TENTH

*E*leanor arrived with concern and sandwiches, soup and love. She came, astonishingly, at Chase's request. It wasn't, of course, the picnic basket of food that Chase needed. He was cooking for Cassandra, feeding her—trying to get her to eat. But . . .

"She's withdrawn from me, Eleanor. Hope will be here this afternoon, but I wonder if you could come. Now?"

Eleanor heard in his voice the same quiet yet frantic despair that, once, Chase must have heard in hers—when she was watching her beloved Andrew die, when Alzheimer's took him away from her and she couldn't reach him, despite all her love, no matter how hard she tried.

"Of course, Chase. I'm on my way."

The bedroom, where the convalescing patient dwelled, was a spacious guest suite two floors below the pioneer's nest where the lovers had lived, had loved. Chase no longer slept in their bedroom. He hadn't for eight years. And since Cassandra's return to the château, Chase, too, slept on the first floor—nearby, to protect, to comfort . . . in case the woman who had withdrawn from him so completely ever needed him again.

Eleanor found Cassandra in the spacious suite, seated by the floor-to-ceiling window, swaddled in blankets from neck to toe, gazing not at the view, but at a crystal vase abloom with roses.

"Knock, knock," Eleanor sang gaily, despite the ravaged loved one she beheld. "And don't you dare stand up!"

"Oh! Eleanor," Cassandra whispered—and wept. "These *tears*. This is what happened the instant Hope walked into my hospital room. I cried. She cried. It was . . ."

"Lovely," Eleanor said. Such an emotional torrent was, she thought, the best way to simply wash away the uncertainties of the past eight years—a nourishing rain that permitted both Hope and Cassandra to admit, without the burden of explaining anything at all, that they were friends. Still. Always. "Hope told me that your very first words to her were how proud you are of her."

"I *am*. So proud of her. And of you, Eleanor. Cateress extraordinaire, belle of the ball, and soon-to-be trophy wife."

"Hah!"

"Aren't you and your young, gorgeous, incredibly nice professor . . ."

"Betrothed? Yes. We are." Eleanor settled into the chair across from Cass and spoke above the cream and pink roses that bloomed in between. "We're all so very proud of you, too, Cassandra."

"Oh! Well."

"All those Academy Awards."

"Nominations, Eleanor."

"You *won* one, and were *robbed* on the others. And, call me old-fashioned—call me archaic—but I, for one, appreciate the fact that PG-Thirteen is as risqué as you get." Eleanor smiled and gazed at Cassandra with her fond, wise, fairy godmother eyes. "How are you, dear?"

"Weepy."

"There's absolutely nothing wrong with tears." *But there's so much wrong with you, Cassandra.* Hope had warned her. The old Cassandra was gone, a change so complete it surely predated the Halloween assault.

Of course it had, Eleanor realized. She had glimpsed it, they all had, in the letters sent—to Eleanor, to Hope, to Jane—the day Cassandra left Montagne Noir. They were thank-you letters, so grateful for their kindness to her and filled with wishes for their happiness . . . always.

They were lovely letters, gracious farewells from a woman who was honestly unaware that she might possibly be missed.

Eleanor saw that lovely woman now. Ravaged, defeated, yet struggling valiantly—for her—smiling softly as she offered more answers to the question Eleanor had posed.

"And bald."

"It's an interesting look."

"And droopy."

"Just between you and me, Cassandra, I always thought your droop was rather . . . provocative."

"And fluffy." Her bony fingers parted the sheath of blankets, revealing the quilted bathrobe she wore beneath. "Hope bought me a colorful collection of down-filled robes and flannel nightgowns, with slippers to match."

"Very stylish."

"Well, cozy and warm." Cass frowned slightly as a surprising yet remarkably untroubling realization penetrated the fluffy cocoon around her brain. "I don't have any other clothes. Not that I need any, I guess. I'm mostly in bed."

"Which is precisely where you need to be. For now. And when you're ready for street clothes, just say the word. Jane and Hope and I will happily go on a shopping spree."

No. Not Jane.

Cassandra's thought came with a fierce yet bewildered expression, which Eleanor could neither miss nor ignore. "What is it, dear?"

"I can't see Jane." *And I don't want her buying anything for me, doing anything for me.*

Now it was Eleanor who was bewildered. "You can't?"

"No. I don't know why, Eleanor. I know it makes no sense." *Jane is so wonderful. So fearless. So generous. So kind.* "But I can't see her. I *can't.* Could you . . . ?"

Eleanor conquered her own confusion and smiled. "Make sure? Without hurting her feelings? Of course I will. There will be no Jane Parish sightings until you're good and ready."

Eleanor paused then, and in those heartbeats of silence a new expression appeared on her face. New, yet familiar— for it belonged to the fairy godmother who had convinced Cassandra to spend the summer at the Domaine, the deceptively innocent and decidedly determined look of the merry Mrs. Claus.

Indeed, Eleanor began as she had eight years ago. "It's so wonderful that you're here. Not the *reason* that you're here, of course, but that you *are,* and in time for Christmas, too. It's going to be a *marvelous* Christmas. I feel it in my fossil bones. Marvelous—wondrous and wonderful—for us all. For once . . . at last."

Chase will give you, even you, Cassandra, a chance. That had been Eleanor's message eight years ago. And she had been right. Chase had given her a chance, and for a while there had been pure magic.

Now the merry Mrs. Claus was promising more magic, Christmas splendor, and even though Cass knew that she would be long gone by Christmas—she had to be—something compelled her to ask, "For once, Eleanor?"

"I imagine that Christmas has always been somewhat difficult for Chase and Hope, at least since the death of Grandpère. That was when he died, you know, just before what would have been a Tessier family Christmas at the Domaine. Always before, the children and Grandpère would meet Frances and Victor somewhere else."

"Because Victor didn't want to be in Napa at Christmas-time."

"That's right," Eleanor said. "How did you know?"

"I don't . . . Oh, yes I *do* remember. On Frances's birth-day video she teased Victor about a Christmas gala so grand that even he would have to spend Christmas in the valley." A frown furrowed her translucent brow. "At least I guess that's how I know. It feels as if I know something else . . . something more."

"Something Victor told you, maybe? Hope said you were happy to see him when he visited you in the hospital."

"That's true. I was." Happy to see the man who made Chase dismember the Domaine? Yes, for some reason, *yes*. "I was."

"Have you and Victor become friends over the years?"

"No. *No.* I'd never even seen him, except on videotape, until a party we both attended four nights before Hallow-een. He came to my home the following afternoon and . . . This is so weird."

"What, dear?"

"It seems so unlikely that Victor and I would have talked at all, much less about anything of substance."

"But you did."

"I think so. Yes."

Yes. For there he was. Victor. A shadowy image in her shadowed memory. He looked, that image, so much like Chase, and he was so tormented that she—his daughter-in-law—had refused to speak to him at the party, wondering what that meant, worrying that Chase loathed him for what he had done. He was an anguished shadow, and such a lonely one that Cass had invited him into her home.

And they had talked. About? She didn't know. Her conversation with Victor Tessier lurked in a twilight memory, a place that was not entirely black yet was too shadowed to see. But the emotions, from the gloaming, were crystal clear. Even now a surprising—yet confident—assertion was forming in the fluffiness of her mind.

"Victor needs to spend this Christmas in Napa. He needs to talk to Chase and Hope." A lovely smile, wan and droopy, touched Cassandra's face. "I haven't the foggiest, and I do mean foggiest, notion why."

Eleanor smiled and hesitated, as if debating whether she needed to say more; then decided that she did . . . that the ravaged woman beyond the roses was not—not yet—including herself in the Yuletide reunion at Montagne Noir.

"My Andrew died at Christmas."

"Oh, Eleanor. I'm sorry. I didn't know."

"It's all right, dear. Although it wasn't all right then. He was still my Andrew, even though Alzheimer's tried its best to steal him away. I told you how healthy he was, even as his mind was being destroyed. Healthy, vital, strong—for years, Cassandra, *years.* But that September, the same September when Frances died, Andrew's heart began to fail. His heart, and then his lungs. Years before, when we were both alert and young, we talked about dying. *He* talked

about it. I would have put such discussions off forever. But Andrew felt it was important, and in his matter-of-fact—and infuriatingly male—way, he made his wishes, and philosophy, perfectly clear. When one's time came, it came. Heroic interventions were not his cup of tea. Nor, he told me, was living as less than the man he wanted to be—for me; or ever, *ever,* as a burden to me. If such a time ever came, he said, he would simply end his life."

"Oh, Eleanor, did he?"

"Kill himself? No. He *would* have, years before, if he'd realized what lay ahead. But Alzheimer's is so insidious, Cassandra, so wicked. Early on, when Andrew was aware of what was happening, he was convinced he could conquer it. He was so bright, so brilliant, really. Surely it was merely a matter of concentrating, focusing his keen mind ever harder. But it was more than that, of course, and then it was too late. He no longer had the mental capacity to kill himself, to make the decision and follow through, even though there were times—oh, there were times—when I'm certain I saw that thought, that solemn promise, haunting him, bewildering him, making him so sad."

Eleanor stared at the pastel roses, her wise eyes glistening with remembrance. "I was grateful he couldn't follow through, *grateful,* in a terribly selfish way. So what if he wasn't the same Andrew I had loved for forty years? That Andrew was inside somewhere, inside the vague, bewildered shell. I wanted him with me—forever, no matter what. That fall, when the physical deterioration finally began, I insisted that the doctors do everything they could. And they did. But everything wasn't enough. I could tell he was in pain, and there were times when he gasped for air, gasped frantically—not understanding why. He was suffering, *suffering,* and only my selfish wish to have him with me, no matter what, was keeping him alive. Well. I

owed the man I loved far more than such selfishness. I couldn't do it myself. Alone. I needed someone with me, someone I trusted, someone who would understand."

"Chase," Cassandra whispered. "Chase helped you."

"I *asked* him to help me, to help me help Andrew die. In retrospect, I can't believe I made that call. It's a terrible—impossible—thing to ask of anyone, much less a twenty-six-year-old man already tormented by worries about Hope. But I did call Chase, ask Chase, and of course he said yes. 'Yes, Eleanor, I will help you.' But Andrew died that night, in his sleep, on his own, as if he knew what I was planning to do for him, and knew, too, how impossible it might have been." Eleanor's eyes glistened still. But as she looked at Cassandra, they shone bright and clear. "I imagine you've guessed that there's a moral to this story."

So many morals, Cass thought. So many truths about life . . . and love.

The moral might have been about Mrs. Claus, that she had forced herself to survive without her Santa, then permitted herself to love again.

But, just as eight years ago, Eleanor's story, and its moral, were for Cassandra.

"You can tell Chase anything, dear, *anything.*"

Oh, Eleanor! No. I can't. Really. I can't.

Eleanor saw her reaction. The sudden exhaustion. The heart-stopping fear. "I've worn you out."

"No," Cass assured her. "This just *happens.* One moment I'm awake—wide awake—and the next, and without any warning at all, I simply crash."

"Well," Eleanor said. "Then it's time to tuck you into bed. Dream about this Christmas, Cassandra, at Montagne Noir. Visions of sugar plums—and sparkling champagne."

$\mathcal{H}$ope arrived at the château ten minutes later. She found Eleanor in the mauve-and-cream kitchen.

"The conquering heroine," Eleanor greeted her.

"*No*, Eleanor. We just had a very good jury, and a very good case."

"But without a very good—the best—assistant DA, who knows what might have happened?"

Hope smiled. "Well, anyway, it's over."

"And you're here."

"For a while."

"Are you feeling guilty?"

"Absolutely . . . except when I think about Cass."

"Keep thinking about her, Hope. She needs you. They both do."

Hope knew it was true. She had dropped by Chase's office—adjacent to the foyer—on her way in. Chase looked as he had eight years ago, in those first months after Cassandra disappeared. Restless. Haunted. Tormented by a fate he was powerless to control.

"Is Cass asleep?"

"Yes. She naps a lot, she says—and she especially wants to be rested for tomorrow's meeting with Mallory Mason."

"I'm afraid that's going to be exhausting no matter how much rest she gets."

"Couldn't it be postponed?" Eleanor asked. "Until she's a little less fragile?"

"It could. But there's a criminal out there. Even though Cass can't remember the actual assault, she may be able to shed some light on the assailant."

"Is Mallory Mason good, Hope? Do you know?"

"I know her reputation. She's a smart, tough, aggressive prosecutor. That's lawyer-speak for good." Hope smiled. "*Very* good."

"Well, she'd better be." Eleanor smiled, too, as she

shifted topics. "Meanwhile, Hope Tessier, have I got a plan for you. For *us*—a one-man show, opening this evening, at Jane's gallery. It will be a display, she says, of the most extraordinary paintings she's ever seen."

"Oh, Eleanor, I don't know."

"Are you avoiding Jane, too?"

"No. *No.* I'm not. And I'm sure Cass won't be, either, for long."

"I hope not," Eleanor said. "For the time being, I thought I'd just tell Jane that Cassandra's too fragile—and too tired—for company."

"Which, after all, is true. It's true for me, too, Eleanor. The tired part. And except for Jane, I'm not really that involved with art."

"But you *know* this artist."

Hope frowned. "I do?"

"You do. His name is Nicholas Wolfe. According to what he told Jane, the two of you met thirteen years ago, in Montana, at Willow Ranch."

That's where we met. But there was that other day, four years later, on Montagne Noir. That dancing, devastating day.

"Nick is here? And he's an artist?"

"Yes to both. He lives in the carriage house at the old Mariposa estate on Zinfandel Lane. It's called the Belvedere now. He takes care of the owners' horses—and paints. He's an incredible talent, says Jane. He just wandered into her gallery one day, wondering if she'd take a look at some canvases he'd done. They were rolled up, and not even finished, but Jane couldn't believe what she saw. She's been raving about Nicholas Wolfe—the man and his art— ever since."

"Have you seen his paintings, Eleanor?" *Have you seen him?*

"No. No one has—except Jane. Nor have I met Nick,

although Jane talks about him all the time. In any event, and it will *be* an event, the grand unveiling of both the artist and his art will be tonight. Come with me, Hope. Cassandra will be sleeping, and Chase will be working, and Samuel's off consulting on a dig, and my old eyes—and old reflexes—really shouldn't drive after dark." Those eyes, not old in the only ways that mattered, sparkled at Hope. "Come on. Jane will be thrilled to see you. So, of course, will Nick."

Will he? Hope wondered. And what did Nick remember most? The dancing, or the devastation, of that long-ago September day. . . .

FIFTEEN

BLACK MOUNTAIN
SEPTEMBER, NINE YEARS AGO

here are a few things I need to take care of, darling. Then I can leave with a clear conscience and you and I can play from San Francisco to Carmel. How does that sound?"

"Fine," Hope murmured. Wonderful . . . unbelievable. Five mother-daughter days. A chance to talk, Frances said, really talk.

"I'll need about an hour, Hope." Frances glanced at her diamond-encrusted watch. "Actually, can we make it an hour and a half? A delivery—the final one!—should be arriving any moment, and I really should check the furniture that was uncrated yesterday. I'd invite you to help, but I want everything about the château—including today's delivery—to be a surprise. Will you find a sunny spot in the meadow? And read for a while? You did bring some of your romance novels, didn't you?"

"No." Hope was going to live *her* life for the next five days—hers, not the lives of the fictional heroines she admired so much. "I didn't."

"Oh? Well, the library inside is fully stocked with mine. You're old enough to read them now—seventeen, and off to college in just ten days! Wait here while I grab my latest."

"That's okay, Mother. I'm fine for now. I'll just look at the view."

And think, and dream . . . and dance.

The impulse to dance began the moment Hope reached the meadow, as if her feet were friends with the ancient volcano, had caressed before its once molten soil.

Hope knew she was an impossible ballerina, ungainly and large. But at this dancing moment she felt feather light—and so confident, so bold, that she made a dancing promise to herself.

We're going to talk, really talk, about my weight . . . and about the way I feel inside, how I loathe myself, my heaviness, every moment of every day.

Do I truly look worse, Mother, when I'm thin? Maybe I wouldn't look so bad, now that I'm older, and taller, and my hair is so long. And no matter how I look, wouldn't it be better, healthier, to be slender?

Hope felt slender now, healthy, better. She was Maria, from *The Sound of Music,* a whirling dervish of boundless courage and spinning joy. This meadow, these hills, were alive with music, and she could climb every mountain.

And she would.

She *would.*

Hope danced and twirled, unaware that she was being watched—or that she, *she,* could spin a delicate web of enchantment for jaded blue eyes.

For Nick's eyes.

He hadn't imagined that Hope would be in Napa. But he had come, at last, to the verdant valley—as she had said that he should, that he *must*. He had arrived last evening and spent the night prowling deserted streets and shadowed alleyways, forsaken places where the rich housed their air conditioners . . . and tossed their trash.

Nick had come, needing to see this place at last, to hate it, and then to leave. But Nicholas Wolfe didn't hate what he saw, not even at night, a moonless darkness as black as his nightmares—and most surely not in the burnished gold of this September day.

And now, in this mountain meadow, Nick beheld a splendor that far surpassed the harvesttime glory of the valley he was born to despise.

Her long cinnamon hair caught the sunshine as she twirled, a golden red corona of spinning light, and there was such grace, such joy. The tomboy had become a ballerina, teetering with exquisite delicacy on the very edge of womanhood—and of happiness and hope.

The joyous ballerina saw him then . . . and her graceful pirouette came to a shuddering halt.

"Nick."

Nick, to whom at thirteen she had been able to confess every truth. But whose eyes now were far too blue. Far too intense. And to whom the most important truths could not possibly be revealed—that he was even more handsome than she remembered, and she remembered him all the time, thought about him . . . all the time.

Hope's gaze fell from his too blue eyes to the harsh sensuality of him. It was a fleeting glimpse of denim, and something—a knapsack, perhaps—in his strong, lean hands; and at his feet a surprising softness.

"Who's this?" she asked, dropping to her knees on the sea of wildflowers as she extended her ballerina arms to the coal black cocker spaniel puppy.

"Molly," Nick said.

Molly, who was wriggling excitedly, so curious about Hope, but who remained close to Nick . . . until her quivering journey toward Hope became possible because Nick was journeying, too.

"She's just a baby," Hope murmured as her hands greeted the soft, trembling, silken fur.

"Four months old," Nick confirmed as he knelt, too, on the blossoming meadow. "Hope?"

"Yes?"

"Hi."

She was touching Molly, staring at Molly, a gaze that encompassed as well her own dimpled thighs, a grotesque reminder of her laden, jiggling, ungainly self. But with his gentle "Hi" came another reminder. Nick was her friend, her *friend,* and she was so happy to see him.

"Hi," she echoed, looking up. "You're here."

So are you, he thought. He had called Chase's office at the Domaine, to ask him about her, never thinking to ask *for* her. Chase was away for the day, and Nick planned to call later, to find out how she was, to be certain she was well, and happy, and soaring, and free.

Which she was, and soon he would leave. Had to leave. But for these sunlit moments in the flowers . . .

"I'm here," he said softly. "The gate was open, so I drove right up. That's quite a place."

"The château? It's a wedding gift, it will be, from my mother to Chase. She's going over the finishing touches right now. Did you see her?"

"No. I just parked my truck and headed in the direction of the view I'd heard so much about."

Hope looked from his too blue eyes to the panorama of Napa Valley beneath the bright September sky. "It's a good view, isn't it? Beautiful?"

"Very beautiful," Nick agreed as he beheld the breathtaking tableau of cinnamon and sunshine. He looked away after a moment, made himself look away, and removed from the knapsack he carried a flask of bottled water, a red plastic bowl, and a small bag of puppy food. "The perfect spot for Molly's afternoon snack."

"And for your afternoon cigarette."

"I don't smoke anymore."

Relief shimmered in her sparkling green eyes. "You don't?"

"Not a puff."

"Because of Molly," Hope said, a conclusion, not a query. "Because the smoke would be bad for her little puppy lungs."

Nick let the gentle assumption glitter in the warm autumn air, even though it wasn't true. He had stopped smoking long before Molly—and because of Hope. Because every time he lit up he saw her earnest young face, worrying about him, not wanting him to kill himself.

It wasn't the image of worry that made him stop, or even the specter of his own searing, gasping demise. It was the image of her, the reminder of her. He missed his lovely little friend, a longing that persisted long after every vestige of soot had vanished from his lungs—a haunting memory of a rare and quiet peace.

Talk to me, Hope Tessier.

Nick's silent command danced a perfect, if frantic, pas de deux with hers. Hope wanted to talk to her friend, this *man*. It had been so easy four years ago, and now . . . what did she have to say that might possibly interest *him*?

The dancing wishes swirled in silence. Butterflies soared. And birds sang. And the grass glowed gold beneath the harvest sun.

Beside them a baby creature lapped fresh water from her

bowl, and when her thirst was quenched, she crunched loudly, lavishly, and happily on puppy chow hand-fed to her by Nick.

When Nick spoke at last, his voice was slightly hoarse, parched from the long journey across the barrenness of his life.

"So," he said. "This is Black Mountain."

"Yes," she answered in a rush of relief—such a rush that more words, perhaps not interesting in the least, came spilling out. "I used to come here all the time, with Chase and Grandpère."

All the time. She said it with such certainty. But was it true? Yes. *Yes.* Once, long ago, a young ballerina had danced here, twirled here, dreamed here.

"Grandpère?"

"My grandfather. He believed you could grow vines on the mountain."

"And could you—could he?"

"I don't know," Hope murmured. "He died."

"Grandpère," Nick said quietly. "You never told me about him. Will you?"

"Really?"

"Really."

Grandpère. The images flooded her, a deluge of remembrance and joy. "He was wonderful. So gentle, so *kind*. He made us feel as if we, his grandchildren, were the most fascinating little people ever placed on the planet."

Her head tilted thoughtfully, a slight yet monumental gesture, for it cast a curtain of burnished copper across her face, as if she intended to shut him out, unwilling to share—with him—her faraway memories of love.

But she was generous, Nick's ballerina. She looked up, to him, and the curtain fell away.

"Well, sir," she murmured.

"Well, sir?" Nick echoed, swamped by forgotten—forsaken—memories of his own.

"That was one of Grandpère's favorite phrases. 'Well, sir, Hope,' he would say to me—and of course I would giggle. And he would wait, smiling and patient, until my giggles subsided, as we both knew they would, because we both knew that whenever Grandpère began a sentence with 'Well, sir' it was always terribly important."

"Like what? Tell me an important 'Well, sir.' "

Hope met the intense and interested—intensely interested—eyes of this harsh and sensual man who was her friend. "I'll tell you the most important one of all. 'Well, sir, Hope, I do believe I know where the vines will grow.' He wasn't talking about here, in this meadow, or even on this side of the mountain. Grandpère believed that grapes would grow only on the other side, nurtured by the rainbows and the mists. It sounds like a fairy tale, doesn't it?" Her head tilted anew. Shutting him out? No. Including him—including *him*—in this fairy tale. "And I suppose it was. But there *are* mists and rainbows on the other side. And, Grandpère said, if you planted vines in the exact spot where the rainbows touched the mountain, well, sir, that's where they'd grow."

Nick had no fairy tales to share. But softly, softly, he shared what he could.

"I once knew a man who said 'Well, sir.' His name was Hank. He taught me about horses, how to care for them, how to ride."

"And whenever Hank said 'Well, sir, Nick,' you knew it was important."

"Very important," Nick murmured. *No matter how trivial.*

Hope waited for Nick to tell her about the man named Hank.

But Nicholas Wolfe was silent.

"Did Hank ever say 'Wow, boy'?" she asked.

"No. Did Grandpère?"

"Oh, yes. 'Wow, boy, Hope, will you look at that rainbow?' 'Wow, boy, Hope, the wild mustard has turned the entire valley into a floating cloud of gold." Hope smiled, shrugged, and pointed with a ballerina's grace to a distant building far below. " 'Wow, boy, Hope, there's Courtland Medical Center, where you were born.' "

Nick looked at the distant yet imposing L-shaped structure that rose from the valley floor. *So that was Courtland Medical Center.*

Silence fell.

Pain fell. Nightmares fell. For Nick.

Hope rescued him—with pain of her own.

"You may have noticed that I've gained quite a bit of weight."

Nick looked at her with serious blue eyes. "Have you?"

"*Yes.*"

"Because you were lonely?"

Lonely. It was the reason she had shared with him on that first day in their golden loft. Did he remember, as she did, every conversation of that Willow Ranch summer?

"I guess," she replied.

Lonely, and sad, and desperate, and . . . and Hope had learned, during the past four years, the myriad reasons that one ate. She knew everything there was to know about being aware of her weight, every second of every day, so terribly aware—always—of her heavy cloak of weakness and of shame.

Sometimes, late at night, in her dreams, she would vow to cast off forever the loathsome cloak. She could do it. She *could.* But in the morning she would awaken to hunger, to heaviness, to weighted memories of how miserably she had failed. And she would eat and eat—hating herself all the more with each frenzied bite.

"And," she confessed quietly, speaking to the memory of her great failure, "there wasn't much point in being thin."

"Because?"

"Because my mother seemed so disappointed when she saw me after that summer at the ranch."

"Seemed?" *Seemed?* "What she did say?"

"Nothing really. But . . ." But Hope had learned to interpret even the most subtle of her mother's frowns. She saw Frances's disapproval—a scowl that was impossible to miss—during the weeks in London after she left Willow Ranch; disapproval—and disappointment—that were more obvious, and more significant, than her mother's displeasure when she was fat.

"What about Chase?" Nick asked. "And Victor?"

"I'd gained quite a bit of weight by the time I saw Chase that Christmas. And I didn't see Victor for almost two years."

"Two years?"

"That's how long they were separated."

"But they're back together now."

"Yes." Hope smiled. "Really back together. Everything seems good between them, especially this summer."

Nick saw her smile and remembered the twirling ballerina amid the flowers, the graceful dancer who teetered, on point, on the very verge of womanhood—and hope.

"You seem good, too."

"I *am.*" Hope's fervent assertion was part determination, part wish. "My mother and I are going away together, just the two of us, and we're going to talk, really talk." *Like you and I can talk.* "Oh."

Oh. The realization pierced them both.

"Leaving when?" he asked gently.

Hope frowned at her watch. "I'm supposed to meet her at the château in ten minutes." She looked up from the timepiece that signaled the end of their sunlit moments in the meadow. "How long will you be in Napa?"

Forever, he thought. Forever in this place he was born to despise but didn't, couldn't. Not when he felt such peace.

But nothing had changed—except that she was a ballerina, teetering on the edge of joy, poised to leap toward a future of sheer grace.

So the man without a future smiled, for her and all the happiness that lay ahead—beginning, ten minutes from now, with her mother.

"Just for another ten minutes," he said. "I'm on my way to a horse ranch in Nevada."

"You and Molly."

Nick looked at the coal black puppy sleeping peacefully beside him, a nap amid wildflowers, her small body touching him, needing to touch, to be safe. "Yes. Little Moll is definitely part of the package."

"You really love animals."

Love? No, Hope Tessier, I do not love anything. I don't dare. "In another life, I suppose, I might have been a veterinarian."

"You still could be a veterinarian."

No, I couldn't. Not in this lifetime. "Now I know where 'Hope springs eternal' comes from. You."

"Oh! *No.*"

He held her with his dark blue gaze. "Yes."

The pas de deux was no longer frantic, just perfect, just exquisite. But it was time for the curtain to fall on the gentle ballet.

"Well, sir, Hope," Nick said. "I think we should wander back to the château."

$\mathcal{F}$rances was waiting outside, standing on the marble steps.

"Hope, darling."

"Hello, Mother. I'm sorry I'm late. I . . . This is Nick, and Molly."

"Hello, Nick." It was a waving greeting of flawless diamonds and satin mauve nails. "And Molly."

"Nick and I met at Willow Ranch."

"*Oh.* And now Nick has come for a visit? What perfect timing. This makes everything *so much* easier, Hope. I won't feel quite so guilty."

"Makes what easier, Mother? Guilty about what?"

"I was just about to write you a note. What it is they say? Writers write. But it's far better just to tell you. More difficult, but better. No incriminating notes, *nothing* to destroy."

Except your daughter, Nick thought. He wasn't certain what was coming, only that this woman, this mother, was about to inflict great harm.

Again.

And that she couldn't care less.

Frances Tessier was flying high—on cocaine, Nick guessed; a euphoric stratosphere in which she soared far above her lovely daughter's fragile heart.

"Mrs. Tessier . . ."

"Please, Nick, call me Frances."

"Frances. Hope is really looking forward to going away with you."

"I *know* she is, Nick. And someday Hope and I *will* stroll the sands of Pebble Beach." Frances looked from the savagely handsome cowboy—with his oddly savage attitude toward her—to her daughter. "But for these five days,

Hope, you're going to have to stay here. It's not the end of the world. This is a rather magnificent château, if I do say so myself. And that special delivery I was expecting? *Food,* lots and lots of goodies, all your favorites, ice cream, cookies, chips—the works.''

Those were not, Nick knew, Hope's favorite foods—at least not the ones dutifully recorded in her Willow Ranch diary and shared, in quiet confessions, with him. They were, quite simply, Frances Tessier's vision of *fat girl* foods, just as to her mother, Hope was, quite simply, a fat girl.

As Frances *wanted* her to be? Nick wondered. Had the glamorous novelist felt threatened, perhaps, by the gaunt but beautiful daughter who had emerged from her summer of starvation at the ranch?

It was possible, Nick thought, especially given Frances's suddenly single—and nearing forty—status at the time. In fact, it seemed likely that this woman, this self-absorbed mother, would greatly prefer the role of sympathetic and cherishing parent of an overweight teen to the one into which she was thrown by Hope's striking beauty: rival for admiring eyes.

"I've put your suitcase in the foyer," Frances, unfazed by Hope's distress, was saying. "Sleep wherever you like. Each and every bedroom is a celebration of romance. *You'll see.* I'd planned to unplug the phones, so you wouldn't answer by mistake. But you're so smart. I *know* you won't forget. You mustn't answer the phone, and you *mustn't* leave."

Frances Tessier's manicured fingers traced the arc of diamonds that encircled her neck. "I need to be with him, Hope! Five days, five *nights,* with him."

"But he hasn't finished writing the score for *Duet.*"

"Oh, you mean Victor." Frances touched, still, the glittering gift, from her husband, on the occasion of her forty-second birthday. "I'm going away with Gavin, darling. Gavin, not Victor."

Gavin? The architect for the château? *Sibyl's* Gavin? "I don't understand."

"Yes, you *do*," Frances insisted. "You know how Victor treats me, how he has always treated me."

What Hope remembered was how wonderful this summer had been, how relaxed and happy her mother had seemed, and how, two hours ago, Frances had given a smiling Victor a teasing, loving deadline to finish the music he was composing by the time they returned from Carmel—or else!

"I thought everything was okay."

"No, darling. *Not at all.* Just because Victor and I don't scream and yell doesn't mean . . . This summer has been awful. *He's* been awful." Frances paused, the experienced novelist shifting the scene—with an improbable segue. "But, my love, Victor *cannot* know. Nor, of course, can Sibyl. They would be so furious, *too* furious. It would take months to unruffle the feathers—*especially* Sibyl's—which would positively ruin all the plans I've made for the Christmas ball."

"But if Victor is so awful to you . . ."

Alarm, and irritation, shadowed Frances's beautiful face. This was *her* story, and Hope was supposed to believe every fiction without question.

"He *is* awful," she insisted. "But not always. I *love* Victor, I *do*, for better or worse. But I *need* Gavin, Hope. I need this time with him."

A bright red Ferrari roared up the drive. The handsome man who emerged roared as well . . . for, quite clearly, Gavin had not expected a group.

"Frances?" he demanded.

"Oh, relax, my darling! Hope is my dear friend, my *best*

friend. I trust her absolutely. Her allegiance is to me, her *mother,* not to Victor."

"Dammit, Frances. You've been using cocaine."

"Just a whiff or two! There's plenty left for you, Gavin, for *us.*"

Gavin scowled at his euphoric lover, then gestured impatiently at Nick, who was holding Molly, had been holding her from the moment the Ferrari sped up the drive. "Who is *he?*"

"Oh! This is Nick. Hope's gorgeous, sexy cowboy. Like mother, like daughter—impeccable taste in men. You *will* be staying here with Hope, won't you, Nick?"

"Mother."

"Yes, Frances." *I will stay with this lovely, mortified ballerina you have so willfully destroyed.*

Nick's eyes were blue ice—a cold fury that Frances Tessier could not, or would not, see.

"See, Gav?" she asked breezily. "Neither Nick nor Hope will tell a soul. Why should they? We're all going to have *much more* fun than Hope and I would have had in Carmel." Frances's beautifully manicured fingers drifted suggestively from Gavin's frowning face toward the buckle of his belt. "Oh, for heaven's sake, Gavin! Let's go. We're taking my car. It's so much . . . roomier. But *you* drive."

In moments Frances and Gavin were on their way, a pantomime of lust in the fading rays of the autumn sun. One silhouette—his—was trying to drive, while the other touched and teased. And as they vanished around the first of so many winding twists and turns, her laughing silhouette listed toward his and disappeared.

"Okay." Nick's voice was astonishingly calm, given the fury he felt. Cruelty did not surprise him, of course. He expected it. But to intentionally harm Hope . . . "Time to check out this rather magnificent château."

"No, Nick."

Nick heard her despair, saw it on her lovely, bewildered face.

"Listen, Hope," he began softly, apologetically, in anticipation of the revelation he was going to make, the truth Nicholas Wolfe had known, he had lived, his entire life: that there were very few human beings worth—

The revelation was preempted—and eclipsed—by the sudden scream of brakes . . . followed by the crush of metal tumbling down the unyielding steepness of an obsidian slope.

"Go inside and call 911," Nick commanded as he handed Molly to Hope. Then, before running to the place where the crumpled metal had come to its final rest, and the horror that would greet him there, Nick issued another command. "And wait here."

*S*ibyl didn't hear the crash. The windows of her gold-tone Mercedes were shut, and her air conditioner was on, and she was straining to hear the infuriatingly quiet—and infuriatingly unemotional—voice at the other end of her cellular phone.

"You may *want* to believe that Frances is faithful. But *Victor*, within two years of your marriage you knew it wasn't true. I'm not sure *how* you could have forgotten—given that Hope is a constant symbol of that infidelity. And surely you know that during your two-year separation Frances was hardly a nun."

"I know, Sibyl. And I haven't forgotten anything." But Victor Tessier had his own mistresses—not flesh-and-blood beauties with whom Frances could easily compete, but elusive, invisible ones. This summer's mistress—the music for

Duet—was his most demanding lover ever; for she, this love story set in Napa, lured him on emotional journeys that he wanted to make . . . and could only travel alone.

"Don't you care, Victor, that your wife and my lover have betrayed us?"

Care? Yes . . . and no. He deserved Frances's faithlessness. He had, after all, been unable to love her as she needed to be loved—unable, or perhaps simply unwilling, ever to love that much again.

Victor was, however, surprised by what Sibyl was saying. Despite the demands of *Duet,* the time spent with Frances had been undistracted—consciously so—and these months in Napa had been among the best in their twenty-year marriage. And maybe . . .

"Gavin is the architect for the château," he said. "It's not surprising that he would be stopping by."

"Victor! You're not listening to me! I *knew* it. Okay, one more time. Gavin called, claiming to be in San Francisco, about to board his flight. *Fifteen minutes later* his Ferrari was speeding toward the château. And now I discover that Frances is also planning to be away for five days. In this case, my dear Victor, two plus two equals *five*—five disgusting days of infidelity."

With Hope as a witness? Victor wondered, aching for the lovely teenager he scarcely knew. *He* deserved Frances's retribution. Hope did not. "If what you say is true, Sibyl, they're taking great pains to conceal their affair. It's transient. A whim."

"Meaning we pretend not to know? *You* may be able to do that, Victor. You've done it before. But not me. If Gavin honestly believes I would ever take him back— Oh, my God, Victor! Something has happened. The police are here, racing up the drive. . . . *Victor.*"

Victor heard, through the phone, the scream of sirens

. . . and the shocked silence of Sibyl's fear. "I'm on my way, Sib. Stay where you are."

*N*ick heard the sirens, too, just as his grim task was coming to an end.

Nick had nothing to offer them, these torn and crumpled bodies, except for privacy—and dignity—in death. He carried them from the smoldering wreckage to an island of grass on the steep volcanic hill.

And he covered their faces. Their faces needed to be covered . . . as did Frances Tessier's neck. It was almost severed, the razor-sharp slash of flawless diamonds into fragile flesh.

The necklace, too, was severed. It spilled to the ground as Nick carried Frances—so carefully, cradling her dangling head. The diamonds glittered as they fell, sunlit tears and bloody ones. There was torn skin, too, amid the bloodied gemstones—a discovery made by Nick as he curled the severed necklace in his palm before climbing up the cliff.

To her. Hope. Nick saw her as he began his ascent, as the sirens screamed in the shattered air. She stood at the cliff's very edge, holding Molly, clutching Molly, staring at the devastation below.

How much had she seen?

Enough, he realized as he saw her stricken eyes and ashen face. Too much.

Everything.

Nick's pale blue workshirt was drenched with Frances Tessier's blood, and in his hand was curled a broken strand of diamonds—bloody, too, and cloaked in Frances's severed flesh.

Nick removed the workshirt as he neared the ravaged

ballerina and, into the denim nest it made on the ground, he dropped the crimson diamonds. Beneath the pale blue denim, he wore a night-black T-shirt. It, too, was wet with blood; but the darkness of the fabric concealed the sodden stains.

Nick reached Hope just as the police and paramedics were screeching around the final bend. Nick met her eyes and saw pain too deep for tears—a loss too great to truly comprehend. Yet.

"Come with me," he said quietly.

And she did, crossing with him to the other side of the road, to a gentle slope of long, golden grass.

"Stay here," Nick told her after she had settled, on her own, into the soft golden nest. "You and Molly stay here while I talk to the police."

*S*ibyl and Victor arrived together—and learned, together, the fate of the clandestine lovers.

"No," Sibyl cried. "I don't believe it! Victor? *Help me."*

He had no choice. Sibyl collapsed into his arms, limp and sobbing. He whispered reflexively, meaningless words of comfort—to which, after a while, Sibyl began to reply.

She did not whisper, however, and her words, easily overheard by the paramedics and police, weren't meaningless in the least.

Not meaningless. Merely untrue.

"If *only* I hadn't asked Gavin to stop by the château," she moaned. "To bring Franny to *me.* I could have gone to *her,* to show *her* the plans for the ball. But I didn't, and now my best friend and my Gavin, my *love,* are dead."

Victor pulled away, glared at her. "What the hell are you saying?"

"Shhh." Sibyl leaned into him again. "Do you want the entire valley to know the truth?"

"I don't give a damn what the valley knows. The only one who matters is Hope, and she already knows."

"Hope knows?"

Sibyl's surprised query was answered by Victor's precipitous retreat toward the golden slope of grass where Frances's orphaned daughter sat. A small black dog was curled against her, and a sable-haired man towered above, a solemn sentry standing guard.

Nick had been watching Victor Tessier from the moment the maestro arrived on the scene. Nick had witnessed Victor's searching gaze—for Hope—his restless worry, his immense control.

Victor's wife was dead. And quite clearly the gifted musician cared very much about that horrific death.

But Victor suppressed his own anguish, for Hope, the daughter who was not his.

As Victor neared, Nick saw something else, something extraordinary from the man who appeared to have such supreme control: a look of sheer helplessness. And as Victor's solemn gaze met his, Nick saw gratitude, toward him, *whoever he was,* for helping Hope . . . as Victor himself might be unable to do.

As she would not permit him to do.

Hope's rejection of Victor screamed from every cell of her trembling body. As he approached, she curled even tighter within herself, a cocoon of despair veiled by shimmering copper.

Still, Victor Tessier crouched on the grass before his wife's stricken daughter. And the maestro's hand reached to touch. But his impending caress of comfort veered, at the last moment, and fell on Molly instead.

"Hope?" Victor implored softly. "I'm so sorry."

The burnished copper parted. "You *should* be sorry! It's all *your fault.* You ignored her. You were *cruel* to her. You killed her, Victor. *You!*"

"I know," he whispered in the heartbeats before the coppery curtain fell anew. "I know. I'm going to call Chase. Right now. He'll be home very soon. In the meantime, I'll wait here, by my car. I'll drive you back to the Domaine, to Chase, whenever you're ready. All right?"

Victor waited, crouched before her, for her reply. But there was only the ferocious silence of her hatred. After a few moments, as if sensing his pain, Molly licked his hand, a velvet soft affection that tore at his already ravaged heart. But Victor Tessier responded to the gentle creature in kind, a thoughtful pat of her silken head, a tender gesture of immense regret.

Eventually he rose, nodded solemnly to Nick, and turned to bid farewell to Frances. Victor's leaden journey toward the mangled body of his wife was impeded by Sibyl.

"Victor?"

"What?" he asked wearily. Warily.

"Who is that man, with Hope?"

"I don't know." *A stranger she trusts far more than me.*

"You don't know? My God, Victor, what if he's involved? *Responsible.* Remember when Gavin fired one of the stonemasons—*fired* him, Victor, at Franny's insistence!—and there were all those threatening phone calls? What if that's *him?* What if he tampered with the brakes?"

Nick heard Sibyl's queries and watched as a police officer, with *his* bloodied shirt, joined the fray. The officer's words were hushed, but the diamond necklace, encased in plastic to preserve his prints, glittered and glared.

"He's a thief!" Sibyl proclaimed. "A *grave robber* for certain, and probably a *murderer,* too. Arrest him, Officer! Arrest that man, *now.*"

Sibyl Courtland Raleigh expected to be obeyed. She always had been. And Nick witnessed prompt obedience now.

The policeman's journey was halted, however, at its very onset, by the hand that had wanted to touch Hope, to comfort Hope, but had patted Molly instead. And after a few hushed commands from the master conductor, the officer shrugged and turned away.

It was a stay of execution, granted by Victor, a chance for Nicholas Wolfe to make his escape.

"I have to go."

The soft voice drew Nick's gaze from the drama of Victor and Sibyl—a life-and-death drama for him—to Hope. She was standing before him, her tear-free eyes determined and bright.

And comprehending now—having heard every word.

Murderer. Grave robber. Thief.

And did she believe any of Sibyl's vicious epithets to be true?

No. *No.* But . . . "Go, Hope? Where?"

"Home. With Victor."

"Take Molly with you."

"No. I . . . couldn't. I can't."

"Okay," he said softly. "We'll see you tomorrow, then. We'll visit you at the Domaine."

"No." She trembled as the vanishing harvest sun left in its golden wake an icy chill. "You need to leave Napa, Nick. *Now.*"

She was right, of course—for even though she didn't believe him guilty of any crime, she knew his prints were on the severed diamonds, and that Sibyl—spurned and vengeful—was out for blood.

So Hope was leaving, so that he would leave, too.

"Not a chance," he said. "I'll be at the Vineland Motel, waiting for your call."

"But I won't call. I *won't.* I'm leaving, too—soon—for college. Please leave the valley, Nick. *Please."*

But it was Hope who left, a joyless ballerina, and such a courageous one. She walked toward Victor without a backward glance . . . without a backward glance toward the rest of her life.

Nick waited for her call.

And for the cops.

But neither came.

Two days after Hope Tessier left the valley, Nicholas Wolfe left Napa, too.

SIXTEEN

VINELAND GALLERY

ST. HELENA

SATURDAY, NOVEMBER TENTH

rava," Jane Parish greeted Hope with a hug and a smile. "I love it when the bad guys get theirs."

"Well. It's nice when the criminal justice system works."

"Amen. I'm so glad you came. Nick will be, too."

He will? her racing heart wondered. *Just* her racing heart? No. Every cell in her body, the cells she knew so well, laden once, engorged with sadness; but delicate now and trembling with hope.

"We haven't seen each other for nine years."

"But," Jane said, "friends are friends. And that's what Nick says the two of you are."

He does? "Is he here?"

"Not yet. In fact, he may be quite late. In the meantime, why don't you wander amid these spectacular works of art? You'll see what an incredibly gifted friend you have."

Hope did see Nick's gift . . . and so much more. The conflict, the emotion, the soft edge of wonder, the harsh edge of pain—skies so blue they punished your eyes; and vineyards burned to ash; and the majesty of a newborn day; and the bitter farewell at daylight's end.

Hope saw, in Nick's extraordinary paintings, *her* Napa, the temptation and the torment, the devastation and the dream, the paradise where ancient ghosts haunted moonlit splendor.

The remembrance . . . and the rage.

The conflict was present, consuming and compelling, in every canvas—until the final one, that is, the last painting on display. It was a portrait of springtime, and of untarnished joy: the entire valley afloat on a golden cloud of wild mustard blooms.

As Hope gazed at the portrait, remembering, remembering, her heart set a truly treacherous pace, and awareness trembled recklessly, and now there was something warm, and trembling, too, at her feet.

Trembling? No. Wriggling, as a small eager tail wagged an entire dog.

Hope knelt to greet the excited softness, to run her welcoming hands through shining black fur.

"Molly," she whispered. *Molly.* Which meant . . .

"Hello, Hope."

She stood, and faced him, and smiled. Somehow. He was the startlingly handsome man of her dancing—devastating—memories. But more handsome, more startling. Harsher. Harder. More fierce.

And his eyes, so very blue, were as punishing as the skies he painted.

"Hi," she said. "You're here."

"So are you," Nick answered softly.

Hope looked from his devastating blue eyes to his painting of a memory that would dance forever. "This is magnificent, Nick. All of your paintings are, but this one . . ."

"I just painted what you told me."

"You haven't seen spring in the valley?"

"No. Not yet." *Perhaps never.*

Nick had been in the valley for less than two months, had returned to Napa—to its nightmares and its dreams—after nine years of trying to resist. He might have stayed away. Could have compelled himself to do so. But Nicholas Wolfe had made the decision, the choice, to run no more—to risk not running. He was tired of flight. Of being invisible. Of remembering the temptation—and the torment—of peace.

And what of the tomboy who had become a ballerina? She would be married, he had decided. Happy and soaring and free. But they would talk, his friend and he, and he would paint pictures for her children, intrepid climbers of willows all—just as Jane Parish painted images on glass for the children who were not hers.

That was the *possible* dream, the *safe* peace. But there had been another dream, impossible and dangerous. She would be free, his ballerina, and he would confess to her every hidden truth, and . . . and here she was, grown now, a woman now, and uninvolved, according to Jane. Unmarried—except to the career that she loved; a career that was so very far from dancing that—to protect her—he must never share with her any secrets at all.

"Does it have a title?" Hope asked, in the silence that had fallen—and gazing still at the golden cloud.

Some of his paintings did have titles, Hope had noticed: evocative words transcribed in Jane's elegant script, inked on the small ivory-colored cards that were engraved "Vineland Gallery" in gold.

But no ivory card was tacked to the wall beside this portrait of joy. And perhaps there was no title, for Nick didn't answer right away.

But then the answer came, harsh and soft—conflicted, like his paintings.

"I call it *Wow, Boy.*"

"Oh," she whispered. Wow, boy—for her, for Grand-père, for the memories shared, with Nick, in a meadow of wildflowers. "You never told me you could paint."

He shrugged. "I didn't know I could. I had sketched a little as a kid." And then not at all for years. Nothing for years. Invisible for years. But he had begun to paint, needed to paint, when he thought about the temptation and torment of returning to Napa. "You never told me you could prosecute."

Hope shrugged, as he had. "I didn't know I could."

"But you can."

"Apparently."

"And you like it?"

"Yes. Very much."

The determined click, click, click of approaching heels distracted them, and as Sibyl Raleigh rounded the corner, Nick scooped Molly off the floor.

"Nicholas Wolfe?" Sibyl queried. "Oh, and Hope! You're a heroine, my dear. One small step for the assistant DA, one giant leap for womankind. Not that *all* men should be locked up." Sibyl smiled appreciatively, approvingly, at Nick. "The talented ones should be permitted to roam free. You are the artist, aren't you? You *must* be." She frowned slightly at the coal black creature nestled securely in Nick's arms. "Jane said you were last seen wandering in this direction in hot pursuit of your dog."

"Molly."

"What?"

"Her name is Molly."

"Oh. Yes. Anyway, Jane also said that the reason you were late, and almost didn't make it to your own show, was because of a sick horse."

"I thought he might be sick. Fortunately, I was wrong."

"Meaning otherwise you wouldn't have come?"

"Meaning I'm glad he wasn't sick."

Sibyl Courtland Raleigh was many things, none of which was an idiot. This was not, she realized, the moment to admonish this gifted—if temperamental, if hostile—artist to abandon the care and nurturing of horses and devote himself entirely to his art. Especially given her own plans for him.

"Well, I'm glad he wasn't sick, too. In any event, I just wanted to introduce myself—I'm Sibyl Raleigh, by the way—and tell you that your work is utterly fabulous."

"Thank you, Mrs. Raleigh."

"Sibyl, please. And you're welcome. Now, I really must be running along. But we'll talk again, Nick. I *know* we will."

As Nick watched Sibyl retreat, Hope watched him.

His heart beat slowly in his neck, a strong pulse, steady, controlled. And his hands, such talented hands, stroked Molly with gentle calm.

But there was punishment in his eyes.

"She doesn't recognize me."

"No."

"Of course, she never really got that close." *Would not deign to.* "Your father, however—"

"Victor Tessier is not my father."

"Oh, that's right. I wonder, though, if charges were ever filed."

"Don't you know?"

"No." His calm blue gaze said the rest. He didn't care,

not for himself. But . . . "You're obligated to check, aren't you? As an officer of the court?"

"There's no warrant, Nick. There can't be. You weren't going to steal the necklace, and as for . . ."

His smile was slow and easy. "Murder? Why don't you check, and let me know?" *Tell me if my fingerprints on diamonds pointed a blood red path to more distant murder, more ancient carnage.* "This time, Hope, I'm not running away."

"You didn't run *then*, even though I wanted you to."

It was true. He had run that other time, that earlier time. "Didn't I? How do you know?"

Because when I called the motel days later, a week later, the clerk said you were still there. You were there, Nicholas Wolfe, as you had promised you would be, risking so much, risking everything—for me.

SEVENTEEN

MONTAGNE NOIR
SUNDAY, NOVEMBER ELEVENTH

*M*allory Mason arrived at the château at three.

"Very impressive," she commented to Chase as he escorted her to the living room. "This place is just as secure as you promised it would be. And very impressive, Hope," she praised when Hope and Cass came into view. "Not a reporter to be seen. Hello, Cassandra. I'm Mallory. We met briefly at the hospital."

"I remember."

"Oh, good. But still no memories of the day in question?"

"No. What were you saying about security, Mallory? Is there danger?" *Because of me?*

Mallory cast a questioning glance at Chase. "What have you told her?"

"Nothing."

237

"Because I haven't asked. But I'm asking now."

"Good," Mallory said. "Since I'm going to tell you everything I know."

It might have been a tea party. Scented candles flickered in prisms of crystal on the mantelpiece, and comfortable chairs encircled a glass-top table crowned by a sterling silver tea service and laden with delicacies that Eleanor had baked.

The three women sat in the cushiony chairs, as if settling in for goodies and girl-talk. But one woman removed from her bulging briefcase a canary yellow legal pad, and another gazed with support—and worry—at her friend, and that friend, bundled in a raspberry-colored robe, was bald, fatigued, frail.

There was tea, but it wasn't a party.

"Here's what we know," Mallory began. "You were found unconscious at seven P.M. on October thirty-first. There were signs of forced entry, and your jewelry was stolen."

"My jewelry?"

"Whatever was in the jewelry box in your bedroom as well as a necklace that was on loan to you from Castille."

"Fantasy Impromptu." As Cass whispered the name of the famous necklace, a rainbow of precious gems, she recalled for the first time the Halloween gala. It was her event, her idea, her cause. Even the name—"Over the Rainbow"—had been hers. She never borrowed jewelry, had never done so before, but rainbows and Castille were gloriously entwined, and when the jeweler had contacted Natalie—*Natalie*. How strange she hadn't heard from her, and how like the cocooning mists that enveloped her brain to shelter her from that worry. But Cassandra was unsheltered from the worry that Mallory Mason had just revealed. "I need to call the jeweler at Castille, to tell her that I'll cover the cost of the loss."

"That's not an issue," Mallory assured her. "Fantasy Impromptu was fully insured against theft."

"Oh. Good. So you need to know who knew I had the necklace?"

"That might be of interest. Actually, Cassandra, what interests me most is your relationship with Robert Forrest."

"With Robert?" Cass frowned, shrugged. "It was just . . . a relationship."

"But a serious one."

"I . . . Define serious."

"We're on the same team here, Cassandra. You sound like you're rehearsing for your cross-examination by the defense."

"The defense?"

"He's already hired the best criminal attorney that money can buy. Lucian—which should be Lucifer—Lloyd."

"He? You mean Robert? I don't understand."

"Did Robert Forrest ever rape you, Cassandra?"

"I really don't understand why you're asking me that."

"Just answer, please. Did Robert ever rape you?"

"Define—Sorry. He was . . . insistent . . . sometimes. Is that rape?"

"Did you feel raped?"

Yes, of course, because Robert wasn't Chase. *Chase.* The cocooning mists had permitted her to answer Mallory's questions as if Chase weren't here.

But Chase *was* here. He stood by a wall of windows, staring toward the place where mists swirled and rainbows shimmered and dreams were born. There were no rainbows now, and the dreams—her dreams—had long since died, and the mists were dark smoke.

Chase Tessier's jaw was taut, his fists clenched, his eyes the color of steel. Taut . . . yet controlled—and forewarned,

Cassandra realized. Mallory's questions, such a surprise to her, were expected by him. Chase knew already what lurked in the blackness Cassandra could not see.

"Cassandra?" Mallory pressed. "I'm sorry to be so abrupt, but I know your energies are limited, and we have quite a bit of ground to cover before you . . ."

"Crash," Cass said. "I understand." She looked at Mallory. "What was the question?"

"Did you feel raped by Robert Forrest?"

Cassandra still didn't reply. She merely stared at the platter of petit fours Eleanor had baked, noticing for the first time the decorative motif: poinsettias, candy canes, snowflakes, and wreaths—more foreshadowing, in sugar this time, of Christmastime wonder from the merry Mrs. Claus.

"Robert said you liked rough sex."

Cass looked up from the cheerful Yuletide confections. "He said that?"

"Is it true?"

"No."

"So. Robert lied. Maybe he *had* to, because he knew the sex on the thirty-first would look rough to an experienced physician. Which it did."

"Wait. Please. I wasn't *with* Robert on the thirty-first. I couldn't have been."

"Why not?"

"Because we weren't seeing each other anymore."

"As of when?"

"Early October."

"Who ended it?"

"I did."

"Why?"

"I just . . . did. Robert says he was with me on the thirty-first? And that we . . . ?"

"Had sex. Yes. And there's ample physical evidence to support his claim. He also claims that it was he who wanted to break up, and that you were desperate to hang on. Another lie?"

"Yes."

Mallory jotted a note on her legal pad and underlined it. "Who knew the relationship was over?"

"No one."

"No one? You'd been with one of Hollywood's most celebrated actors for almost a year—"

"Only seven months."

"—and didn't mention the breakup to anyone? Didn't confide in a single friend?"

A *single* friend? As if she had more than one. As if she'd had any friends since Hope. "That's right. I told no one."

"But this explains why you weren't surprised by Robert's absence after you woke up."

"I wouldn't have expected him to visit me. Or wanted him to." *After you woke up.* Cassandra frowned. "Did he visit me?"

It was Hope who answered. "Yes," she admitted. "In the beginning, before Chase threw him out."

Cassandra glanced toward the wall of glass and spoke to the steel-eyed warrior reflected in its crystal panes. "Thank you."

Chase drew his dark gray gaze from the swirling mists, a gaze of swirling fury. "Don't thank me, Cassandra. I'm the one who let the son of a bitch near you in the first place."

"You didn't know, Chase." *How could you know?*

His expression softened, for her, and behind him a valiant shaft of sunlight sent the promise of a rainbow, and for a glorious moment the mists became the color of champagne, and Chase and Cassandra were alone in their château.

Explorers.

Farmers.

Pioneers.

And lovers.

"Did Robert ever hit you?" Mallory's question splintered the nascent rainbow—its memories, its promises, its dreams—into an infinity of gray, weeping shards.

"Is this necessary?" Chase demanded, even though he knew. The crime was attempted murder, and Robert's lies had upped the ante, and no one wanted the monster behind bars more than Chase. "Sorry. I know it is."

I'm so sorry, he thought as he gazed at his lovely, battered Tinkerbell . . . the wounded soul he had vowed to love, to cherish, to protect.

"Cassandra?" he asked, so softly. "Did he hit you?"

She looked at him still, and at the charcoal gray skies beyond. Unbidden, and wonderingly, her fingers touched her battered skull, the translucent flesh laced with slashes the color of her fluffy robe. Touched, then fell.

"Hit?" Cassandra echoed at last, her gaze leaving Chase as she stared at the pale fists curled tightly in her lap. "No."

"But was there something, Cass?" Hope's question was gentle, coaxing, and necessary. "*Some* kind of violence?"

You can tell Chase anything, Eleanor had said. Anything. And this was so trivial, of no consequence at all, compared to the secrets she could never share.

As inconsequential as this confession was, Cassandra made it not to Hope, not to Chase, but to the bloodless knots that were her hands. "There were three . . . incidents."

"Okay," Mallory said. "I need to know the details of each."

Once upon a time an enchanting muse, a modern-day Scheherazade, had enthralled tourists at Domaine Tessier.

But that amber-haired enchantress had vanished, a be-witching mirage.

Cassandra's story was as skeletal as she, and there were no cocooning mists around these memories.

"The first time was in June," she began, looking up to Mallory as she spoke.

"Hold on a minute," Mallory said. "Let me get a few things straight. You and Robert became involved when?"

"In February. We were in a movie together." *It was a love story, you see, between a woman so much like me, who I was when Chase and I met, and a man so much like*—how deluded she had been, had permitted herself to be; and how masterfully Robert had sensed her delusion, her need; and how cleverly he had reprised the role, *his* role, just enough, just often enough, that she didn't leave.

"Did you live together?"

"No."

"Was it an exclusive relationship?"

"I didn't see anyone else."

"But he did."

"I think so."

"Okay. What happened in June?"

"I got a part in a film that every actress in Hollywood wanted, a part Robert encouraged me to try for, even though my chances seemed slim."

"Wait a minute," Mallory interjected. "I'm sorry to in-terrupt, Cassandra, but I've been doing a little reading about your career." Such research was effortless, of course. Since the Halloween assault, articles about the wounded actress were everywhere. Mallory had read *People* maga-zine's account today, during her flight from Los Angeles. " 'Phenomenal' would be an understatement."

"Well. I've been . . . very lucky."

It wasn't luck, Mallory knew. It was talent and hard

work. According to superagent Natalie Gold, Cassandra Winter was the hardest-working actress in Hollywood. Almost compulsive, Natalie had said, about starting something new within days of completing the last.

"So why," Mallory asked, "would your chances of getting that part have seemed even the least bit slim?"

Was it because, her expression embellished discreetly to Hope, there was some psychological battering as well?

Cassandra answered with a shrug. "Anyway, I got the role, and on the same day Robert lost a part he'd been counting on."

"So he took his rage out on you."

"Yes."

"How?"

"He accused me of sleeping with . . . everyone, including the director who denied him the role *he* wanted. Then he grabbed me. Here." Her pale fingers pointed to her upper arms, cushioned now by plush layers of raspberry fluff—but with such meager flesh, such fragile bones, beneath. "He watched me bruise."

"And enjoyed watching?"

"Yes," Cass said softly. "Very much. For a while. Then everything changed. He became apologetic, despondent."

"And begged you to forgive him?"

"Yes."

"Which you did."

"Yes." *Because when his pathetic pleas weren't working, would never work, he changed again, becoming the man in the love story, becoming*—what a willing participant she had been, what an accomplice to her own destruction. "I did."

"And he was on his best behavior until?"

"Mid-July. The film we'd done together was in postproduction, but since Robert was the movie's co-producer as well as its star, he was actively involved in that phase as well. He decided to add a love scene. It would be authentic, he said, compelling, since we were . . . together . . . in real life."

"But you never do love scenes." It was another statement of fact gleaned from the many articles Mallory had read.

"No. I never do."

"But Robert wanted you to make an exception. For him. With him."

"Yes."

"And when you refused?"

"He went crazy. We were . . . in bed. His bed. He wanted me out. Shoved me out."

"Did he *kick* you out?"

"Yes."

"And did he keep kicking you, even after you were no longer in his bed?"

"Yes."

"Where?"

"I was on the floor."

"I meant where did he kick you?"

"My chest." And . . . it was trivial, it didn't matter, but still she couldn't say it.

But Mallory Mason could, and started to. "And also—"

"In my lower abdomen." *My womb.* "Yes. There, too."

"You didn't do the love scene."

"No. I was too badly bruised." *Robert made sure of it.* Cassandra drew a breath, a gasp for nourishing air that came up absolutely empty. "I'm sorry. It's happening. I'm suddenly very tired."

"Can you hang on just long enough to tell me about the third time?"

Cass inhaled again and was empty still, exhausted still. But she submitted to Mallory's request. "It was late September. He accused me of being involved with someone else. It wasn't true. I told him it wasn't. He pushed me against the stone fireplace in my home."

"And?"

"He left."

"Leaving you injured?"

"Yes."

"How long was he gone?"

"A few days."

"And how badly injured were you?"

"There was blood in my urine for a while. It made sense. The bruising, from where I fell against the stone, was over my kidney. I didn't see a doctor. The blood went away. And when Robert reappeared I told him to go away, too."

"Was he angry?"

"No. Not at all. He said he was sorry, and that he understood."

"Did he call you after that? Do anything to try to convince you to change your mind?"

"No."

"All right, that's enough." The voice was soft, gentle, and right behind her. The warrior prince had moved with stealthy grace from the place where rainbows had shattered and dreams had died. "Come on, Cass. I'll walk you to your room."

In another lifetime, Chase Tessier had stood behind her on the veranda at the Blue Iris as a mauve sunset filled the sky. The sexy wine wrangler had suggested a field trip . . . to grapes that tasted like the wind and emeralds that splashed from the sea.

Chase was offering a different journey now, to her first-floor bedroom just down the hall, and the eyes that had glinted with amusement on that pink summer night were fierce and solemn with concern.

Far too much concern. "I'm fine, Chase. Thank you. But I can manage."

"Just two more questions," Mallory implored. She was delighted, of course, with what Cassandra had already revealed. The scenario was classic—including the near fatal ending. Cassandra had placed herself at great risk, the greatest risk, when she dared to tell her batterer good-bye. Mallory had enough, she believed, the state of California had enough, even without Cassandra's eyewitness account of the actual assault, and even if Cass said no more. But if there *was* more . . . "Please?"

"What questions?"

"How did Robert feel about your trips to Seattle?"

"My . . . how . . . ?"

"We found receipts."

"He never knew."

"Okay. We're almost done. I need you to look at this."

Mallory placed the eight-by-ten glossy on the glass-top table in the only area where there was space, beside the platter of Eleanor's petit fours. The blowup of delicate pink roses with long golden stems embedded in a circle of silver might have been the perfect accompaniment to the tiny cakes iced with Yuletide joy—had it not been for the thick frosting of blood.

"You were wearing this ring on the day of the assault."

No. I couldn't have been. I would never have permitted myself to wear it. Never.

"Someone wanted it off," Mallory continued. "The damage to your finger tells us that. But you resisted. Ferociously. Your finger was so badly swollen, in fact, that the emergency room physicians had to cut the ring to remove it."

The minor surgery performed on her wedding ring had been accomplished with a small electrical saw designed expressly for such purpose. And Westwood Memorial's expert trauma team had done a neat job. A thin line sliced through the layers of blood—and silvery gold—without pruning a single pink blossom from a single pink rose.

But her ring, the only piece of jewelry that had ever mattered to her, and which had not been stolen after all, was severed through and through.

As it should be. As the marriage had been.

"Did this ring mean anything to Robert?"

"No. He'd never seen it."

"So it wasn't a gift from him?"

"No." The answer was very quiet and very male. "It was a gift from me. It's Cassandra's wedding ring. Our wedding ring."

"Which means," Mallory mused, "that Robert might very well have been infuriated once he learned what it was."

"I'm sorry. I really have to lie down."

But first Cassandra had to stand, a feat accomplished through sheer will and forsaking the hands that reached to help her. Hope's hands. Chase's hands. Cass was too tired, too battered, to speak. But her sunken eyes spoke volumes. *I need to do this on my own. Please.*

And she did, on her own, then she walked away, a teetering skull atop a mass of quilted fluff, her feet shuffling in frothy slippers too heavy to lift. When she reached the farthest edge of the living room, she stopped and turned, a wobbling pirouette.

She gazed for a moment at the three people at the opposite end of the room. All were standing, all had stood as she'd begun her journey, as if, by standing, they might in some way lessen the immense weight that was crushing her.

But Cassandra was weighted still, crushed still, and

now, as she made the quiet pronouncement, her frail shoulders seemed burdened even more.

"You believe he did this to me," she murmured. "You believe Robert beat me . . . and left me to die."

EIGHTEEN

*I*t was almost midnight. She had been asleep all this time, and he had been waiting nearby, all this time, for her to awaken.

Chase waited, silent and near, even after he heard her stir. He hoped she would make the short journey to the kitchen. But Cassandra crossed to the alcove by the window, settling there, and after a brief journey of his own, Chase spoke softly through the bedroom door.

"Cassandra?"

"Chase."

"May I come in?"

No. No! "Of course."

There were no stars on this November night, and no moon. The mists that shrouded the mountaintop were far too dark, too dense, to permit even a single shaft of heavenly light.

251

Cassandra was a shadow in the alcove. And he was a shadow, too, elegant, graceful, and carrying a mug.

"Hot chocolate," Chase explained as he offered the sweet warmth to the shadowed darkness.

Cassandra managed to take the mug without touching him. "Thank you."

"You're welcome." Chase sat across from her without invitation. Without daring to ask for one. He couldn't see her face, only the luminous glow of her naked skull—and of the thin white fingers curled around the mug. She might not sample the steamy chocolate. In fact, she probably would not. But at least she was holding the warmth. "We need to talk."

Her fingers tightened around the mug, a clench so fierce that Chase feared the glazed stoneware might shatter. Perhaps Cassandra feared such destruction, too, for she set the mug on the table between them, its nourishing heat abruptly forsaken.

When she spoke, Chase heard icy tendrils of fear.

"About what?"

Us, he thought. About why you left—the truth, not the lie—and why you were wearing our wedding ring on Halloween—and a thousand other restless questions he could not ask.

Yet.

"About," he said gently, "where Mallory Mason would like to go from here."

The delicate wave of her glowing, empty hands forecast her relief even before she spoke, as if to say "Oh *that*"—a trivial topic, attempted murder, compared to the questions she sensed and feared.

"All right."

Chase drew a breath, dark and deep. "All right. Mallory wants to issue the arrest warrant right away, and—

assuming Roberts pleads not guilty at the arraignment—to convene a grand jury to indict. The grand jury proceeding is secret and, in essence, the prosecution's show. Neither the defense nor the defendant would be there. You would need to be there, though, to tell the jury what you told Mallory today. We'd drive to L.A., so you could sleep en route, and we'd stay at the Hotel Bel-Air, where our privacy would be assured, and we'd have a limo waiting to return us to the hotel the moment your testimony was through. But no matter how streamlined the process was, it would be an ordeal for you. Exhausting for you."

We, Chase? Us? But she knew he would have it no other way. Her hands curled into tight fists in her lap. "I see."

Chase saw the luminous balls of fear—of him, of *him*—and forced the frustration, and the fury, from his voice. "There's more to see, Cassandra. Convincing the grand jury to indict will be easy compared to securing a conviction in the criminal trial. Unless your memory returns, the forensic evidence is going to be critical. It has to be impeccable and unimpeachable—which, thanks to Jack Shannon's meticulous stewardship, Mallory believes it will be."

"The forensic evidence?" she asked, wary anew, fearful of whatever other monstrous revelations—perhaps already known to him—lurked in the blackness of her battered memory.

"Prints, fibers, that sort of thing," Chase reassured her. "The prosecution needs to establish beyond a reasonable doubt that the only people in your bedroom on Halloween were you, Robert, selected paramedics, and the police. The definitive forensic analysis will take a while, which means there's no urgency about issuing the warrant, convening the grand jury—anything."

"But Mallory wants to move forward."

"Yes."

"And can't without my testimony?"

"No."

"What does Hope think?"

"Hope agrees that given what you revealed this afternoon, there's more than enough to convince a grand jury to indict. Having said that, however, she would still defer filing charges until after the final forensics are back."

"Because she's worried about my strength?"

"That," Chase confessed. *We both are.* "And because she's a careful prosecutor in her own right. She likes to have her *i*'s dotted and her *t*'s crossed before starting the legal clock ticking toward such things as speedy trials. She's quite surprised, in fact, that Mallory's in such a rush." *It's as if*, Hope had mused, *Mallory has some personal vendetta against Robert Forrest himself.* "In any event, there may be very valid reasons to delay, not the least of which is your health. You don't need to decide now. We'll let Mallory know when you know. Okay?"

"Yes. Okay." Her luminous skull tilted thoughtfully in the shadows. "What do you want?"

"What I want, Cassandra, is to kill him."

Her head snapped to attention, and the glowing bones that were her hands flew to the lopsided mouth he could not see. *"Chase."*

His face was as shadowed as hers. But Cassandra heard his smile, deadly and wry.

"You asked." After several measured heartbeats of silence, Chase spoke again, the smile—but not the deadliness—gone from his voice. "You must have loved him very much."

"No." *No. "I didn't."*

"But you stayed with him even after he hurt you."

"I . . . it didn't matter." *Nothing mattered.*

"What does that mean?"

Her delicate fingers fluttered briefly, the faint trembling of fragile wings, then vanished into the luxuriant pockets of her quilted robe—just as she, his fluttering Tinkerbell, had trembled with exquisite delicacy and luminous joy . . . then vanished from his life. "Nothing. I don't know."

"Well, Cassandra," Chase Tessier replied very softly. "Maybe I do. Maybe I know about a little girl named Sandra Jones."

"You can't." It was a plea and a prayer. *You cannot know about the pathetic witch everyone despised . . . the girl for whom faces drooped, a sag as ugly as hers, whenever she appeared, and who smiled—as she could not smile, not as a girl—when it was time for her to leave.*

"But I do." *I searched for you, Cassandra, after you left me. And I learned so much, discovered so much, even though I couldn't find you.* "I know about a baby girl, born on Halloween, in Southern California—not a small town in Vermont. Her mother's pregnancy was difficult, as was the baby's delivery, and during the first year of her life her parents' marriage fell apart. I wonder if that innocent little girl might—somehow—believe she was to blame."

Somehow? Of course she was to blame. Her parents' marriage had been perfect—an eight-year liaison of passion and success—until they decided to have a baby. *Her,* the grotesquely flawed infant who caused such disruption, such devastation, to their lives that by the time the divorce was final even the memories of love had been destroyed.

The baby witch cast her evil spell from the womb, causing such sickness in her pregnant mother that her career faltered, and such bloating—and such irritability—that even her once enraptured husband stayed far away. The delivery of the demon brought even more torment, more torture, culminating in a distress so fierce that the intern—covering the maternity ward while the senior physicians were scrubbed—used forceps too soon, and with a novice's zeal.

So she emerged, hopelessly damaged, irrevocably imperfect. She, this daughter of the once perfect love. The damage was only skin deep—nerve deep—the doctors assured them. But baby Sandra's parents knew the truth— that the droopy face was merely a symbol, and a forecast, of deeper flaws still to come.

And they were right. Their defective newborn screamed around the clock—pleas for food, her doctors decided when her first postpartum visit found her to be startlingly small.

They *had* been feeding her, of course. Trying to. But it was difficult. She was so difficult. Milk splattered from her droopy mouth, and she cried and cried, and "Never have children," the little girl would overhear her mother advise in the years to come. "It was the biggest mistake of my life."

The Joneses made, together, the decision that became such a monumental regret—although in the bitterness that ensued, each blamed the other for the irrevocable rocking of what had been a blissful marital boat.

Within a year of Sandra's birth, both parents wanted out of the marriage—and of the responsibility for her.

In an ancient world, three millennia past, a king named Solomon had proposed, as a test to distinguish a true parent from a bogus one, that a disputed infant be cut in half. But there were no true parents in the world of Sandra Jones. Neither wanted custody, but each accepted what was required, a precise and equal sharing of expenses, and of time.

The baby girl was divided, her life was severed, and her lopsided face was the symbol of that as well—as if, in fact, from the moment of her birth, some malevolent force had known the infant would be sliced in two.

To her mother, baby Sandra looked like a damaged version—as he deserved to be damaged—of the husband who was no more, and to her father, the defective little girl resembled the worst of the woman he once, so foolishly, believed he had loved. And to everyone else she was a freak.

And to Chase, the man who loved her?

"*She* hadn't failed," he said so gently, "that little girl with the droopy face. But she must have felt that she had, never really welcomed, teased and taunted for the way she looked."

"You saw how she looked?"

She was asking, the woman in the shadows with the vanished hands and trembling skull, if he had seen photographs of the unwanted girl.

Chase hadn't seen any images from her childhood, although he had asked both her father in Denver and her mother in New Orleans for snapshots of their little girl. Sandra Jones's parents seemed authentically bewildered by the request, just as they could not fathom his interest—the interest of such a handsome and powerful man—in the blemished daughter they had spawned. *They* had no interest in her, of course; had bade adieu, forever, the day she'd finished high school.

"Didn't I see how she looked, Cassandra? The day she arrived at the Domaine?" *And the day she left Montagne Noir?*

Yes. *Yes.* And somehow Chase had discovered the truth of the small unloved little witch, and he had forgiven her lies; at least it sounded in the blackness as if he had, and there was such tenderness in his voice—but it was too late, far too late, for there was that other lie, that final truth, which no one, least of all herself, could ever forgive.

Remembrance returned with a vengeance, a glaring pain that severed the mists cocooning her ravaged brain as, once, golden shafts of sunlight had parted the mists of Montagne Noir.

But no promise of rainbows came with this piercing shaft of pain—only the certainty of greater pain, of piercing heartache, the longer she remained on the mountain of dreams.

"Chase?"

"Yes?"

"I want Mallory to file the charges now. I'm ready to meet with the grand jury as soon as it can be convened." *I will be strong enough, healed enough . . . strong and healed enough to leave.*

NINETEEN

MONTAGNE NOIR

FRIDAY, NOVEMBER SIXTEENTH

*T*he call came in the early afternoon. Hope answered, which was just as well—it was Hope to whom Mallory Mason wanted to speak.

"I'm calling to let you know when I'll need Cassandra. The hearing is scheduled to begin on Tuesday, the twenty-seventh, and should be finished by the twenty-ninth. My witness list is still a bit tentative, but at the moment I expect to call, in approximately this order, Jack Shannon, Amanda Prentice, Westwood's chief of neurosurgery, the neurologist from Courtland, our two forensic experts, the soap-writer neighbor, and finally Cass. I probably won't need her until Wednesday afternoon, but I'd like to meet with her here, on Monday, to go over her testimony before the hearing begins."

"The *hearing,* Mallory?"

"Haven't you been watching the news?"

"No."

"Well. Before we could convene the grand jury, Lucian Lloyd started ranting and raving—quite publicly—about 'veils of secrecy' and 'rushes to judgment.' "

"So there's going to be a preliminary hearing instead?"

"The accused has rights, as you well know. Thanks to Mr. Lloyd, Robert Forrest is exercising them all."

Those rights swirled in Hope's legal brain. The grand jury proceeding was secret, private, without the defendant or the defense. A preliminary hearing, however, was a mini-trial. True, there was no jury, only a judge; and as with the grand jury, it was, in essence, the prosecution's show. *But* Robert and his defense counsel would be present, and Lucian Lloyd would be permitted to cross-examine the witnesses, including the state's star witness, who was also the victim; and where were *her* rights?

A postponement could, quite legitimately, be requested on the basis of Cassandra's health. And although Lucian Lloyd would object loudly and legally, such a request was unlikely to be denied. But, Hope knew—she feared—that given the option of the rigors of a preliminary hearing soon versus the prospect of an indefinite delay, Cass would choose the hearing. In a heartbeat. For, quite simply, since Sunday, Hope Tessier's frail and battered friend had been willing herself to heal.

"The hearing is scheduled for eleven days from now?" Hope asked.

"That's what the defendant wants. Demands."

"Can you be ready?"

"I have to be. And will be, Hope, with your help. I need you to prepare Cassandra's testimony, as well as rehearse her for cross."

"So you want me to conduct the direct exam at the hearing."

"No. Thank you. I'll handle that. I'll need your notes, of course. It's the cross I'm most concerned about. I'm sure you're aware of Lucian Lloyd's reputation for ripping witnesses to shreds."

The breath Hope drew had no impact whatsoever on the misgivings she felt. "I'm aware of Lucian Lloyd. I'll make certain Cass is ready for his cross."

"Good. Thanks. While I've got you, Hope, maybe you can help me decide who should be seated on our side of the courtroom. Robert Forrest is going to have some big-league celebrities lined up for miles. They're already lining up, including Natalie Gold, by the way, who used to represent them both. We need a few heavy hitters of our own. Despite her phenomenal success, and her respect within the industry, Cassandra is not well-known—personally—by the Hollywood elite."

"She's very private."

"Yes. Obviously. Which is fine, except for the fact that Robert Forrest is known, and loved, by everyone."

"Anyone who loves Robert Forrest is loving a batterer."

"Which," Mallory said, "is precisely what we're going to prove. In the meantime, however, Cass needs an impressive show of support. You, of course, and maybe Meryl Atwood, and even though he's on location in Spain, Adrian Ellis has offered to come, and I'm wondering about Victor. He's so gorgeous and elegant. Like Chase. In fact, in a way, I wish Victor could be in court as a surrogate for Chase."

"*What?*"

"I know. I know. As her husband, Chase needs to be there."

"He will *want* to be there."

"That's even better. And, let's face it, your brother's hatred of Robert is terrific, as is Chase's fierce protectiveness of his wife. But you saw what Cassandra was like when Chase was in the room. Inhibited, unemotional, flat."

"This is a preliminary hearing, Mallory. No jury, just a judge—who, I assume, will be completely uninfluenced by peripheral theatrics."

"I assume so, too, given that it's Nancy Barnes. A very lucky draw, by the way. There won't be a jury, Hope, but there will be that all-important court of public opinion."

"Oh, no," Hope whispered as realization dawned. "There *cannot* be cameras in the courtroom."

"I'm afraid there can, and will. The decision has already been made."

*H*ope needed time before sharing the news with Cass and Chase. She didn't think. She just drove. Away from the château, down the winding road, past the spot where Frances and Gavin had soared to their deaths and where she had stood, on that day and on so many days since, remembering, and trying to forget.

Her journey seemed random, a purposeless meandering in the pale glow of the November sun, until she found herself driving along Zinfandel Lane, then turning through the massive stone pillars engraved "Belvedere," then veering left, toward the stable, the carriage house, *him.*

The carriage house was both substantial—two stories— and quaint: a cedar-shingled cottage silver with age and adorned with an abundance of wisteria.

As she neared the front door, Hope heard voices within.

One voice. His. Soft, low, coaxing.

For a moment she was at Willow Ranch, outside his room in the stable, coming to say good-bye. Then as now, her knock was an intrusion so quiet that, if he chose, it could easily be ignored.

That *was* his choice, Hope realized as her hushed rap evoked taut silence.

Then, taut too, and low and rough. "Yes?"

"It's Hope, Nick. I—"

"Come in."

She passed beneath a lavender arcade of wisteria blossoms into the single space that was living room, breakfast nook, and kitchen all in one.

The hardwood floor, shining and pegged, was at the moment home to both man and dog. Nick knelt, and Molly sat, her paws touching his denim knees even as she cast an imploring gaze at Hope. Her velvet black muzzle was laced with snow white foam, and there was more bubbly whiteness on Nick, a frothy spill from toothbrush to fingers to palms.

He was brushing Molly's teeth. Hope couldn't quite meet his blue, blue eyes. But she felt the intensity, and the intimacy, of his searching gaze.

Hope focused instead on the eyes that were brown, and mournful and pleading, and embellished by a questioning tilt of her cocker spaniel head. "I think she wants me to call the SPCA."

"She does." A slight smile touched his voice. "It's part of the tooth-brushing ritual—her expression of shock, as if she's never had her teeth brushed before, and of horror, at the sheer torture of it all."

"And how long has this been going on? The ritual, not the torture." There was, of course, no torture; only gentleness, only caring: a gifted artist painting mint-flavored foam on beloved canine teeth.

"Every day. For about six years." Nick looked meaningfully at Molly. "Okay. We're done. You're off the hook."

Molly understood at once, even before Nick moved to wash her toothbrush and his hands. She galloped, a wriggling mass of black fur and flying foam, to her savior.

Her Hope.

Hope wove her hands into the energetic fur and asked on a soft laugh, "You have healthy teeth and gums, don't you, little Molly? And you know Nick would never hurt you. Never. He loves you. You couldn't have a better daddy."

Hope heard her own boldness and looked at Nick. Was he embarrassed by his obvious affection for his little dog? No. Of course he wasn't. Not at all.

But Nicholas Wolfe was something, intense and fierce.

"So, Hope, have you come to arrest me?"

"What? No." *No.*

His ice blue gaze was calm, unreadable, only vaguely interested in his fate. "Meaning no arrest warrant?"

"I have no idea! But if there is, Nick, there shouldn't be."

A glint of indigo—deep and dark—glittered in the impassive blue eyes, as if it mattered very much that the soldier of justice believed him to be an innocent man.

He looked at her, this prosecutor in blue jeans, her cinnamon hair unbound and falling free. Tomboy. Ballerina. Warrior. She was all three, standing before him, intrepid, graceful, proud.

"So," he asked softly, "why are you here?"

"I needed to talk."

Talk to me. Talk to me.

"Okay," he said even more softly. "Let's talk, and walk. Molly needs to nap, and she won't if we're here—well, if you're here."

The truth of his words wriggled at her feet: a dutiful, if fatigued, shimmy of fur. It was her job, after all, as a dog, to be relentlessly enthusiastic, even as her lids grew heavy over her huge brown eyes.

"Sleep time, Moll," Nick whispered.

It was what Molly needed to hear, those precise words,

spoken with that exact fondness. She trotted to a nearby couch, to retrieve a nylon bone, then to a stack of comforters folded neatly in a warm, shadowed corner of the room. She settled, with a sigh, into the billowy softness.

"She doesn't sleep with you?"

"She did, in the beginning. But at about six months, a fairly impressive independent streak appeared. Since then Molly's had her own agenda."

"Which includes naps." *On plush comforters surrounded by her toys—special toys, thoughtfully selected, because you know how much such treasures mean.*

"We'd better go," Nick said. "She's not going to close her eyes until we do."

Nor was Molly going to close her eyes until Nick patted her, a reassurance from his gifted hands that it was safe for her to sleep, that he would be here when she awakened.

Nick patted Molly and murmured something Hope couldn't hear, then looked at Hope, and shrugged, and smiled.

It was an extraordinary smile. Sexy? Yes, of course. A smile, on his lips, could never be anything else. Anything less. But this smile, this acknowledgment that she had witnessed yet another gentle ritual in the life of Nick and Molly, could only be described as lovely.

They walked outside, through a tangle of lavender, and began a leisurely stroll toward the pasture where Nick's equine charges grazed into the muted lilac of the November day.

Muted. Gentle. Like Nick's gentleness with Molly. Hope wanted the gentleness to last, even as muted—and such gentle—thoughts danced inside.

Who do you sleep with, Nick? Who?

But she asked, "How did you and Molly find each other?"

"I was working on a horse ranch, Thoroughbreds only. The owners raised pedigreed spaniels as well. I'd seen horses foal, many times, but I'd never witnessed a canine birth. And wanted to. It was a big litter, beautiful, healthy pups—save one. She was very tiny, and so weak she couldn't even crawl to her mother, much less fight with her sibs for a chance to nurse."

"So you offered to nurse her, to feed her, by hand."

Nick hesitated, so tempted to tell the lie. *Yes, Hope, that's exactly what happened. And if I hadn't volunteered to care for her, her owners would have. They would have kept her tiny body fed and warm; and they would have slept with her, so she wouldn't be afraid; and they would have whispered to her, and kissed her, when she cried.*

It was such a tempting lie, such a hopeful lie, for Hope.

But Hope Tessier knew firsthand the cruelty of human beings. Nick had been with her when she'd learned. And it was important, temptation and torment, that Hope know this about Molly—and him.

"The owner asked me, actually told me, to get rid of the runt."

"Get rid of her?"

"To throw her in the trash, I suppose, on my way back to the bunkhouse. She wouldn't have lasted long." *Only a few desperate minutes of crying—alone and unheard and unloved and blind—in the midnight cold.*

"I can't believe . . ."

"What?" Nick heard his harshness, as cold as the night air in which the tiny puppy would have perished. "That someone would throw a baby away? It happens all the time. You know that, Hope. You see contempt for innocent life every day."

"Yes," she whispered. "I suppose I do."

Their stroll toward the golden pasture was leisurely still.

But the topic shifted from innocent creatures to brutal crimes.

"You're worried about the preliminary hearing."

Her golden red head tilted. "Yes. Very. You've been watching the news. I wish I had been. When Mallory called today I was completely taken by surprise. She wants me to prepare Cass for her testimony, as well as for what's going to be a grueling cross."

"Which you don't want to do?"

"It's not that. It's . . ." She shrugged.

"You think he's abusing her still. Robert. Abusing her, humiliating her, forcing her to appear in public while she's still so ravaged by what he did."

"Yes," Hope murmured. "I'd been trying to figure out why this bothers me so much. But that's the answer. Robert *is* abusing her, as is Mallory, and now I'm a co-conspirator as well."

"Couldn't Cassandra, or her doctors, say no? That she's simply not well enough to testify?"

"Yes. They could, and her doctors would, but Cass won't. Which makes her an accomplice, too." An accomplice—returning to her batterer, as if deserving more abuse. "This is so wrong."

"But you'll make it right."

"I will?"

"You will." Nick smiled. "When you can't convince Cassandra to agree to a delay, you'll make certain that she's absolutely prepared for whatever nastiness Lucian Lloyd plans to throw her way. That's a friend, Hope. Not a co-conspirator."

Nick's pronouncement, another gentleness on this lilac day, came just as they reached the pasture. The long, swaying grass was gilded emerald, and the horses, three of the four, were the colors of autumn: shining bounties of gold, of chestnut, of roan. The fourth, a dapple gray, gleamed faintly lavender beneath the lilac sky.

These were magnificent creatures, impeccably bred, hopelessly pampered. Majestic. Arrogant. Proud. Yet they bounded, like eager puppies, to Nick.

Nicholas Wolfe had no food. No apples in his pockets, no sugar lumps in his palms. But the regal beasts didn't care. They wanted Nick, just Nick, his attention, his affection, his low whispers and stroking hands.

The gifted artist didn't have enough hands, not for all four velvet muzzles. Hope joined in the patting, the whispering, too.

"You've been around a few horses since Freckles."

This whisper, soft and low, was for her.

"Yes," she confessed. "I have. I took riding lessons during law school. And I ride, now, whenever I can. There's an academy in Golden Gate Park."

"I know."

"Oh? Have you worked there?"

"No." *I just died there.* Dreams died. Hope died. This November day was dying as well. The sun was leaving, as it had years ago, a sudden chill in which the devastated ballerina had walked away. Today, soon, this chill would drive her away—far away, as she needed to be, as he wanted her to be. So whose voice was it, such a soft and gentle voice, that suggested such danger—such temptation and such torment—to the fading rays of gold? "If you're in the mood, Hope, between prep sessions with Cassandra, I could use a little help exercising these four rascals."

"Really?"

"Sure. If you want to."

"I want to, Nick." *I want to very much.*

TWENTY

MONTAGNE NOIR

SATURDAY, NOVEMBER SEVENTEENTH

*T*hey sat in the mauve-and-cream kitchen, at the round wooden table in the breakfast nook, its shining surface home to steaming hot coffee and warm blueberry muffins. Hope's canary yellow legal pad was filled already with pages of notes—her own compulsive preparation before this all-important preparation of Cassandra even began.

"First things first," Hope said. "You're going to need a mantra."

"A mantra?"

"Some soothing internal chant that you can repeat over and over while Lucian Lloyd is cross-examining you."

"I'm going to need to be soothed?"

"Absolutely. The esteemed—and evil—Mr. Lloyd is going to do whatever he can to rattle you. Anything and everything, Cass, including—especially—personal attacks.

It's all he *can* do, of course, because you've done nothing wrong. But no matter how prepared you are, it's going to make you mad. Furious. Which is exactly what he wants. Your mission is to stay calm."

"Hence my mantra." Cassandra gazed thoughtfully at a muffin. "How about 'Hope'? Or 'friend'? Or 'Hope *is* my friend'?" The questions wobbled, quavered, as tears flooded her sunken blue eyes. "Damn! I want to tell you this, if I can. I've *missed* you, Hope Tessier."

"Cass," Hope whispered, weepy, too; flooded, too. "I've missed *you.*"

Cassandra tilted her battered skull, and a faint wry smile curved her droopy lips. "It occurs to me that you might have been upset when I left."

Hope's laugh was startled and soft. "That's *just* occurring to you?"

"I didn't want you to be upset." *To feel betrayed.*

"I know," Hope said gently. "Your letter made that very clear. Still, I missed you."

"And I missed you." Emotion flowed anew, a torrent of dampness swiped by her pale, impatient, and trembling hands. Cassandra sighed theatrically and managed a smile. "I think we've established the mantras that *won't* work."

"I think so," Hope agreed, swiping too, and smiling too. Then the girl who had once been an eager lady-in-waiting to an imperious princess of Wales herself gave a grand and theatrical sigh. "Okay, Cassandra, enough! Let's get today's prep session under way—so you can work on your mantra and I can go riding with Nick."

She was not the princess of Wales, the frail woman who sat across from Hope. Nor was she the sultry Blanche. She was, instead, the old Cassandra, ferociously impassioned—for her friend. They had not, of course, discussed boys—men—in college; especially not Hope's. But Cassandra's sparkling blue eyes gave fair notice that that was about to change. "Forget the prep session, Hope Tessier. *Who is Nick?*"

The man I love.

The man I *have* loved for a very long time.

The answer sang, a joyous chorus, for the next eight days, as Hope galloped across pasturelands with that man . . . and talked to him, they talked to each other—as always.

"Does Cassandra believe Robert is guilty?" Nick asked one afternoon as his dark blue eyes surveyed billows of smoke above a doomed vineyard.

"I'm not sure," Hope admitted. "But it would be so awful, wouldn't it, to know that someone you loved, who was *supposed* to love you, wanted you to die . . . left you to die?"

Nick's gaze narrowed against the gray black sky. "Isn't that what your mother did to you?"

"What?"

Nick looked from plumes of smoke to dancing tendrils of cinnamon fire. "She betrayed your trust, your love, then she died, leaving you to die. But," Nicholas Wolfe added softly, "you didn't."

Didn't I? Haven't I?

No. Not when she was with Nick, when her entire being hummed with thrilling awareness and unsurpassed joy . . . and when she felt so safe—and so precarious—all at the same time.

"Have you made peace with Victor?" he asked.

"With Victor? No. Not officially. In fact," she confessed, "not even unofficially, which is to say emotionally. I know, rationally, that what I said to him on the mountain was terribly unfair. Part of me knew it even then. I had, after all—we had—just seen my mother's selfishness in action."

Yes, Nick thought. We both witnessed Frances Tessier's self-absorbed conceit. But . . . "What you didn't see, Hope, on that day, was how much Victor wanted to help you. How much he cared."

As he had cared about Chase, she realized, as Cassandra lay dying in the ICU . . . and as he had cared, once, about a thirteen-year-old girl in Vienna. "I owe him an apology."

"I doubt he expects that."

"Well." *Someday Victor Tessier and I will talk. We must.* "Does Jane ever mention him?"

"Jane?"

"Years ago, Sibyl intimated that there was some an-cient, and negative, history between Victor and Jane." And now, after her mysterious conversation with Victor, Cass was adamant in her refusal to see Jane. "I wondered if Jane might have said something to you."

"She's never mentioned Victor."

"But you're close, aren't you? You and Jane?"

Yes. It was a surprising closeness. The bond, he sup-posed, of artists. Yet it seemed more than that, stronger. For Nick knew that if Jane Parish ever needed him, he would be there. And he was quite certain, astonishingly so, that if the reverse were true, Jane would move heaven and earth for him.

"Jane does," he said, "have my undying gratitude for keeping Sibyl Raleigh at bay."

"With pleasure, I'm sure. What does Sibyl want?" *You?*

"She'd like me to paint portraits for her parties, guest of honor canvases, that sort of thing. It isn't a bad idea, ex-cept for its source."

"Do you do portraits?"

Nick hesitated. Frowned. "That remains to be seen. For the past few years, I've been working on a quartet of portraits. The same person over time."

"Oh," Hope mused, recalling her art history courses at Val d'Isère. "Like Monet's paintings of the cathedral at Rouen, the same subject painted at different times of day and in varying light."

Nick smiled. "Something like that. The concept, not the quality."

Her sparkling green eyes begged to differ. "Does your quartet have a title?"

"Seasons of the Soul."

Oh. The title evoked so much, far more than images caught at dawn, at noon, at dusk. *Seasons.* Birth. Growth. Harvest. Death.

"Are the paintings of you, Nick? Portraits of the artist as a young—and evolving—man?"

"Hardly." His laugh was soft and harsh, and his wintry blue eyes flickered with surprise, as if amazed that she could imagine, in his soul, any season other than the one that was the most bitter cold.

*T*hey rode.

And they talked.

And far too soon the eight days came to an end.

It was the Sunday before the preliminary hearing. Chase and Cassandra were driving to Los Angeles, to their two-bedroom bungalow at the Hotel Bel-Air, and Hope was returning to San Francisco, to prepare for the sentencing hearing for convicted cop Craig Madrid.

The Madrid hearing was scheduled for Wednesday afternoon, precisely when Cassandra was likely to be on the stand in Santa Monica. Hope might have, could have, turned over the sentencing hearing to someone else. But Cassandra, the bride who hadn't wanted her loved ones to witness the intimacy of her wedding vows, wanted no one—except Chase—in the courtroom as she confessed to the watching world the intimate violence she had endured.

Nick had met neither Cassandra nor Chase, nor would he meet them on this Sunday afternoon. They would be gone before he ascended the winding road to Montagne Noir.

On a September day, nine years ago, a mother's lover ascended that tortuous road a few crucial minutes late, and on this Sunday in November, Nick—and Molly—arrived precisely on time.

But Chase had been detained by an overseas call, which meant that he and Cassandra and Hope were walking toward Chase's car just as Nick brought his old blue pickup truck to its gentle stop.

Despite what Hope had told him—and she *had* told him—Nick was unprepared for Cassandra, the skeleton that she was, so battered, so frail.

She was a very stylish skeleton, in her charcoal gray coat, and high-heeled boots, and the light pink scarf purchased by Hope. And a valiant skeleton, surviving on fumes, gossamer vapors of courage and will.

And Cassandra was a smiling skeleton, too, her eyes bright and blue, her lips with scarcely a droop.

"Nick!" she enthused as he neared. "At last we meet. And Molly."

Molly wagged, of course, and Nick smiled.

"Hello, Cassandra," he greeted her. "And Chase."

Chase, who was stylish, too, ravaged, too.

As Nick shook Chase's hand and met Hope's brother's

solemn gray eyes, it was as if he was seeing Victor Tessier as well—Victor, on that day of carnage, offering a silent and solemn thank-you to Nick for helping Hope.

I'm not helping her, Chase. She's helping me. And it has to end. It must end—for her sake.

"Nick?" Cassandra smiled still, a ray of sunshine in her translucent face; a sunbeam that was drooping now, drooping noticeably, as her meager energy began to wane. "Did Hope tell you that I've decided to go with your suggestion—'vermin'—as my courtroom mantra? Not the 'critters' definition," Cassandra swiftly assured the man who, according to Hope, cared about creatures great and small. "But the one that defines 'vermin' as a particularly loathsome human being."

"I hope it helps."

"It *will*. Armed with 'vermin' and 'allege' and 'claim'—which, whenever the vermin utters such verbs, I'll promptly restate as fact—how can I go wrong?"

"You're going to do great," Hope said.

"Well." Cassandra shrugged, a lift of frail shoulders against the cashmere coat that had become a weighted cloak of armor. "I'll try."

"We'd better go." Chase spoke softly to his wife, his gray eyes dark with worry at how quickly she had fatigued even with this most friendly repartee.

"Yes. Okay."

In moments they were gone, leaving Nick and Hope to watch their departing silhouettes as they had watched another pair of silhouettes depart nine years before. This shadowy pair, limned in sunlight, was quite different from that long-ago duo. These solemn shadows didn't flirt, didn't tease, didn't lust, and this black-haired driver guided the car slowly, cautiously, ever mindful of the precious cargo in his care.

Nine years ago, just before Frances and Gavin vanished from sight, the author-seductress herself had vanished, an ultimately fatal dip. And did Cassandra make such a provocative motion, such a carnal lunge?

No. Her fragile silhouette was motionless still. But a ray of sunlight caressed her ravaged skull, illuminating the faint golden growth of hair just so—so that, in that moment, a delicate halo glimmered and glowed.

There were no similarities at all in the silhouettes that departed Montagne Noir. But both Hope and Nick silently counted the seconds after Chase's car vanished around the bend, and counted still, and for many heartbeats beyond, the time when they had heard the scream of brakes and the crash that was thunder.

Hope turned to him at last, exhaled her relief, and smiled. "I'm glad you met them. What did you think of Cass?"

"That she's strong," he said. "And fragile. And terrified. And very much in love." *And terrified, most of all, of that.*

"As is Chase."

"Yes."

"I'm so afraid she's not coming back." Cassandra had been informed on Friday that neither the prosecution nor the defense required, any longer, the Brentwood crime scene to be preserved. Which meant that the blood-splattered walls could be repainted, the crimson-stained carpet replaced, and Cass could live again in the place where the stone fireplace had caused her kidney to weep bloody tears . . . and where she herself had almost died. "It should be enough, shouldn't it? Love?"

Hope was asking him, of all people?

But it was him, of all people, from whom the hopeful ballerina—turned impassioned prosecutor—needed to hear the truth.

"But it's not, Hope. Love is not nearly enough."

Nicholas Wolfe would have left her then. Should have. But Molly had other ideas. A car, carrying lovers, had departed the mountain safely, without tumbling over obsidian cliffs into a mangled fireball of steel.

So, her wriggling body seemed to ask, why not reverse that entire September day?

As she began to trot, to bound, toward the meadow of wildflowers, Hope whispered, "She can't possibly remember."

"Yes, she can," Nick countered. "Animals can."

But we can't, Hope. We cannot, should not, remember that gentle peace.

Molly, however, left them little choice. The creature with her own determined agenda had already disappeared.

They followed . . . to the meadow that was an emerald sky adorned with clouds of flowers—as it had been on that September day. The light was different, however, on this November afternoon.

Sublime. Serene. Mature.

And closer to winter.

And in the distance, far below, Courtland Medical Center shimmered a silvery gray.

Monet would have cherished the chance to paint this heaven of wildflowers in this muted light between seasons. And the artist who, for years, had been working on a suite of portraits entitled *Seasons of the Soul?*

Nick saw the September ballerina, spinning and twirling in the harvest sun, a portrait of such grace. Such joy. So lost was he in that image, so captivated by remembrance that he asked, although he shouldn't have, "Do you still dance?"

"No." *No. Not since that day.*

"You should."

Yes. *Yes.* "Maybe I could," she said softly. "For you. With you."

She was such a courageous ballerina, this new ballerina, this November dancer in the wintry light. She was suggesting a different dance, sublime and mature, the pas de deux of love, of loving, between a woman and a man.

Hope was offering herself *to him,* with grace, with joy, and now her ballerina arms were reaching to touch him, to begin their exquisite ballet, and—

"I don't dance."

Her arms halted in midair, then fell; graceful still, but with shattered joy. "But I thought . . . You don't want me?"

Want you? More than life itself. And if it were only my life, I would give it without a thought.

But it was her life, Hope's life. And she belonged in a September meadow, dancing beneath a harvest sun, not in the cold pale rays of winter—with him.

"No, Hope. I don't."

The dark blue eyes, where Hope believed she had seen such desire, were steel gray now and bitter cold. But she looked at him still, this man with whom she had always felt so safe—and recently so precarious—and to whom, always, she had been able to talk . . . to confess.

Hope confessed to him now. "I feel so foolish."

"Don't."

"This sort of thing happens all the time, doesn't it?" she asked without bitterness; not needing to ask, not really, for of course she knew. She had seen, had learned, at Willow Ranch, how much, and how desperately, this sensual man was wanted. "Women throwing themselves at you?"

Nicholas Wolfe's cold gray gaze traveled to the shimmering L-shaped structure that rose from the valley floor below.

"All the time," he said softly. "It happens all the time."

TWENTY-ONE

SANTA MONICA COURTHOUSE

THURSDAY, NOVEMBER TWENTY-NINTH

*A*ll the networks were there, camped outside the venue of justice. Their satellites tilted, like massive inverted umbrellas beneath the swaying palms, and their reporters wandered, like renegade chess pieces, on the emerald lawn.

Both Main and Fourth were cordoned off. Only the cars—and limousines—of those most intimately involved were permitted to pass. The principals, and their advocates, could speak to the press, if they so chose . . . if they ventured to the bright yellow barricades that kept them apart.

It was from behind such a barricade, a false sunbeam on this overcast day, that Beth Quinn spoke to Global News Network's legal anchor—and to the world—toward the end of the lunch recess on what was believed to be the third and final day of the preliminary hearing in the matter of the *People of California* versus *Robert Forrest.*

"I want you to recap this morning's testimony, Beth." Gregg Adams spoke from the anchor desk in the network's Manhattan studio. "But first, please, describe Cassandra Winter's appearance. For those of us watching the proceedings from a distance, it's quite startling. Disturbing, in fact. Is it any less so in the flesh?"

"Not at all. Of course, it's often surprising to see in person a celebrity known only from the silver screen. But even the Hollywood press are struck by how thin she is, how frail, how small—even though she's wearing her signature clothes, a stylish ensemble in ebony and cream with her trademark high-heeled boots."

"To those of us in the studio, as well as to the numerous viewers who have e-mailed and faxed, the image she presents is hauntingly reminiscent of a cancer patient having been ravaged by chemotherapy. Adding to this image, of course, is her baldness. The purple scars on her skull look like those markings used to show radiation therapists where to direct their beams."

"She isn't really bald," Beth Quinn countered with obvious regret. She was loath to contradict the network's most popular anchor—and celebrated trial attorney in his own right. But she felt constrained as a journalist to report the facts. "I'm sure that's far more apparent in person than on TV. What little hair she has is very light, a pale, pale gold."

"In any event," the anchor replied, bristling, "one wonders why Cassandra Winter isn't wearing a wig. The drama of having her remove it, as Ms. Mason surely would have had her do, would have been, it seems to me, quite shocking."

"We hear, from sources within the DA's office, that Mallory Mason very much wanted that shocking moment.

Indeed, as one of the tabloids is reporting today, a Rodeo Drive wig maker was commissioned to make a wig that would resemble, as closely as possible, the luxuriant mane for which the actress is so well-known."

"But?"

"Well, again according to sources, Cassandra refused to participate in the courtroom theatrics. Having watched her testimony this morning, I believe that's true. There's been quite a battle between the prosecutor and her star witness. Cassandra's recounting of what, let's face it, are three episodes of rather savage violence has been matter-of-fact, unembellished, without emotional enhancement of any kind."

"And Ms. Mason was pushing for more drama, more outrage?"

"That's the sense we had in the courtroom. If anyone *could* deliver such emotion, it would be the actress known for the dramatic—even harrowing—roles she's chosen to play. At the very least, she might have appeared fearful of Robert."

"But she didn't?"

"No. Not at all. It was as if he wasn't there. As if he were invisible—or she was."

"The invisibility of the victim," Gregg Adams mused. "We've heard expert testimony about that, in other cases covered by GNN. But, if memory serves, the sense of invisibility, the utter loss of self, more typically occurs when the trauma is inflicted when the victim is quite young—a child, for example, who has been raped. Is that what you recall?"

"Yes. Absolutely. And in this instance, the way she's *not* seeing him is as if, to her, Robert Forrest—and their relationship, for that matter—was never truly real."

"Even though her testimony seems very real."

"Very. Frankly, at least in the opinion of the press on the scene, Cassandra's flat—even battered—recitation made what she was saying all the more authentic, and chilling. It also made that one moment of sheer emotion quite stunning. I'm not sure if you or our viewers—"

"If you're talking about the moment when Ms. Mason handed Cassandra her bloodstained wedding ring, yes, we all saw it, felt it. The witness seemed lost for a moment, wanting to hold the ring, to keep it, to never give it back. I know my thought at the time: For heaven's sake, let her keep it."

"Yes," the reporter agreed. "That was my thought as well."

"Well, Beth, our time is running short. Please tell us what to expect this afternoon, from the much anticipated cross-examination of Cassandra Winter by the famous— some might say notorious—Lucian Lloyd."

"Expect a ballet, Gregg, performed by the Nureyev of criminal defense attorneys. Mr. Lloyd has to destroy her— without, of course, appearing to be as vile a batterer as his client is alleged to be. He must deliver a fatal blow; must, because as it stands Cassandra Winter has been an extremely credible witness."

"Who does, however, have some vulnerability."

"Yes. Definitely. And you can count on Lucian Lloyd addressing her as Mrs. Tessier, as a reminder of that vulnerability—her deceit, the marriage she concealed from everyone, including her lover."

"This may be painful, and artful, to watch. And our viewers will have that opportunity, just moments from now. In the meantime, following a brief commercial break, we'll get an update on the other legal news of the day— including the extraordinary hearings being held in the nation's capital. So stay with us for that update, and for the cross-examination of Cassandra Winter Tessier. . . ."

$\mathcal{G}$ood afternoon, Mrs. Tessier."

Smile, Hope had advised, when you can, when the vermin's pretending to be pleasant to you. But don't be deceived. He is vicious. "Good afternoon, Mr. Lloyd."

"Let's begin with your wedding ring."

No. No! Vermin. Verm—

"I noticed the way you touched it, Mrs. Tessier. I think we all did. It's obviously very important to you." Lucian Lloyd gave his *Father knows best* smile, as if he were the kindest man on the entire planet—and was so devastated that Cassandra was being subjected to this disagreeable charade that he was bound and determined to set things right. "Although I haven't had the opportunity to discuss this with Ms. Mason, I do have a suggestion to make." The defense attorney looked from the witness to the judge. "We have abundant photographs, Your Honor. We know the blood is hers, and that there are no usable prints. I see no reason, therefore, to impound the ring. My suggestion, if Ms. Mason agrees, is that we return Mrs. Tessier's wedding ring to her—now."

"Ms. Mason?"

"I have no objection, Your Honor."

"No?" Judge Barnes's expression conveyed surprise—a reaction that was clarified for the viewers at home by GNN's attorney turned anchor.

"This is extraordinary," Gregg Adams remarked. "A prosecutor knows to object, in principle, to any suggestion a defense counsel makes. Especially a suggestion as emotionally charged as this one is. But perhaps, as GNN's reporter Beth Quinn suggested earlier, emotion is precisely what Mallory Mason wants from her witness—no matter who evokes it."

Lucian Lloyd reclaimed the ring, an exhibit no longer, and removed the bloodstained gold from its protective plastic bag. The impeccably attired defense attorney eschewed the usual latex gloves, as if he—and therefore his client—knew that Cassandra's blood was untainted. Then, after dipping his own fine linen handkerchief in a defense table water glass, he meticulously wiped away every trace of trauma, taking special care to thoroughly cleanse the place where the eternal circle had been severed through and through.

"May I approach the witness, Your Honor?"

"If Ms. Mason doesn't object."

"No objection."

"This is unbelievable," GNN's Emmy Award–winning anchor informed his viewers. "Hope Tessier would—will—go ballistic when she sees the tape."

Lucian Lloyd approached. But he didn't hand the ring to the witness—would not presume to actually touch the prosecution's trembling star. Cassandra Winter Tessier *was* trembling, her bone-thin hands were, even as they rested, clutched in her lap.

"Go ahead, Mrs. Tessier," Lucian Lloyd coaxed as he placed the shining gold symbol on the varnished wood railing that blocked, from every view but his own, her tremulous clasp. "Put it on."

"It's as if," Gregg Adams whispered, "in the tradition of Dirty Harry, Lucian Lloyd has just said, 'Go ahead, Mrs. Tessier, make my day.' "

There was a single camera in the courtroom. Mounted. Stationary. And providing the same—and sole—video feed to every network: the witness, the judge, the prosecution, the defense, in each and every frame. The solitary camera could not swivel, nor could it tilt or zoom.

Which meant that only those fortunate enough to be

in the courtroom knew what caused the sudden commotion in the gallery. Everyone else—viewers and commentators alike—could only guess at its source . . . until Lucian Lloyd spoke anew.

"Maybe Mr. Tessier could approach, Your Honor? It's clear that he'd like to."

"Ms. Mason?"

"It's fine with me, Your Honor."

Within instants Chase Tessier came into view, and the camera faithfully transmitted his approach to the witness stand, his worry, his dignity, his grace. He seemed, this elegant man in the charcoal gray suit, a philanthropist in its purest sense, about to grant a ravaged woman her dying wish. The camera didn't know, and it was easy to forget, that this robustly handsome man and the translucent creature he approached were husband and wife.

Any speculation about the charity of Chase Tessier, his generosity to mankind, was dashed the moment he reached Cassandra. Chase knew where the camera was and positioned himself between the prying lens and his trembling bride. He sheltered her, sheltered their privacy, in a cave created by his charcoal tailored torso—and his love.

No one but Cassandra saw his eyes, glittering and tender and gray.

And no one but she heard his words, tender and glittering, as he slipped the roses onto her finger, a gentle journey over scarred and tattered flesh.

"With this ring, Cassandra, I thee wed."

"Chase." *Oh, Chase. No. No.*

He was upsetting her, rattling her. Chase saw it, felt it, and smiled. "Cassie? Give the vermin hell."

He touched her ashen cheek, a private caress of farewell, then turned, his expression unreadable as he returned to his seat.

"I'm sure you're very tired, Mrs. Tessier," Lucian Lloyd resumed solemnly. "You've been through a horrific ordeal. So I'll keep this very short. We've already established that you claim to have no memory of the assault."

"I *have* no memory of it," Cass clarified mechanically, so well rehearsed by Hope that even as her entire being quivered she restated as fact what he had "claimed."

"Mrs. Tessier . . ." Lucian Lloyd gazed at her as if she were a beloved yet naughty child. "This is your first, and hopefully last, experience with criminal cross-examination—"

Mallory Mason leapt to her feet. "Your Honor!"

"Mr. Lloyd." Judge Barnes's expression communicated quite clearly that it was the defense counsel who was naughty. "The Court doesn't need your predictions of its ruling in this matter, nor will subliminal suggestions work. Not with this Court. Or any court. I hope."

"Of course not. Thank you, Your Honor. I just wanted Mrs. Tessier to understand that there is a light at the end of this tunnel."

"I'm quite sure she's aware of that. You were, I believe, instructing her in the art, and rules, of cross-examination. Perhaps it will save time if I do that." Judge Barnes addressed Cassandra. "You need to wait until he asks you a question, even if he's making an assertion with which you don't agree. He's not permitted to testify, and I'm quite aware of what the testimony has been, so you needn't be concerned. Okay?"

"Yes."

"Good. Mr. Lloyd? Please continue. A question for the witness would be nice."

"Thank you, Your Honor." Lucian Lloyd looked from the reproving judge to his wary prey. "You never told Robert that you were married?"

"No," Cassandra whispered as a frisson of relief twined with the quivers of despair. The vermin was back to the script at last, asking a question for which she was fully prepared.

Back to the script . . . fully prepared . . . except that she was wearing her wedding ring.

"And you never told anyone—anyone *at all*—of the violence which you now allege?"

"I never told anyone of the violence which *happened*," Cassandra replied. *Vermin. Vermin.* The mantra came unbidden and with trembling calm.

"Very good, Mrs. Tessier. Someone has prepared you well." Lucian Lloyd made a slick transition from vermin to snake, a well-trained cobra about to strike. "And what about your *baby*, Mrs. Tessier? Did you ever mention *that* to Robert?"

Mallory Mason was livid. "Your Honor! This is outrageous. Mr. Lloyd is examining the witness on evidence not introduced on direct."

The Judge looked at the defense. "Mr. Lloyd?"

"Ms. Mason opened the door, Your Honor. If you'll refer to People's Exhibit Twenty-one, the report of Dr. Amanda Prentice, the gynecologist who examined Mrs. Tessier on October thirty-first. Dr. Prentice described Mrs. Tessier's cervix as parous, which means—and I'm quoting now—'having given birth one or more times.' Dr. Prentice, the prosecution's own witness, sailed through voir dire. Is Ms. Mason now questioning her expertise?"

"Ms. Mason?"

"What the People are questioning, Your Honor, is relevance."

"And your response to that, Mr. Lloyd?"

"It goes to credibility, Your Honor. Mrs. Tessier didn't tell Robert about her marriage. Nor did she mention to anyone, it seems, including the always interested Hollywood press, the episodes of alleged violence. Now, Your Honor, we have a never before disclosed baby—perhaps *Robert's* baby."

"Speculation!" Mallory Mason insisted.

"Yes, well," Lucian Lloyd replied. "I'm sure Mrs. Tessier can clear that up, once I'm permitted to proceed. Credibility is the issue here, Your Honor. Credibility—and facts. The prosecution has built its case on allegations of physical violence, for which there isn't a shred of evidence. There is abundant evidence, however, that Mrs. Tessier concealed her marriage, as well as at least one child."

"I'll allow the question, Mr. Lloyd. But be very careful."

"Thank you, Your Honor. Mrs. Tessier, did you tell Robert Forrest, your lover, about your pregnancy?"

Vermin. Vermin. Vermin.

"No." It was a whisper of grief, spoken to her hands, to the ring of roses that seared her flesh like molten gold.

"Was it his baby, Mrs. Tessier? Robert's baby?"

Please. Please. Please.

"Mrs. Tessier?"

Baby. Baby. Baby.

"No."

"No? Then would you care to tell us whose baby—"

"Objection!"

"Sustained. That's enough, Mr. Lloyd. There's no jury here, and I get the idea."

"Thank you, Your Honor."

Cassandra Winter Tessier was a crumpled marionette. Whatever invisible strings had kept her skeleton erect and her skull from rolling had snapped the moment Lucian Lloyd said "baby."

Cassandra had crumpled.

But Lucian Lloyd had persisted.

And somehow she had answered him.

Now, spurred on by Cassandra's own complicity in her demise, the esteemed defense counsel persisted still.

"Isn't it true, Mrs. Tessier, that all you *ever* do is lie?" The defense counsel's sneer was a mirror image of the scorn worn by Robert when he had attacked her. "That everything you've told this Court, absolutely everything, is patently false? You lied to Robert from the very beginning, concealing a marriage, *and a baby.* And when Robert couldn't stand the deceit, and wanted to be free, you decided to get even by doing what you do best—telling lies, this time attempting to destroy the reputation of a fine, decent, gentle man. I have no further questions of this witness."

It happened then. The strings from heaven attached anew. Or perhaps the marionette found new life, different strength, from something deep inside.

Robert Forrest had succeeded in his battery of Cassandra because it didn't matter, she didn't care. And for a while Robert's defense counsel had succeeded in battering her, too, kicking her when she was already down, curled and crumpled and wishing only to die.

But Lucian Lloyd miscalculated grievously when he launched an assault on the people Cassandra loved.

She straightened, frail and proud.

"Wait a minute, Mr. Lloyd. *Wait.* You asked me some questions. I have a right to answer." She looked at the judge. "Don't I?"

"Yes. You do."

Cassandra's nod was decisive, not a precarious bob, and her eyes, bright blue and huge against the gauntness of her face, found Lucian Lloyd.

"What I've said today, *everything* I've said, is the truth. My marriage is a private matter. And as for my baby . . ."

She faltered, trembled. Then recovered, for that baby; stronger than ever, and ever more fierce. She looked from the abusive attorney to the abuser himself and pointed at Robert, the coward and the bully, who was invisible to her no longer. "You would want *that* man to know about a baby, Mr. Lloyd? That man who kicked me, and meant to damage me, in the only sanctuary unborn babies have on this earth? If I *had* been pregnant, Mr. Lloyd, when your client kicked me, the baby I was carrying would have died. *Would. Have. Died.*"

Her bright blue gaze returned to the defense counsel, and the hand that pointed fell.

The hand.

And nothing else.

"Bravo," Gregg Adams whispered.

And Judge Nancy Barnes arched an approving brow.

And Lucian Lloyd? "I have no further questions of this witness at this time."

"Ms. Mason?"

"Nor do I, Your Honor. Cassandra has already, and rather elegantly, addressed the essential points I would have explored on redirect."

With that, Cassandra Winter Tessier was permitted to step down, and every network executive in the country made a solemn vow: When this case went to trial, and it would, they would make certain there were many cameras in the courtroom, one for each of the principals—at least— including Chase Tessier. And if the trial judge balked? Surely the First Amendment litigators who argued such things could come up with convincing reasons why the public had a right to see every bit of drama simultaneously and at close range.

As it was, Cassandra vanished from the frame before reaching her husband, and Robert and his attorney were huddled in a way that only a zoom could have conquered, and the most interesting observation that could be made in what might have been this most monumental courthouse moment was that Mallory Mason's skirt was, perhaps, a little too short.

Judge Barnes brought to an end the interlude that felt, to network execs, like an eternity of lost opportunity but was, in fact, quite brief. "Any more witnesses, Ms. Mason?"

"No, Your Honor. The People rest."

"Shall we take a recess before closing arguments?"

Mallory had a ready answer. "In light of the hour, Your Honor, we would urge the Court to move forward, without recess, until the conclusion of this hearing."

"Mr. Lloyd?"

"We, too, are interested in swift resolution. Which is why, Your Honor, in lieu of a recess we would like to call our first witness."

"Excuse me?" Mallory glared at Lucian Lloyd. "This is a preliminary hearing, not a trial."

"And, as we all know, a preliminary hearing is the prosecution's show." Lucian smiled at Mallory, then addressed the judge. "But, Your Honor, we have the right, do we not, to offer an affirmative defense? To present exculpatory testimony if we have it?"

"And do you have exculpatory testimony, Mr. Lloyd?"

"Yes, Your Honor. We do."

"This is the first the People have heard of such an offering."

"The witness has just come forward."

"Maybe we do need a recess," Judge Barnes observed.

To which Lucian Lloyd looked perplexed. "The prosecutor has just said she doesn't want one, and why. We concur. We would like this matter settled this afternoon. We believe the testimony we're about to offer will do just that."

"The People have been sandbagged, Your Honor."

"It looks that way, Ms. Mason."

Lucian Lloyd, master of the spin, offered a positive view. "If the case goes to trial, you'll have more than a glimpse of our defense."

"If?" Mallory Mason echoed.

"All right," the judge intervened. "That's enough. Call your witness, Mr. Lloyd."

"Thank you, Your Honor. The defense calls Nicole Haviland."

"Nicole Haviland," Gregg Adams murmured, searching his own memory as GNN's research crew scrambled to retrieve data stored in network data computer banks about this surprise, yet famous, witness. "She's an actress, of course. Her most recent film, at least the one I recall seeing most recently, I believe was called *The Second Sister.*"

The anchor's ad lib was hardly necessary. Most of GNN's viewing audience was quite familiar with the glamorous superstar . . . who in mere moments was seated in the witness chair and being addressed by the defense.

"Good afternoon, Ms. Haviland."

"Good afternoon, Mr. Lloyd."

"Will you tell the Court, please, how long you have known Cassandra Tessier?"

"I had believed it was three years. Since all of *this,* however, I've been reminded that Cassandra and I actually met eight years ago, in Napa Valley. I was starring in Adrian Ellis's *Duet,* and she was spending the summer at Domaine Tessier."

"Let's just deal with the past three years. How would you describe your relationship to Mrs. Tessier?"

"We're friends."

"Close friends?"

Nicole Haviland sighed. "Not close enough, apparently, that Cass felt comfortable sharing secrets with me."

"By secrets do you mean episodes of domestic violence?"

"No! There *were no* such episodes. Cass told me how gentle Robert was, *always.* Gentle and tender and kind. She also told me that Robert wanted out."

"So she confided to you that there were problems with her relationship with Mr. Forrest?"

"Oh, yes. She confided that. But she neglected, it seems, to share with me the truth of her marriage, her pregnancy . . . Lord knows what else."

"Your Honor!" Mallory implored.

"Ms. Haviland," Judge Barnes admonished, "kindly answer the questions with as little embellishment as possible."

"Oh, yes, Your Honor. Of *course.*"

"Now, Nicole," Lucian Lloyd continued, "please tell us about your relationship with Robert Forrest."

Lucian Lloyd's voice was smooth and soothing. But still the actress sighed with dismay. "We were lovers."

"Were?"

"Since the day Cassandra was injured, Robert and I have felt so awful, so conflicted, so *responsible,* that we've . . . stayed apart."

"In what way responsible, Nicole?"

"Well, if Robert had been with Cass, instead of with me, when the burglar broke into her home—"

"Wait," the judge interjected. "Ms. Mason, I'm making your objection for you. Ms. Haviland, please try to address your answers to the question that was asked, and to avoid speculation of any kind. Okay? . . . Good. Now, you were telling the Court that you and Mr. Forrest were lovers."

"Yes." Nicole gazed at the judge, penitent, eager to comply. "We were."

"For how long were you and Robert lovers?" Lucian Lloyd asked. "Prior to the assault on Mrs. Tessier?"

"A month."

"And was Mrs. Tessier aware of your affair?"

"Not until that day. She knew only that Robert wanted out."

"Which troubled her?"

"Yes. She was bitter, angry, *vengeful.*"

"Your Honor!"

"Relax, Ms. Mason," Judge Barnes advised. "There is no jury."

And Lucian Lloyd moved on. "Now, Nicole, tell us about the day of the assault."

"Robert told Cass that their relationship was over, and he also told her about us."

"And you know that how? Because Robert told you?"

"No. Cass told me. *Mrs. Tessier* told me."

"When?"

"At three o'clock on the afternoon of October thirty-first."

"Which was Halloween? And also Mrs. Tessier's birthday?"

"Yes."

"You're certain of the date?"

"Absolutely."

"And of the time?"

"Yes. I was staring at the clock, waiting for Robert to return. He had gone to Cassandra's about one, and when the phone rang I was sure it would be him."

"And you were where?"

"At my home, in Bel Air."

"Which is how far from where Mrs. Tessier lives in Brentwood? If you know."

"I don't know precisely. Not far. A few miles."

"Okay. Let's return to the phone call you received at three P.M. on the afternoon of October thirty-first. The caller was not Robert?"

"No. The caller was Cassandra."

"And what did she say?"

"This calls for hearsay, Your Honor," Mallory Mason insisted. "Cassandra has no memory of the alleged conversation, so can't possibly refute it."

"She *says* she has no memory," Nicole murmured. "Did anyone see *Echoes of Darkness*? In which Cass portrayed an amnesiac wife?"

"Your *Honor.*"

"I know how to weigh hearsay, Ms. Mason. And I would like to hear what Ms. Haviland has to say." Judge Barnes looked at Lucian Lloyd. "Proceed."

"Thank you, Your Honor. Please tell us, Nicole, what Mrs. Tessier said."

"She was angry, but also threatening. She warned me to stay away from Robert, and insisted that her hold on him was so strong, so *sexual,* that he would never leave her. She said, in fact, that they had just made love."

"You mean Robert was with her at the time of the call?"

"No. He was with me. He walked in while Cass and I were talking. *I* was angry by then, furious that what she said about their making love might have been true. Then I saw how upset *he* was, and all the blood on his shirt."

"The blood?"

"Cass had scratched him, deep claw marks all over his chest."

"You saw these marks?"

"Of course."

"Did Mrs. Tessier tell you that Robert had assaulted her?"

"Hardly. She described, in lurid detail, their hot, passionate sex."

"Did your conversation with Mrs. Tessier end when Mr. Forrest walked in?"

"My part of it ended. Robert talked to Cass for a while. He was very honest with her—honest to the point of cruelty. Robert is *not* a cruel man, which is why, within a few hours, he decided to accompany her to the Over the Rainbow ball. He didn't want to make up, only to make things easier. *Kinder.*"

"Did you attend the ball?"

"No."

"So there came a time Robert left your home?"

"Well, yes and no. There came a time, shortly after his conversation ended with Cass, when Robert and I left together."

"Why did you leave?"

"We were worried that Cass might come to my home. Neither of us wanted a scene, another scene."

"So you and Robert left, together, and went where?"

"We just drove around for a while. We worried that she might drive to Malibu when she discovered we weren't in Bel Air. We reached Robert's home, in the Colony, at about five. That's when he called her. To apologize. To offer to take her to the ball."

"Can you tell the Court a little about the ball?" Lucian Lloyd queried as if it were an impromptu thought. "It was a charity event?"

"Yes. At the Beverly Wilshire."

"And what charity benefited from the Halloween soiree?"

"Various adoption agencies. I'm not sure which ones."

"Adoption isn't one of your causes?"

"Well, of course it is. I support adoption. Who doesn't? Mrs. Tessier, however, was a little rabid on the subject."

"Rabid? You mean foaming at the mouth?"

"Not literally. But, yes, she felt very strongly, *extremely* strongly, that the best interests of the child weren't always served by remaining with the biologic parents. Which, of course, they're not, but . . ."

"This is very interesting," Gregg Adams murmured, his tone implying, quite clearly, that Beth Quinn might have spent a little more time investigating Cassandra Winter's obsession with adoption and a little less noticing the few golden hairs on the actress's battered skull. "And pertinent, especially in light of the revelations made about a baby."

Lucian Lloyd, having made that pertinent point, moved on. "You were saying, Nicole, that Robert called Mrs. Tessier to escort her to the ball?"

"Yes. And when he got only her machine, he assumed she'd already left."

"And at some point Robert left?"

"Yes."

"Is adoption one of his causes, too?"

"Oh, yes. One of *many*. Robert gives generously, both in money and in time, to any number of charities—especially those involving women. And children. I suppose, of all the issues Robert supports, it's domestic violence that concerns him most."

"Your Honor," Mallory Mason implored. "If Mr. Forrest would like to take the stand, and tell us how much he cares about battered women, we would be delighted to hear that testimony—as well as answers to other questions the People might have—under oath. But this is, well, gratuitous."

"But Robert's *been* there," Nicole Haviland insisted. "He's attended candlelight vigils, and spoken at rallies, and—"

"Stop," Judge Barnes commanded, and silence fell. "Okay. Mr. Forrest is against domestic violence. I think it's fair to say we all are. Mr. Lloyd, let's proceed with the events of the day in question."

Lucian Lloyd's solemn countenance belied his delight that his superstar witness for the defense had managed to get in what she had. "You were saying, Nicole, that at some point Robert left his home."

"Yes. And I remained in Malibu. I was still there, at Robert's home, when he called to tell me what had happened."

"Did Robert drive himself to the Beverly Wilshire?"

"No. He took a limousine."

"Was that usual?"

"In that setting, yes. When there are fans and paparazzi. And, because he was still so upset about Cass, he wanted someone else to drive."

"Do you recall what time the limousine arrived in Malibu?"

"At six."

"You saw it?"

"Yes. And the limousine driver—his name is Charles—saw me, too."

"And recognized you?"

"Of course."

"So. In summary, is it your testimony, Ms. Haviland, that you spoke to Mrs. Tessier at three P.M. on Wednesday, October thirty-first?"

"Yes."

"By the way, would that be a toll call? From her home in Brentwood to yours in Bel Air?"

"No. It wouldn't be."

"Is your phone number unlisted?"

"Of course."

"But Mrs. Tessier knew it."

"Yes. We were friends."

"And is it further your testimony that Mr. Forrest arrived at your home while you were still speaking with Mrs. Tessier?"

"Yes."

"And that there was blood on his shirt?"

"Yes."

"And that you saw scratches on his chest?"

"Yes."

"And that those scratches were still bleeding?"

"Yes."

"And is it your testimony that you and Robert were together continuously from three until six, when a limousine driver named Charles arrived in Malibu to drive Robert Forrest to Beverly Hills."

"Yes. That's my testimony."

"One final question, Nicole. Why have you just come forward? Surely this extremely important information should have been shared with the authorities weeks ago."

"I know it should have been. But even though I could *prove* that Robert could not have committed this horrendous crime, he didn't want me to come forward—because of Cass. It was a matter of honor. He was protecting her from the humiliation of our affair, as well as her desperate behavior on that day. Her *birth*day. He was protecting me, too, of course. Robert has always had faith in the criminal justice system. He was certain there wouldn't be an indictment. How could anyone possibly indict an innocent man?"

"But somewhere along the line Robert's faith faltered?"

"Not Robert's faith. *Mine.* Robert is not happy that I'm here. But enough is enough. Obviously, if an indictment were handed down, I would have come forward right away. So why wait? And so what if it's a little embarrassing for me—*or Cass.*"

"At the beginning of your testimony, you sounded apologetic about your affair, regretful of its impact, perhaps, on Mrs. Tessier. Now, it seems, you're a bit less sympathetic."

"I guess I'm conflicted. There's the woman, the *friend*, I believed I knew. Then there's that *other* person, the one who tells such lies."

"Thank you, Ms. Haviland. I have no further questions."

Judge Barnes arched an inquisitive brow at the prosecution table. "Ms. Mason? You've been remarkably, astoundingly silent."

"Because I *am* astounded, Your Honor. This carefully scripted performance did not just happen. Mr. Lloyd and Ms. Haviland have obviously done more than a little rehearsing, which means that the defense counsel has been aware of her version for quite some time. And yet failed to mention it to the People."

Lucian Lloyd looked utterly surprised that anyone could imagine he would be so sneaky. "Your Honor, Ms. Haviland was a reluctant—indeed, unwilling—witness."

Mallory's angry retort was preempted by the judge.

"The question is, Ms. Mason, are you going to cross-examine Ms. Haviland?"

"May I have a moment, Your Honor?"

"Of course."

As Mallory Mason conferred with her co-counsel at the prosecution table, legal analysts throughout the country speculated about what would happen next. The prosecution would drop the charges, most experts opined, at least for the time being. Since double jeopardy did not attach until a jury was empaneled, charges could always be filed again at a later date.

And, the commentators said, although the prosecution could proceed with its closing argument, it seemed risky to do so—for unless and until Nicole Haviland could be thoroughly impeached, the evidence simply wasn't there to compel Judge Barnes to bind the defendant over for trial.

By the time Mallory Mason spoke, at least for the viewers at home, her announcement was an anticlimax.

"Your Honor," she said, "the People withdraw their complaint against Mr. Forrest. For now."

TWENTY-TWO

SAN FRANCISCO

THURSDAY, NOVEMBER TWENTY-NINTH

*T*oo damn bad about Cassandra."

Detective Larry Billings's smirk belied his words. He was pleased—in fact, thrilled—to be the first to share the news with Hope.

He was the first, he knew. Hope had been in the courtroom, crucifying his best friend, while he and that best friend's father—retired police officer John Madrid—waited for their chance to offer a defense, a plea for leniency, for Craig.

In the room reserved for those scheduled to testify on the defendant's behalf had been a television, tuned to Global News. Which meant that Detective Billings had seen it all.

"Too damn bad," he repeated.

"I don't know what you're talking about," Hope said as casually as possible given the racing of her heart.

"I know. Would you like to? Sure you would. Let's see, while you were in here destroying a decent, law-abiding cop, Mr. Lucian Lloyd was making mincemeat out of your sister-in-law's so-called story of abuse. We should have hired Mr. Lloyd for Craig." The detective looked beyond Hope to John Madrid and made a solemn promise—and in Hope's case a warning—to them both. "We *will* get Mr. Lloyd, when we appeal Craig's bogus conviction. Sure, Lucian is pricey. But that's not a problem anymore. Donations will come pouring in now that the world has seen the lies your witnesses are willing to tell—and how they shatter when those lies are exposed."

"I'm quite sure Cassandra didn't shatter."

Detective Billings was not about to concede that, in fact, the actress had managed a rather dramatic, if ultimately futile, recovery. "If that's not shattering, I guess I don't know what shattering is. I should probably find a dictionary and look it up. Speaking of which, Hope, you need to improve your dictionary skills, beginning with 'parous.' It's far too late for Cassandra—she's already shattered—but it might help the next victim you decide to use in your crusade against men."

Parous. Hope knew what it meant. As did any prosecutor who handled sexual assaults—assuming that prosecutor read, with meticulous care, every word of the physician's report.

Quite obviously Mallory Mason had not. And *she,* Cassandra's friend, and a meticulous prosecutor in her own right, should have insisted, as a quid pro quo for preparing Cassandra for trial, that she review every scrap of data the prosecution had.

But Hope hadn't insisted, and now . . . Cass had given birth? To Chase's child?

Detective Billings seemed to read her thought. "That lit-

tle bombshell—the missing and presumed Tessier baby—
was just the beginning of Cassandra's downfall. Then came
the alibi witness, in the person of Hollywood's sexiest actress. And let's face it, Hope, even before she turned into a
walking skeleton, your sister-in-law was never in conten-
tion for that title. But Nicole Haviland definitely is. I hope
you set your VCR to record the festivities down south. It's
really riveting—and educational—TV."

"Thank you *so much*, Detective Billings, for your support." The sarcastic words did not belong to Hope. She'd
been so focused on what the gloating detective was saying
that she didn't even see Meryl Atwood arrive. But the DA
had definitely arrived and was undeniably annoyed.
"Now, if you don't mind, Ms. Tessier and I need to confer
before the recess is over."

"Sure, Meryl. Confer away."

As the detective ambled over to John Madrid, Hope and
Meryl withdrew to a vacant courtroom across the hall.
Hope spoke the moment their privacy was assured.

"Did you see it, Meryl?"

"Yes."

"And it was bad, wasn't it? I should have—"

"I knew it! I *knew* you'd blame yourself. Of course, I'm
not alone. Jack Shannon knew it, as did some other very
nice people named Eleanor and Nick and Jane, all of whom
have called." Meryl waved a handful of pink phone message slips. "Their message, which is also my message, is
that none of this was your fault. Mallory blew it, not you.
Mallory—who, by the way, has not yet bothered to call."

But Nick *had* bothered. Hope's already whirling mind
reeled further at the news and swiftly spun to the truth:
Of course Nick had called. Why wouldn't he? Just because
Nicholas Wolfe and Hope Tessier could not dance, would
never dance, didn't mean Nick wouldn't offer words of
consolation to a friend.

"I'm wondering if I should handle this afternoon's cross," Meryl said. "Not because you can't, but because you may want to give your brother and Cassandra a call."

"Chase and Cass need to talk to each other, not to me," Hope said quietly. "And besides, Meryl, you really can't cross-exam John Madrid. It was difficult enough for you to prosecute his son, even from a distance."

"His son is a rapist."

"But John isn't. He's a good man, who has been your friend for a very long time. I'm fine, Meryl. Truly."

This is what I do.

This is my life.

B aby.

The small, precious word was a jagged-edged knife. It had plunged into Chase's heart the moment it left Lucian Lloyd's lips; and plunged again, and again. And twisted.

Yet once Lucian Lloyd had starting battering Cassandra, and even though it was she who wielded the knife, Chase had moved toward her, to rescue and protect her. The bailiff had impeded the impassioned journey almost at its outset, an obstacle that would have been trivial had Cassandra not rescued herself—a crumpled marionette shattered no more.

Chase had stood on guard throughout the remainder of her testimony, waiting to escort her away, *and then what?* The answer was postponed, delayed, for the Tessiers remained in the courtroom until the hearing was over.

It was over now, all over, and the skies above Los Angeles were sunny and bright, as if approving of the events of the afternoon. Palm trees swayed in the balmy November breeze, and joggers jogged, and when Chase and Cassandra reached the Hotel Bel-Air and walked in silence to their secluded bungalow, snow white swans glided in the indigo pond nearby, and songbirds warbled in the eucalyptus trees overhead.

Then they were alone, in the living room of their two-bedroom suite.

And then what?

His silent query was answered, in silence, by her—by the skeletal fingers that tugged on the white gold band of roses, the severed circle of pink blooms and private vows.

"Leave it on," Chase said, breaking the silence, shattering it with his solemn command. "I want you to wear our wedding ring while you tell me the truth about my baby. The truth, Cassandra. For once."

Cassandra spoke to the ravaged flesh, the bulky scar that made it so difficult to remove the broken band. "She . . ."

She. The single syllable twisted ever deeper the jagged-edged knife. He had a daughter. Chase's voice softened for that faraway little girl. "She's in Seattle, isn't she?"

"Yes."

"She was the someone else, wasn't she? She was the reason you left." When Cassandra nodded, when her tarnished golden skull bobbed once with weighted anguish, Chase asked, softly still, "Why, Cassandra? Tell me why."

"I don't know," she whispered. "I don't *know.*"

She moved then, fluttered then, sinking into the plush pillows of the living room couch. It was a billowing creation of floating fabrics and tropical hues, like the plumage she once had worn, her witch's disguise, combat gear for the wounded soul who was so complex—and at this trembling moment so terribly confused.

"It seemed . . . so clear to me that I had to leave. That I had no choice." That the fairy tale would end. That the rainbows were destined to die. That midnight would come, for Cinderella, with its promised vengeance. After a frowning moment, and bewildered still by a clarity that had been so persuasive—and so false, she repeated, "So *clear.*"

"Because of me?" All softness vanished from Chase Tessier's voice. "Because I told you—once—that I didn't want children?"

More than once, she thought. For hadn't he told her again during their months of love on Montagne Noir? Hadn't he said that his life was perfect, precisely as it was, with his mountain, his rainbows, and her? Perfect . . . just as her parents' marriage had been perfect—until her.

"You *didn't* want them." *Did you?*

No. Not until I fell in love with you. "Neither did you," Chase said quietly. "What did you do with her, Cassandra? The baby—our baby—whom you did not want?"

"I *wanted* her, Chase." *From the moment I sensed her inside me.* "I wanted her. So much."

"But you believed I didn't? Wouldn't? That I would abandon my child? Did you think so little of me?" *Believe me to be such a despicable man?*

Her cloudy blue eyes cleared, for him; a brilliant clarity—for him.

"No, Chase. *No.* Never. That's why . . ." the memory came with a pain that stole her breath. *He loves you. He will love us.* The voice, so bright, so confident, had come from the tiny life that danced within.

"Why what, Cassandra?"

"Why I was coming back to you," she confessed softly. "Why *we* were coming back."

But you didn't come back. The thought pierced, twisted, plunged. "But, instead, you gave her away."

"No," she whispered. *We were coming back, Chase, to you. We were coming back!*

But that night, the eve of her return to him, Cassandra's nightmare had returned to her. She was falling, falling, and when she awakened, gasping and damp, some of the dampness, *most of it,* came from the drenching deluge of blood.

"She died, Chase. Our baby girl died."

The knife sliced then, clean and swift and all the way through.

Since the revelation in the courtroom, and the testimony—about adoption—that surrounded it, Chase had believed that his daughter was alive: seven years old, and living in Seattle with a family handpicked by Cassandra, and smiling and happy and—

And in the past few moments, Chase had even begun to understand why his wounded Tinkerbell had found a Grandpère—and a Grandmère—for their blue-eyed, amber-haired girl. She wanted, for their daughter, parents whose love would never shatter, and who would love their little girl always . . . as Cassandra—as Sandra Jones—had not been loved. Had never been loved.

And who, Chase realized now, had left Montagne Noir, left him, because she believed she would not be loved—not really, not forever, not by him . . . despite the promises of love he had made.

She had left, wounded, uncertain, and so confused. But she had decided to return—a decision of courage, of trust, of love.

But Tinkerbell had not returned to Montagne Noir, nor had she given their daughter away. Their daughter . . . who was not smiling, not dancing, not laughing after all.

"She died?" Chase repeated at last. His grief was numb, still, stunned, still. But hers . . . he saw the raw pain on her ravaged face. "Can you tell me what happened?" *Tell me, if you can—if talking about the sadness will help.*

Chase wasn't certain that it would, or that she would.

But after a moment she met his gentle gray gaze and began to speak.

"I was in my seventh month." *And we were coming home, Chase, coming home.* "I went into labor."

"So she was premature." *Too tiny, too precarious, to survive.*

"Yes. But there was something . . ." *wrong with her.* Cassandra could not say the words. How could anything have been wrong with the joyous little life who danced inside her?

"Something?" Chase pressed gently.

"Something . . . developmental." Her gaze fell to the tightly clasped knot of bones—and severed roses—that were her hands. "I suppose I wasn't giving her what she needed."

She sat, small and frail amid a vivid tableau. But nothing, neither brilliant hue nor billowy fabric, could disguise the anguish of the unloved little witch.

Did she truly blame herself? Chase wondered. Of course she did. She had been taught, from birth, that she destroyed even the most perfect love.

"It's not your fault."

Cassandra frowned at her severed wedding ring, hearing in his words echoes of the assurances spoken by the doctors who had cared for their baby girl. Not your fault. Not your fault. Nothing you could have done.

"You can't know that," she whispered to a delicate pink rose.

"But I can," Chase said softly. "And I do. I know you're at your most ferocious when someone needs you. You took wonderful care of our daughter. I know you did."

She looked up, to him—and disbelief, with just the faintest shimmer of hope, fluttered in her sky blue eyes.

"I tried. But . . ." The shimmer died.

Chase gazed at the woman he loved, and he felt searing fury—toward himself. He had vowed to cherish her, to protect her.

"I should have known you were pregnant. You never had a period." *I would have known if you had.* "I should have known, should have realized."

"But how could you, Chase? *I* didn't know. And you knew it wasn't unusual for me to go six or eight months between periods. And I used my diaphragm—always."

"*We* used your diaphragm, Cassandra." And they had used it carefully, compulsively, correctly, despite the urgent demands of their passion. "But you didn't always wear it, did you? Not that final night." *When you reached for me, so desperate, so needy.*

"No," she confessed. "I knew I was pregnant, and I . . ."

"Wanted nothing between us. I wanted that, too." *Always.* "I should have been with you . . . With both of you." Chase drew a ragged breath. "You were in Seattle?"

"Yes. I worked at the art museum, giving tours." *It was easy, Chase, and lovely. It reminded me of giving tours at the Domaine—and of you, and of magic.*

"It was cold that winter." So cold, Chase thought, the winter you left me. He remembered that winter so well, searching for her, wondering about her, hoping—whenever he saw the news reports of record snowfalls and storms of ice—that she was somewhere south, somewhere warm. But she had been in Seattle, the Emerald City—which, that winter, had been particularly hard hit. "Seattle was very cold."

"Yes. But *she* wasn't cold, Chase. She was *never* cold."

"I meant you." *My lovely Tinkerbell.* "I meant you."

"I wasn't cold, either." *Not with her inside me. Not with you inside me.* "I was fine, and she was fine. And then she was born, and she was so little, Chase, and so beautiful, and so brave. She fought so hard to survive. So *very* hard."

"Her mother's daughter." Chase walked toward her then, toward the frail loveliness amid the billows and hues. And when he was close enough to touch, he extended his hand to hers. "Come back to me, Cassandra," he whispered, touching her only with that spoken caress. "Come back to me."

"Chase," she breathed in shimmering disbelief—even as the entire room began to shimmer, filling with a most wondrous mist, the color of champagne, that dancing gold color that promised rainbows. "Chase."

"I love you, Cassandra."

She saw his eyes, misted, too, and gray with love, and her own tears began to spill, as they had spilled that other time, that first time, amid a tangle of chardonnay.

"Is that so bad?" he asked gently, as he had even then.

Bad? No. But he was loving her, loving *her,* even though she had left him. And now her gray-eyed sorcerer was bestowing even more gifts. For this magician who could taste the wind and make emeralds fly from the sea was conjuring, from this champagne mist, a rainbow.

And in that shimmering pastel mist, his hand seemed to shimmer, too. To tremble. And then she was reaching for that hand, so warm, so strong, and then she was standing, and touching.

She was touching *him.*

Her hands, one of which wore roses, the vows for both of them, fluttered to his lips, his jaw, his cheek . . . and lighted, astonished, beneath his tired, loving, uncertain eyes.

"Say it, Cassie."

And she did, this woman who was most ferocious when

someone needed her. As he did. Unbelievably. *As he did.*

"I love you, Chase," she whispered. "I love you, too."

*T*hey made love beneath the rainbow he had made for her, their own pastel mist of joy. Chase kissed her scars, cherishing, lingering caresses of tenderness . . . and the place where Robert had kicked her . . . and where, with such courage and such care, Cassandra had loved their baby girl.

And, as they loved, Cassandra made a rainbow, too. For him. It shimmered in her eyes, clouded no more, and it promised, that brave and fluttering rainbow, to love him, to trust his love, always.

TWENTY-THREE

I knew you'd be at home—and working?"

Of course. Hope frowned. "Sibyl?"

The voice wasn't precisely Sibyl's. It wasn't precisely anyone's. But the smoky whisper, patrician in both its affect and its style, was pure Sibyl . . . who, if silence was an accurate barometer, wasn't the least bit pleased to have been identified so swiftly.

Fine, Hope thought, vaguely annoyed. "Who is this?"

"Someone who cares about justice. As you do, Hope. Don't you?"

"Yes. Absolutely."

"Good. Because he did it to me, too. He *raped* me, too."

"Who raped you?"

"Robbie, who else? The famous Robert Forrest. He raped me, just like he raped Cassandra—and beat her, and left her to die."

The affectation remained Sibyl's, identical to Sibyl's, but . . . "Who is this?"

"Someone who knows everything, including, you'll note, your unlisted home phone. You know how I got that? From a sheet of paper in Robert's locked desk. You're on that list, Hope, as is Cassandra, and someone named Eleanor, and Dr. Amanda Prentice, and Cassandra's soapwriter neighbor."

Hope forced a calmness into her voice that she did not feel. "You said you know everything."

"I *do*. Such as the fact that Nicole lied. He *made* her lie."

"About?"

"Her friendship with Cass, the confidences they shared, and, of course, her own whereabouts at three P.M. on Halloween."

"She wasn't at her home in Bel Air?"

"No. She was at *his* home in Malibu. But Malibu is a toll call from Brentwood. And Cassandra didn't call Nicole that day. How could she? She was dying. Robert *left* her to die."

"And you know that because . . ." you're Nicole? Hope wondered. The whispering voice could easily belong to Nicole. The actress, betrayed now by the lover she had lied for, could effortlessly affect a patrician accent and would have no qualms about approaching Hope as if they knew each other—as they had, that summer at the Domaine, when Nicole Haviland had lusted after Hope's hair.

"Because Robert *told* me," the smoky voice repeated. "If I wasn't careful, he said, he'd do to me what he'd done to Cass. He's obsessing about her, Hope. Obsessing. And plotting."

"Plotting what?"

"Her *murder*. Robert's convinced he's bulletproof—which he is, as long as incompetents like Mallory Mason are on the case. You'll notice *her* name isn't on his enemies list. But yours is, because Robert knows how good you are. He has to be stopped, Hope. And you can do it. *We* can do it. I want to show you the list, and I have some other things, other *proof.* Would that be possible?"

"Certainly."

"Soon? Robert has begun talking about a Christmas surprise, a special Christmas gift for *himself.* I'm so afraid he means Cass."

"Or someone else on his list."

"No. No one but Cass is truly at risk. I'm sure of that. The list is just further evidence of what an egotist—what a megalomaniac—Robert is. The only danger is for Cass. She's the *only* woman on earth Robert Forrest cares about."

"I can be in L.A. in two hours."

"Thank you, Hope. *So much.* But I have to come to you. If Robert finds out, he'll kill me. And he *will* find out, if we meet in L.A. His friends, his spies, are everywhere. How else did he get your unlisted number? The police adore him. Maybe even the police up there. They can't be involved, Hope. Not yet. Okay? Please?"

"Yes," Hope agreed. "Okay."

The mystery woman with the aristocratic accent and the terrifying news would call when she arrived, which gave Hope ample time to place calls of her own.

The first, to Montagne Noir, remained unanswered after twenty rings.

But it was all right. Expected. The memory came with a flood of relief. At this hour, on this Friday evening before Christmas, Chase and Cass wouldn't be at home.

The second Napa Valley number Hope dialed was answered right away.

"Eleanor, it's Hope. You're still there."

"We're leaving in the morning." Eleanor frowned. Hope knew their plans. She had specifically asked, just last night, when she'd called to wish them the merriest of Christmases with Samuel's children—and grandchildren—in Santa Fe. "What's wrong, dear?"

"Nothing! I was just wondering if you know where Chase and Cass and Victor are dining tonight."

"No," Eleanor replied. "I don't know. Were you hoping to join them after all?"

"No. I still can't. You know me. *Work.* Actually, Eleanor, something is wrong."

Hope told her. Everything. And they hatched a plan. Hope would phone likely restaurants in the city, until call waiting signaled either that the Tessiers had been found or the mystery woman had arrived, and Eleanor and Samuel—from their separate lines—would canvas Wine Country restaurants while making periodic calls to the château.

That resolved, Eleanor addressed a more immediate concern. "Your first call, Hope, needs to be to the police."

"No," Hope countered quietly. "It doesn't. She's scared, and if I betray her trust, she may simply disappear. Besides, my relationship with the police remains a little shaky."

"Not with all the police."

"True. But it's at its worst with Detective Larry Billings, who's working tonight, and is the senior officer I would logically call."

"I think, logically, you should call *someone.*"

"I'm fine, Eleanor. Really. I've met with terrified women before—many times. This cloak-and-dagger paranoia is common, in fact typical, especially in a battering situation. It will be okay. More than okay. This just may be the beginning of what you've been predicting for months—a wondrous and wonderful Christmas. What could be better than having Cassandra's assailant behind bars?"

Eleanor could think of even better things—happier and more wondrous—for Hope. But she admitted, "That would certainly be a dandy start."

"Promise me, Eleanor, that you won't call the police."

"As long as you promise to be careful."

"I do!"

"Then I promise, too." *No police, just the man who—I believe—would protect you with his life.*

Eleanor didn't know that man's phone number, nor could Directory Assistance provide a listing for him.

In truth, Eleanor scarcely knew Nicholas Wolfe at all.

But she knew from Cassandra how happy Hope had been during those November days, and that Hope had not mentioned Nick's name since. And Eleanor knew from Jane that although Nick never mentioned Hope, either— never would, not even to Jane—his silence spoke volumes.

Eleanor reached Jane in her home, and studio, on Sage Canyon Road.

Jane answered the studio phone, its receiver a palette of bright smudges. Jane always answered her calls, even when at work. Her muse wasn't that fragile, not fragile at all, and as for paint . . . it was mother's milk to an artist. This artist. Teal green splotches adorned Jane's cheeks even now.

Jane answered cheerfully, then sobered as she heard Eleanor's voice.

"You sound worried."

"I am. I'm looking for Nick. I was hoping you'd know how to find him."

"I do. In fact, I'm looking at him right now." Looking at the lonely man she had invited over on this holiday evening, on the pretense of needing Nick's artistic advice on a painted glass window she had agreed to design. "I'll put him on."

"No, Jane. Wait. I'll just tell you, and maybe you can tell him? It's about Hope."

"Hope? You're making me very nervous, Eleanor."

"With reason." Eleanor's recap was even more succinct

than Hope's had been, and extremely focused. After explaining the situation to Jane, she said, "I was hoping you would convince Nick to drive to the city, to Hope's apartment, and follow her when she leaves."

"I'm quite sure it won't take any convincing. Let's see. I'll need Hope's address. I have it somewhere, but if you're within reaching distance of your cloth-covered book?"

"I am. She lives on Laguna, in Pacific Heights. The street number is . . ."

Jane transcribed the information, bade good-bye to Eleanor, and looked up at Nick. "Hope needs you."

His blue eyes darkened. "Okay."

Nick listened, restless but absolutely still. And silent.

When Jane was finished, she offered him the sheet of paper on which she'd written Hope's address. But the strong, gifted hands of Nicholas Wolfe did not move.

"Have you been to her apartment, Jane?"

"Yes."

"Then come with me. Show me the way. It will save time."

"All right."

"Cell phone?"

"In my purse," Jane answered, grabbing said purse as Nick collected Molly.

In moments, and in unison, Jane Parish and Nicholas Wolfe murmured, "Let's go."

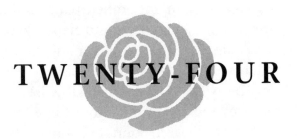

TWENTY-FOUR

PACIFIC HEIGHTS
FRIDAY, DECEMBER TWENTY-FIRST

*H*ope? I'm here."

"Good. Where?"

"Nordstrom's on Union Square."

"I'll meet you there, in the main lobby. Will you recognize me?"

"Oh, yes. I saw your press conference the day the jury began its deliberations on the rapist cop."

"Okay. I should be there in about twenty minutes."

A car was parked behind hers on Laguna Street. Hope had assumed, until a whisper came through the open window on the passenger side, that the lightless vehicle wasn't occupied.

"Hope?"

A cloud of smoke wafted with the whisper, shrouding its owner in a murky haze . . . its owner, who had not been calling from Nordstrom's after all.

Hope saw hair, a luxuriant amber mane, and a gloved hand holding a lighted cigarette, and half a face, a shadowy profile, curtained by the fall of hair and concealed further behind large, dark glasses.

Could this be Nicole Haviland in disguise? Yes. Definitely. Nicole, wearing a wig similar to the one Mallory had wanted Cassandra to wear in court. Or, Hope thought, this could be Mallory herself, her personal vendetta against Robert suddenly explained by a troubled relationship of her own with the abusive actor.

"I take it Robert also had my address."

"I should have told you," the smoky whisper apologized. "I know. But I didn't want you to freak and call the police. You don't seem that freaked."

"I'm not." Hope was a little unsettled, perhaps, but okay. In fact, this entire scenario was a rather reassuring déjà vu of her first encounter with Craig Madrid's frightened wife. After arranging to meet with Hope at Fisherman's Wharf, the detective's wife had appeared on Hope's doorstep, apologetic, anxious, and so terribly afraid that Hope would rescind her offer of help. Hope did not, of course, rescind. Indeed, she had invited Rosemary Madrid into her home. But that had been in broad daylight, with a woman who wore neither sunglasses nor a wig, and who had been forthright, from the outset, about who she was. "Why don't we go to Ghirardelli?"

"There's a problem." The dark glasses came off even as the amber-tressed head turned. The face, fully exposed, was unfamiliar—neither Mallory nor Nicole—and beautiful, a Hollywood glamour, with dramatic makeup artfully applied—except, that is, for the enormous purple bruise that extended from temple to jaw. "I could have covered this, but I didn't. Just as Cass refused to wear a wig. It's his shame, Robert's shame, not ours. Isn't that right?"

"Yes. That's right. Robert did that to you?"

"Of course! I was defying him, you see. Trying to be me. But Robert wanted Cassandra, only Cassandra, *always* Cassandra. That's why I have this wig. Robert bought it for me. He makes me wear it whenever we're together. This coat is identical to the one she wore to court, and she owns this exact pair of gloves. Robert would go crazy if he knew I was smoking, or that I was wearing tennis shoes instead of high-heeled boots. But it's safer, you know, for driving? And I'm still a little dizzy from this." A gloved hand pointed to the bruise.

"Robert makes you dress like Cassandra," Hope reiterated quietly.

The self-deprecating smile on the bright crimson lips confirmed what Hope already guessed and explained further the extreme reluctance to involve the police.

"I'm a hooker, a *whore*—although, until Robert Forrest, I was, by all accounts, a high-class, and very classy, call girl. I fell in love with the bastard. Can you believe it? And he did this to me, brought me so far down . . . but not out. I'm ready to see if a battered prostitute can bring Hollywood's golden boy to his knees. With your help."

"You'll have it."

"Thanks. Can we just talk here? In my car? I'm more comfortable in shadows."

Hope felt a faint frisson of concern. But she fought it, calmed it. There was so much at stake. "All right."

"Let me make everything more comfortable for you." The gloved hand extinguished the cigarette, turned the ignition enough to awaken the controls, then lowered all the windows and set the air conditioner at full blast. "This should take care of the smoke, and I won't light up again until we're through."

The smoky assurance brought even greater calm. It was

so typical of a battered woman to be at once apologetic, grateful, and desperate to please. "It's all right if you do."

"Well. I'll try my best not to damage your lungs." A soft clicking sound indicated that the passenger door had been electronically unlocked. "Okay. I think it's safe to get in."

But it wasn't safe in the least.

The windows were being raised even as she was getting in, and her door was locked the moment she closed it, and as the car's engine began to roar, Hope inhaled, amid the lingering smoke, the scent of Promise, Cassandra's signature perfume.

From rain-slick lane to rain-slick lane the car darted— impatient, it seemed, to outpace, and outdistance, every other vehicle on San Francisco's congested roads. Nick followed in his pickup truck, close enough to maintain visual contact, yet far enough to avoid alarm.

They rode in silence, Nick and Jane, and even Molly, seated between them, seemed at once anxious and subdued.

Nicholas Wolfe drove masterfully and decisively, even as Hope's mystery woman led him ever nearer the place haunted by his own impatient ghosts. They had been wanting him to return, those restless phantoms, promising retribution and revenge.

Nick drove. Masterfully. Decisively. Hope mattered. Was all that mattered. He would not permit the ancient ghosts to distract him.

When the distraction came, on Fulton, along the northernmost edge of Golden Gate Park, its cause was human, not demon—a boy, little older than Nick had been when the torture began.

The boy was lost in dreams, perhaps, visions of brightly wrapped Christmas gifts under a pine-fragrant tree. Or maybe he was fleeing demons of his own.

For whatever reason, and without the slightest glance toward traffic, the boy stepped off the night-darkened curb into the rain-drenched street—directly behind the car in which Hope rode and in front of all the rest.

Brakes squealed. Cars swerved. Traffic shuddered, skidded, stopped.

And the boy? He would be all right. A slow-speed fender-bender of gleaming chrome and preteen flesh. Everyone would be all right, as soon as the burst of adrenaline, reflexively released, stopped flogging their hearts.

The adrenaline that flooded Nick's veins, and pummeled his heart, was far more than a single burst. It was a gushing river, at flood stage now as he realized that the car in which Hope Tessier rode had vanished from sight.

It must have turned off Fulton and into the park. And it must have turned at *that* entrance, the Thirtieth Avenue entrance, his own private entrance to hell.

*W*ho are you?" Hope demanded, not for the first time—but with ever-increasing urgency.

"Don't you know?"

She did, of course she did, an awakening terror that was becoming a horrific knowledge.

"Robert."

Despite the darkness, ever darker as they drove deeper into the park, Hope saw the shimmer of triumph beneath the false eyelashes and powdered lids.

"Bingo." The smoky whisper yielded to the male voice known to the world. "Impressive, wouldn't you say? The costume *and* the role. I really have the battered woman nonsense down, don't I? The fear, the paranoia, the irratio- nal hatred of men. I guess it's fair to say that all those do- mestic violence rallies I suffered through finally paid off. Admit it, Hope. You're an expert on this mumbo-jumbo. I had you totally convinced."

"You're wonderful, Robert. A sensational actor and a truly terrific guy."

"Oh, we're being sarcastic now. Not very charming, Hope. Not charming at all. And you can stop fondling the door handle. I'm afraid it doesn't work. You're in the car, with me, until I decide it's time to let you out."

"What do you want?"

"I'm sure you know what I want. If not, you'll find out very soon. We've almost reached the spot where some lucky early morning jogger or rider will jog or canter upon . . . well, you get the picture. Or shall I spell it out? Picture this: Hope Tessier, dressed only in a necklace—Fantasy Im- promptu—and her own debutante blood. For inquiring minds such nakedness will answer a question that has been tormenting me ever since I first saw you: Can her cin- namon hair possibly be real? If so—"

"You're sick."

"Actually, I'm feeling very well. Except for this." With a flourish, Robert Forrest tossed the amber-tressed wig into the backseat. "And these." He tugged from his hands the skintight gloves, the covering that had concealed, until it no longer mattered, the masculine shape. He flexed and stretched his freed fingers. "There. Circulation at last. What was that famous—or should I say infamous—little ditty? If the gloves don't fit, you must acquit?"

"You won't get away with this."

"Sure I will." Robert discarded, too, the long cashmere coat. He wore black beneath, an executioner's garb. "I'm bulletproof, remember? The platinum blond whore who paid, in cash, for this car doesn't exist, and the car itself is destined for death in the bay, and without boring you with the technology, suffice it to say that phone calls are being made, from my Malibu home, even as we speak. Apologetic messages recorded onto machines of friends who are out for the evening. Which all normal people are, you know. Parties with friends, rendezvous with lovers."

There was nothing even remotely normal about the madman who scoffed at her with painted lips and powdered eyes.

"You're not partying with friends."

His crimson lips smiled with menacing glee. "I'm not? I'm afraid I don't agree. There's no party I'd rather be at than the one that's about to begin in Golden Gate Park. Speaking of which, here we are. So. Let the party begin," he enthused as he retrieved a small bag from beneath his seat. "I've taken the liberty of bringing a few props."

Robert Forrest extracted, first, Fantasy Impromptu, the necklace of rainbowed gemstones created by Castille and stolen from Cassandra's home on Halloween. He slipped into a black pocket the precious creation of gems, then dipped into the bag anew—retrieving this time a roll of duct tape.

To bind her wrists. His intent was clear, even before he made his move, such an effortless move, despite her struggle to resist. The car was small. She was locked inside. And he was empowered by madness, ever more powerful the harder she fought.

"I wonder about taping your mouth," he said once her wrists were secure. "Well, why don't we just see how things go? Pleas for mercy appeal to me. Really, they do. Cassandra was so disappointing in that regard—in most regards, if truth be known. She never pleaded, never implored, never *begged*. No one will hear you, Hope. Not here. Not even if you scream. Maybe I shouldn't have told you that. Now you'll be silent, like Cassandra, just to torment me. Well, Hope, I can torment you, too."

One of his false eyelashes had dislodged during the pitifully brief struggle as he bound her wrists. Robert pulled the dangling lash from his lid, swiping makeup with it, then extracted the two remaining items from the bag: a vial of snow white powder and a shining silver knife.

He looked at her through gleaming eyes, one lushly female, one starkly male, both utterly insane.

"Would you care for a little cocaine? It might make this entire experience—this ultimate trip—even more, well, ultimate."

Hope didn't answer, nor did Robert expect her to. After helping himself by dipping the tip of the knife into the snowy white drug, he began a soliloquy of sorts. He was an actor, after all. *Hamlet*. The prince of the Danes was not, however, pondering the existence of being or of not being. His queries were practical, not philosophical; but he caressed his prop, the knife, as if it were poor Yorick's skull.

"They say this doesn't really hurt. But who, I have to ask myself, are *they?* Survivors of slashed carotids and severed jugulars? I don't *think* so. Well. We'll see, and maybe hear. I promised not to damage your lungs, remember? And I'm a man of my word. So please, Hope, feel free to scream. Okay. Let's party. Just to show you how gallant I am, I'll come around and open your door."

*J*ane?"

Nick's query broke the silence that had traveled with them since Pacific Heights. They were inside the park, at the point where the road offered a choice, a decision that must be made, whether to journey west or east.

Jane knew that Nick was asking for her help with the monumental decision. But . . . "I don't see any lights at all."

Nor did he. Not even the faintest flicker. He would simply have to guess which way the car had turned, to sense where Hope was, to hear her silent calls.

But what Nick heard, all he heard, were the cackles of his own haunting ghosts, beckoning to him, goading and taunting, daring him to turn. Left. To them.

Nick *did* turn left, compelled by some invisible force—benevolent or evil—to drive toward the demons who would devour him . . . and, *please,* toward the cinnamon-haired angel he must save.

But there were ghosts, only ghosts, in the darkness, their screeches ever louder, their cackles ever more shrill, as he drew ever closer to the blackness in which they dwelled. This is the wrong way! they taunted. You need to turn around. For her. For *her*. But you can't, can you? *You are seduced.*

Then he saw it, they both did, they all did, for Molly, too, was suddenly on alert. *It,* the gleam of a knife. And then the luminous whiteness of an angel's flesh.

"Call 911," Nick told Jane as he switched the headlights to their brightest glow and opened the door.

The golden beams were floodlights on a sinister stage. As Nick approached, both actors stood frozen in the brilliant glare. The knife was at Hope's throat, and her wrists were bound, and her clothes, slashed and torn, were ragged proof of her courageous fight. But she was outmatched by the other actor on the glittering stage—the grotesque idol who even now believed he was in complete control.

"You'd be very smart to just turn around and drive

away," Robert advised the approaching shadow limned in gold. "Whoever the hell you are."

"Not a chance."

"*Nick.*"

"Oh," Robert mused. "Someone we know? Someone little Miss Hope called despite her promise to me? But you're not a cop, are you, Nick?"

"They're on their way. It's over, Forrest. Let her go."

" 'It's over, Forrest, let her go?' You've seen one too many Dirty Harry movies, Nickie boy—correction, one too few. You are woefully unarmed, bud, not a Magnum in sight."

It was true. Nicholas Wolfe had no gun, no man-made weapons of any kind. But he was definitely armed, lethally armed, with the power of his love and the fury of his ghosts.

"The cops have guns."

A darkly penciled brow shot up, astonished. "But they can't use them, Nick, not in real life—especially when I have such a real-life hostage as Hope. Of course, given the regard in which this particular prosecutor is held, San Francisco's Finest might just lay down their arms and hail me as a hero for killing her. Either way, Hope dies. You don't really *care*, do you, Nick? About Hope? Aren't you just the Good Samaritan dropping by? Too bad, Nick, because now you both die. First her. Then you. I gotta tell ya, Nick, your arrival on the scene, and the possibility that you really called the cops, makes me more than a little angry. I was planning to carve her up. *Slowly.* Oh, well, I'll do the carving after, if there's time. So. Let's see. As I recall, it's possible to slash all the way to bone."

"Wait." Nick commanded, so harshly that Robert withheld the lethal slash—for the moment.

"Something you want to say, Nick? Go ahead. Far be it

from me to preempt a supporting actor's lines. Or maybe it's something you want to *do*. I've been noticing you moving ever closer. You're stealthy, Nick, I'll give you that. Might there be a little Indian—excuse me, Native American—blood in your veins?" Robert studied the face that drew ever nearer and answered the question himself. "The cheekbones are definitely right, high and noble. And you have the look of a proud, if doomed, brave. You should have gone into acting, Nick. The casting directors would have eaten you up. You'd need the right name, of course. Nick Dances-with-Shadows, something like that, assuming your real name, your *reservation* name, isn't already perfectly good."

"It's Wolfe." The name he had chosen years ago, when he'd needed a new name, a different name—a name with which to flee his ghosts. "Nicholas Wolfe."

"Nicholas Wolfe. That'll do nicely. Pardon me, *would have done* nicely. Oh, well."

"Oh, well?" Nick echoed conversationally.

It was working, this conversation with the madman. As Nick drew ever closer, Robert drew closer as well—ever closer to dropping his guard. It wasn't yet safe for Nick to make his move. The knife was angled still into Hope's throat.

But in time, in this conversation of cocaine and madness, it would be safe. Time. It was as sharp edged, and as potentially lethal, as the knife itself. If Nick moved too soon, the blade would sever Hope's vulnerable flesh, and if he waited too long, the scream of sirens would fill the night air.

Nick needed a distraction—a surprise, not a warning. But what? How?

The answer, the who, came from the shadows, a small black missile launched by the Lakota woman herself.

She was an unlikely weapon, that gentle pet with the meticulously brushed teeth. But Molly's instincts were as old as time. She dashed not toward the man she loved, but to the feet of evil.

Surprised—but not significantly wounded—by the furry intruder, Robert nonetheless looked down, and in that unguarded moment Nick freed Hope from the madman's embrace, spinning her away even as he became a human shield.

Hope twirled, twisted, fell. Hard. Nothing broke her fall. Nothing could. Her hands were bound.

But she was safe. *Safe.* For now.

And even if she were badly injured, Nick believed that his courageous ballerina, his glorious dancer, could will herself to walk, to run, away.

Nick willed such flight now.

"The truck, Hope," he commanded even as Robert lunged at him. "You and Jane *go.*"

A distant corner of Nick's artistic mind painted a reassuring image: Jane, sitting the driver's seat, motor running, prepared to gun the engine the instant Hope climbed in.

It was a comforting tableau. But a false one. Jane was nearby. The stealthy she-warrior—carrying her secret weapon—had traversed the shadowed edges of light. Now Jane emerged from those shadows, ready to do battle, to help Nick vanquish his cocaine-enhanced foe.

During that summer, on an indigo screen at the Domaine, the "girls" had enjoyed myriad Hollywood offerings. They had wept together at the most romantic fare, and together—and fiercely—had scoffed as motion picture heroes fought to the death while their whimpering, useless womenfolk cowered nearby.

Jane Parish neither cowered nor whimpered. Nor was Jane frozen by fear. But she was useless, and perhaps harmful, to Nick's cause.

Her intrusion into the fray might easily distract the wrong man. Even Molly's well-intentioned interference could spell disaster for Nick. Jane unbound Hope's wrists and scooped Molly into her arms, and the three of them watched, ever vigilant, searching for the moment when it would be safe to join the dance of death.

Kill him, Nick, the two women silently implored, believing it would be so simple for Nick to murder the monster—knowing how easy for them, effortless really, such a willful killing would be.

But such lethal violence, it seemed, was not easy for Nick. He was trying to subdue Robert, not kill him, forsaking again and again what seemed perfect opportunities to plunge the knife.

Neither woman knew—how could they know—that Nick was battling a single madman and an army of ghosts: ghosts that wanted him to kill, goaded him to kill, especially when he felt Robert's heart pounding against him, as another man's heart had pounded, with violence, with lust.

Lust. Nick felt it now: Robert's carnal desire for blood. But Nick had almost made it. The sirens were blaring now—and near.

He could do this. He could hold both the madman and the ghosts—of his hatred and his rage—at bay until the police arrived.

But as Robert, too, heard the sirens, awareness dawned. And maybe, in those heightened moments before death, Robert Forrest sensed what his death would do to Nick: that Nick would die as well.

For the actor smiled, a grin of crimson and madness, as he twisted the knife toward his own heart—and grinned still, with satisfaction and triumph, as the razor-sharp blade pierced his flesh.

TWENTY-FIVE

*W*ell, well, well." Detective Larry Billings yawned as he surveyed the carnage, and carnival, of the scene. "What have we here? A disheveled prosecutor. A woman with green paint on her face. And an inconsequential pooch going crazy beside a blood-drenched cowboy who is hovering, strangely riveted, over a dead-as-dirt transvestite."

"Not just any transvestite, Lar," a fellow officer reported from the body. "I think it's Robert Forrest."

"What?"

"I really think it's him."

"It is," Hope confirmed.

"Suddenly I'm interested." The detective glared at Hope. "What's the story, Counselor? When your pal Mallory Mason couldn't get a conviction against an innocent man, you just decided to execute him anyway?"

Hope glared back. "You've got me, Detective. I asked Mr. Forrest to disguise himself as a woman and drive me, against my will, to this remote spot, where I insisted that he bind my wrists and slash my clothes, before my accomplices, one of whom was a cocker spaniel, leapt out of the shadows and killed him. Robert Forrest tried to murder me, Detective Billings. *Murder* me. He would have succeeded, too, if . . ."

Emotion caught up with her, gratitude toward these loved ones who had saved her life.

The loyal pet.

The courageous woman inexplicably denounced by Cass.

And, of course, the man who didn't want her.

And yet had come here.

For her.

Willing to die.

Perhaps Nick had died, was dying. He stood, transfixed, over Robert's body, oblivious even of Molly's whining pleas.

I need to go to him, to comfort him, for as long as I can— until he pushes me away. The thought came with urgent foreboding, as if each passing second sounded the death knell of Nick's life.

But Hope couldn't go to him. Not yet. There was the red tape of the law to wrap around this crimson carnage, not to mention the problem of the hostile cop.

"Robert Forrest was a *monster*, Detective. He tried to kill Cassandra, and very nearly succeeded in killing me."

"But he died instead."

"Yes. Are you disappointed? You'd rather be investigating two counts of murder one, I suppose, instead of a routine case of self-defense. But self-defense is what you've got, Detective. Self-defense, with two extremely credible witnesses. So, if you don't mind—"

"A few details, Counselor. Please." Detective Billings looked at Jane, truly seeing her, and authentically surprised by the beauty he beheld. She was quite striking, this mahogany-haired woman with the teal green cheeks. Striking and fierce—in a fierce, striking, quiet way. "You are . . . ?"

"Jane Parish. I own an art gallery in St. Helena."

"And why are you here?"

"Because a friend, a woman named Eleanor McBride, called me this evening, looking for Nick. Eleanor wanted Nick to follow Hope, to protect her, while she met with the mystery woman who claimed to have information about Cassandra's assault—but who was in fact Robert Forrest himself."

"And you knew where Nick was?"

"Yes. He was with me, in my studio. When I started to give him Hope's address, he asked if I knew where she lived and would show him the way. Of course I said yes."

"So the pooch is yours," the detective deduced.

"No," Jane countered quietly. "She's Nick's."

Detective Billings sighed. "Nick. Nick. Nick. It's time for me to hear from the man himself. Nick? Oh, Nick? Talk to me."

Talk to me. Talk to me.

Nick looked up at last, an expression as stark as death. His ravaged blue eyes did not find Hope, or Jane, or the beloved creature at his feet.

Nick looked instead at the detective who was so like that other bully, that other cop, the man whose heart had pounded with lust, with violence, so very close to this haunted place of death in Golden Gate Park.

Nick's voice was as bleak as his eyes. "My name is Nicholas Doe."

"Doe?" Detective Billings echoed. "I don't believe I've

ever met a *Nicholas* Doe. Lots of Janes and Johns, of course, corpses found in alleyways, stiffs that no one claims."

Or wants, Nick realized vaguely. Except for the season of his birth, he would have been John, not Nicholas, but *Doe* either way. And now the life of Nicholas Doe had come full circle, ending as it began, a human being no one knew, no one missed, no one wanted, no one claimed.

Nick's calm blue gaze found Hope. "Will you do something for me?"

"Yes." *Anything.*

"Take care of Molly." *Love my little Moll.*

"Of course," she whispered. "But you can take care of her, Nick. You will."

A slight smile touched his blood-splattered face. Then the warrior, drenched in authentic war paint, looked at the Lakota warrior with teal green cheeks. "Will you call the Tylers for me, Jane? Tell them they need to find someone else to look after the horses."

"I'll look after the horses, Nick, until you—"

"I won't be coming back to Napa."

"Nick," Hope implored him, "what's going on?"

"Yes, *Nick,*" Detective Billings mimicked. "What is going on? I have to confess I'm getting real intrigued. Care to give me a hint?"

"I wonder," another officer mused. "There was a murder, just a block or two from here, maybe eighteen, twenty years ago. The victim was a cop, Al Garrett, one of the most decorated men on the force. And now that I think of it, Al's partner was John Madrid. Craig's father."

"Lordy, Lordy . . ." Detective Billings fairly salivated at the revelation. "This gets better by the second. A murder, you say?"

"A real brutal one. Al and his wife—Iris, if I recall correctly—believed in giving every kid a chance, no matter how disturbed or delinquent the hellion was. The Garretts took in kids from the street, fostered them, cared for them."

"And?"

"And his charity cost Al his life. He was stabbed to death, in his sleep, by a fifteen-year-old psychopath named Nicholas Doe. . . ."

TWENTY-SIX

*T*he tabloids went wild, issuing special weekend editions, which were gobbled up by hordes of shoppers, even as they purchased gifts of Yuletide cheer.

Traditional Christmastime items—sightings of Jolly Saint Nick over Iceland, Rudolph saving the day at a foggy O'Hare—were replaced by stories of another Nick, not jolly at all, and the brilliant crimson of savagely spilled blood.

Art critics and forensic psychologists alike pored over the paintings of Nicholas Wolfe, née Doe—until Jane Parish realized who they were. She tossed them out of her gallery and bolted the doors, but not before insisting that they print her assessment of Nick: that he was one of the finest men she had ever known.

Jane's pronouncement was carried by all the tabloids, as were the evaluations of the psychologists and critics who

341

had managed to catch a glimpse of Nick's work before Jane threw them out. Their analyses were surprisingly sympathetic and uniformly laudatory. Nicholas Doe was an artist of immense talent, they proclaimed. His paintings of conflict and of rage contained all the torment, all the self-loathing, and all the genius of Van Gogh.

The mainstream press steered clear of the tabloid psychobabble, but they most definitely joined the fray. And why not? The story, as sensational as it was, was true—hence news.

Indeed, the *Chronicle* had extensive archival information on the brutal assassination of Al Garrett. Nineteen years ago, as the murder of the celebrated cop went unavenged, Bay Area journalists had moaned aloud and in print their sorrow, and outrage, that the teenage killer had vanished without a trace.

Now, in whispers and off-the-record, members of the fourth estate marveled at how magnificently the story had aged, like the finest of wines, so much more interesting, more *complex,* than had Nick been captured at age fifteen.

The Robert Forrest twist alone made it worth the wait. Was the famous actor really a transvestite? Had Cassandra Winter Tessier known his sordid little secret and threatened to reveal all to the Hollywood press? Was that why the cross-dressing Thespian had wanted her dead?

But it was the Hope Tessier ingredient that made the impeccably aged story the remarkable vintage that it was—even without Robert. Indeed, although the police investigation was still open, the death of Robert Forrest would, even the tabloids agreed, be ruled self-defense.

But there remained that extraordinary coincidence, surely *not* a coincidence: Hope's zealous prosecution of one Craig Madrid, whose father had been the dead cop's partner—and best friend. Had Nicholas Doe regretted not executing Al Garrett's partner, too? the tabloid journalists queried. Was that why Hope, as a gift to her *lover* Nick, destroyed John Madrid's only son?

The mainstream press alluded, only in passing, to the potential legal battles the cinnamon-haired prosecutor might face: disbarment for harboring a fugitive; and reversal—or at least mistrial—in the matter of the *People* versus *Craig Madrid.*

Most legitimate legal pundits preferred to cast Hope in the role the citizens of San Francisco knew well—that of avenging angel of justice. The passionate prosecutor had had no idea, the legalists opined, that the artist Hope knew as Nicholas Wolfe was, in fact, a killer.

And now that she knew?

She would not, of course, be prosecuting the case. She could not, without the appearance of conflict, seek to convict for murder the man who had saved her life, especially given the potential penalty for that crime.

The issue of punishment was a fascinating one: the sparkling bubbles in an already perfectly vinted champagne. Had the teenage murderer been apprehended at age fifteen, his likely punishment would have been incarceration, in a juvenile facility, until he was twenty-one. Nicholas Doe would have walked free after that, an assassin who had been given a clean slate.

But the teenage killer had run, and in estimation of the jurists polled, special circumstances definitely applied for the boy who was now a man. The victim was a cop, after all, and the many, many stab wounds made the crime a particularly heinous one, and it was only luck that Al Garrett's wife, Iris, had herself managed to escape the lethal blows.

It was a capital case, the experts agreed. A death penalty case. And, they concurred, despite the debt Hope Tessier herself owed Nicholas Doe for saving *her* life, the soldier for justice would not necessarily attempt to save *his*. She would remain mute, remain remote, while her colleagues in the DA's office made the decision about the punishment they would seek.

On Sunday a new twist appeared. COP-KILLER LINKED TO DOUBLE MURDER IN NAPA, the tabloids declared. NICK KILLED HOPE'S MOTHER!!! PROSECUTOR OUT FOR REVENGE!!!!

The accompanying articles liberally quoted their principal source. "I knew he was a thief," Sibyl Courtland Raleigh avowed. "And I *suspected* him of tampering with the brakes. I wanted the police to arrest him, then and there. But Victor [Tessier] convinced them not to—not only that day on the mountain, but several days later as well. That's *so* Victor. He's a brilliant musician, of course, but when it comes to seeing *evil,* well, dear, brilliant Victor is *more than* a little blind."

By contrast, according to Sibyl, her best friend Franny's beloved daughter was "perfectly sighted, and incredibly smart. Hope is *passionate* about justice. For all I know, the reason she became a lawyer—a decision made shortly after Franny's death, Franny's *murder*—was so that she could put men like Nicholas Doe behind bars, *and in the gas chamber,* where they belong. When Hope saw him again—can you believe he had the nerve to return to Napa?—she vowed to avenge Franny's murder. At last. Will Hope encourage her fellow prosecutors to seek the death penalty? You can *count* on it."

Hope read the latest tabloid offering on Sunday afternoon, shortly before her visit to the county jail.

She was going to see Nick. She had to. And would. Somehow.

Nick had made it very clear, achingly clear, on Friday night that he didn't want to see her. Not ever. And not Jane, either. Or the public defender assigned to his case.

But Hope had to see him, and she was dependent on others—hostile toward her—to deliver to Nick her impassioned plea. The jail guards were police officers, after all, and now, on top of the enmity she'd engendered by convicting one of their own, came the speculation that she was linked, as Bonnie was linked to Clyde, to the brutal murder of a man in blue.

The guard stationed at the locked door through which Hope needed to pass was, in fact, reading a tabloid. Today's tabloid. But when he looked up at her, Hope saw undisguised interest and a flicker of respect—as if she were, in fact, an avenging angel who would not rest until Nicholas Doe met his death in a suffocating mist of fumes.

"May I help you, Ms. Tessier?"

Hope shifted tack, from Nick's friend—imploring that she be permitted to visit—to the attorney she was, the prosecutor who was wedded, above all else, to justice. She was dressed for the part and even carried her briefcase, and she managed a most professional tone as she placed her request.

"I need to see"—Nick—"your prisoner."

Hope didn't need to clarify which inmate. The jail, at least this cell block, was virtually empty on this afternoon two days before Christmas. The cop killer was imprisoned here, in a remote and unmonitored cage.

Nicholas Doe didn't seem the suicide type, someone decided. The psychopaths never are. And if the prisoner hung himself in his distant cell, to be discovered only after the deed was done? So what? The taxpayers would be thrilled.

"Come on in," the guard invited her.

"Actually, I wonder if you would tell him that I insist on seeing him, but that the choice of venues is his. I want to do this by the book. If the prisoner would prefer to meet with me in an attorney room, I want to honor that request. Okay?"

"Sure. I've been meaning to wander on down there and tell him about today's headlines anyway."

"Tell him?"

"He doesn't seem too keen on reading the papers himself, so I'm keeping him informed."

"Maybe you should defer telling him about the most recent revelations until after he and I have met."

The guard grinned. "Good idea."

"In fact, it would be best, for now, if he knew nothing about our interest in his involvement in the Napa fatalities."

"You got it."

The guard ambled off, with an unmistakable eagerness in his arthritic gait. Hope watched him lumber away, down a long gray ribbon of scuffed linoleum and eventually out of sight.

When the guard returned many minutes later, he was smiling.

"He doesn't want to see you. Not at all, and in a very big way. I told him that was too damn bad. In which case he prefers an attorney room to his cell. We'll meet you there."

There. Hope arrived, many minutes before Nick, in the soundproof room where attorneys met with clients and where this prisoner chose to meet with the assistant DA.

This prisoner . . . her Nick . . . who did not, perhaps, want her to see him in his cell, a caged beast.

But this was even worse, Hope realized when, at last, he appeared.

For Nick was caged, still, in his own private prison. And the beast was chained. His graceful gait, once so powerful and so free, was crippled by the shackles at his feet, and a heavy chain, wrapped twice around his waist, also bound his hands.

"You want me in here with you?" the guard asked as he shoved his shackled prisoner into the soundproof room.

"No," Hope replied as an avenging prosecutor would, calmly, professionally, even as her heart screamed. *Unchain him! Please. I'm safe with him. So very safe.* "Thank you. I'm fine."

"Okay. I'll be right outside."

The door closed, and they were alone, in the thunderous silence, facing each other across the scarred wooden table where criminals and their attorneys pondered life and death.

Nick saw what worrying about him had done to her—tainted her, tarnished her, touched her with sadness where, for her, he only wanted joy.

And Hope saw what being caged, being chained, had done to him. His eyes, once so blue, were gray, and from their clouded depths came a horrifying truth. He was dead. Already.

Already dead.

Even his voice came from the grave.

"I asked you not to come."

"I know. But I need your help."

The faintest wisp of blue glittered in the deadly gray, the tiniest glint of light, of life, for her. "I'll tell whomever you want, as often as you want me to, that you knew nothing about me."

But I know everything about you, Nick. Almost everything.

Hope had access to all the files on Nicholas Doe—the murder investigation conducted nineteen years before, as well as the investigation into the teenage murderer himself, everything that could be uncovered about the first fifteen years of the young killer's life.

Hope knew things the press did not, revelations the police were unlikely to leak, ever, about their fallen colleague.

Those revelations were reason enough for murder, motive enough for the brutal slaughter that Detective Garrett's slaying had been.

"I know what Al Garrett did to you."

Nick shrugged, weighted by chains, yet unweighted for her. It was nothing, his shrug said. *Forget about me.* "Big Al was a violent guy. He liked beating people up, loved it, actually, especially when his victims were smaller, weaker, than he."

"I mean, I know that he raped you."

You can't know that. I don't want you to know that.

"His partner, John Madrid, came forward after his death," Hope continued. "Al got drunk one night and confessed all." Everything, including a cruelty that was perhaps even worse than rape: for the abusive cop had revealed to Nick the horrific circumstances of his birth, *and where he was born,* and had taunted the boy, raped the boy, with that appalling truth. "Detective Madrid warned his contemptible partner that if he didn't promise to stop abusing you, immediately, he would turn him in. Only you know if Al Garrett kept his promise, if he left you alone during the two months before his death."

Of course he didn't. He couldn't. There had been even more lust, and more violence, during those final months, as if Al Garrett knew the ravishment was coming to an end and hated that closure even more than he loathed his own disgusting need, his perverted obsession—and the small, beautiful boy who evoked it. The detective had been attracted to women only, and only to grown women—until Nick. *Nick* was to blame, Al Garrett reasoned; Nick, who was *trash.* Worthless trash who had seduced him.

Hope looked at the man that beautiful boy had become. The beauty was harsh now, ruthless and raw, and the boy who had been so small and so frail—even into his teens— was powerful and strong.

"Why didn't you leave?"

Nicholas Doe's sensual gray eyes, so sensual even in this living death, did not care. Refused to care. "Al wasn't the first adult male who'd been interested in me. I knew he wouldn't be the last. It wouldn't be any different anywhere else, and there were things I liked about living there."

"The horses in the park."

"Yes."

"And Hank."

Nick hesitated a long, harsh, aching heartbeat.

"Yes," he admitted quietly. "And Hank."

Hank . . . whom Nick had told her about on that long-ago September day, when she was telling him about rainbows and fairy tales and her own beloved Grandpère. Hank was Nick's Grandpère, the man who had taught Nick about horses, and who had never hurt the little boy, and who had cared about the orphaned Nick just as Jean-Luc, her own Grandpère, had cared about the orphan Chase.

Hope's voice softened, for all of them, the cherished grandfathers and the orphans they loved. "Hank's statement, taken the following afternoon, is paraphrased in the police report. But I'm sure I know his exact words. 'Well, sir, Officer, I know for a fact that Nick didn't kill anyone. I know, because he *told* me.' "

"Hank was an old man. Why shatter his faith?" Nick's eyes were as harsh, and as unrevealing, as his face. But his vision was quite unimpaired. Nicholas Doe saw Hope's faith, and it scared the hell out of him. "You said you needed my help. Please tell me what you need." *Then leave.*

"Okay. What I need, Nick, is for you to permit me to represent you."

"No."

"Please."

"You're a prosecutor."

"But I don't believe in prosecuting an innocent man."
His gray gaze told her nothing. Did not flicker. Did not
glow. "If you're worried about my abilities as a defense attorney, then will you at least let me—and Chase and Cassandra and Eleanor and Jane—get you the best trial lawyer
money can buy? We want to, Nick. We all want to."

All. Especially Chase. Hope had revealed to Chase only
the physical abuse Nick had endured from Al Garrett's brutal fists. Chase didn't mourn the cowardly cop any more
than he mourned Robert Forrest. But Chase mourned Nick,
mourned *for* Nick, and Chase wished with quiet fury that
it had been he who'd killed Robert, as he had wanted to.
Chase Tessier could have murdered Robert without re-
morse, and with his bare hands, master vintner hands unsullied by a long-ago—and entirely justifiable—crime.

"I'm not worried about your abilities, and I'm grateful
for your offer. For all of your offers." Grateful, and
stunned. So stunned that the ravaged corpse almost jolted
back to life. Limitless money they were offering him. And
boundless love. And never-ending faith. Extraordinary
gifts. But far too late. "But this isn't going to end well."

"*Yes it is.* It has to, Nick. For Molly. She misses you, desperately. *Frantically.*" Hope had not planned to tell Nick
that truth, had wanted to spare him such pain. And now?

Now his eyes were as gray as the mists of gas in a chamber of death. "My arraignment is Tuesday. I'm going to
plead guilty."

"You *can't.*"

He almost smiled. "Sure I can. And will. I'm not interested in an abuse-excuse defense, Hope. In any defense. So,
I think we're done."

Nick was not a dancer, or so he had said. But there was
such grace as this man, this chained beast, hobbled and
bound, stood up from his chair. Where another man, in

shackles, might have struggled, Nick did not; and his balance, where others might have teetered, did not falter.

He was a solitary dancer. He had to be. He could not permit even the first movement of a pas de deux; could not allow the copper-haired ballerina to offer her graceful hands, her helpful touch. He had to get away from her. For her.

Now.

"Wait, Nick. Please. Just one last thing." Hope withdrew a sheet of paper from her briefcase. She couldn't hand it to him, he had no hands, so she set it on the wooden table in front of where he stood. "Do you recognize this?"

"No."

"You didn't even look at it! Look at it. Please."

Nick obeyed. He looked down at the paper, for a while. Then he looked at her. "I don't recognize it. Sorry. Is that all?"

"Yes, Nick. That's all."

*M*olly greeted Hope at her apartment door, sensing Nick, searching for Nick, and frantic when he wasn't to be found.

"He's not with me, Moll." Hope patted the trembling fur. *He will never be with me.* "But he's going to be with you. Soon."

Hope's impassioned promise was undermined by the message that blinked on her answering machine, news from the private investigator she'd hired twenty-four hours before. Hope was absorbing the blow when the phone rang.

It was Cassandra, calling from the château, her voice laced with worry but bright with cheer.

"Have we got a deal for you, Hope Tessier. Chase and I thought we'd mosey on into the city, do a little last minute Christmas shopping, then pick you up and bring you here. We're ready to mosey now, or whenever you say. We'd really like you to come today, and spend an extra night at Montagne Noir—as many extra nights as you like."

Hope stared out her window, at the spectacular view from her Pacific Heights perch, the famous tableau of bridge and bay. The frigid water, on this wintry afternoon, was shiny and smooth, a shimmering silver platter on which was being served, to the City by the Bay, the rock island known as Alcatraz.

"Actually, Cass, I was just about to call you. I can't make it for Christmas Eve, after all. Or for Christmas. I really can't."

"You *have* to."

Because of Victor, Hope thought. Victor—with whom she needed to forge some kind of peace. "I know Victor has something important to say, and all things being equal I'd like to hear it. But you can tell me what he says, and at some future time he and I will talk. But not now. There's simply too much going on here for me to get away."

"Too much, Hope? Like what? Like reading the police files for the zillionth time? And worrying about Nick, wishing you could see him, knowing he'd refuse if you tried?"

"I saw him."

"Oh . . ." Cassandra's voice softened. "And?"

"He's innocent, Cass."

"Hope, I know that's what you want to believe."

"No. He *is* innocent. Which I will prove." *Somehow.* Her mind was already whirring. There were other witnesses, potential witnesses, she would instruct the private investigator to find. Long shots, admittedly, but . . . "I *will*."

"I know you will," Cassandra, prophetess—and

friend—swiftly concurred. "But please come to Montagne Noir. At least for Christmas Eve. Forward your calls, and come. Let *us* come get *you*. Please? The change of venue will do you good."

But Nick won't have a change of venue. He will be in jail, caged, chained, forsaken. On Christmas Eve *of all days*.

Hope's gaze fell from the view of Alcatraz to the trembling creature at her feet. Molly needed her comforters, her toys, the beloved gifts and scents of Nick from the carriage house at Belvedere.

Hope would retrieve as well, from Belvedere, clean clothes for Nick: denim unstained with blood, to wear—in lieu of a prison jumpsuit adorned with chains—to his arraignment . . . and to wear again, without bondage of any kind, the day he walked free.

"All right. I'll come. I'll drive myself. I'll be there tomorrow afternoon, in time for whatever it is Victor has to say."

TWENTY-SEVEN

MONTAGNE NOIR

MONDAY, DECEMBER TWENTY-FOURTH

*T*heir houseguest—their *châ-teau*guest, Victor—had gone for a drive, and Hope and Molly wouldn't be arriving for a while, and together, Chase and Cassandra had already prepared the meal and set the table . . . and so, together, on this Christmas Eve afternoon, they took a nap.

Cassandra took such revitalizing catnaps almost every day. And Chase joined her, whenever he could, making love to her before she fell asleep, and again when she awakened in his arms.

They had loved on this afternoon, and now she was awakening to the strong, sure heartbeats of the man who wanted her, who needed her, in his life. For the rest of his life.

Cassandra turned in his arms and met his clear gray eyes. "Hi."

"Hi." Chase kissed the golden curls that framed her face.

These curls, this cap of shining amber, knew his kisses very well. The soft golden cloud was, perhaps, so luxuriant because of his nurturing, these caresses of such tenderness that had begun that day, a month ago, when Chase was permitted to love his Cassie again.

They were pioneers still, explorers still, discovering ever more about each other as they lived their love. Cassandra looked at him now, at the silver gray eyes that welcomed her, trusted her, to see so clearly their most intimate depths.

"What?" she asked softly.

"I was thinking about Victor."

"Worrying about Victor."

His smile, this intimate smile, was only for her. "Yes. Worrying about Victor."

"If I'd known how difficult it would be for him to be here at Christmas, I probably wouldn't have suggested that he come."

"But you do know," Chase countered gently. "At least, your hidden memory knows about Victor, and Christmas in Napa, and whatever it is he's planning to tell Hope and me. Victor wants to tell us, whatever it is. He wouldn't have accepted our invitation if he didn't."

"Well," Cass murmured. "Whatever it is in my memory, and Victor's past, I guess we'll find out soon enough. Something else is worrying you. Hope?"

"Sure."

"And Nick."

"And Nick."

"And something else."

"I spoke with Dr. Dane."

"Oh," she whispered.

Dr. Dane was Cassandra's obstetrician in Seattle, the doctor who had delivered, and cared for, their baby girl. Cass had given Dr. Dane permission to speak with Chase, to share with him the medical details she remembered only vaguely. The details hadn't mattered, not then, because there was the overwhelming truth: the prediction, offered gently, from the start, that her newborn daughter was going to die.

But the details mattered now, to both Cassandra and Chase. And he knew them now, and his loving gray gaze was worried. And sad.

"Oh," she whispered again. "Was there something genetic, after all?"

"No," Chase reassured her softly. "Not genetic. Developmental. Just as you remembered. A very rare anomaly that had nothing to do with you."

"Or with you."

"No."

"And which would be unlikely to happen again?"

"Extremely unlikely." Chase smiled, for her, as he hid from her what else the doctor had said. The experienced obstetrician had never before seen an infant with such an anomaly achieve any hope of viability on its own. But this baby, their precious little girl, had been so loved by her mother, had been welcomed in Cassandra's womb with such care and such joy, that she had survived to be born . . . only to struggle for four valiant days . . . only to die.

Chase could not tell his beloved Cassie that anguished truth. Could not possibly.

So Chase Tessier smiled, and wept inside, and after a moment permitted worry to darken his gaze anew.

"But?"

"But Dr. Dane said you nearly died."

"After *she* died, Chase. After our baby died. I told you that."

She had told him so much. Everything. Every truth to this man she loved. She had wanted to die, wanted that desperately, wanted nothing more than to sleep forever with her baby girl. But there were hospital bills, substantial ones, which Cassandra was determined to pay as soon as she could—gratefully pay. Everyone had fought so hard for their daughter, every second of those days and nights in the ICU.

In the beginning it was the bills, and her gratitude, that kept Cassandra alive. She returned to her job at the Seattle Art Museum, was welcomed back—even though it seemed unlikely that she would truly be able to work. She was so changed from the Cassandra who, just ten days before, and with such hope, such joy, had told them she was returning to the baby's father.

It seemed impossible that the devastated creature who returned, instead, from such loss could actually resume her tours—any tours, much less the lively, intelligent romps that drew raves for the pregnant mother-to-be.

But Cassandra did resume the tours, her tours—precise replicas, exquisite encores, of what had come before. She was an actress, after all—and she needed to do this, in a bittersweet and punishing way. She needed to remember the baby girl who danced inside, wanted to, and the pain was necessary, too—for despite the vague memories of being told it wasn't her fault, she knew it wasn't true.

It would take a while to pay the bills, which was fine, this pain was so deserved. She was working still, dying slowly—still—when Adrian Ellis became the talk of the town. The famous director had come to the Emerald City to shoot a film, and he had brought with him an ensemble of Hollywood's most glittering stars.

The location sites, listed daily in the morning paper, were mostly downtown, just blocks from the museum, an irresistible chance for stargazing that was seized, whenever possible, by every employee but Cass.

She didn't accompany her co-workers. But she was so very aware of the emotional magnet beckoning to her, daring her to journey to memories of magic, when Adrian Ellis's *Duet* was on location at the Domaine. . . .

It was the pain, the punishment, of those memories that compelled Cassandra to Pioneer Square. She stood in the crush of the crowd, a huge gathering despite the drizzle, her blue eyes seeing only the past—including the image of Adrian Ellis arriving with his video of her winery tour and telling her to consider it her screen test should she ever pursue an acting career.

Then, in the drizzle in Pioneer Square, Adrian was there, speaking her name—and remarking, when at last she focused on him, at the spectacular coincidence. "Kismet," he would later say—for he had a script, and he'd actually thought of her the moment he read it, and then there she was, standing in the Seattle rain.

It was kismet, she realized; her own inevitable destiny. For dying was too easy, not punishment enough. But this, her surrender to the self-destructive urge that had taunted her since childhood, was better, *harder*. This: the willingness to be someone else, anyone else, and to deny herself, her *self*, entirely, and to acknowledge that the loss, the death, of the real Cassandra was really no loss at all.

So she became the actress that she had both dreaded and been destined to be. And it wasn't about fame, just about work, about working all the time, as much as possible—denying Cassandra, hating Cassandra, losing Cassandra . . . then came the role that was Cassandra, the real Cassandra, the woman Chase Tessier had loved . . . and Robert was there, pretending to be Chase, but not Chase, never Chase . . . and then she had almost truly died . . . but she had awakened to him. To Chase.

To whom, in the past few weeks, she had confessed everything.

Everything.

"Chase?" she asked softly. "I told you I wanted to die."

"Dr. Dane isn't talking about after," he said quietly. "She's talking about at the time. You lost a lot of blood, she said." *Too much, she said, to do what you did, what you insisted on doing—spending every second of her life with our baby girl.*

"And I was *fine,* Chase. Dr. Dane is so nice, and I know she was worried about me, and that you are, but you don't need to be."

Her hands touched his beloved face, and she smiled, until he did, and after a moment he kissed her fingers and then her palms. And, smiling still, Chase studied her wedding ring.

The golden band was severed still, the neat and shiny incision between roses quite unrepaired. Despite numerous discussions, at first solemn and then teasing, Cassandra had resolutely refused to relinquish her wedding ring, their wedding ring, even for a moment.

"What are we going to do about this?" he asked.

"Nothing!"

"I suppose, with the proper kind of shielding, it could be soldered back together right where it is."

"No, *thank* you. At least not anytime very soon." Her eyes teased no longer, but they were brilliant—bright blue—with love. "The slice permits lots of room to expand, so I can wear it, and keep wearing it, no matter how puffy and pregnant I get."

"Cassie . . ."

She shared his worry and his fear. Another pregnancy scared them both, for reasons that were different and yet the same. Each was terrified, most of all, for the other. Cassandra did not want, for Chase, the immense sadness of losing another child. Chase feared such sadness for her as well, and now there was the terror of losing her, too, if she had such excessive bleeding again.

Cassandra met his worry with a glorious smile. Cassandra Winter Tessier was not going anywhere. She would not be lost, never be lost, ever again. She was going to give this man, this orphan who had never wanted children until he fell in love with her, a family. His family. To cherish. To love.

"It will be fine," she assured her silver-eyed sorcerer. "Everything will be just fine."

They were protected, forever, by the shimmering pastel rainbow he had conjured just for them, the misting arch of crystalline sunlight and glittering gems.

She and Chase were safe. He had made them *so safe*.

But Cassandra wished, how she wished, that she could sprinkle a little rainbow dust—even a single pastel sparkle—onto Nick, onto Victor, onto Hope.

*V*ictor Tessier roamed to familiar places, dangerous places, on this dangerously familiar day.

Even the weather, on this Christmas Eve, was treacherously cold, the kind of bitterness that promised ice as day became night.

"Victor!"

The voice was familiar, and not dangerous in the least. "Hello, Sibyl."

"You're *here*."

It was a generic "here"—the valley—and a specific one . . . this oak-shaded street in Rutherford near what had been, long ago, the cozy pub where one drank, at Christmas, steaming mugs of hot buttered rum.

"I am."

"Why?"

"Chase invited me. Chase and Cassandra."

"Before the Nicholas Wolfe—Doe—fiasco?"

"Yes."

"Well. It's wonderful that you're here, for many reasons, not the least of which is that now you can speak to the police. I've tried, but they're in a disgustingly holiday mood."

"The police?" Victor echoed, caught in the netherworld between present and past. *The police can't know, can't ever know.* "Why?"

"Because of *Nick,* of course. Because he probably did tamper with Franny's brakes."

"You know damn well he didn't."

"I know damn well that he stole her necklace, tried to."

"I doubt that, too. But so what if he had? He would have been welcome to it."

"What?"

"Nick helped Hope that day in a way that I never could. And, Sibyl, Nicholas Doe saved Hope's life last Friday night. He and Molly and—"

"You're not planning to see her. Victor, *please* tell me you're not going to see Jane."

On that cold, gray Christmas Eve thirty-four years ago, nineteen-year-old Sibyl Courtland had made a similar plea, with comparable passion—and equivalent horror. Yes, Victor Tessier had told her then. *Yes. I am.*

But today, beneath these foreboding pewter skies, Victor said, "No, Sibyl. I'm not."

A glimmer of satisfaction replaced her horror, followed by another plea, smiling and soft. "But we are going to have dinner, aren't we, Victor? Just the two of us? For old times' sake?"

"I'll have to get back to you on that, Sib. I'm not sure how much longer I'll be here." *How much longer I can stay.*

Victor and Sibyl parted as they had on that long-ago afternoon, with a promise to speak again later.

On that distant afternoon, within moments of leaving Sibyl, Victor had gone to Mariposa, the estate on Zinfandel Lane where Jane Parish lived with her parents in a carriage house cloaked in wisteria.

Jane's mother was the estate's live-in cook, and her father was the keeper of horses—and of the gate as well, when it came to his precious only child.

"But we love each other," that beloved daughter implored. "Victor and I will love each other—always."

Thomas Parish did not doubt his daughter's love for the Tessier heir even though at seventeen Jane was an innocent and Victor, at twenty, was fully a man.

The gap between Jane and Victor was far greater, however, than the disparity in their experience or their age. It was a vast abyss, and it doomed the young lovers from the very start. In the end, Thomas Parish knew, Victor Tessier would not choose the half-breed daughter of servants. The wealthy, worldly virtuoso would play with her, a dilettante's toy, then cast her aside.

Which is precisely what happened.

Victor shattered Jane's heart.

And his own.

Jane would not let him inside on that long-ago Christmas Eve, would not open the carriage house door more than a most slender crack. But Victor saw her face through that frugal opening—saw the anguish in her dark, lovely eyes, and the limpness of her mahogany hair, and her cheeks, sunken and sallow, beneath her proud Lakota bones.

"Victor?" Her once lush voice was as pale, as drawn, as her flesh. "Why are you here?"

"I've come to apologize, Jane, to tell you that I miss you, and love you, and want us to be together—always."

"Oh, Victor. No."

"*Yes.* Will you let me in? Please?"

"I . . . can't."

Her parents should not have been here, not at this hour on Christmas Eve. Her mother should have been in the mansion, preparing the feast, and the horses needed tending, as always, even on this festive day. But perhaps one, or both, were inside. "We'll meet later, then. Okay? Later, Jane. Whenever you say. Give me a chance to explain. Please."

"No. I can't. It's too late, Victor, don't you see? It's far too late."

"Jane . . ."

"We're leaving, Victor."

"Leaving?"

"Moving away. Tomorrow."

"Where?"

"I can't tell you."

"I'll find out, Jane. I'll find out, and I'll find you, and—"

"No, Victor. Please. *Please.* I have to go. Now. I *do.* Good-bye."

Jane closed the wooden door framed in wisteria and fragrant, on this day, with a pine-scented wreath. She closed the door quietly, but with a thunder Victor Tessier would never forget.

He stood in the fragrance of pines and the bounty of lavender blossoms, waiting for the door to open anew, hoping, praying—and leaving only when he was compelled to do so.

"How dare you come here?" Thomas Parish demanded when he returned from his chores. "Haven't you done enough?"

Now, on this dangerously familiar day thirty-four years later, the maestro was returning to the estate on Zinfandel Lane. It was an impulse, foolish and mad, but not dangerous on its face. Jane lived here no more. Perhaps no one did. "Mariposa" had been abandoned in favor of "Belvedere," and maybe the carriage house had been abandoned, too, the era of servants—and their quarters—long since past.

But, Victor discovered, someone did live in the silvery cottage. Someone who might be alarmed by the sight of a stranger, especially a tormented one, appearing out of nowhere on this holiday eve.

Might be? Would be, for whoever lived here was home. An old blue pickup truck was parked beneath the carport, and a shining green Infiniti angled across the pebbled drive, and lights glowed from within the cottage, golden beacons of welcome on this dark December day.

No pine-fragrant Christmas wreath adorned the familiar wooden door, but the wisteria blossomed lavender still. And the door itself, sealed so tightly then, was ajar, and where there had been thunderous silence, there was commotion, excitement . . . and then a small black nose . . . and then paws, *paws,* reaching up to him as if she had been waiting for him, missing him.

Desperately.

It was a welcome of love for Victor Tessier—here, in this place where love had perished. Victor curled the enthusiastic bundle into his arms and spoke through the wild lapping on his face.

"Well, hello there. Who are . . ."

But he knew. According to Chase, Nicholas Wolfe—Hope's Nick—lived at Belvedere, an equestrian estate nearby; and since Friday night, Hope had been caring for the cocker spaniel that Victor had met, once before, amid the tragedy on Montagne Noir.

"You're Molly," he murmured. Molly, who couldn't possibly remember him and yet perhaps sensed, by the uncanny sympathy of gentle creatures, that he was hurting, aching. *As was Hope*—in this charming cottage where his love, and hers, had lived . . . and died. "Molly? Let's go find Hope."

What Victor found, inside the cottage, was a stack of comforters, and a trio of bowls, and a vast assortment of canine toys.

But no Hope.

"Where is she?" Victor asked as he gently lowered the cocker spaniel to the shining wooden floor. "Where's Hope?"

Did Molly understand? Probably not . . . and yet Nick had spoken to her for nine years, this creature who simply loved the sound of his voice, had confided things to Molly he had never told another living soul.

Most likely Molly just wanted Hope to see Victor, the wonderful new treasure she had found. After a single circle of sheer energy, Molly bounded up the hardwood stairs to the second floor.

Hope was in Nick's studio, having been led there, lured there, by Molly, in her frantic search for Nick.

He's not here Molly, sweetheart, Hope had whispered as she followed. Oh, little Molly, he's not here.

But Hope stopped following when they reached Nick's studio, for there it was, Nick's *Seasons of the Soul*, his quartet of paintings.

Of her.

In one, perhaps the first one painted, she was a ballerina, twirling in a meadow of wildflowers. She had been heavy on that day, or so she had believed. But this ballerina was neither heavy nor thin. She—her soul—was merely dancing, merely soaring, merely free. This was summer, Hope supposed. The season of celebration beneath a golden sun that cast no shadows.

And such a stark contrast to the portrait beside it, the dead of winter that had come that same September afternoon, when Hope had stood on the precarious edge of an obsidian cliff, clutching a midnight black puppy as she'd witnessed, as her soul knew, such carnage, such betrayal, such death.

But you didn't die, the artist had told her. And she had wondered if it was true, if she had really been alive, again, until him. But there she was, before she ever knew that Nick had returned to the valley. She stood on the courthouse steps in San Francisco, addressing the media, her hair swirled by the wind, her face damp with rain, her gaze determined and proud. This was autumn, the season when the soul realized its bountiful harvest—when *her* soul yielded its gold-and-cinnamon-hued abundance of passion, her passion, for justice.

Then there was the fourth portrait, the final portrait. Of her, in springtime. The springtime of her soul. The portrait was just painted, just finished, before the artist journeyed to a winter from which he seemed resolved never to return.

Hope stood again in the meadow of wildflowers, but she was a woman, not a girl, awakening to love, blossoming to desire, a flower so confident, so bold, that she gazed courageously at the glowing sun, knowing it wanted her . . . that *he* wanted her. She was so ready for his touch, this springtime flower, so willing to feel his fire and his heat.

"He loves you very much."

Nick. *Nick.* Was he truly here, behind her, confessing his love? No. Hope knew he couldn't be. The deep, gentle voice could not possibly be real.

It was, she knew, merely a phantom of her wishes, a hallucination of her fatigue.

But Hope Tessier turned toward that gossamer wish, unafraid to face the apparition, longing to see the beloved mirage.

"*Victor*. Why . . ." *are you here?* What had begun as a demand drifted into bewildered silence.

"Why doesn't matter," he said very gently. "What matters, Hope, is that these portraits were painted by a man very much in love."

"He's innocent, Victor."

"I believe you. And if I can help . . ." He shrugged and smiled a little, a wry and sad reminder of the other time he had offered her his comfort.

Hope had rejected such comfort on that day of death on Montagne Noir—a searing refusal fueled by betrayal and loss.

But on this Christmas Eve, in this place of love for both of them . . .

"Thank you," she whispered.

"I mean it, Hope."

"I know you do," she answered softly, believing it, knowing it. *I know.*

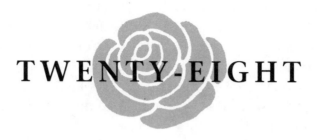

TWENTY-EIGHT

MONTAGNE NOIR

CHRISTMAS EVE

*V*ictor Tessier had been on stage all his life, performing for enraptured audiences around the world. But it was the music that truly performed. He was merely a conduit, had merely been blessed with a wondrous gift.

And so it was, as he sat before Cassandra and Chase and Hope, this most important audience of his life, the virtuoso felt distinctly ill at ease . . . even though, for this performance, the setting was cozy and festive. Red orange flames crackled cheerfully in the living room fireplace, and scents of bayberry and pine wafted from glowing candles within the prisms of glass.

"I don't usually talk about myself," Victor began. And the talented musician usually had something to do with his gifted hands, violin strings to vibrate, the familiar smoothness of a conductor's baton. But the hands that created the magic found a touchstone here. Since opening the door to him with her nose, Molly had been a constant shadow. She was curled against him now, a determined warmth against his leg, and whenever the talented fingers that caressed her became still, she looked up to remind him that she was there . . . and needed more of the touches that comforted her so.

"But," he said, idly stroking the coal black fur, "Cassandra believes this is something you need to know."

"It is." Cass smiled. "Whatever *it* is."

Victor looked at the conductress who had orchestrated this confessional. He had told Cassandra so much, too much, for she had been able to guess the rest. As a consequence of the assault, however, Cassandra remembered only that there was something, some shadowed part of what he had said, that Chase and Hope needed to hear.

Victor would tell them that part. He wanted to. But he would conceal—forever—the rest. He had to.

Politely, and casually, although it was so terribly important to him, Victor asked of the conductress, "Still no memory?"

"Still no memory," Cass confirmed. "Just the unwavering belief that there's something Chase and Hope need to know." She frowned slightly, a little amazed. "I've also deduced that I must have told you about our daughter."

"Yes," Victor said. "You did."

"You must have been awfully persuasive—and insightful."

"Not really, Cassandra." I was just lonely, he thought. As you were. Lonely, and so tired of the secrets that separated us from love. Victor smiled gently at the kindred spirit to whom he had confessed, had wanted to confess, so much. "My admissions came first, after your ferocious attack the instant you opened the door. You demanded to know what kind of man I was, what kind of father."

"And you said 'despicable,' on both counts. That I remember. I also know it isn't true."

"Yes," Victor countered. "It is. Nothing, and no one, prevented me from embracing Chase as my son." He looked at that forsaken son, the boy—and then the man—who had been so loyal to him. "At the very least, Chase, I should have given you the Domaine."

"You did," Chase said quietly. "After Grandpère's death, when I needed it most. You wanted to sell. I think you wanted that very much. But when I asked you to let me stay, you did, without any hesitation at all. I have a feeling it would have been the same if I'd asked eight years ago."

"But you didn't ask."

"No. I didn't. For my own reasons, and also, Victor, because of what you said."

"What I said, Chase?"

"When we were discussing closing the Domaine forever, you said that Grandpère might not approve, but that he would understand. Grandpère knew what it was that haunted you, tormented you, about the valley. It haunted him, too."

"But he never told you what it was."

"No," Chase replied. "I guess Grandpère decided it was your secret alone to share."

"Not it," Victor said softly. "He. My son."

"Who died," Cassandra whispered. "Like our daughter died."

Victor looked at her, a little worried that her memory was not as shadowed as it needed to be, *as he needed it to be,* but mostly gentle, because of the sadness they shared. "Both babies were premature. Your daughter. My son. Both were too tiny, too fragile, to survive. We would have given our lives for them. We wanted to. But we couldn't. We could only touch them, and talk to them, and pray for them. And when they died, we died."

"And you told me, didn't you, not to make the same mistakes you had made?" Her expression was thoughtful, and golden, in the dancing glow of the crackling flames. "I don't remember, Victor, but you must have. You must have said I had to risk loving again, to risk the joy—and the pain. That must be why I was wearing my wedding ring on Halloween."

"That is what I told you, Cassandra, although we never discussed your ring." Victor's solemn gaze turned to Chase. "And what I need to tell you, Chase, is how sorry I am. You could have been my son. You should have been. Grandpère knew it. He knew it was destiny for a six-year-old boy to need our love six years after my newborn son had died. You were his grandson. You know that, don't you?"

"Yes," Chase said. "I do."

Chase smiled a gentle smile, so much like Victor's; a smile for the man to whom Chase Tessier had been bonded, always, by the love of Grandpère, and to whom Chase was bonded now, irrevocably bonded, by another truth: that of a father, like Chase, who had lost a child.

Victor smiled gently, gratefully, in reply. Then he looked, his smile forsaken, at the other forsaken Tessier child. "And Hope? I could have raised you as my daughter, could have told Frances that was how it was going to be. But I didn't."

Hope didn't answer at once. But after a moment she said very quietly, "I remember Vienna."

"Do you? So do I."

Hope spoke to him, and to the memory. "You were my father then, Victor. You wanted to be." *You were so nice.* Nice. Her word for Victor—and Nick's word for her. *Nick.* She drew a ragged breath. "And maybe . . ."

She faltered. But Victor was there.

"Yes," he said. "Maybe if your mother and I hadn't separated that summer. But we did, and . . ."

And he faltered. But Hope was there.

"We couldn't have seen each other then. It would have been impossible, for me. My allegiance was to her. I would have felt conflicted . . . guilty." But you knew that, didn't you? Hope thought. Of course he did. And the father who was not her father would never had done anything to undermine her relationship with the mother she loved. No matter how flawed that mother was. "Victor?"

"Yes?"

"I don't feel so guilty, so conflicted, now."

"No?" he asked softly. "I'm glad."

"So am I," Hope murmured. *So am I.* She felt it then, such peace . . . and then a sudden restlessness. "Was he my brother, Victor? The baby who died?"

"No. He was born long before Frances and I ever met."

"So his mother was . . . ?"

"My first love." *My only love.* "She died the day he was born."

"Oh, Victor," Hope whispered. "I'm so sorry."

"Don't be!" Cassandra exclaimed, even as she frowned, bewildered at the words, such callous words, that seemed to come from nowhere. But not from nowhere—from the twilight shadows of her memory that were suddenly, stunningly, bright. "*Don't* be sorry, Hope, because it's not *true.* She is *very much* alive. I remember now, I have to remember, Victor, because Chase and Hope need to know the truth."

"No, Cassandra, they do not."

Victor's expression—an intense worry that verged on fear—might have halted her. Would have, for Cassandra cared about Victor Tessier very much.

But it was already too late. Cassandra had already announced that Victor's first love was still alive—and for neither Hope nor Chase was the puzzle difficult to solve.

There was, after all, in Napa, the woman with whom Cassandra once had been close—and now inexplicably refused to see.

"Jane," Chase murmured even as Hope was saying:

"The baby's mother was Jane."

"Yes. *Jane.*" Cassandra gazed at Victor, apologetic yet determined. "Chase and Hope need to know the truth, Victor. They deserve to know it."

"It's not that simple, Cassandra."

"Yes. It *is.*" All traces of apology vanished, trampled by a resolve that was truly fearsome. Cassandra became a ferocious Scheherazade, with a far from enchanting story to tell. "To begin with, Victor's son—Jane and Victor's son—may *or may not* have been premature. He was tiny, however, and destined to die—because he had been *starved* in utero."

"Starved?" Hope echoed with alarm.

But Hope's alarm paled in comparison with Victor's. "We don't know that, Cassandra."

"We *did*, Victor. *You* did, just a few months ago. You even tried to *defend* it, to take the *blame*. Jane was so young, you said, when the two of you broke up. But seventeen isn't *that* young, and no matter how upset you are, or how angry at the baby's father, you don't take it out on your unborn child."

It began then, as if Cassandra and Victor were dueling attorneys, offering heartfelt presentations to a jury of Chase and Hope.

Victor Tessier pled, with a quiet passion, that the Yuletide jury return an innocent verdict for Jane.

Victor began his case by calling on their memories of

the man they all had loved. "Like Grandpère, I'm dyslexic. I cannot read. Not a word. Not a letter. Not at all. As a boy, it was very difficult for me. I felt lost, displaced . . . blind. Then I discovered music, and it was all I ever wanted—or ever wanted to be—until Jane. When I fell in love with Jane, my music was forgotten. Everything was forgotten. Nothing mattered except her. I felt myself—my self—begin to disappear. It terrified me. I was lost again, blind again. I ended our relationship with no explanation except that I wanted out."

"How could you explain something you didn't truly understand?" Cassandra, the prosecutor in the case of the *People* versus *Jane Parish* wanted to know. Her query was urgent, for she was perceiving sympathy, far too much sympathy, from the Montagne Noir jurors. "You were *feeling*, Victor, not *thinking*. Now, a few decades later, you have lots of insight. But then . . . you fell in love, fell so hard you became lost in the vortex. So you broke up. Young lovers break up all the time. But they don't *all* kill their babies."

"Jane didn't—"

"*Yes.* She did." Cassandra clarified for the Tessier jury. "Victor returned to the valley at Christmastime, and went to Jane to beg her forgiveness and ask her to marry him. But Jane wouldn't permit him into her home, would not allow him to see anything other than her painfully thin face. Jane kept her pregnancy hidden from Victor, but she forgot to conceal the more horrendous truth—that she had been starving herself *to starve her child.*"

"We don't know that, Cassandra. Jane may not have even realized she was pregnant. She might have had morning sickness without knowing what it was, and lost weight—"

"Without knowing what it was? Thinking it was *love-*

sickness, perhaps?" Cassandra stopped abruptly, halted by her own holier-than-thou contempt.

What right did she, of all people, have to hold anyone in such disdain? She had, after all, fled from the man she loved, so confused was she by her own pregnancy; and after losing her daughter, and her husband, she had almost died of lovesickness herself.

So how dare she be so unforgiving of Jane? And why was she so convinced that Jane had—so willingly—caused harm to her unborn son?

There had to be something more, hidden in the shadows, something Victor had told her in October but was withholding now—a revelation so damning that even as she listened to Victor plead for mercy for the woman he loved, Cassandra would not yield. The memory was hidden. But its emotions were not. "Jane starved that innocent little life, Victor. She starved your baby, your son, *to death*—a death that was inevitable from the moment he was born. In my book, that's murder."

With that, the faux prosecutor rested her case. And the counterfeit attorney for the defense?

Victor was silent, fearful that Cassandra might remember the rest—the part, the crime, that the authentic prosecutor in the room would be obliged to pursue.

"Well," he said finally, softly, but with determined finality to Chase and Hope. "Now you know. You'll have to decide for yourselves how you feel about Jane. I really hope—"

"When was he born?" Hope interjected.

"What?"

"When, Victor, was your baby boy born?"

Victor frowned but replied. "Thirty-four years ago."

"On Christmas Eve?"

Ice cold fear filled his veins, a glacial terror that was at odds with the warmth, the heat, pressed against his legs. He had, during his impassioned defense of Jane, stopped patting the coal black creature at his feet—and Molly had stopped demanding his caresses. But she had curled against him, ever more close.

"Victor?" Hope pressed softly, but with determination of her own. "Was he born on Christmas Eve?"

"Yes."

"And was he found in a Dumpster? Behind the old bakery in Rutherford?"

"*Yes,*" Cass whispered, remembering everything and understanding her own venom—at last. "Jane called the Domaine that evening, just hours after she and Victor had talked. 'Your son treats women like trash,' she told Grand-père in a whispered hiss. 'Now your grandson is learning exactly how that feels.' Jane threw her newborn baby, her *starveling,* in the trash, covered only with her blood. She left him to die, to freeze to death, on Christmas Eve. That's not willful, Victor? That's not *murder?* How can you even think about defending her, protecting her?"

Because I love the girl I once knew. I love her . . . still. "She told us where to find him, and he was still alive."

"But he died, Victor," Cassandra insisted. Then, gently, so gently for this man, this father, she admired, "And so much of you died with him."

"Victor?" Hope asked. "When did he die?"

"On January third." Victor looked at the authentic prosecutor—who knew now of the most serious crime—and with whom just moments before he had forged a quiet peace. "Jane was so young, Hope, so wounded. She had no idea what she was doing. You know her, Hope. You know it wasn't Jane who did this. It was some other part of her, a part she must loathe every day of her life."

"Please, Victor," Hope implored in reply. "This is so important. Did your son have a name?"

"Lucas," Victor whispered. "I named him Lucas."

"So the hospital would have a record of Lucas Tessier."

"No," Cassandra answered. "Victor—and Grandpère—protected Jane even then, beginning then. They told the police and the doctors that they just happened to hear his cries coming from the Dumpster, even though he didn't cry. And as for their vigil in the ICU? Anyone who knew Jean-Luc Tessier would expect such compassion for the foundling no one claimed."

"You took him to Courtland Medical Center?" Hope asked.

"Yes."

"Did Sibyl know?"

"Sibyl? Yes. The emergency room staff notified her father—he owned the hospital—within minutes of our arrival."

"Did Sibyl know the baby was yours, and Jane's?"

"Yes. She knew. Sibyl and I were friends, had been good friends, for many years."

"And did Sibyl disapprove?" Hope wondered. Did she condemn Jane's Lakota blood? And the valiant half-breed infant who was so welcomed by Victor and Jean-Luc?

"Sibyl disapproved of my relationship with Jane, but not of Lucas. Hope, I don't understand."

"I just have to be so sure. So *sure.*"

"Before pressing charges?"

"No, Victor. There won't be any charges." But oh, how she would love to file charges against Sibyl Courtland Raleigh. Yet she couldn't, couldn't, because . . . "The statutes have run out on everything but murder. And there was no murder here."

"Thank you."

Hope looked at Victor, and Molly, and saw so clearly despite the sudden mist in her eyes. The baby cocker spaniel, who would have been thrown in the trash to die had Nick not rescued her, was curled as close to Victor as she could possibly be.

As close as Molly would have curled to Nick.

Molly knew. She had known all along. From that day on the mountain when Molly had licked Victor's hand.

"There was no murder," Hope said at last. "Because that baby boy, your beloved Lucas, is still alive."

TWENTY-NINE

*T*his is Victor Tessier," Hope told the same guard who had been on duty when she'd visited the jail the day before. She paused a moment to permit the guard to recall what he had learned from yesterday's tabloid about the famous musician: that Victor prevented the police in Napa from investigating Nick nine years ago, because—according to Sibyl Courtland Raleigh, who knew, who knew so well—Victor Tessier was quite blind to evil.

"Oh, yes," the guard murmured, and frowned.

"I'd like Mr. Tessier to speak with Mr. Doe."

The guard's frown deepened. Understandably. Was Hope Tessier, warrior for justice, capable of taking the law into her own hands? Had she chosen Victor Tessier, whose wife Nicholas Doe had also murdered, as her Christmas Eve assassin?

381

The guard couldn't care less about the fate of the cop killer—well, yes, he did. He wanted Nick to die. But the guard was loath to have such carnage occur on his watch.

"That seems unusual."

"I know." Hope smiled. "What *isn't* unusual about this case? But Victor and I just breezed through the metal detectors, and my thought was that their meeting would take place down here, not in an attorney room."

"With the prisoner behind bars," the guard clarified.

"Of course," Hope agreed.

$\mathcal{V}$ictor Tessier made the journey alone to his son's cell. His footsteps echoed in the deserted gray hallways as Christmas carols drifted overhead.

Silent night.

Holy night.

All is calm. All is bright.

On that faraway Christmas Eve, Victor had found his son, cloaked only in blood, cold, alone, dying—and silent.

And on this night before Christmas, Victor found his son again. Alone, cold, dying—and so silent, so calm within in the unholy darkness of his desolate cell.

Nick stood in the shadows, not restless, not pacing, not searching frantically to be free. His powerful body was quiet, absolutely still. Waiting for death. His cloudy gray eyes greeted Victor with neither interest nor surprise.

Nick had given up hope.

He had given up Hope.

Victor spoke to the darkness and to the shadowed soul caged within.

"I had a son, once. I loved him very much. *So much.* His name was Lucas, after my own father, Jean-Luc. I named my newborn son on Christmas Eve, during our desperate drive from a Dumpster behind a bakery in Rutherford. We took him to Courtland Medical Center, where he survived, survived, against all odds. We didn't leave him, his grandfather and I, not until the tenth night, when his doctors insisted that we go home to sleep. He would be all right, they assured us. He was stronger, better, and we needed rest, the doctors said, even more than he. Just before dawn, a friend—I believed she was a friend—arrived at the Domaine. My son had died, she said. My Lucas had died."

He had wanted to see his baby, his precious Lucas, to hold his son's small dead body against his heart—to kiss him good-bye and wish, for him, eternal peace. Victor Tessier had wanted, desperately, that final farewell with his son.

But it was too dangerous, Sibyl had told him, reminded him—far too dangerous . . . for Jane. His son had died, a consequence of the crime committed by Jane; and if he went to the morgue, demanding to hold—and kiss and cherish—the cold body of the foundling, questions would arise about his true relationship to the abandoned boy.

So he hadn't bade that last adieu to his son, and in a few days Sibyl arrived with a silver urn of ashes—collected, perhaps, from a Christmas blaze at Courtland Manor.

"But he hadn't died, my Lucas. And my supposed friend—with the help, I assume, of her father—arranged for his transfer to San Francisco, to the neonatal ICU at UCSF. He was named there, named again, a Christmas Eve baby the doctors christened Nicholas Doe."

Victor's vision was adjusting to the blackness, or maybe he just knew how to see into the darkest shadows of pain. He saw Nick's ashen face, a pale glow in the darkness, and the powerful fists clenched tightly at his sides. And Victor saw as well that Nick was listening, straining to listen, as if hearing a language he had never heard . . . a language Victor would speak, and keep speaking, until the shadow spoke in reply.

"She handled all the paperwork, too, that friend. She could read, and I couldn't, and neither could Grandpère. Had I been able to read the piece of paper she claimed was my son's death certificate, I might have realized my son was still alive. I would have found him, and loved him, as I love him now."

It was too much, this alien language of love lost and life discarded. Nick moved away, deeper into the shadows, farther into darkness.

But still Victor spoke to his son.

"He's an extraordinary man, my Lucas. Twice already he has risked his freedom, his very life, for the woman he loves. Twice already, and he's doing it again, protecting her even when—this time—it's he who needs her help. But she's extraordinary, too, the woman he loves. She's fighting for him, and will continue to fight. As will I. He might have committed the crime for which he stands accused. It would be understandable, *forgivable,* if he had. Even the gentlest of creatures will lash out, will kill, if wounded badly enough." *Your mother, my Lucas, is the gentlest creature I have ever known. But even she could be pushed, was so cruelly pushed by me, to the very edge of humanity.* "But Lucas didn't kill the monster who raped him. He couldn't have, you see, because my son, like his grandfather and like me, can neither read nor write—and Al Garrett's murderer left a note."

Victor sensed, in the shadows, a breath of surprise . . . and of hope.

"Hope didn't know that Lucas Tessier was dyslexic, not with absolute certainty, until yesterday. But she read the records of the little boy who had been a ward of the state, too sickly, too frail—as an infant—for anyone to want to adopt, and too silent and withdrawn as a toddler, and too difficult as a child. He was a discipline problem, the social workers said: inattentive in the classroom, except when it came to art. Dyslexia was never mentioned. But as Hope read about that boy, she thought about the man who never looked at her Willow Ranch diary, even though—she says—she sometimes left passages open for him to read; and who would have been a veterinarian in another life; and who returned to Napa without checking for a warrant for his arrest; and who, last Friday night, asked a friend"— *asked his mother*—"to guide him to Hope's apartment, an unfamiliar address that might otherwise have taken him far too long to find.

"Hope's diagnosis of dyslexia was merely an educated guess, until yesterday, when she showed Lucas the note—a copy without the splatters of blood. 'I'm not sorry,' Al Garrett's killer wrote. 'The bastard deserved to die.' It was written in what Hope calls block print, grandiose and bold—the sort of lettering a vengeful teenager might choose . . . or a choice, perhaps, of an emotionally ravaged spouse. My son didn't write that note. He couldn't have. Any more than he could have committed the murder for which he stands accused."

The accused man, the condemned man, stood unmoving in his cell. Beneath the soaring promise of Victor Tessier's words Nick heard another sound, primal, rhythmic, ghastly, raw.

It was the sound of tempered steel slashing human flesh, the sickening sound of death that had awakened him that night. The noise, ritualistic and methodical, came from the bedroom where Al and Iris slept . . . and where, among other places, Al took Nick when Iris wasn't home.

Iris Garrett was in the conjugal bedroom on this night,

on the conjugal bed, straddling her already dead husband, mutilating him still, an unpitying destruction for the endless beatings she had endured.

Nick wrested the knife from her bloodied hands, and held her while she sobbed, and formulated a story for the police, a fable that began with the truth—that Al had hit her this evening and had threatened, as he so often had, to kill her while she slept.

Iris went to bed with the knife beneath her pillow, they would say; and she awakened, confused by a nightmare and groggy from sleeping pills, to see her husband hovering over her, poised to make good on his murderous threat.

So Iris murdered him first. In self-defense.

In fact, Al Garrett's death had been carefully planned, a murder-suicide, plotted weeks in advance. Iris had already taken a small handful of sleeping pills, and the remainder, far more than a lethal dose, were on the nightstand, splattered with her husband's blood. The sheet of paper, beneath the crimson drugs, was used by Nick to gather the remaining pills and flush them away, after which he tossed the crumpled paper into the trash.

Nick altered the story, and the crime scene, for Iris, and when she was calm, it was he who called the police. He was with the younger children, calming them, soothing them with lies, when the police arrived . . . when he overheard Iris Garrett's impassioned account—that she had discovered Nick savaging her beloved husband, carving his body long after he was dead.

Had Iris Garrett finally confessed? The question brightened, for a moment, the shadows. But darkness returned with a vengeance. Of course she hadn't. He would not be here if she had. In fact . . .

"She's dead. Isn't she? Iris is dead."

Victor didn't respond at once, for at last his son had spoken . . . and Victor heard such despair.

"Yes," he admitted quietly. "But we're going to find the other children who were there that night."

"They were downstairs. Asleep."

"But maybe she told one of them something. Confessed before she died."

Nick closed his eyes, hearing again the words Iris Garrett had used to betray him. Iris believed her own lies. She had, within minutes of her crime, convinced herself that it was Nick, not she, who had murdered the batterer she loved. It was unlikely that she had confessed. And the note, a confession in itself?

It proved only that Iris Garrett's story to the police was not entirely true—that she had been, at the very least, an accomplice. The note didn't absolve Nick of the crime. His fingerprints, inked in the murdered policeman's blood, were everywhere. In the bedroom, on the knife, on the note.

And he had run.

This isn't going to end well, Nick had told the cinnamon-haired angel who wanted to defend him. And it wasn't going to.

Couldn't.

Victor Tessier sensed Nick's anguish, felt his hopelessness as surely, as piercingly, as Victor had felt his own desperation the day he was told that his baby had died.

"We had only ten days together, my son and I. I touched him whenever I could, whenever the doctors told me it was safe. He was very tiny, my baby, my son, as was the opening in the incubator through which I was permitted to reach. It couldn't accommodate my hand, just a finger or two—fingers that until then had been useless. Oh, there were those who maintained that I created emotional magic on the strings of a violin. But it was such false magic, such inconsequential emotion, compared to what happened when my son curled his tiny fingers around mine. I felt his courage, and his love. I pray, I have always prayed, that he felt mine."

The opening in that infant's incubator had been very small. But the spaces between these jail cell bars, in this cage where Victor's son now dwelled, were more than wide enough for a hand.

For both of Victor Tessier's gifted hands.

Victor reached. Through the bars. To his son. In the darkness.

It seemed, for a moment, that Nick would walk to him. That father and son would touch. Again. At last.

But the infant who had been left to die, cloaked only in his mother's blood, had been destined to wear more blood, so much blood—spilled in lust, in violence, in rage. Al Garrett's blood cloaked him now, as did Robert's, as did the splattered claret of Frances Tessier and her lover Gavin.

The death blood of others drenched him—thick, pungent, clinging, cold—and so brilliant, its deadly hue, that even the shadows in which he stood were tinted, tainted, red.

"Nick?" Victor implored. "Lucas?"

"Forget about me," Lucas Tessier whispered from the bloodied shadows. "Please. Just forget about me."

THIRTY

MONTAGNE NOIR

CHRISTMAS DAY

*L*ong ago, Chase Tessier had read for Grandpère, and on this Christmas morning, in the cheerful mauve-and-cream kitchen of the château, Chase—and Hope and Cassandra—read for Victor.

They scanned the day's papers, searching for the revelation that would inevitably surface once the sensationalism of Robert Forrest in drag—and of the ancient murders in San Francisco and Napa—had become old news. The journalists would turn then to the ancient history of the murderer himself. And they would discover rather quickly that the ward of the state had been found in a trash bin in Napa on Christmas Eve.

"Nothing here," Chase said as he finished his survey of the latest tabloid.

"Or here," Hope concurred as she completed her *Chronicle* scan.

389

"Or here." Cassandra looked up from the Christmas edition of the local paper once edited by Eleanor's Andrew.

"Nothing yet," Victor amended quietly. "But I need to see them both. And I'm going to. Today."

"Both?" Hope asked. "You mean Jane and Sibyl?"

"Yes."

"Why?"

"Because," Cassandra replied, "Victor's protecting Jane—still. He knows that in order to deflect scrutiny from her own wrongdoing, Sibyl would talk and talk and talk about Jane's crime. So Victor's going to offer Sibyl an incredibly generous deal: her silence about Jane in return for his silence about *her*."

Victor's expression, as he looked at Hope, was a solemn confirmation of what Cassandra had said. "The four of us know the truth. And Jane and Sibyl will know it, too. But it can end there, can't it?"

The maestro was a blindman still, relying on the meticulous prosecutor's careful read of every document in Nick's files.

"Yes," Hope said. "It can." *Because even thirty-four years ago you protected Jane so well.* Lucas Tessier did not exist, except in the hearts of his father and Grandpère. "I'd be happy to speak to Sibyl, Victor. In fact, I'd be delighted to."

"As," Chase offered, "would Cassandra and I. Seeing Jane will be enough for you, Victor. More than enough."

"And," Cassandra murmured, "it would give me great pleasure to speak with Sibyl."

There was more, of course, for Cassandra—her memories of Jane, who had always been so wonderful to her, and who cared so very much about Nick, and who, with her unlikely but perfect canine weapon, had helped Nick save Hope.

Those were Cassandra's authentic memories of Jane Parish. And the other images? Grotesque and hateful? They were conjured only—and perhaps, perhaps, entirely wrong. Maybe Jane hadn't realized her pregnancy until the startled moment of her baby's birth. And maybe the frightened and frantic teenager believed that her son—who would have been so beloved—had been born dead. And maybe Jane Parish didn't *throw* her infant away, but merely *placed* him . . . unlike Sibyl, who coldly and calculatedly severed Nick from the love, the family, the life that was rightfully his.

Cassandra's blue eyes glittered with ferocious passion—and fierce hope. "I'd really love to focus every single negative emotion I've ever had about Jane squarely on Sibyl instead. I *want* to do that, Victor. And I need to, don't I, for all of us? Let me be the one to tell Sibyl that we all know just how evil she truly is. Please. It would be, for me, a most spectacular Christmas gift."

"Are you sure?"

"Absolutely."

"So," Chase said. "That's settled. We'll take care of Sibyl, while you see Jane." He glanced from Victor to the creature who would not let Victor out of her sight, her touch. "You and Molly."

"Thank you," Victor whispered as the kitchen phone began to trill. "Thank you all."

Chase answered the telephone, exchanged the most efficient of words, and looked at Hope. "It's Meryl Atwood. For you."

"Oh." Hope moved to the phone. "Meryl?"

"Hello, Hope. I just got a call from John Madrid. He wants to see you, and me, and Larry Billings—today, as soon as you can get here. John doesn't give a damn about Christmas, not with Craig in prison. I assume you're not celebrating, either."

"No."

"Nor am I. So?"

"So, yes. Of course." Even though, Hope thought, this Yuletide meeting of prosecutors and police might make Detective Billings's Christmas—especially if, as she feared, John Madrid was about to formally retract the statement he had made nineteen years ago about Al Garrett's sexual abuse of Nick. "I'll be there, Meryl. I'll leave right now."

Hope returned the receiver to its cradle, recounted the facts, and, for Victor, came up with a far more hopeful reason for the Christmas meeting. "This probably has nothing to do with Nick. John Madrid's probably just choosing this festive moment to announce what the tabloids have been predicting for days—that because of my bias, he's going to get his son's conviction overturned. I guess this means I won't be going with you to see Sibyl."

"We'll be all right," Chase said. "Cassie and I have the easy part."

*J*ane Parish's cottage on Sage Canyon Road was hauntingly, beautifully, reminiscent of the carriage house on Zinfandel Lane. Its cedar siding, too, had silvered with age, and wisteria spilled, in a bountiful lavender cascade, from its eaves. The wreath, on the cottage door, was a circle of gardenias and pine, sparkling with delicate glass ornaments painted by her.

Victor stood before Jane's door, not yet chiming the bell, not yet ready to; but sensing she was here. Nearby. At last.

Jane *was* nearby, kneeling on the floor beside her tree. The Christmas tree was a blue spruce, alive and flourishing in its wooden planter, a gift from a long-ago lover—and too heavy, for many Christmases, for her to carry inside.

But here it was, this year, because of Nick. He had carried the tree and its weighty planter inside her cottage, after which she had asked him to decorate, with her, its teal green boughs. Asked . . . and then insisted, as Nick's uncertainty made her wonder if he had ever trimmed a Christmas tree before.

It was a lovely tree, this spruce decorated with Nick, and it was surrounded by presents, brightly wrapped still, a bounty for the generous artist who always gave so many gifts herself. Jane needed to open her Christmas packages—the ones labeled "To Aunt Jane" at the very least. There were children, innocent and eager, who expected to hear before day's end just how much Jane loved what they had made, or chosen, for her.

It was the specter of those phone calls that was most daunting to Jane. She had to sound happy and gay for those children who were not hers.

But how could she?

Jane was contemplating a package, its gift wrap midnight blue with silver stars, when her doorbell chimed.

She stood, crossed the short expanse of hand-woven rug, and opened the gardenia-and-glass-adorned door.

And then, oh then, there was more silver, shimmering silver, streaks of starlight in his night black hair. And there was midnight blue—the darkest blue laced with gray—in his eyes. Such troubled eyes. So worried. So weary.

So beloved.

"Victor," she whispered. *My Victor.* "And Molly."

Molly wagged in greeting. But she stayed close to the man who reminded her so much of Nick, stayed close to the father . . . not the mother.

"Hello, Jane." *Hello, my Jane. My Jane.* "May I—may we—come in?"

"Yes. Of course. Victor, has something happened?" As if

anything more could happen. Except things *could* happen, horrible things, to an accused cop killer in jail. Jane had seen the venom, the hideous glee, of Detective Larry Billings that night in Golden Gate Park. "Victor? Why are you here?"

"Because of Nick."

The delicate hands that had loved him with such bold passion, such unashamed joy, flew to her throat. "Oh, no. Something *has* happened. Nick has been hurt, or, *Victor—*"

"Nick's all right, Jane. Nothing has happened. You care about him, don't you?"

"Yes. Very much. If you're asking me if I'd be willing to help him, the answer is yes, anything, *anything*. Surely Hope knows that."

"She does. But there's something about Nick that you don't know."

"I know that he's innocent."

"I know that, too." *And we can convince him, you and I, that he must permit us to fight for him. Then we will fight, you and I, for the life, for the freedom, of our son.* It was a glorious thought, a soaring fantasy, a wish that flew high above the truth. The wish crashed, shattered, just heartbeats before Victor Tessier said very softly, "What you don't know, Jane, is that Nick is my son."

*M*erry Christmas," Sibyl greeted, a disingenuous welcome that became even more false as she realized that Chase and Cass were alone. "Where's Victor?"

"With Jane."

"With? I trust that's not a euphemism for s-e-x." Sibyl shook her head in disgust. "So. You two are here because . . . ?"

"Because of what you did," Cass replied. "What you convinced your father to do on January third, thirty-four years ago."

Alarm flickered briefly, very briefly, before being repackaged as imperious surprise. "January third? Thirty-four years ago? I can't imagine what I would have wanted that I hadn't already gotten for Christmas. We Courtlands were always very practical about specifying, in advance, every Christmas gift we hoped to receive."

"This particular request wasn't born until Christmas Eve."

"Oh. Well, then, you must be talking about Galahad, my champion show jumper." Sibyl frowned, as if, despite her ageless beauty, old age was definitely catching up with her mind. "I'd forgotten his birthdate."

"You *know* what we're talking about, Sibyl," Cassandra insisted. "Victor's baby, Victor's *son*, the ten-day-old infant you shipped to UCSF, after which you told Victor his son had died."

Sibyl arched a perfectly penciled brow. "This is such an interesting fantasy, Cassandra. I can only assume it's a consequence of the head injury you sustained on Halloween. I'm not sure how you've managed to snare Chase—and Victor?—into your delusional system. But you're a *pro* at pretense, aren't you? You always have been."

"We have *proof,* Sibyl," Cassandra lied. But it was an honest falsehood. Surely they would have such proof if they bothered to ask. "The doctors and nurses who cared for the foundling know he didn't die, and they have assumed, all these years, that Victor and Jean-Luc knew it, too. Courtland Medical Center's health care providers remember, quite clearly, that the baby boy was transferred— just as Victor remembers, vividly, your arrival at the Domaine, in tears, to tell him of his son's death. Victor *knows,* Sibyl. He knows *exactly* what you did."

Sibyl Courtland Raleigh's expression changed then, from haughty and disdainful to vulnerable—and young. Her voice changed as well, as she asked, as she implored, "And does he loathe me? Does Victor *loathe* me?"

"I guess," Chase said softly, "that Victor just doesn't understand."

Sibyl looked at Chase, beckoned by the softness of his voice and the gentle sympathy on his face. A faint, sad smile touched her perfectly painted lips. "That's the problem, Chase. He never did."

Your son, Victor?" No wonder I care so much about him. No wonder I love Nick as if—

"My son, Jane . . . and yours."

They were devastating words, the shattering truth, and Victor had dreaded them so; dreaded inflicting on her such excruciating pain.

But there was no pain.

"I don't understand." *Are you saying, Victor, that you will share your beloved son with me?* "Victor?"

"Nick is the baby boy born that Christmas Eve."

"I don't know what you're talking about."

Don't know? The realization came to Victor with a flood of relief. Jane's memory had gone to darkness, just as Cassandra's had, mercifully shadowed, irrevocably black, spared from reliving forever a trauma so immense it might not be endured.

"It's okay," he reassured her gently. "It's okay."

Jane wanted to remain forever in the embracing warmth of his tender gaze, to be seventeen again—oh, she was seventeen now—and promising to love each other always.

Jane Parish had never broken that vow. Not in all these years. *All these years.* She was jolted, a gentle jolting—for she saw such gentleness still—to the present.

"What's okay, Victor?"

"That you don't remember that Christmas Eve."

Nor, he realized, do you remember how cruelly I broke up with you months before. That trauma, too, had surely been consigned to blackness.

How else could one explain her expression when she opened her gardenia-fragrant door? As if she were opening to him, welcoming him, loving him? And how else, other than such blackness, could one explain the way Jane, his Jane, was looking at him now?

"And I think," he added softly, "that you don't remember, either, the months that came before."

"But I *do* remember," she answered, her voice as soft as his. "I remember everything. You were right to end our relationship. We were young, and there were so many obstacles, too many. It couldn't possibly have worked out the way we wanted it to. It took me a while to realize that. But I *did* realize it, and I was just beginning to adjust, I had almost made it, when you appeared at my door that Christmas Eve."

"You were so haggard. So thin."

"So were you. I saw how difficult it had been for you, too. Oh, Victor, I wanted to pull you inside the cottage and never let you go. But I couldn't. I knew—I believed—that if we tried again, it wouldn't last. I couldn't survive loving you again, only to lose you. I almost didn't survive the first time."

"But our baby survived." *And together, my Jane, we will survive this. But first I must tell you. First, you have to know.* "You gave birth that night, that Christmas Eve. You gave birth to our son."

"Oh, Victor," Jane whispered. "What I would have given to have had your child. And if that baby, that son, had been Nick . . ." She drew a ragged breath. "I've never been pregnant, Victor. Never. There have been men since you, men who've wanted me to have their children. But I couldn't. Yours was the only baby I ever wanted to have. If Nick is your son—and oh, Victor, I pray that he is—and if he was born on that Christmas Eve, then . . ."

Then Victor had betrayed her, even as she was struggling to survive the loss of his love. He had slept, then, with someone else. . . .

*V*ictor never understood that *we* were meant to be together." Sibyl Courtland Raleigh's voice was far away. "We were friends, *just* friends, even after we made love. For me our lovemaking was . . . unbelievable. And for Victor? It was a moment of idiocy, and far too much champagne; a moment Victor Tessier regretted even while—well. He *kept* regretting it, apologizing for taking advantage of me, for coming to see his good friend Sib when he was so upset about his breakup with Jane that he wasn't in his right mind. Do you know how it makes you feel to have someone *regret* having made love with you? And to feel *disgust* with himself? And *guilt* because of the woman he'd betrayed? *Do you?*"

"Yes," Chase said quietly. "It makes you feel like trash."

"*Yes.* Trash. Just like the cancerous growth Victor left inside me. I hated that baby, wanted it to go away, would have gotten rid of it had I realized in time."

"So you starved him instead."

"I starved *myself,* until there wasn't a clue, even in skin-tight clothes, of the tumor within. I'd never looked better.

Even *Victor* said so, when he saw me, that Christmas Eve . . . when he told me he was going to see Jane, to tell her how *sorry* he was, and how he wanted her back."

"And she played right into your hands by refusing to let him into her home."

"*No.* Jane ruined everything. As *always.* It never occurred to me that she would refuse Victor's offer to reconcile. I imagined she'd be with him, celebrating their joyous reunion, when I called the Domaine . . . and that they'd discover, together, Victor's dead son in the trash. I didn't identify myself to Grandpère. There was no need. Victor would know it was me, and that the baby was mine, *ours,* and he would feel such guilt about the way he had treated me that he and I would . . . Well. So much for best-laid plans. Victor assumed the baby was Jane's, and he protected Jane and loved her baby—*my* baby. I was with him at the hospital, Victor wanted me to be, and I listened, good friend that I was, to the way he blamed himself for hurting Jane. I'd never felt closer to him, and for a while I even wanted the baby to survive. We would get married, Victor and I, and I would raise Jane's bastard son as my own, and Victor would never know the truth. But when it became clear that the baby might actually survive, do you know what Victor did? He began talking about finding Jane. He needed my help, of course. I could read, and he couldn't. He wanted me to find out where the Parishes had gone, the reservation—I assume—to which they had fled. He wanted Jane's address, and her phone number, so he could explain to her that it was his fault, his cruelty, that had made her throw their baby away. And then—here's the best part—he was going to ask her to marry him."

"And you couldn't stand the thought of that. Of any of that."

"That's right, Chase. I couldn't."

"So you threw your baby away—again."

Sibyl Courtland Raleigh smiled. Haughty again. Imperious forever. "Why not? I had every right to throw him away. *Every* right. I was his mother."

THIRTY-ONE

DISTRICT ATTORNEY'S OFFICE

SAN FRANCISCO

CHRISTMAS

*H*ave you read my state-
ment in the Al Garrett murder file?" John Madrid asked of
the prosecutor who had convicted his son.

"Yes. I have." *And I won't let you recant it.* "Why?"

"Because there should be more, something I should
have added thirteen years later, and that I must add now."

"What is it, John?" Larry Billings pressed, his smug tone
implying that he sensed John Madrid was about to ham-
mer the final nail into the pauper's coffin of Nicholas Doe.

John Madrid answered his son's loyal partner with a
gaze that was solemn, thoughtful—and sad. Then, with
somber resolve, the beleaguered father looked at Hope. "I
promised Iris that if Nick was ever caught, I would give this
to the police."

"This" was a sealed envelope.

"Oh," Hope whispered. "Her confession?"

"Yes. She wrote it shortly before she died."

"Do you know what it says?"

"She told me. Al was already quite dead, she had already more than killed him, by the time Nick entered the room. Iris told me more, told me everything, so if there are gaps in what's written down, the necessary details can be provided—by me."

The necessary details that would set Nick free. It was a gift, on this Christmas, from the father whose son Hope had sent to prison . . . and for whom Meryl Atwood had always felt such enormous respect.

"You didn't have to do this," Hope said very quietly to that honorable man. *You could have taken this secret with you to your grave.*

"Yes, I did. For Iris. But mostly for Nick. I knew him, you know. Al was my partner, my friend. We had family get-togethers, the sort of thing Norman Rockwell liked to paint." John's weighted sigh was eloquent testimony to how far the image of innocence was from sordid truth. "Nick was very small for his age, and he was beautiful, truly beautiful, and quiet, and serious—perfect bait, in short, for a bully. Like my son."

"John," Detective Billings implored. "What are you saying?"

"The truth, Larry." John Madrid sighed anew. "The truth. Nick ignored Craig's taunts, always ignored them, no matter how punishing or cruel. Then one summer day, when we were all at the beach, there was a dog, trotting back and forth at water's edge, while his owners skied in the bay. My son, *my* son, decided it would be great fun to throw rocks at that abandoned pet. But before he could launch the first missile, small, frail, beautiful Nick grabbed Craig's arm and hung on for all he was worth."

"That kind of courage," Meryl Atwood murmured, "that kind of compassion, is worth a lot."

"I suppose that's why I knew, even before Iris told me, that Nick hadn't murdered Al."

"And it's why," Hope added softly, "you permitted Nick to get away."

"Wait a minute," Detective Billings commanded. "John Madrid would *never* permit a murderer to go free."

"But Nick was *not* a murderer. *Is* not." Hope's eyes shone with gratitude as she looked, once again, at John Madrid. "And you *did* permit him to escape. You knew enough about Nick to realize that the first place he would go, that night, would be the stables in the park. But the interview with Hank—*your* interview, John—didn't happen until late the following afternoon."

Hope's speculation was neither confirmed nor denied. But John Madrid said, a quiet confession of sorrow, "I would have been proud to have Nicholas Doe as my son. Far more proud than I am of the son I have raised."

"Well, *hell,*" Larry Billings muttered.

"You've changed since working with Craig," John told his son's partner and friend. "You need to change back, Lar. *You have to.*"

It was the beginning of a conversation these two men would have, must have. Sometime. But this was not the time, and there was an innocent man, a bloodied shadow, dying in a distant cell.

"Okay," Meryl said. "Here's what's going to happen next, what must happen given the media scrutiny of this case. Larry and I will meet with Nick—right now—and get him to tell us the truth. You can't be involved, Hope. You know that."

"Yes. I do know. But . . ."

Meryl smiled. "You're worried that I might not be able to convince Nick to talk? Trust me, Hope. I've been at this a very long time. Besides, I plan to tell Nick the truth—that we have Iris Garrett's confession and all he has to do is come up with a story that matches what she said."

"He will."

"I know. And you know, Hope, that even if we establish in minutes that Nick's account is an exact replica of what Iris Garrett wrote, the process of getting him released, that red tape of freedom, will take a while. *Quite* a while. So," Meryl Atwood advised, "why don't you make a slew of phone calls, and find, for Nick, something to wear that's not covered with blood?"

"His clothes are in my car."

"Well. After you get them, why not talk, for a *very* long time, to the good folks in Napa?"

$\mathcal{T}$ he red tape of freedom, that bright and glorious ribbon around this Tessier Christmas, took almost until midnight. But it didn't matter. Eleanor's bold forecast of Yuletide wonder, that astonishing pronouncement from the merry Mrs. Claus, had already come true.

Hope's phone calls to Napa found Victor with Jane. He would be with Jane always. And Cassandra reported that Sibyl Courtland Raleigh, who was many things, many horrible things, but never an idiot, had already booked a one-way ticket to the south of France.

And any moment now Nick would be free. *Free.* To live as he wanted, without fear. To love as he wanted, anyone he chose.

And Hope was fine, too. She *would* be fine. She had found peace, and perhaps a beginning, with Victor, and there was her bountiful passion for work, that autumnal harvest of the soul.

But now Nick was walking toward her, his sable hair

damp, his clothes loose, and his gait, without chains, a motion of sheer grace.

He was a man walking free, walking to peace.

Walking home.

He was very solemn, this sensual, graceful man.

And his eyes had never been more blue.

"Dance with me."

"Nick?"

"Dance with me, Hope. I have loved you for so long. Dance with me. Please. Always."

*T*hey danced, in her apartment overlooking the bay, a ballet of loving, and of love.

There was a rainbow, on that Christmas night, a pastel caress of mist and moonglow. The rainbow arched high above Montagne Noir and enveloped them all.

Chase and Cassandra.

And Nick and Hope.

And Victor and his Jane.

And Eleanor and her Samuel.

And Molly. Of course, Molly.

There was something else that night, a sound in the wind. It was a murmuring. A soft duet of grandfathers.

Well, sir, the wind whispered on that shimmering pastel night.

Well, sir, Hank.

Well, sir, Jean-Luc.

I do believe I see a family.

That gentle wind, that *well, sir* zephyr, would whisper forever in the valley, and it would live, as well, in the dancing bubbles of the champagne known as Montagne Noir.

But that spring, as newborn leaves appeared on the

vines, and wild mustard bloomed in clouds of gold, a new murmuring could be heard, a springtime whisper, too young, then, to be discerned.

It grew, that soft whisper carried in the wind, crescendoing throughout the summer and into fall. It sounded like *baby* as it rustled through the vineyards, and *love* as it caressed the roses. And to some, the sound, this nascent duet, could have even been *woof*.

But that fall, at harvesttime, when Lucas Victor Tessier was born to Nick and Hope, and Eleanor Jane Tessier was born to Cassandra and Chase, there could be no doubt about the joyous whispers of the wind.

Wow, boy.

Wow, boy.

Wow.

Boy.